INSIDE THE RAIN

and

SWEET OPIUM

TWO NOVELLAS

BY

ROSARY HARTEL O'NEILL

\ə⁺'mer⁻ɔ⁻kən 'dog\ *n* 1: a book company

Inside the Rain
Sweet Opium
Copyright: Rosary Hartel O'Neill
Published: March 2021
ISBN: 978-0-578-78154-9

ON THE COVER: Maria Mason and Barret O'Brien

For

Bob Harzinski and Anne Pincus

Literary champions for hope

FOREWORD

As a journalist, I frequently have the opportunity and honor to meet and interview many creative people yet Rosary O'Neill stands out as being one of the most fascinating individuals I have ever come across. A Ph.D.-holding scholar, historian, and professor who once served as the Artistic Director of the Southern Repertoire Theater, Rosary is also a multi-produced playwright and published author whose works are typically fueled by two driving forces: her fascination with historical figures and her Southern roots. Rosary's contributions to the literary world have earned her numerous Fulbright Scholarships and her plays have been performed in front of prominent political figures.

Although Rosary now spends much of her time in New York, she was born and bred in New Orleans, Louisiana. Her background infuses itself into every aspect of her writing; especially when she is chronicling the lives of wealthy characters who are, on the surface, rich and privileged but whom nonetheless cope with incredible emotional and psychological turmoil bought on by fate, bad choices, unfortunate circumstances, or a mix of all.

Rosary hails from a prominent family and she writes about wealth from the perspective of an insider. Her uncanny ability to capture dialogue with regional accents, phrases, and idioms transports readers to the exact place and era in which her stories are set. Yet it is her ability to depict the multiple aspects of a character, not as merely good or bad but *believable*, that enables her to truly connect with readers regardless of their backgrounds, conveying the realities of the human condition with poetically-laden words.

Sweet Opium and *Inside the Rain* are both examples of Rosary's Southern-tinged writing. Both take place in New Orleans and both focus on characters whose wealthy families are part of the fabric and history of the city, mirroring much of Rosary's own life and family history. Yet the former focuses on a teenaged girl confronting dysfunctional family dynamics in the Summer of 2005—just days before Hurricane Katrina devastates the city—and the latter deals with a man coping with his impending demise from cancer. Although both stories are dramas, they shine through with humor and wisdom which are hallmarks of Rosary's writing style.

Although these stories will undoubtedly hold special interest for those who reside in New Orleans, anyone who enjoys dramatic character studies with layered plots will find Rosary's work well worthy of their time.

Sincerely,
Meagan J. Meehan
Author, Artist, Journalist
December 26, 2020

INTRODUCTION

Rosary O'Neill is a New Orleans native. Her storied ancestry anchors her to the culture, sophistication and revelry of the marvelous city that basks in its French, Spanish, African and Native American roots

A dramaturg, NYC theater critic and Adjunct Professor, I became acquainted with Rosary at an International Women's Writing Guild event at the National Arts Club in New York City. Eventually, I interviewed her for a publication I wrote for at the time. Over the years as we became friends, I traveled with her and friends to Paris, Rome and Ireland. Shared interests in theater, furthering our writing careers and erudition kept our conversations lively, as both of us are Ph.D. scholars.

Rosary, a historian, published author and produced playwright had been a theater professor at Loyola University where she served as the Founding Artistic Director of the Southern Repertory Theatre. All of her life she's experienced the ins and outs of New Orleans trends, Mardi Gras festivities and the familiarity of wealthy Garden District social circles. During the course of her annual travels to Europe as a recipient of numerous Fulbright Specialist Program awards, and additional Fellowships, her Southern charm and atmospheric Garden District splendor always endeared her to notables and acquaintances alike.

To my mind Rosary is hardy Southern Gothic with a modern, eclectic twist. Picture exquisite French Quarter architecture, floral balconies and jazz, pop and classical music wafting in the air then folding back into soft silence. That is Rosary and this rich, dense, poetic atmosphere of NOLA characterizes the charged beauty of her fiction and drama.

Like many New Orleanians of mixed French, Irish and German heritage, Rosary's connections and adventurous wanderlust, at times drawing her away from "The Big Easy," have irrevocably informed her work. She has spun her profound understanding of the combined glory and tragedy of the South with its angers, hurts, sorrows, pride and love of European, old-world gentility and lyricism into fiction that captivates. And in an organic revelation this gothic Southern spirit which flows throughout her two novellas *Sweet Opium* and *Inside the Rain* in their settings, characters and plots ignite our imagination to engage with worlds that are no more.

Rosary presents determined, willful characters who are complex and driven, churning with unfulfilled dreams, lusts and regrets. They are captivated by their environment in New Orleans but are equally stifled by it. Whether in their attempt to transform to another identity of their own making or to enhance the accoutrements of their heritage and capitalize on them, her characters seek freedom from themselves, from that integral and inherited nature which would suffocate them in mediocrity and banality.

In her YA novel *Sweet Opium* we are introduced to the intrigues of the wealthy in the Dubonnets and their in-laws who are a New Orleans top drawer family living together for a summer season at Serenity, a 19th century acreage that is their family compound. Serenity includes a luxurious beach mansion at the edge of the Gulf Coast, the once idyllic fairyland of protagonist Sissy's childhood. Natural splendor resides in the sunrises and sunsets shadowing the mansion as ocean waves rock the rhythms of life.

But in July 2005, a teenage Sissy seethes with fury at her indomitable Grandmother Irene with whom she lives ever since her mother abandoned her. Conflict, anger, frustration are everyday emotions for family members. Sissy must ride daily imbroglios, barely keeping her head above the roiling currents of her own misery and the overwhelming tensions of desperation driving family members.

Rosary O'Neill brilliantly sets the stage for the unfolding conflicts and themes as her heroine is caught in the webs spun by her grandmother, her beautiful but destructive Uncle, her fading actress Aunt and her conniving, duplicitous father. *Sweet Opium* is a coming of age tale and Rosary's word craft is her special gift as she grounds us in the lyricism and tragedy of youth and desire.

With facile gorgeousness, she configures Sissy's budding beauty as the engine of development. We understand why Sissy must make the choices she does as her spirit opens with supple sensitivity. Sissy's romantic longing to consummate her forbidden passion enflamed by her stunning Uncle must be kept secret from her Grandmother's watchful eye as she eludes the traps set by family members.

Rosary masterfully rekindles remembrance of youthful desires and leads us to note the edges of adult bondage and freedom as she unfolds this pageant of haunting summer love, regret and loss a month before Hurricane Katrina makes landfall.

The Southern gothic spirit receives further evolution in her novella *Inside the Rain* with the character of a dying young man who must set his house in order before he leaves this plane of consciousness. Rooster is an artist who seeks death as he mourns the passing of his wife Christine and his infant son.

We learn that Rooster's imagination, caught up in grief's spell is also obsessed with his own death, despite his family's wealth and the sumptuousness of the Greek revival mansion which gives him no comfort as his home. Instead, he searches for his soul purpose with a lover in the ethereal realm to help him on his journey away from days of misery, torment and the critical rejection of his art.

When Rooster becomes reawakened by the nurse caring for him, hope's light overcomes his soul's darkness of pursuing death. It is this reawakening which sparks a new life and passion to understand who he is and why he must choose life and not seek the grave where Christine and his son lie.

Inside the Rain is a tour de force which encapsulates the darker themes of death and resurrection and the artist's way toward finding creation. Rosary employs the full force or her talents setting the novella during Mardi Gras revels when the heightened fervency of living to party and "let the good times roll" is Rooster's countdown toward the grave.

Enjoy these two profoundly captivating novellas which embrace the haunting glamor and dissipation of the south in an unforgettable journey through New Orleans' character, spirit and settings.

Carole M. Di Tosti
Drama Desk Award Voter,
Drama Desk,
NYC Skyline,
Theatre Pizzazz Critic
January 2021

INSIDE THE RAIN

Maria Mason and Barret O'Brien, actors, *Inside the Rain*

CHAPTER 1

On the day I find out my cancer has come back, I'm at Mother's in New Orleans.

The clock wails. I'm wheeled inside the gargantuan library. Books on the dead and the resuscitated leer at me. My therapist sits in a wing chair by a skeletal lamp.

Behind him, French doors encase a gray sky spilling thick wide rain. Lean, ash blonde, Dr. Miles is supposed to give active advice, not sit, sloe-eyed and frown. "Your doctor called. Sent your paperwork. 'Prognosis for male 39.' Your chances to beat this cancer are 20%."

My black shepherd, Boon looks up limpid-eyed from his place beside my wheelchair, clinging to me, my ex-wife having fled.

"Unfortunately," Dr. Miles says. "I'm going on vacation."

I stare at a red unicorn tapestry, feel that old bubbling sludge of horror when people I like abandon me. Our relationship has plateaued since he became Ma's mouthpiece.

He adjusts his spectacles, exasperated flips through pages of his journal, noting folded back sections. "I started seeing you in January, 2013. And we talked through Christine's departure in 2015, four years of treatments, 2016 on."

"So tell me what I can do to elevate my chances," I say.

"I don't know. You've had every possible trial, two surgeries."

Everything goes white but I push through positivity. "The Contemporary Arts Center has this huge project. They are going to celebrate fifteen artists in fifteen venues. All people I know. I'm sure I'll be included in the show and I need to be in form for that."

"Has your work been accepted?" Miles scowls.

"I should hear any day," I squeak. "Doubt doesn't get you anywhere," I smile. "Doubt, fear the dark side baby."

Dr. Miles unpockets a mint. "Do you have someone who can advocate for you?"

"No."

Miles says. "Find one. Perhaps your art school friend, Skye." He plops a small box of Kleenex beside me. I glare at the limp tissue. The library expands into a cavern. Miles seems to shrink inside his stuffed chair.

"I'll get better," I say. "*I'm thirty-nine*. Not seventy."

He studies his Gucci loafers. "I can't hear you," he says.

"My enzymes are up in my liver so I can't speak loud." I force the wheelchair to a side table, dribble peach liqueur into a tumbler. I cry out, "Talk more about … about … strength … about … how to be direct and GROW." An ugly black rain falls over the voracious window as my spirit sinks into the cage of pain that is my body. *Lord, have mercy. Christ, have mercy. Lord, have* mercy guts through me.

"You need to have a will," Miles says.

I grab a Kleenex and wipe my brow. "I'm not going to die. That's final." I hope, trust, pray, dream, yearn, plead for one great painting to still be in me. One 'Cotton Office in New Orleans' like Degas, one 'Man with A Guitar' like Picasso, one 'Carnation, Lily, Lily Rose' like Sargent. How can I reconcile this desire with the past months of barely painting, much less my bandaged stomach?

Miles withdraws a book from a satchel. "I brought this for you."

"Goodbye!" I force a shout though my mouth.

He slides the book *Radical Acceptance* across the table. I break out in a sweat, lean forward in the wheel chair, grasping for the book, wheeling over to the trashcan and letting it fall.

Moments later, I'm barely able to dial my best friend Skye, now managing art, not making it.

Skye picks up on ring two. "Hi chum. You okay?" he asks cheerily.

Static comes through the phone. "Where are you? I can hardly hear you," I say.

"The airport. I'm interviewing for that arts position."

"The Deanship?"

"In Virginia, yes."

I imagine him making his way through the terminal, navy jacket, starched shirt, stylish. Healthy. "You okay?" he says.

"Sort of."

"The Contemporary Arts Center rejected you?"

"No. I haven't heard from them." I stare at a metal Buddha pushed between two brown books. "No. Not that. It … is … about my health."

"What?"

I swallow phlegm, focus on a black metal cat lounging on a Carnival book. "The cancer is back."

"What's next?" he says.

Boon nuzzles my leg, somehow knowing.

"Get another opinion." Skye clears his throat. "Sketch something. Tonight."

I peer at a darkened shelf where a Hummel statue, a small boy, forever blows his pipe.

"You got to fight back. Keep painting," Skye says, "Be aggressively hopeful."

Has my life mattered? I think. I worked so much. But what art have I left?

"I know that show at the Contemporary Arts Center will come through," he says.

"Don't worry. Your art will rise to the top. You'll get all the accolades you deserve… Look I got to get my luggage. Hold tight. I'll call you back tonight." He hangs up.

Minutes later, Ma's footsteps click down the hall. My throat catches.

Fear, like an arrow, is thrust into the deepest part of her heart. She vanishes into the corridors and her chauffeur wheels me to my quarters. In my bedroom, I wheelchair past a mirrored side table with a lone hydrangea and a two-way monitor (so Ma and staff can hear me and I can call out). My skin has turned light gray. My eyes shrunk above dark circles, gaunt cheeks. A year ago, before I moved back to the Garden District in New Orleans, my body was fierce from a lifetime standing outside painting canvases. I was a tall, lean thirty-eight, with a lot of dark hair and even darker brown eyes.

I flick the brooding orchestration of *La Pathéthique* on the sound system. Tchaikovsky who worked in the sanctuary of suffering from the time he was four. Whose parents wanted him to be a civil servant, but who never left the keyboard even when quietly crying. Tchaikovsky who went deep into the realms of death, past a mother taken by cholera, a wife institutionalized for violence, past original productions of *Sleeping Beauty, Nutcracker, Romeo and Juliet* that were flops. Tchaikovsky, who attempted suicide by wading into the Moscow River. Tchaikovsky! Who never had the luxury of witnessing his work become an instant success but kept composing, dying in 1903, nine days after dismissal of his last symphony, *The Pathetique*, arrogantly drinking unboiled water and expecting his own body system to be impervious to cholera, the same disease that killed his mother.

Tchaikovsky wrote *Swan Lake* during a breakdown, Mozart his *Requiem* while dying, Debussy *Claire de Lune* when stricken with depression. To paint something great must I too be disintegrating? Oh but the thrill of painting. When the weight of the image is on me fully, and I can feel every bump and contour of it against my heart and hips, there are moments of pure crushing happiness. Chopin's *Study in C Minor*, harsh revolutionary bolts through the speaker. I'm recharged. It's as if we'd pressed our bodies together until Chopin's soul passed through mine. I tell myself I'm safe. Chopin and Keats are on the further side.

I wake hours later in high fever. Dr. Miles words, *You have a 20% chance,* echo through the coldness of my room. A tray of food waits untouched. Beside my bed, Boon watches, waits, as if his presence will sustain me. Light from a cracked door spills onto a canvas of crabs colliding on the beach started three months ago. I imagine myself in my studio outback or in a duck camp at the marsh observing what the sunrise is like and the birds that go by.

Ma's voice bleeds from the hall; she's forgotten to turn off the house monitor. I envision her, her monogrammed silver tumbler in hand, blonde upswing hairdo struggling to stay intact. "Roo's had it all," she's telling someone.

I stare at the ceiling, my legs frozen, fingers clenched.

"Only God decides who's dying." A woman snaps. Touche! It's probably a nurse candidate. The last one Ma fired for stealing tea bags, before Ma passed out on my davenport, a Vera Wang scarf over her face.

Strength in this nurse's voice makes me want to listen. She seems ideal—like she might root for me to get well. "I'm here to return your son to health, Mrs. Dubonnet," she says. "While some might see my job as difficult, I find being with people who are critical a profound experience."

I keep the monitor on, curious why this nurse is championing us failing ones.

She says, "I have volunteered for years. Being in the homes of ill ones and seeing their families, it's incredible the love that people evoke. And it makes me realize this is why we're here; what we do; what we give to each other. And why there is always hope."

Ma's voice constricts. "Well, God seems to have given up on my son. Rooster may not have to land a plane on the Mississippi River, but surviving this cancer is like that."

"All sickness does not go on to death," the woman says.

"You look like you just graduated from nursing school. What professional experience do you have?"

"I was twenty-eight yesterday. I've worked with the dying," the woman says. "I took care of my husband."

"I don't want to learn about your life."

Back in bed, I inch painfully on my side, going in and out of the conversation.

"He's my first patient," the woman says.

"So no references," Ma says. "Lord. I ought to send you back. You should always say it's your second patient. At least your second ..." Ma blows her nose. Coughs.

"Are you all right, Mrs. Dubonnet?"

"I've an allergy," Ma snaps. "You should know ... Roo was seven when he first went up in a hot air balloon, eight when he rode a camel in Africa, nine when he steered a barge down the Nile. All for the sake of educating himself, seeing more as an artist. My son's a subtraction of his former self. Half of his friends are dead by their own hand, and the other half is only alive because they didn't succeed."

My breath is harsh and labored. It's true. God awful, but true. Three of my painting friends have left the arts in the last six months. One evolving into "a real Floridian," whatever that is. Another retreating to Belleview. A third devolving into heroin.

"Rooster should have quit the profession."

"Maybe not," the woman says, cheerfully. "I've some ideas on helping patients with difficult prognoses. Are you familiar with Dr. Moody's, *Life after Life*?"

"Moody, who?" Ma says. "Don't you know Roo's done all this 'woo woo' stuff and it's a waste of time. Your job is to make my son take his medicine, to ring the kitchen staff if he wants a tray."

I push the call bell. Ma is pretty brutal. She thinks if I rest, eat well, follow strict protocols, I'll get the strength to see a specialist in New York.

"We should go in," the woman says, hearing the buzzer again.

"No need," Ma replies. "He'll drift off … I keep telling Roo to get a suite at Sloan Kettering in New York. But he won't listen."

I turn away. I can't submit to Sloan Kettering, to strangers in bright rooms, greasing their machines, hanging their urine bags, waiting for the next chemo to take hold. Life hemorrhaging out of me. For me, creating in my studio in the middle of the Garden District is where I was happiest, where I did my best art. That's why Christine and I came back here. I'm going to imagine myself in that art studio, even though I can't walk.

Shortly before 4 am that weekday morning, I manage to wheelchair around a paintbrush, past Christine's desk to the window. I look at my studio shed, the place where I've painted much of my life. Where I stored palettes, brushes, unredeemed art. I've been away from it almost eighteen months. Already it seems gauzed in dust and disuse. I'm afraid the doctors and Miles may be right. What happens if I accept that? Worry needles through my chest.

* * *

The next morning, cutting pain goes in and out my stomach as someone comes in. Boon growls from the couch facing my bed.

"I'm Monica Falcon, your new nurse," the auburn-haired intruder says. I recognize the strong voice. The body that goes with it is slim, tall, a reddish blonde with green eyes, firm smile.

I blink uneasy. Yesterday I liked her, but today I feel miserable. I can deal better with an achy body if I don't have to talk. "I don't want or need a nurse," I say. "And you're walking on my paint brush."

She picks it up, slaps it atop my desk unruffled.

"I don't want you muscling through here messing up things."

"I'll respect your wishes," she says, firmly. "But I will take care of you. The last nurse my agency sent was bitten by that dog there and has a lawsuit on file."

I sit back disgruntled, annoying pain everywhere. I don't want to fall apart in front of this clearly inexperienced woman. "How much money do you need to go now?"

She chuckles, her thick hair grazing slim shoulders. "Money is a funny thing. I seem to have absolutely none, but I'm not bothered." The clock on the bedside table gongs. She yanks on an old-fashioned lamp, dislodging a leatherette single bird coaster designed by Christine, which Ma has kept.

"Don't touch anything--" I say, replacing the coaster. "You're not hired--If I must have an attendant, it'll be a male. I feel more comfortable with a man bathing me." I'm still privately embarrassed by a woman looking at my genitals.

"And you're an artist," she laughs, then turns to me with a no nonsense look. Blue eyes strong but unbending. "I'm here under the authority of your doctor. Can you get in the wheelchair?"

I slide onto it, grind forward, hoping to make it to the windows. I pass paintings in different stages of development, scrap paper, cardboard.

She commands me to pick some balled papers off the floor. Before her, most of my nurses gawked and tiptoed about as if reshuffling deck chairs on the Titanic.

"So why are you tossing these? Are you successful?"

"Yes, but on a shallow incline."

"Did you paint in this room?"

I wheel away.

"Do you have a specific time you paint?" Monica asks. "A routine? I should know about." She tosses back her shiny hair exposing a slender shoulder and frame. Her neck is long, elegant.

For a moment I'm distracted by the perfect curvature of the woman. "Show me where you paint," she says.

I squeeze a fist, armpits sweaty, shoulders heavy. I can't give my last shred of energy to talk to some neophyte. These medical professionals have no background in art or literature. Educated to confront insurance clerks and pharmacists, they have nothing aesthetic to contribute to a conversation. When nurses were nuns, I'm told, some intellectualism could have been evoked. But the repeated dumping of bedpans today isn't offset with prayer but secretive phone calls to cube dwellers who threaten to cut off support.

I reach for Tylenol. I need to hide inside the blueness of my pills, but she's moved them. I clutch the armrests trying to roll away She grabs the back handles of the wheelchair, sails it around the room, her breath warming my neck, past Boon giving us a jealous look, around and through the spot where my temporary easel used to be. Perhaps I've misjudged her abilities. She has all this boy energy. At another time, I might have followed her to hell.

She comes round reaching for my arms. "Can you stand?" She flips up the metal footrests.

"Away Medusa!" I plunge my feet onto the hard ground. But my legs give out and I collapse in the chair.

She yanks me up, has me stand, strong. No holding on. Despite the cramp in my gut, I feel warmth creeping up my back. Second by second, it starts in my toes and moves up my back. My god, I think, I'm standing. It's been weeks.

She smiles, her large eyes, small nose, full lips and high cheeks all flashing in my direction and I smile back.

"Good," I gasp. "Can I get back in bed now!"

Monica points at the back of the courtyard. "Is that your work shed out there?"

I stare through the blurry rain at a dark brown rambling cottage, a living organic thing, made of cypress bargeboards from the swamps.

"Yes."

She smiles poetically. "Did you get up at dawn, work every day."

"Yes.

"When did you stop."

"A year and a half ago. Before the surgeries."

"I'll be back tomorrow and we'll go look at that art shed."

I dismiss her, press my wheelchair against the bed, head spinning. I don't want to talk about my misses when capturing the cycle of seasons. How I would go out girded letting the paintings chew on me for a while, not liking them, some pieces really putting my nose out of joint. How I would sift through the shit looking for diamonds only to find more questions.

I manage to squish into the icy bottom of the sheets, the fibers cool and strange against my frozen toes. I close my eyes imagining the art shed. It was a place where if you stayed still long enough the vines would grow through you toes, where nature in all its beautiful machinations would come through the cracks of the floor, where images sprouted in the wilderness of the imagination— where I was a small part of a greater thing. Had a soul-deep interest in my life's work?

I flick on *Black Key Etude* by Chopin, grateful for his artistic stimulation. Chopin who wrote over one hundred compositions. Chopin who played his first concert in Warsaw at seven, who believed his work only suitable for small audiences, who succumbed to tuberculosis at thirty-nine and destroyed all his unpublished work. Chopin most remembered for the *Funeral March*. Chopin, who requested his body be buried in Paris and his heart sealed in a jar of cognac and smuggled into Warsaw. On the top shelf of my bookcase orange covered books, *Adam Strange, Montgomery Clift, The Real James Dean* jeer at me. Clift and Dean who died too young and Strange who was suddenly teleported to another galaxy.

I commit to firmly staying here, push out a "Hail Mary Full of Grace," breathe deeply. I'm Roman Catholic. But prayer rarely consoles me now.

CHAPTER 2

The next day, Monica gets a walker from the closet and makes me balance myself on it, weight on my right arm, then quickly on both. This auburn-haired farm girl-turned- nurse is vicious. I crumple over the walker, can barely extend my arms as I straighten my legs, bending over the red Oriental rug.

Monica holds the walker tight to the solid oak bed frame. "Just stand," she says, a Buddhist smile on her plump lips. "If we don't have health we have to have courage."

I knife down on the handlebars, coughing, dizzy, stare inside the red oriental rug, first purchased for my son's bedroom. I study a rabbit in the Jungle design, and relive a short memory of Christine and me before things went bad. How she would tease me with her literary brilliance, her knowledge of Shakespeare, the sonnets, the Medici princes, and Lucretia Borgia, sired by a 16th century pope, who wore a hollow ring on her little finger to poison drinks.

"Water, please." I nod toward a silver service by the bed.

"You neglected to mention what you paint."

Monica hands me water in a monogrammed tumbler. Her pale pink polish glows in the half-light. She looks about, expectantly. Her bright auburn hair sways about her face. "Are any of your paintings hanging here?"

"No." I balance myself to drink.

She studies me. "How long were you a painter?"

"Thirty years. For as long as I can remember. Since before I was born."

I give her the glass, slide my aching body tight against the walker.

"Baby steps," she says, her turquoise eyes intense, her porcelain skin like those saints in medieval miniatures.

We make it past the four-poster, past the soft buttery leather sofa to a Louis XV desk, where I keep Christine's correspondence. Our shepherd, Boon shadows me.

Outside the tall windows, a patio, complete with exotic birdcages calls. And for a second, I see my ex-wife her hand raised to a huge cage and a tiny dove cooing on her wrist.

"What kind of painting do you do?" Monica says whimsically.

I stretch against the walker. "I never did art. It did me."

"Don't you like to paint?" she asks.

"Painters don't paint for fun," I say. "They paint because they have to. It's not a choice." I slip on the walker. Crunch over. What's fun about standing in the rain under a leaky umbrella doing thirty quick sketches, feet sinking in the mud, hands grimy with sweat, exhausted legs cramping? I bite back acid reflux, stare at the sprawling oak (originally there were two), where Christine said she was leaving on an award to Paris. One giant limb still dangles beneath it.

Monica retrieves a grotesque four-footed prong cane. She demonstrates how to walk, planting one foot first then stepping to it. "Try your hardest," she says, passing me the cane. "That's right. Keep the cane four inches outside your foot. One leg at a time. Step right, then pull up the left." We plod through the French doors.

Outside, on the patio, everything seems very, very large: the massive oak sagging with moss, spectral banana trees limp with bruised fruit, oleander stalks flapping bud-less limbs. I get hot when I come outdoors now; it's a skin thing. I wipe my brow, glance inside the Big Mama Oak tree. I want to do all I can to not cry, feel grateful, be different. But I'm a sinister fucked-up mess.

I look ahead at my studio. I haven't been inside it for so long, this place where I magically stargazed... Where I painted Christine tiptoeing about. I've been focusing on trials and surgeries and sketching in my room.

Monica says. "What kind of painting do you do?"

"Wildlife."

"How do you do that?"

I tense, suspecting she's humoring me, trudge forward. "Oh please. . . .I do lots of sketches outdoors. "To find out what I'm thinking," I say. I wipe sweat from my brow. I can't do an Intro to Art course with her.

"And?"

"Also what I see." I took an art survey course at community college. The best artists don't want to live off emotion. They live off purpose."

I smash along averting a fountain I designed with statues of Cupid and Psyche, and elaborate glass-domed birdcages.

Faith causes you to believe good things are going to happen," she says enthusiastically.

"Please." *I almost squash a robin slow on takeoff.* I can't tell her I immerse myself in nature. I remain cracked open— to what comes through the senses . . . to what I want to paint. Why tell her I did about five dozen sketches before starting a piece, filled twenty pages of a sketchbook with scribblings, had to stay with turtles, herons, insects for hours. All things I can't imagine doing now.

"And what do you have to show that people can't see for themselves?" she says determinedly following.

"Are you challenging me," I say.

"You have to be aggressive. Foolish to think we can do the ordinary thing and still have things work out in our life."

I bite my tongue stunned she has nailed my hypocrisy. If painting is a way of coming to terms with mortality – why do I quit it as that day approaches?

Monica slips a band around my waist and holds onto it, her slim arm drawn to her side, but strong. She challenges me over a bumpy path past the aviary.

I steady my quad cane, avoiding a caterpillar straightening his frail spine, a beetle cowering under a stone. Overhead, birds are going off to clouds and disappearing. The white sun is crippling the banana leaves and palmettos, grass balding here and there. Wasp nests blight the gawking trees. Boxwood, ragged like a bad haircut, claws at the breeze. Winter's coming. Even in the south.

"Watch over there," Monica says, her high cheeks flushed. She points to castle-like cages where Christine's doves flutter.

An icy sweat takes hold of my arms. ...Christine painted birds everywhere, on cups, mugs, trays. Blanche and Neige, her rescue doves coo mournfully. They were deeply bonded to her, and although Neige is completely deaf, and has cataracts, Christine had developed hand signal communication with him, and he would sleep in the crook of her arm with his little head on her shoulder every night if she'd let him. But Christine couldn't take them with her to Paris, the airlines only allowing dogs and cats onboard.

I freeze, holding back tears.

Monica heads for the faded studio/caretaker's cottage with big windows and a headless cherub on the porch.

I wobble to a steel grey Pagoda bench, brushing away a few large insects and spiders, sitting with jerky movements. A lizard scatters as Monica returns and settles in Christine's spot. Even when posing, with babe in arms, Christine'd toss her head back and flirt with any man that happened to visit, despite my anger and then rage.

"What were you painting last?" Monica asks.

My thoughts shoot to the classical motif Madonna and Child, where only the hands, face, and neck can be seen. "This Madonna and Child," I say. My chest sags. Christine letting me paint her in the rain took place just a few feet away. Me under a tarpaulin. Her with rain streaming down her cheeks.

I push off the bench with my left hand, and strain on the cane in my right. I move forward to the house, holding onto the solid French doors and plodding across the darkening threshold.

Monica hurries me across the bedroom. Painfully, I swing onto the softly colored patchwork quilt. I pull up and stretch against the solid oak headboard, eyeing the portrait of me as a four year old on Mom's lap. She in green silk, the color associated with wealth in post-classical Europe, her favorite period for portraiture, me in a Little Lord Fauntleroy Suit of black velvet. Everett Ray Kinstler leading portrait artist of US presidents did it at the National Arts Club, New York. My throat is hot as I recall seeing him at one of my unproductive shows there. Monica makes me lie down on my bed as she checks on my wound. The corners of her lips tense as she pulls off the old stomach dressing, from my operation a month ago. She tilts her head to the side. "I thought you painted wildlife. Then why do paintings of Our Lady?" Monica asks.

I bare my teeth. "I DON'T KNOW."

Her mouth turns down.

"My wildlife days are over. I can't spend hours with a rank stinky rotting carcass . . . and sketch the muscles, the bones. Chain myself to a tree to feel a hurricane. Row fourteen miles in a skiff loaded with art supplies."

She grits her teeth, looking down at my eight-inch incision.

"Am I bleeding? Is that wound in my stomach starting to boil?"

"It's a little oozy," Monica says, taking a picture of the wound to send to my surgeon. I press my hands into the sheets, jutting back while she blots my stomach with some fierce alcohol. I gag at the sting, my teary eyes fleeing up inside the Tudor canopy. She changes the dressing on the feeding tube taped to my stomach. "You're still an artist," she says.

"It's like being a nurse with no patients," I yell.

"There are always patients," Monica says, perspiration beading her face. "And even if there weren't, I'd still be a nurse." She smiles at me and says, on leaving, "And you'll be an artist." Is she dispensing deathbed wisdom or is she seriously trying to reinspire me?

We connect with another smile. I feel her sincerity. Emboldened, I dial the Contemporary Arts Center Exhibition Department. They said the end of February for the announcement of winning artists for their exposition. No one picks up the phone. They don't phone, they don't text. You cry waiting for these people.

I reconsider Monica's line, even with no patrons, am I still an artist? I blast on Beethoven's *Ninth Symphony,* shivering. …The rain also starts to scream, a patter at first, then a serious onslaught. I lean against the headboard. It's raining so hard I can't see the patio, just the rain view but I can smell wetness in the air. Feel the pain inside the rain. Rain throws you into a netherworld of doom, which most people can't comprehend. It makes you feel okay to cry, drink, to sleep alone.

I grab the quad cane and despite rapid onset of chills and death fever, I manage to get to the closet. I thrust open the doors, rocking back on my heels at the assault of dust, catching myself on the waxy doorknob. I can hardly stand from the violent shaking at the sight of it all.

Easel and canvases of waterfowl and binoculars flung everywhere. Shelves droop with paintings, blank, prepared but not finished, and water colors--ice blue, mint, and lavender. I reach for a painting behind a box marked, "Fragile. Painted Plates." Pictures sail down like lost airplanes, robins, hummingbirds, blue jays.

Sunshine dresses and winter cashmere squashed by a wall call to be released. A hand-woven Panama hat with a blue velvet bow dives off a nail. I scrunch it atop a tall wooden chest, full of paint tubes, brushes, pencils. The scent of turpentine and oil screams down from a cup with a dried-up paintbrush. Below it is a chest of drawers harboring pictures of rain, rain, more rain, and of Christine in watery blue, hair flung back, Christine in palest pink with a robin perched on an extended hand, Christine on bridges in City Park, Christine nymph-like on the water's edge. And those photos of her with all the Madonnas! How I prayed to Our Lady, my mother the Madonna to help me sleep, to cover me with her mantle of grief so I could sustain it all.

I snap my cane into the floor, catching my breath, eyes misty. Ah yes, Christine's shoe, the sandals in the last painting. And the blue dress. And her socks and underwear, stuffed in that basket. And there . . . under a blanket in the corner, the last painting of pink and blue rain, the one that the dry brush wanted to caress.

Seconds after I unwrap the painting, my heart stops beating and my brain goes dead. Christine stares back from the canvas...heavy blonde hair that falls past her knees, the beautiful complexion, hazel eyes that change color, the full, high bosom. She stands there mouth open, head back in the overlay of luminous blue black rain, shiny diamond sky rain and for a moment I can barely breathe. In her arms the faint outline of a little baby.

2006 Yale, School of Fine Arts

Shortly after we both started in the same grad program at Yale, she posed for me for our Renaissance art class, as a Madonna.

Running to meet me at the workshop studio, whenever it was available, early mornings and rainy days.

"Oh, I forgot to tell you," she said, about a week in. She tossed back her damp blonde hair. "It's a financial arrangement," she said, obstinately. "My being at Yale."

"What?" I stammered. It was hard to talk and paint her simultaneously and it was raining harshly outside.

"But it's a choice to pose for you."

I broke out in a sweat, needing to focus. "Don't talk."

"I want to be your muse. I'm in love with your painting, especially your blue ones. Have been for a while," she said.

"For how long?"

She laughed. "Three months." She fixed me with her stormy blue eyes. "People need idols. It's virginal. I'll move in when you want. Tomorrow. Next week. Just keep painting those blue paintings for me." She hugged me right there in the empty studio. "We were born to coupledom from the start," she said, her hand ripe on my arm her eyes one with my painting. "Artistic coupledom. When you don't know anyone like yourselves it feels like you fell from the sky." Her eyes widened, starlit. A glow drifted from her cheek. "We can inspire and critique each other," she said. "I can lose myself in your art. I will protect you and nurture you and love you. And you will create your blue masterpieces whenever it rains."

Christine was right. When I met her, my art shifted in some way. She opened me up to new things I could do with my art. I was inspired by how focused she was pushing me to become more serious and disciplined. Living with an admirer, despite any undercurrent of tension I moved me forward as an artist. I guess I stayed with her to get back to that feeling. Even now I miss her shield. I wonder how she would have dealt with the director of the CAC. Would she have had the same defiance? Or would her indifference to viewer appeal, her artistic hard heartedness, her complete focus on her own direction have immuned her to his savagery.

* * *

I blink my eyes, returning to the present. I stuff the painting back into the closet. I started the painting in 2012 right after my son was born. Some famous artists have taken months and even years to finish a painting. The 19th-century French artist Ingres took a decade to paint his Madame Moitessier. I worked on it more about three years until right after Christine left. It's unfinished. At one time I thought this was my greatest painting. Because the idea for it came in one full sweep and the lines were strong and deep and something inside the masses of blue and the swaddled baby compelled the eye. There was so much love there. I feel guilty that I can't continue it. The loss of my son, Benno, my move to New Orleans, Christine's departure, my cancer everything collapsed too suddenly. Even now I think if I don't finish the painting, Benno still lives with me in some small way. But what if it was my greatest work?

Regret seizes me. I make it back to the bed. A sound of ambient waves mixes through my head. Some distant voices. Then a crash.

Moments later, Monica bends over me, skin taut, loose hair falling down her cheeks. Her eyes are wide, her nostrils flared. Has my fever spiked?

"A picture fell out your closet," she says.

"Was it damaged when it fell?"

"I don't know."

"I placed it on the desk."

"Let me see," I insist.

Monica whips back the bird-themed quilt. I creep aching and sweating to the desk, relieved the canvas is unharmed, insisting Monica restore it to the closet.

But Monica pauses, holding the painting out at arm's length. "Wow. Did you really paint this?"

"Yes." I hesitate, scramble into the wheelchair. "It's a Madonna with Child."

Monica studies the painting: a woman with heavy blonde hair that falls past her knees, a beautiful complexion, hazel eyes, a full, high bosom.

"Is that Christine?"

"Yes."

"She's very sexy for our blessed lady."

"Yes."

I wrench up tall, push the wheelchair forward, holding my breath as I bolt out my quarters toward the dining room. Perhaps there's some word from the Contemporary Arts Center about featuring me in their next exhibition on noteworthy New Orleans artists.

I scoot down halls with gold-crusted pictures. Magisterial old ladies in Edwardian lace vie with photos of Christine and me. Christine in wedding gown with delicate capped sleeves; me with groomsmen in elegant formal but handsome pose. Why has Ma never taken those down?

Monica catches up with me. Her always-smiling, never-complaining face annoys me as we zoom ahead. Monica lilts along, pausing to study the life-sized lithographs of birds, their colors blinding in intensity, sap green, cad yellow, marine blue, their bodies so tall they seem to spill out the frame, a Red Flamingo leaning by a ledge, a White Swan paddling into lilies, a Great Blue Heron, bending into cattails, a White Owl staring from a tree.

"They're Audubons," I say.

"Who?"

"America's dominant wildlife artist! The Louvre, The Smithsonian, the National Gallery. . . .museums," I clarify. "Ma collects him."

"Why?"

"Because he is famous. Audubon was extreme . . .about his art."

"Such as?"

"Shooting birds then wiring their dead bodies together, so he could paint them anatomically correct. Re-painting from scratch two hundred works eaten by rats."

"Wouldn't you do that?"

"Sure." For god's sake if I knew what it took, I would paint like Audubon. Create a signature style. Go into a meditative state, create visions of the world, document magical moments, master effects of color and light smoke, steam, mist, rain. My one hope left is being featured with top artists under forty at the

Contemporary Arts Center. Why is this show so important? I can't apply to other shows because I may soon be dead.

A bright smile lightens her face and her eyes shine luminous as she studies the paintings on the wall. "Wow. Are all these Audubon?"

"No." I hesitate, pointing to a brilliant painting of a tiny Pelican, a painting even more captivating than one of Audubon's beside it. "That picture of a nestling is Christine's."

CHAPTER 3

A crystal chandelier beams down on Ma in a dining room, lush with Mardi Gras decorations. Servants inch about the table in wilted whites. "Look, my son's graced us with his presence," Ma says. Her blonde hair is intact, despite her poking at it, her repainted face hides deep circles. Sleep problems have caused one eye to sag.

She lifts her old fashioned, knocking off a Birds of Faith coaster, a Christine creation with a Cardinal and the words "Be Strong and Courageous" Joshua 1:9." Ma never totally dropped Christine. Her fame was too glamorous to let go of.

"And Monica," Ma says, "Remove the false smile. We're not supposed to be happy all the time. Change your face to neutral. If for no other reason, it calms my dogs." She points to the white poodle on her lap and the black Bullmastiff at her feet.

The help refill her silver tumbler. "This place in the Garden District," Ma says, "is a pretend house, Monica. . . . The whole idea was for children, grandchildren, cousins to come." Ma tightens hairs into her French twist.

I'm about to exit the cruel embarrassment, (I don't want to talk to Ma necessarily even though I paid a lot of money in therapy to learn how to do it) when Ma nods toward an already opened envelope on my gold-rimmed plate. I look down, beginning to dread the peculiar grim whiteness of the paper. "Despite all efforts, the Contemporary Art Center is dropping you," she says. "Open the letter."

I cradle the envelope as if it's a dead bird.

Her words shriek in my ears. "They have the nerve to send names of all the featured artists—"

I bury the envelope in my lap.

Ma says, "They give you a twenty per cent discount on their gala."

"QUIET." I blot my mouth, little shocks of grief through my heart.

Ma arches back in her chair, lips resolute. "I spoke to several board members."

Oh no. I have to listen to this?

"One said, 'Roo's paintings are highly attractive, I suggest he show them to someone else.'"

I spear a lemon slice. "Attractive," I say, squeezing it in my water.

Ma's eyebrows shoot up. "Another said, 'I wanted to like these, but I don't.'"

"Who said that?" I ask.

She looks at me with horrified eyes.

"Who!" I say shaking my water glass.

Ma scratches her collarbone "Yes. It's so demeaning. These slaps from the museum people. About passion."

I sip water, my throat suddenly hot.

"We've heard that passion slur before," Ma says.

My eyes go red.

"They all said passion was missing," Ma says, pushing the remark down my throat.

"Passion," I repeat, my soul boiling. "What's that mean?"

"You're the artist for gods sake son. Don't you know?"

My brain fogs. I grab a cracker, slapping butter on it. No of course I don't know. If I have passion and paint from emotion and commitment or at least that's what I experience I've done, am I deranged?

Ma smirks. "One colleague even said, 'There's nothing at the base of Roo's work.'" Ma clenches her napkin, her rings glinting. She reaches for some garlic bread, tension in her jaw. "And now, I have to live with these disruptions. God knows how many of these foolhardy shows you are getting involved with." Her eyes bloat with tears.

"You're too old to shame yourself, with these neophytes at the Contemporary Arts Center. Anyone can see tell you're yards above them," Ma goes on, face pallid, "It's like Pollack versus basket weavers."

"Three block rule!" I say, skin hot.

"What's that?" Monica comes over, laying her thin hand on my shoulder.

"This rule where you don't discuss an artist's work until he is three blocks away."

"It's just a horror, so disgusting," Ma says looking at Monica. "I want to believe in Roo but none of the critics do. Now he'll have to donate big time to get hung."

"Three block rule!" I repeat, cold and perspiring.

Ma shakes her head, a vein pulsing at her temple, "I called the Center," she says. "I know I shouldn't have. I told them your situation, but that was as humiliated as I dared get. I've been begging you to leave this crooked profession." Ma opens her compact (red enamel and diamonds from the Russian Collection at the Met). "These lowlife bureaucrats are stonewalling us..... If this two-bit gallery causes your relapse—"

I begin to cough, don't think I can stop. Monica pats my back, tops off my water.

"Let the servants do that." Ma says.

I breathe deep, sip while observing my hummingbird coaster, Christine design, "With God, All Things Are Possible," Matthew 19:26.

Outside thunder yells; each bolt of lightning causing Ma to blench. She cracks off some French bread; "I never really saw Roo's brilliance even when he was somewhat the rage. Of course I believed in him. I paid for all the courses. Hoping with each connection, he'd finally make his mark."

"Don't," Monica interjects. "Health requires safety where no one says anything hurtful."

"Did I say something bad?" Ma says, with a thin smile.

"He asked you not to discuss art," Monica says.

"Thank you," I chime in.

"And I told him to stop entering these fool competitions. The problem is the whole field is shutting down. Too many artists, too few galleries. And it's a youth driven profession. Standing and painting and hiking outdoors." She bumbles the drink to her mouth, guzzling a chunk of ice, blinking at Monica now standing behind me. "Roo was a great fire," Ma says, "who burned bright as a child, and we lived in his warmth for so long. Art is a marvelous pastime. He can dabble in it forever once he does something useful. Like resting now. Studying later. Architecture or finance down the road."

"Three block rule," I shout, hands clutching the envelope, lungs gasping for air, eyelids batting off sweat.

I head for the music room, pushing my half dead body onto the piano bench and plunging into Claude Debussy's "Clair de Lune." Generally, a person is considered dead when blood circulation stops; that is clinical death. But to an artist, criticism feels like death because it kills the urge to create. I pound down on the piano keys raging into Johann Sebastian Bach, the most famous Bach, who was the personal servant and violinist of a duke; who had twenty children but no heirs. God can't give any one artist too much.

Despite acclaim, Beethoven was ravaged with illness: (rheumatic fever, typhus, abscesses, inflammatory arteries, jaundice, chronic hepatitis, cirrhosis of the liver.) He managed to compose with partial hearing by biting a stick, holding it against the keyboard to discern faint sounds and writing his most famous work, *the Ninth Symphony*, stone deaf. But his habit of dunking his head in cold water to stay awake to compose exacerbated bacterial infections, which led to his death.

My fingers, drenched in sweat, slide off the arpeggio chords I press. The wound of leaving the table early won't be healed by music. A strange decaying chill grips my fingers, as if one hand is frozen. A rapid onset of fatigue takes hold.

Ma barges in, her pale cheeks flushing. *"Your art career is finished," she says.*

I look up to see Ma with her discarded dessert, picking at a sugar free chocolate pudding in a cup. Her hair is mussed. Her riding boots scuffed. "This has been the worst spring of my life," she says. "No one can believe you weren't featured at the CAC exhibit."

"Ok," she says, eyes small, mouth wide." I spent the last hour calling the CAC. Making sure they know you want your work back."

"You did what?" I say. "Can't you mind your own—"

"Good news is they sent two tickets to the art show opening. Monica, please encourage him."

The chauffeur comes in smiling, presenting me with a huge box wrapped in red and black.

I slash off the blood red bows, rip open the shiny black boxes to find another velum card and three suits, a grey cutaway, a black tuxedo, and a navy pin stripe suit, tagged the "best seller." (They are two sizes smaller than my old suits.) I contort the boxes interlacing my fingers through the clothes and squeezing them together.

Ma marches to the door. "I think you should try to make the event if you can. Be a good sport in public. That's all I came to say."

I transfer back to the wheelchair and shout, "Back. Mephistopheles. Back! Back! I don't need some identity analysis mother/art therapist/psychic, morbid half-alive, comatose, vice-driven infected sociopath rebuking me.

Monica attempts to follow me out the music room, but I stop her, saying, "I need to be by myself."

Monica leaves and I roll down the hallway diving into memories of the CAC and of my rejection. I tell myself don't think about it, don't look up the website, see the artists accepted, how much the stipend is, where and when is the reception.

* * *

Back in my room, red-winged nightmares seize me trying to tell me something. I'm at The National Arts Club alone, in November 2012. It was a mythopoeic place to see and be seen and my art was the show they were celebrating. How did I fall from being pursued by patrons to where I am now? That day I wasn't tired. The weather was loving me. Barely cold with a touch of snow. Sparkling darkness down torch-lit Gramercy Park and then the resplendent canopied club mansion. I should have insisted

Christine come, but she wasn't interested in patrons spying on us all the time. Declared that talent not "chatting" sold paintings. I didn't know what she was talking about but I came to see what she had to say. I went to the gala anyway. I didn't want to live off patience. I wanted to live off purpose.

I climbed the grand red-covered staircase leading to galleries featuring my art. Chandeliers sparkled. Waiters spun about in tux, champagne tipping on trays. Linen-covered tables offered chocolate, strawberries, flaky Napoleons, goats' cheese, white grapes, kiwis.

I phoned Christine. There was a stunned silence from the other end of the phone. She was sassy. Said she wanted to sit home and nurse her worries and not go out and "spectate." I didn't know she was lonely and she just wanted me to cry with her—so dazed was I, I didn't think clearly. – There was such an easy flow of information back and forth, in the beginning. Perhaps my verbal responses came too quickly. I regret that.

I dodged patrons gushing in my ear, slipping checks in my pocket, handing me Kir Royals, prosciutto, and Beluga caviar.

I phoned her before I left the gallery. Not answering was her way to tease, defy, subdue me. Those days, I was mostly not home. She said she had to protect her inner core. I stayed away, telling myself I was giving her space. Her behavior was justified. She just really wanted a baby.

An artist's employment was based on temporary work in cities. What else could I do? Starve in a garret? Become a house husband? Live at Mother's? Foolish for me to think I could make a few phone calls, jaw hanging open, dripping and snapping shut again, and feel what she was going through. I didn't see her throwing her chin up in defiance, hiding her face, massaging feeling into her fingertips. In dreams, her eye contact was overly intense, face masklike but smiling. But the nightmares vanished.

CHAPTER 4

The next morning, I wake up feverish. Monica's turquoise eyes are flashing. Color is hot in her cheek. She looks full of a rebellious passion despite her golden skin and her soft auburn hair clipped back. She gives me a burning stomach shot. There is no spot that hasn't been injected. Vicious pain rips my gut.

Monica studies my charts on the computer, chewing on the corner of her mouth, then furrowing her brow. "I'm going to need to draw more blood," she says. "Your liver numbers are elevated."

My heart falls. "What's that mean?"

"Enzymes are fighting something. I'm taking you off Tylenol because it's bad for the liver."

Oh no, am I dying sooner rather than later? My eyes wander to the sparrow motif on the cornice bracket, providing no value other than polite distraction from the sharp angle of the wall, and confirming the Biblical injunction to look up.

"Do you want to go to the closet and look at that painting now?" she says.

"No," I say, lips leaden, determined not to argue.

"I see."

"When I'm feverish all I want to do is sit in one place."

Rain drenches the windows.

Monica puts a cool cloth to my brow. Her eyes become driven, opening hard and blue out of kindness. "You look very hot," she says. "I need to check your skin."

"I've plenty of that. Bring me back to life. Me and Lazarus."

She puts her hand fully on my cheek feeling every bump and contour of my throat. I crumble inside the bird quilt. She touches the swollen glands that feel like hard lumps on my neck.

"Are you through yet?" I ask.

"I suppose so."

She treats a spiderlike rash on my arms with biting tonic, chatting to keep me awake. "My husband and I had a lovely white room with long white curtains and a white ceiling fan with three tulip lights."

I can hardly talk to her. I look away from her eyes, so opaque in their greenish-blue

"Outside our bedroom window in Delaware we had all these plants." She tightens my armband to take my pressure. "It's good to be alone," she says, "but it's nice to feel the warm glow of your own bed. You neglected to say when your sweet wife passed?" Monica says.

"Not died, LEFT," I say baring my teeth.

I walk the claw cane to the window where the patio is lifting in the soft rain; I need to see the azaleas. And they are there, the purple-stemmed flowers, rustling and rasping and shivering, so shiny and vital, but with nowhere to hide their flesh, as they bend from the water. I look into the weeping rain.

"So when did she leave?" Monica stands at a respectful distance and looks at me with cold blue eyes. "If you don't speak her name or talk about her, it's like all the good times are forgotten."

I peer out as if the rain trembling the French doors has the answers. "Two years," I say. "She flew to Paris." My legs wobble and I grab onto the porcelain doorknob (with Chantilly Bird Design.)

Monica moves closer, firmness and forthrightness in her step.

I hobble over and fling myself across the bed. She flattens pillows behind me. I plunge inside the pillows.

Monica removes a Bible from a stack by the bed. "Cancer makes some feel hopeless." I think there's a lot we're not supposed to know," she says.

I slide my aching body tight inside the sheets.

Occasionally, we all fear 'death will come up like the sea and take us. Revelations 13:1.'"

I move onto my sore back. My legs are freezing. A heart condition and slight brain deterioration were diagnosed when I was examined last week!

I reach for the dusty Bible. My wedding picture falls out. "The New Orleans Museum of Art--Sculpture Gardens," the card screams.

Monica studies it. "Beautiful. I've never seen those gardens and I'd like to. We could go there tomorrow," she says.

"I can't go out," I rasp. "I suffer black outs. I've been warned not to travel distances." I can barely move. For god's sake, a heart condition and slight brain deterioration were diagnosed when I was examined last week! I stare at the ceiling medallion with it goldfinches perpetually feeding.

CHAPTER 5

Getting out the Uber at the Sculpture Garden, the next morning has to be done discretely. I hold on both sides of the door and make that step down into the shadowy gardens with white swans. I've spent the majority of my life painting in this kind of aliveness, replacing physical love with natural beauty.

Outside, a hard air embraces me and hazes my view of the sculptures. I see Christine feeding a swan, her flimsy top slipping down over her delicate shoulders, the bones showing a little. I blink, keep moving.

So many details to manage--bringing both feet up to the center of the stone slab then putting the cane down, while putting weight on the cane in front. No talking while I'm walking. No looking at the small blue sky; or the birds letting out sharp, high-pitched sounds in their rough, withered flight as we pass.

I walk my screaming body past mountainous statues, huge mossy oak trees, below a bountiful sky. An image of Christine peeks out along the Corridor Pin Blue path from behind a blue safety pin sculpture.

I catch my breath. "Do you know this collection?" Monica asks.

"Sure." I say, moving before a huge ninety-nine-inch bronze of Gaston Lachaise.

"Some of it sat in front of Besthoff's building."

She looks at me perplexed.

"Sydney Besthoff. The guy who donated this Sculpture Court, who had the drugstore chain--."

"He knew you?" she says, wonder-eyed.

I nod. "Once he sponsored an art opening."

Ahead a huge male figure, La Chaise's *Heroic Man, stretches out* his arm as if blessing us. "I used to paint the rain dripping off his fingers," I say.

"Isn't this where you took that wedding photo?"

"Yes. We both had been brain seared into believing we had to be married outdoors. She wore a Givenchy gown and jewel-studded platinum riding boots both endearing and horrifying my family. Riding a white horse in a flowery wedding gown to the ceremony."

I talk quickly, gasping over breaths, moving past the sculpture, the black earth, blue sky and gold sunlight. "People like me need people like Christine to give us strength. I remember her now the way she was. So lithe, defiant, hopeful."

"You don't need to talk about her," Monica says. She puts a hand to my waist as I move forward with weakening limbs.

I'm having a hard time catching my breath. "The only way I'll get through this Sculpture Court," I joke, "is imagining these poor clouts in the gutter. I've got to tell myself that nine hundred and ninety-nine out of one thousand artists die homeless, unrecognized, and at least the suckers in this Sculpture Court were for a time heralded."

"You have to function as if success is possible." Monica's face is inwardly soft and connected.

I need to get on without Monica, and hold my own. I spot a bench and sit, limp bodied, heart dulled.

"I brought your notebook and pencils. Do you want to draw something?"

"I haven't sketched for a while."

"I know." She excuses herself and wanders off for a time. Clumsily, I sit. People walk by, and in front, scarcely seeing me. She has given me space to work on my art. If only I could find some sculpture that inspires me. I take the sketchbook and begin to doodle.

In the distance, Henry Moore's bronze cast, *Mother and Child*, gigantesque and powerful lures me. I move closer, sit on a welcoming bench. Its moving stillness, nearly audible, the stone mother's voluptuous arms call me... I start playfully drawing them, sketch the shape and the curves of muscles, add lines to indicate direction. So far so good!

But my mind drifts to Christine, her arm holding the baby at the Birthing Center. She wanted me to sketch her as a Madonna to fix this yearned for experience into long-term memory. I shake her off, draw the basic part of the sculpture's head.

At the end, I think Christine unraveled. Scowling faces in the driveway. Hesitant lovemaking. I make the lines corresponding to the form of the large neck, shoulders, hands, body, breasts, and legs. I sketch the statue's elbow and the wrist. ...draw the fingers ...more realistic nails. ...Add in details.

I began painting Christine in the rain. Outside she didn't call up the hurt feelings. She liked the dampness under her feet and wetness on her cheek. Inside the rain was where she felt at peace.

I draw the statue's chest. Nice curves. Rib cage. The details make it work.

Christine distanced herself in small ways at first, saying she was tired, she didn't feel well. Women have not been feeling well for years. Men understand that. Was she seeing someone else (possibly), watching porno movies (probably not)? I was in pain a long time, and I suppose she was too.

I look at the sketch. It's not too bad. I do have passion and it's hurtful others don't see that. I go to show the sketch to Monica, but I can't find her.

I discover her with head tilted down, blotting her eyes by the LOVE Statue. Her skin is no longer slick and glowing and even her auburn hair seems faded. We connect on some level of pain and uncertainty. Before us, the huge LOVE, Red Blue lettered installation aluminum with enamel. Red on the outside, blue on the inside.

I stoop over her. "What's wrong," I ask, voice tight.

Her face tenses, her eyes are puffy and red. "I've lost a spouse too, you know" She sighs. She looks up with a sweet smile. "Many have, many will."

Oh no. "But you talk a lot about him. I knew he was sick, but—"

"He died just 6 weeks ago."

Coldness runs through me. Yes I recall mom's interview with her mentioning something about caring for an ill husband.

"Speed?" I say.

"Yes. He got that name from playing football."

"I'm still greatly mourning his loss," she says. "I think it's because we had to look out for one another so much."

I sit by her on the bench. She calms to an almost Zen-like state.

"Are you afraid of death?" I ask.

"For those I love, yes. For myself, no."

"Why not?"

She laughs, "I'm a nurse. In training, I saw a lot of severe illness."

"And it was easy?"

"Most times. . ."

"But you didn't know the people."

"I knew my, my. . . husband, since high school." I didn't want him to die," she says. "But I didn't want him to suffer either. He was exhausted and needed a rest." Her eyes fill with tears.

Oh my. I had no idea she was in such grief. "I'm sorry," I say, swallowing hard. Intent on distracting her, I point to a carousel in the distance. "Lets go there."

We Uber to "Flying Horses," a wooden carousel with green-striped canopy and twenty-five larger-than-life fairytale horses. We climb aboard, zig zag past camels with faux gemstones, flying white stallions with real horsehair tails. We ride in silence in golden chariots surrounded by giraffes.

"What was your husband like?" I find myself saying.

Her throat catches. "Nice. He liked cookouts with friends. Spring. Our patio when the delicate pink azaleas were in bloom. "And your wife?"

"She liked the moon through the window and trees at night," I say. "We met at an artists' retreat in Indiana-- a monastery. Beautiful white snow. Everyone there was young, broke, and becoming."

Monica sits square beside me, her blue eyes strong but gentle, her expression inscrutable. "How did you deal with your wife's leaving?" she asks

I drag myself up, looking out where wind tears leaves from the trees. "Not well."

Her eyes twitch. "You were angry," she says.

I nod. "I thought I deserved more. I wanted to curse God."

"What did you do?" she asks.

"I took meds till one night at three am, I found myself in my shirt and sandals in Wal-Mart."

She laughs, breathes quickly, through parted lips.

"I don't know how I got there," I whisper. "I just had my car keys in my hand, no wallet. I made it to my car."

"How did you finally get over—the loss?"

"You never get over it. You get used to it. I went to bed for a week and sobbed. My neighbor had to drag me into the shower. It was like a closing of the chest. Everything became very, very small. But the hard part was choosing what to keep and what to toss. Holding on to her clothing. Not wanting the hurt--the missing to stop."

Monica was cold but listening.

"Since then," I say, "I don't do funerals. I don't do wakes. Don't linger with the depressed if I can help it. When I feel really blue, I always go outside."

Monica's eyes are speckled with a dark light. "You've got to get back to working with other artists and practicing. Don't give up on painting just because you don't know what to do. In the doing you'll find out things."

"A lot of artists have resignation. Ever heard of that?" I say.

"Resignation kills," she says. Overhead loose roof tiles clatter. "'But they who wait for the Lord shall renew their strength; they shall mount up with wings like eagles.' Isaiah 40:31."

"Right," I say. I drag my legs tight to the chariot. Before me, the oak trees creak, their roots rising in a sudden vicious rain. A paper blows along the yard, and an umbrella, turned inside out sails like a large bat. I hear Christine's laughter. "Either we are going to have a good time or we are going to die."

CHAPTER 6

The next morning, I awaken flailing. Monica puts on cold compress on my forehead. My eyes ache. "I dreamed I was burning to death," I say. "I kept calling for someone to save me."

"And did they?"

"I don't know. The dream said, 'Go out.' And I said, 'How do I know if I can?' You don't think I'll die, do you?"

She turns away, dropping and tightening venetian blinds.

I say, "Because I want to live till I'm old. . . ." I stick my sore feet out the sheet. "Is it hot in here?"

"No. It's cool as anything." She gives me warm tea with lemon, her hand cradling mine for a second.

"Sometimes you can slip back a bit," Monica says.

"I fear I'll sleep and never wake up," I say.

Monica rubs my hands and feet for numbness. "You won't die," she says, staring at me. "The doctor said there is nothing to worry about if symptoms only last for a day or two and your sleep goes back to normal." She's so positive I'm not sure we are speaking to the same doctor.

Morning shadows crawl over me. Monica opens a little Bible. I fear I know what's happening. She is preparing me for my death. Taking me to dreamy places. Reading high poetry. "Did you want to read the Evangelist Luke?"

"No."

Monica's blue, all-seeing eyes seem disappointed. "Both you and Luke are artists and have a special way to reach people . . ."

I look up at the ceiling medallion.

She leans in insistent. "Luke goes to great pains," she says, "to write beautifully to tell the truth. And that's what you do, with the right shapes. "

I scrunch my eyes closed.

"Do you want to paint now?" she says.

I shrink down in the sheets, appalled. "You don't start any canvas when you're in my condition. It could take weeks."

"I thought you cared about your art," she says. Her insight unnerves me.

"That feeling is gone."

"That quick?" She looks at me flabbergasted. "At the Sculpture Court, you were sketching and now you're feeling sorry for yourself. What are you so afraid of?" she says, nudging me into a seated position and handing me a club cane. And I find myself despite myself going to my studio to paint.

Outside, there's a violent sleepiness to my studio like it might come alive at 12 pm. or 3 am. Everything is bone dry. Even the weeds in the unwatered plants seem dead. Inside the dreaded studio an almost sinister privacy prevails. I'm struck by the bitter odor of charcoal, linseed oil and dust: nine hundred square feet of carriage house with shelves, a big worktable, and a double bed. Art and "art in progress" everywhere. Tiny glass bottles in shades of blue and green, framed silhouettes, antique cameras and a mounted deer skull and horns.

My legs contract as I steer over paint-spattered floors. "I've got to guard my energy."

"You're going to start painting," she says with a fearless look. "You had a bad night but you'll have a good morning."

I grab my worktable for stability. Nearby on an easel resides the smoldering last rain painting. "You can work on   . . . this canvas a little a day," she says.

"You went in my closet," I say, shocked. "Look I can't paint this. . .here now."

My eyes skim the unfinished canvas. Its colors scream at me: ribbons of blue rain and elsewhere rain, crab-colored or dark as gravel, surrounded by a bluish-white hoar of frost, and Christine in pale pink, her hand in the air, the purplish density of oaks beyond.

"Look," I gasp, "finishing this painting won't console me at the end."

"Why not?"

"I don't know."

She's not listening to me now. "If you aren't going to paint," she says, "let's practice your leg exercises."

"You wanted me to come back to the studio and I'll do your exercises about muscle strength and so on. But I can't work with someone jabbering about me. "You got to leave when I do art. . . Or try to do art."

She nods. We march in place first. "Hold on to that worktable," she says. "And one, and two, three." She demonstrates the movement. There is something young and bright in her fair cheek, and her quick eyes.

"I'm sorry for my brusqueness." I say, guiltily. As an artist," I say, "I've rarely taken the time to hold back. . . ."

"Why?" she says.

I speak over clenched teeth. "I've lived mostly in a society . . .where we feel we're never painting enough. . . . going fast enough . . . being good enough . . .selling hard enough. I thought as a man, I'd be like Jackson Pollock," I say, tensing past a stomach cramp, hallow legs."

"Who?" she asks. "Four, five, six."

"The abstract expressionist. . . Canvas wall art?" Oh no, she knows nothing!

My leg caves and I moan.

"It's good to feel pain," Monica says, blindly encouraging me, "as long as it's not the last thing you feel. Didn't you have your own gallery?"

I tilt my head down, starting to exercise. "Yes, I was . . .known. . . .in New Haven."

"And what did you do there?"

"Things . . . with . . . Unusual colors ..."

"And people loved it, I bet. Seven eight, nine."

"That fine work almost . . . killed me because I had to work incessantly..." My eyes burn. "I had to raise money constantly."

"Is that bad?"

"Yes. . . . I'm an artist not a . . .a . . . banker."

"But your mother is. . .Ten, eleven twelve. Next leg."

"When I came home to New Orleans I just thought . . . I'm going to paint brilliant work . . . and people are going to love it." I stumble away to get water. I hate to feel so absorbed by this pain.

"When you're an itinerant artist, it's great because . . . you're free . . .you don't ...have to please anybody." I gulp more water, grind my teeth. But you have to attract others based on the sheer value of the project or your personal charisma even if you're lying to yourself." Tears well in my eyes. I blow my nose. "It's so artistically unacceptable breaking down."

She nods. "The first time I cried in front of a patient I felt stupid. The patient loved it. Now's your chance to be a real artist—work from passion and from pain." She switches the quad cane for a metal therapeutic one with a spongy handle and a strap.

We walk back and forth before canvases tacked on the walls, stopping in front of each painting, a Golden eagle, a Mississippi buzzard, a Louisiana fox. Birds, fishes, animals, racehorses, livestock. "My, oh my," she says. "I like them," What are they called?"

"The medium is watercolor." Her naïveté is so annoying.

"They're the prettiest paintings I've ever seen."

"Have you never been in a studio or museum," I ask, sarcastically.

"No." Her eyes narrow, likely with embarrassment. "We could put some in your room."

"No, thanks." I rest on a stool, debating a flight to the small bathroom on my left.

She shakes her head, her eyes luminescent. "The light beneath the paint seems alive. ..."

"Impressionism it's called," I say, rushing life in my numb foot, easing back on the stool. I chuckle.

"The number of . . .of --It looks like you keep starting over." Monica says, wide-eyed, before a painting.

Bang. That hurt. "Yes I did. I do." I'm feeling uneasy with her now.

Monica is glued to my work, squinting at it with curiosity. She goes to my worktable, grabs jars of brushes, paint tubes and brings them to me. "At some point," she says, "Are you going to.... finish something?"

I jolt back. Second slap. She's touched something in me and I don't have the strength to fight. "Please go," I say. "I'll work now."

She leaves for the house, turning at the door to say. "I'll be back."

* * *

I stumble to my easel, where Monica has now placed the unfinished canvas. I can't speak. I'll sob. But if I don't paint, what else is left.

I mix paint, balance and lift the brush. For a second I recall fun expeditions with Christine: crawling through marshes, sleeping in an overturned boat, smoking hand-rolled cigarettes and watching dragonflies. Tenderness seizes my joints. I totter, recover, paint.

Christine loved a rainy day - the sound of raindrops gently tapping through the trees, hair flapping in her face. Oh and kissing in the rain. It was hot. Just was.

I collapse into an ebony armchair with swan's heads, one of two that commanded Dad's office. Christine drew her little wet sparrow series from here. Rain starts and I try to rest, closing my eyes, tossing aside the angry bird chair pillow, recalling how a bird's solo flight from a storm inspired it. I look up and see Christine's dew drenched body: heavy blonde hair that falls past her knees, smooth complexion, marble eyes that change color, full, high bosom.

When rain trapped Christine and me here, she held fort about the Medici princes, and Lucretia Borgia, sired by a 16th century pope, a predatory blonde who wore a hallow ring to poison drinks.

As I paint, I begin connecting to Christine behind the rain. Her face shining inside the iridescent tiny drips, the bright blue streams, her hair flying about. I paint till I can't anymore and stop.

Moments later someone steps over the ledge into the frustrating studio. It's Monica. I shrink inside myself, collapse in the swan chair.

She slides off a drenched raincoat, blots her wet skin, which breathes life. I'm annoyed how fit she is, how young and bright with her full hair, and quick eyes. She glances at me compassionately, with curious far-seeing eyes, picks up the balled up sketches.

"Are you finished working?" she asks.

"Yes."

"Tell me about it."

My ankles feel like rocks. My brain like muck. Pain bites my stomach. My nose runs, my eyes water. I fling back inside the chair then thrust forward on my hands.

"Is there a place where you stopped?" she asks.

"Don't talk about my art. EVER"

"Easy," she smiles, moving to the right of the easel by the painting sink, where she sets up an exercise station, hand grippers, bar bells, red therabands. "I'm not going to besmirch your artistic effort. But if you live your life stunted in doubt you'll never go anywhere."

Moments later, I sit gripper in hand, refusing to squeeze. Her bare hand touches my shoulder, her face bathed in a newly bequeathed light. It's sickening.

"To have ups and downs in work is perfectly normal," she says, demonstrating an exercise with a hand gripper. She fixes me with her glowering blue eyes, counts slowly "on--e, tw--o, th--ree. Yes, four, five, six." Her voice is stern. "You're just going through a temporary slump, seven, eight, nine."

I release a crick in my neck, face hot. Outside, deep brown finches find tiny seeds on the window ledge.

She takes a step to me, her hair wavy and auburn, her face fresh. Her hair has volume, I think as she leans beside me, it's living, it grows.

"Work can take a lot out of you." She makes me squeeze the gripper. "Thirteen, fourteen, fifteen."

"Now switch hands," she says. "And one, two, three."

I'm breathing quickly. Still she holds my bare arms out, and I continue exercising with two grippers despite the prickling sensation all over my body.

"Four, five, six," she says.

I tilt my fists upwards and watch the tiny pinprick of sweat ease up through the skin. Monica sends me a large soft smile, counts, "Seven, eight, nine . . ."

"I can't do this," I say, muscles tight.

Her eyes look warm and kind. "Push on that fourth and fifth finger pad," she says.

I grip hard with the left hand. With the heavy squeeze comes weakness.

She switches out the grippers for bar bells and counts as I lift. "One, two, three. Maybe you just need to let go and, act like a kid again. Four, five, six."

"I don't do fun!" My heart races. I glance outside. A woodpecker hides in a tree cavity. A thrush eats berries. Christine's bird friendly garden provides food, shelter and water.

But Monica is still counting. This healthy woman with her fresh, clumsy sensuality that invites scorn. "Seven, eight, nine," she says.

I extend my bare arm gripping the barbell, perspiration rising between my fingers.

Monica's eyes are large and soft, unlike Christine's fierce driving ones. A skin of certainty about Christine should have been my first flag.

"Ten, eleven, twelve," Monica says, with an unanticipated flash of a smile. "Shall we turn on some funky music? Thirteen, fourteen, fifteen?"

My shoulders ache. Still, I tilt my barbells upwards and watch outside the rain running in tiny streams on the water soaked ground. Birds pile into Christine's single roost box to conserve heat. Others find cavities she has designed in the sides of trees. If only like that small owl I could hide inside some hole till I die.

But Monica is tireless in making me exercise. There is no personality, just sheer routine and force. She uses the quenching rain to drive me onward. Then come the leg lifts, swings, spinal stretches, knee bends, marches, squats.

"Why exercise?" I say, gasping for air, "when you are dying?" I stop the exercises, leaning on the counter, panting for breath. I'm at my breaking point.

"Not all of life is painful." Monica urges me onward, pushing a curl behind her ear with curious swift, soft movement, doing leg lifts herself. "One, two, three . . . you can delight in the moment. Now ...four, five, six. . . . Speed and I used to enjoy the magnolias in bloom, trees at night, Audubon Park on our evening walks. We'd marvel at the beauty and quiet of nature."

Talk of her late husband is so irritating. I know you're sincere," I say, "But you're sincerely wrong. "Go and let me draw."

That was the good thing about Christine. She only encouraged me to create. Knew time spent even fiddling with a paint brush could lead to magical things bursting on the page.

"We're not finished exercising," she says with a penetrating smile. "Exercise."

Black spots appear before me as I sit up.

She stares into my eyes, with a perfect, fearless, impersonal look. "Do simple steps and avoid sudden movements," she says. She demonstrates sidestepping in slow motion back to the easel. "Can you make it here?"

I go to the easel, where my painting idles, moldy and undefined. She points to some pictures behind it. "What are those diplomas?" she asks.

"Christine and my awards. She graduated receiving the biggest financial award and me the second." (Ma said because of all the women's issues no white male could graduate first.)

"How did you feel about that?"

I touch the rim of the painting, my fingers almost grey in the half-light,

lifting off grime. "I believed in Christine's superiority. Everyone at Yale did."

The stool topples.

Monica catches me. I look up, grateful for the attention. I want to hold her there. She blinks a few times, stays a generous moment, then removes my arm around her. And makes me do toe-heel stretches. I'm woozy at first, but she holds my leg in place. She has nice hands, fingers long, nails taken care of. She holds my arm makes me do leg squats.

Then pain strikes my abs. I back off, feeling my heart contracting pushing blood around my body. I ask for water, she brings it. Outside a simpler wind sings through the trees.

She remains for a moment, handing me a bar bell to work, then she goes to the sink by my workbench. Monica smiles, her white slim back curved over a big pail, in which she ducks each brush.

"Tell me about Christine," she says.

Reluctantly, I flex my cold hands as I pick up the bar bell, desperate to quit talking. "There was a time when all I saw was Christine," I say definitively. "Even at the end she dazzled me."

Monica begins cleaning brushes.

"She was so confident," I say. "So hypnotically brave in her perspective."

"What does that mean?" Monica scrapes off excess paint from a brush.

"She functioned as if success was possible."

"Isn't it?" Monica says attentive but aloof.

"No. In art, you are either famous or nothing." I raise a bar bell overhead, squint as I lift it side to side.

"So you had to be famous," Monica says with a confused look.

"Right. People will be jealous," Christine said, "screw them. Success is our birthright."

"Pretty extreme."

"Yes. I drop down the bar bells. "Christine was so epistemologically headstrong, coming from Yale, believing she knew what was on the other side of the tapestry." I grab a theraband stretch it wide overhead. "In rainstorms, I say, "she sang through the trees, sending loose leaves flying."

Monica peers over her shoulder, and says, "Wow. How did that make you feel?"

"I was hesitant, conversing with my inner critics, working and reworking each part of a painting."

Monica looks perplexed as if millions of degrees remote from any understanding of me. She moves aside a bird dishtowel with the embroidered words, "A cardinal is a visitor from heaven." Then suddenly Monica leaves. I lie down for a catnap.

* * *

Ma comes outside to the studio with an embellished snack tray. Her silk blue trousers, grey cashmere scarf are all soft and damp. She walks to my cot with furrowed brow. "Your walk-in tub arrived, and they have started replacing the old tub and tile. I need your opinion on these things. You need to come inside."

I have no choice but to emerge slowly from the covers. I check my cell phone. It's still early, about ten am. I push up slowly on the bed because fast movement on waking can trigger nausea.

I had lain down for a brief nap and unfortunately Ma thinks I'm really ill.

She brushes a leaf from her tight jacket.

I nod, looking out the window as droplets splatter on the outstretched glass.

She appears uneasy, being alone with me in the empty studio after so many years. She inspects the room for drafts, tightens a window, "It's too cold," she says. "This place was meant for summer. Cushy plants and chatting people."

I switch on the sound system, searching for inside-by-the fireplace music, under-the-blankets music. Handel's *Water Music* plays. Handel whose eyesight failed after being operated on by the same oculist as Bach.

"I brought you a rose from the gar—den, Ma says," lowering the music. "It's a red beauty."

"Thanks, Ma." I study the creamy vase with bird design.

She snatches the rose from my too thin arms and places it on the workbench table. She is slim through denial, her body light like delicate china, but with no gleam and sparkle to the flesh.

She arranges the light repast she has brought on a table, claps down the sparrow placemats, unscrews the porcelain jar with wren design. "Eat something," she says. "I've your favorite Peregrine Peach jam." She squeezes onto the workbench, her back to the wall, below my old watercolors of crabs, monarch butterflies, foxes.

"Careful," I tease. "Even old paintings need protection."

Ma adjusts the bench cushion with its birds on wire embroidery. The diffused gray light over her sallow face shows she's been crying. "You're holding on," she says with a cold tone, "but just by a thread."

I plump the bird-face pillow beneath my head and ease back down on the cot.

Ma coaxes me to the worktable, where she prepares English Breakfast tea. I drag my legs over the side of the bed. The rain has shadowed the floor to brackish brown. My feet touch the floor, cramping on the damp wood. I wobble with each step careful not to slip on the beige bird rug.

Ma nervously cracks off a piece of croissant.

I make it to the workbench. We sit and she dresses our places with napkins featuring a blue bird, flowers, and scripture, Joshua 24:15 "As for me and my house we will serve the Lord." Outside there's no breeze anymore

I study my tea, one sugar lump rapidly disintegrating. The myriad of brown hues now punctuated with white.

Indigestion takes hold. I blow on the too hot English breakfast tea. I can't even talk. I rip a Stevia packet into the brew. Outside wind builds weaving through the trees.

Ma studies me, as she squeezes some lemon. "What went wrong?" she says.

I cringe, swallow, the burning tea. Suddenly it becomes grey and thick with brown sweeteners clawing the bottom.

"You hesitate," Ma grins. Within minutes she is refilling my tea. Light-headedness takes hold. I bite into a piece of lemon, swallow it whole, choke down more tea. Rain falls, cascading, slashing the windows as if demanding entrance.

Ma's eyes shrink. "You can't stay out here. You have to be cared for by someone."

"And that someone is you?"

Ma says, "you're physically restricted and your impulses need to be controlled. If you don't restrain yourself, God knows what will happen."

"Please, Ma." I reach for the ceramic bird coffee mug with scripture - psalm 103:5 'He fills My Life With Good Things.'

Ma takes a smidgen of margarine. "Listen to me, son," she says. "I know how necessary it is for you to be . . ." She searches for words, "alone quiet. But some days, you should read, relax." Her eyes are concerned again, suspiciously warm and gray, and somehow kind. "Let me remind you, I let you paint as long as I could, opened your mail, answered your calls, ordered your food, did all to conserve your energy for creation."

I stumble back to the cot, put on musky socks and shoes. "I'd like to make a request for family counseling sooner rather than later," I say. "Don't 'babyfy' me!"

Ma says, "I must. You LIE to me. I thought you had learned enough not to paint the rain, a . . .topic that excites you to be outdoors in bad weather."

"I'll be careful."

"And now," Ma says, "I see your old rain painting on the easel. I hope to god you're not reaching out to Christine."

"Please."

"Her departure put you in the psychiatric ward--escaping on sheets and painting the wall trying to get out."

I grab my cane, pressing my feet against the floor, intent on reaching that canvas.

Ma cries, "I believe in you and your talent, but the market for paintings, like that for board games, has gone. Don't make me watch you kill yourself."

"I won't." I half smile, detour, cracking the window so I can hear the steady drumming of rain. If only like that owl I could perch on a thick branch very close to the house, sleeping through the storm while tightly clasping that limb.

"Why won't you listen to me?" Ma says. "You haven't listened to me --." Red splotches pop out on her forehead. "I phone you. You don't answer."

"I'm busy--"

"I text you a warning, you send me a happy face." She fixes me with her glowering grey eyes. "You are not YOUNG. I hate to say it."

"Then don't--"

"Men are dropping dead now at 40, 50. Your father at 67."

"He had a heart murmur."

"And you have stomach cancer," Ma says.

"You're upsetting me, Ma."

"I hope it is scaring you." Ma rails a hand to her cheek, her face chalky, one eye bloodshot. "I walk the floor at night, pray to Our Lady, wondering what I can do to save you. Everything comes down to caution in the end. You haven't got real choices. Day in and day out, one thought fills my mind. I'm responsible for keeping you alive. It's my obligation." She sobs.

"You've been the most concerned person," I say, twisting painfully toward her.

"Where's it gotten me? Your father's dead. Your sister's gone. Your nephew's flunking out of school. And you're going to have a final relapse. I'm sure you will. All it takes is for one little abnormal cell to take charge of your body."

"Why don't you let me find out?"

"Because you act stupidly."

"I recognize what you've contributed, but it's my life!"

"You're selfish."

"All artists have to be. We live with people who don't know, care, no actually HATE what we do. We are trying to see clearer, make the world a kinder place, not prioritize everything on money."

"Shut up. You. I'm on five heart pills, because of you. There isn't one mother with an artist son who doesn't have some physical defect from the experience. Either we're overweight, or we shake. I've got cataracts on both eyes."

Ma rises, slams a window shut. "Painting out here is impossible what with the drafts, dampness. Not to mention chemicals in the paint. You can die any minute and you will." She shakes her head, grabs her umbrella, and goes out. I hear her struggling with it, as the drops are bigger than grapes and pelting down.

I take a step out under the awning. The soil that was fried so hard last summer is mushy with rainwater. Outside the grass looks normal but one step forward would tells an angry story. Any pressure will sprout water, soaking the foot. For a second I imagine Christine walking across the yard with her suitcase, every step causing a temporary puddle. I spy the roost box she created for backyard birds to keep warm in the rain. I see her talking to a robin, before she departs through the garden but her expression evades me.

A menacing wind goads me to turn to the rain painting. "Go ahead try," it sneers, "now you're alone. Paint."

Inside, I glare at the rain canvas and the details elude me. A plane flies overhead and I stare at the easel where the picture rumbles. I hold my bare arm out to paint her, it falls to my side. I squint at the image on the canvas, but I don't see the rain colors. I pull a stool up close to sit while I paint, but Christine's voice grates my ears. "Remember to draw with an eraser," she says, "Leave only the tiniest glimpses no one else perceives."

My blood runs cold. Her face looks too small in the painting, too vague.

The subtleties of tone and smokiness of her expression keep eluding me like they did at the beginning.

I retreat to my worktable with its ashy smells of charcoal crayon and clay. I sketch Christine's face, tear it up, only to draw and toss three more sketches.

* * *

Am I missing something? Was there something I didn't do for or neglected seeing in her? I think back on the lack of understanding I chose to have in Rhinebeck, 2011 when Christine was pregnant. Were we doomed to be brokenhearted? Love can draw upon extremely selfish emotions.

It was raining. An unusually blustery October heralding an even more vicious November. I was late rushing back, soaked, from a gallery preview in New York City. A desperate Puccini aria invaded our tiny living room (table, sofa, desk).

"Didn't you hear me phone?" Christine said, clutching her round belly. "I could be in labor. I'm eight months." She looked Botticelli beautiful in her stretch orange top with brown velour jacket.

"I left my cell at the gallery," I said.

"You missed the birthing class."

"Sorry." I dropped the heavy damp backpack.

She said, "I could send a car for your phone or have my agent drive it here tomorrow."

"I may have to go back."

"You can't go to New York in this rain! This is your baby."

I went to kiss Christine, but she gave me her cheek.

Was there something redemptive I could do? "Oh honey," I said, "This is my first solo show in New York. Everyone feels it will launch..."

"You to what? Where?" She whipped a hand though her blonde mane jarring a loop earring.

I studied the belly of the refrigerator in the next room. The wound of her unplanned pregnancy hadn't healed. I was still mad at her though I knew being 32 and childless had terrified her. I didn't tell Christine I had nightmares about dead babies. Instead, I presented her with a five-pound box of Godiva, which I'd managed to secure before boarding, and which I couldn't afford ($290).

She popped off the limp gold bow, grinned. "The only good thing about today is you're home." She guided me to the green couch facing the road to the train, moved her textile sketches aside. "Let's sleep in tomorrow, do late breakfast at Bread Alone?"

I looked out the flooding windows. The trick was not making the hurt worse than it was. I hated to feel so absorbed in my thoughts, so broken as an artist that I rejected her. But my opening was that weekend. I knew my shows weren't as glorious as hers. Still if I didn't try, nothing would definitely come of my art. Christine had galvanized our professors at Harvard, her painting selling in the thousands her first year of grad school. Each bird she sketched was an immediate sensation.

"Let's live off my money for a while," she said. "You can just make art. My manufacturers will take a look at your designs for other consumer products. They'll drive up here."

I clawed the armrest. "Don't start. I'm trying to get something going for myself. I thought when we got this place you'd be happy. . . You keep wanting me to be something that I'm not. A family man. A lets stroll in the park man. Watch a sitcom and drink beer, man. Try to understand and be reasonable," I said. "I want a life for myself in New York." (I didn't see then, she was right.)

"Haven't we already seen that doesn't work?"

"For you, no." I looked out the streaming windows. Blue light was ash scattered through the air. "I can't just lose myself here."

"Can't you go into teaching or art management?" she said. "There are schools and interesting people in Rhinebeck."

"Really?" I said. She shook her head. "You find plenty of time for all these outlets in New York. Can't you find time for our pregnancy? We don't need the money. Can't you just do your art?"

"Without an audience how do I know I'm any good? Look," I said," I should go back to New York. The rain has let up and there is going to be a downpour tomorrow."

"Where would you sleep?"

"In the train station. The car. What do you care?"

"I want you here with me."

"That is not what you want. You want me to shrink into some puppet," I said. "I can't control you. I say what I need, and you discount it."

"I'm seeing Mark again," she said.

"Your therapist?" My stomach revolted. "That bastard," I said, "you haven't talked to him for five years. Colluding with Mark. Calling me, 'the tarantula.' Based on some history of god knows what, you load up ammunition against me. I'll take the car and sleep at the station at 42nd Street. I hate it here. I feel like I'm drowning."

She stared at me through eyes gone hard. "Maybe our teachers at Yale didn't have it all wrong. Maybe art has turned you into an egomaniac. You're so full of yourself you think you can do and say anything. Other people have needs, wants. *If you leave, don't come back."*

The next morning, I awake, happy to not be in Rhinebeck. Monica's wants me to attend a show at the New Orleans Museum of Art insisting this event has two values: seeing art and helping the community. But dare I trust Monica? Or reveal how tired I am. In his narrative poem the Metamorphoses, Ovid describes how distrust led to murder among the gods.

That night, we white-knuckle it in an Uber as we do a slick turn. Of course, Monica wanted to go to the fundraiser not realizing its stratification, handed down since the Civil War when defunct planters sought ways to avenge themselves on the Yankees with private parties and public parades.

Monica, spry in a long blue gown, grabs a wheel chair from the coatroom, and smiles at me. "I think it will do you good to get into the world and be a great artist again," she says.

"No wheel chair," I say, cringing at my limitations moving out in the museum. I cane walk in my too loose tuxedo despite the pain. The guard steps back creating a space for us to pass. "You don't need to get checked, Mr. Roo. I know you." I smile thankful for the tiny recognition.

The parlor with eight-foot crystal chandeliers ribboned in purple, green, and gold abhors me with its lavishness as does Georges Peal, the director of the CAC who sent me the rejection letter. He's all new in navy linen & silk, caught up with men in white suits, women in pale pinks, ice blues and waiters serving freshly baked scones. I explain who he is to Monica. Her face falls as if she realizes her mistake in bringing me here.

My breathing increases but I pursue Georges, despite Monica's protests, past girls in creamy cotton materials and boys with designer sunglasses. He stands there with sly downcast eyes, his sweaty fat hands clutching a ribboned creamy program. Garden

District ladies intent on themselves approach him. They are beyond Chanel. So much plastic surgery when they blink their faces don't move. I wave once, twice, tell myself he doesn't see me. For a panicked brief moment, I reflect on how bad off I look. Monica tags me. We pass a trio playing Liszt, a composer whose talent so outstripped his sinfulness the Pope titled him, Abbe.

"You don't need to do this," she says. "You're getting upset. You should go back to your studio and paint."

I break out in a sweat, turn to her and say, "I need to stand up for myself." When I move, a fragility takes hold--twitching my limbs when I don't want them to, jerking my spine when I don't want it to, weakening my ankles till I feel they will collapse.

The director ducks into a nearby exhibit. "No Dead Artists." Immortal works by Picasso, Braque, Dufy and Miro. I'm dizzy, wobbly. For a moment I think I'm not going to be here when they take these down. Monica forces me into a wheelchair, tries to distract me, rolling me to a painting of Weeping Evangeline. But I push off the chair and seize the cane. I stumble pass stanchions of too sweet roses, gray haired women drinking Cabernet, "debutante delights,"(the name for available bachelors under 45)—. I make it outside to tents where delicacies are set up. Platters sale past: petite Brie en croûté, lump crabmeat, oyster patties. Waiters in full dress whiz by with silver platters of petite crawfish on toothpicks. The director of the CAC stands gloating, clotted cream pastry in hand, smiling at couples to the left, to the right: people who have gotten used to being at a certain level, who wouldn't know how to cope going down. The proud bunch ignores me. I'm the same man who graduated summa cum laude. But artists don't provide a service that people can live without. And by forty we're all damaged.

I grab a Bloody Virgin full of hot sauce, pickles, beans. Oh, I want to kill that man, knock him down, pulverize him. Part of my mind is literally flying up in dark flecks. I go to Georges roaring inside, cautious outside.

"How are you," he says with a surprised worried look. I put down my drippy glass. "I got your rejection letter."

He steps back, his brow steaming with sweat. Wind hollers outside. Former friends from Tulane Art School, wide eyed and with lifted eyebrows, strut past like penguins in their full dress.

The director turns to leave but I tap his foot with my cane, saying, "The doctor told me to call if I had a fever higher than 102 degrees. But with your letter my fever is constantly higher you see."

"Think I need a refill," the director huffs watery eyes raised as if to call for help.

"Not just yet," I say.

Monica waves. She pushes through cold women in sparkly ball gowns, their elbow-length kid gloves flung open so they can grab lipstick from inside pearl-studded purses; men in tux, waggling eyebrows, sending her lecherous smiles.

I speak on, "Your form letter refused ALL of my art."

Monica arrives just as Haydn's *Farewell Symphony* starts playing.

"Did you know," I say to director Georges, "this symphony calls for musicians to depart one by one as they complete their parts?"

"No" he says, keeping a steely gaze ahead.

Monica bends in close pretending to be in a hurry. "Can we leave?" she says.

Waiters holler in the distance. Seared scallops with asparagus, gratin of crawfish tails pass by me. I glare at the director, grinding my eyes into his cheek, seizing his arm, putting indentures in his shiny black sleeve. "Now," I say. "I'm in a frenzy . . . Feel like I got to kill someone."

Georges looks about for help.

"And you! You contemptible bastard. I can't figure what to do . . .with all those paintings you dislike!" I say.

"Things will get better," Georges says, reaching for his cell phone.

"That's what I believed," I say, blotting my mouth, noting a drop of blood. "Joseph Haydn's symphonies were written at 60. But what if my body gives out and your letter is my legacy?"

Monica grabs my arm, "We must go," she says.

Georges glares at me. "You think my letter could kill you?"

"Telling me I lack passion. What the bloody world is that supposed to mean." Like I don't see deep enough or hurt bad enough.

"You're not operating on a practical level," he says.

"PRACTICAL. What kind of word is that to fling at an artist?"
Waiters gather. Onlookers close in.

"I didn't mean you had no talent," he says. "Your focus on technique or getting a niche holds you back in some way."

"Why would it, when I've nothing to lose now?" I scream. I lean on the cane, then wave it like a sword. People about me back off. "My paintings are strong, unique, and masterful," I cry.

He reaches for his cell.

"You'd like to crate them, throw them in the ground, and bury them. But they'll work their way up and out into eternity. And you'll go down in history as the man who tried to destroy me."

"Preposterous," Georges says, still searching for his cell.

I grab his collar.

He gasps, "Security."

I pull him to me. "You sniveling idiot. I've seen you on the backstreets of the Quarter with your 'little friends.' Who dote over you? You don't even have an art degree. You got your pathetic job because you slept with the right boy. . . One day soon before I die, I'll sign all my paintings. That's what Turner did? He had his sons bring him all his paintings at the very end. I'm going to throw all my stuff in a room, and whoever finds it, finds it...."

Georges hollers for security. The doorman grabs my arm, attempts to throw me out. Faces around me loom with outrage and pity. The grand tent area shushes behind me into silence then a mounting hum as stunned guests wander about. But Monica shoves me in a wheelchair and wheels me up and away inside to the Degas gallery, now empty.

I think pity is the worst thing for me. My breathing has increased noticeably. I tell myself to calm down by meditating on Degas. But *The Portrait of Estelle* isn't there. This museum is so small they have to rotate their great art. I forgot. They switch masterpieces out in winter. I'm flushing hot with humiliation. I need to see that *Portrait,* to rest inside the bleak downcast eyes of Estelle, the long fingers of her ghostly hands touching the gladioli, the moaning images of darkness, of rain in the distance. But the wall is garishly vacant.

* * *

Skye Evans gives me a fierce hug, steps back, shocked at my bony structure. Lets face it 85% of people with my type of cancer would already be dead. He's visiting from back east, just got back from a round of job interviews, and enjoyed my attack on the CAC director.

"I tried to call you several times," he says. "You don't answer."

"Sorry. I've been a little low."

"I saw your pompous ass director. I have faith in you. Have faith in yourself."

"Are you here for long?" I say, forcing a smile, so rugged is he in his fitted tux with starched shirt, and designer shoes with fringe.

Skye tosses back his full streaked blonde hair like a stallion, masking his eyes and other tiny imperfections. "I'm moving into the scene in New Haven," he says. "I'm an art critic now. Soon I'll to be dean of an art school, I hope."

I pull up tall on my cane, encouraged. Skye and I had a mentor in New Haven whose painting elicited this *je ne sais quoi* that makes for great as opposed to proficient art. Skye insists on visiting my studio almost pushing me to his car. I'm annoyed I can't keep up but text Monica to go home without me.

"Get your paintings out there and then the fame and respect comes," Skye says, slapping my back. "If you make this journey alone, you'll feel terrified — and crazy."

Come east where the intellectuals are. When you don't know artists who confirm you, it feels like you fell from the sky."

"I've done so little good painting since I left," I admit, "my art is on a diet."

"You're going to always have to be in NYC part of the time because that's where it is for you. You are a painter." Leaning back in the Subaru, stretching his neck, he says, "Look we all want to feel better. Having cancer is a lot of pressure. Artists are not equipped to deal with these maintenance issues."

CHAPTER 8

Back home in my studio, Skye surveys my paintings on the walls, smiling cynically, shifting his weight, contemplating each composition. I rearrange a basket with pencils, leave Monica a second message.

"There's a kind of priestly cast to your recent art," Skye says. "I like that."

"I toyed with taking the four minor orders and even the priesthood," I say.

"I didn't know that.

"For me, art was religion. I was called to it, and when I stopped because I was ill I felt like I'd broken some primordial pact."

He helps me to prop up some rain paintings on the worktable, and seems glued to them transfixed.

Outside, the moon appears and the sky that had been so dark is suddenly light.

"Oh my!" he says, "The timing is really strong for these." He puts a soft hand on my shoulder. Vulnerability is key. We have to hear how hard it is. And we do. These will sell."

"Please." I push out the crick in my neck, moving away. People with his stature are always promising things. Hopefully he's not trying to seduce me. I daren't think it.

His piercing green eyes catch me, the lids flickering every so slightly. "How's your ex-wife?" he says.

"She never calls. And yours?"

He lets out a churlish laugh. "I was married a very long time. Three weeks. But yes she's fine. Calls every few weeks." He purses his lips and says dramatically, "I'm sorry about Christine. I found her great fun if difficult to be with."

Strangely queasy, I pass a mirror and see my skin, cool to the touch, has turned light gray. A patch on my neck is reddish blue. My dark brown eyes are watery.

"Look," I say, grabbing the back of a chair, "I need to rest."

But Skye is letting out a cry and creeping to the painting of Christine that Monica has brought here and set up on an easel next to the worktable. I sit on the cot in an effort to divert him from the Christine painting, which seems fiendishly alive as if it is crying out.

Skye paces before the paintings. "Oh my! The timing is really strong for this. I'm not speaking randomly. I get $5000 for each artist I place. I suspect a part of me knows what will sell because I've a keen sense of what the upper crust are lacking and what they think the art they buy can supply. Is it possible to imagine them suffering—divorce? A loss of fortunes? Or a business? Something that would connect them to your current sense of loss."

Again he squeezes my shoulder.

I release my tense jaw. He is trying to seduce me I fear, or sexually telling me something. He's unmasked and stands before the unfinished painting of Christine in the rain, smiles provocatively. "This is the painting I want. When you finish it." He squeezes my shoulder. "Name your price and where you want it hung."

My eyes are watery. "Look," I say, "I've got to go the doctor's tomorrow morning."

"Why?"

"I go twice a week for transfusions."

His face constricts. "Oh gosh. That's right. I'm sorry, Bro." He hiccups nervously and leaves his card.

Oh my, was he in love with Christine? Is he attracted to me? Or, does he want to sell the painting based on Christine's fame? I couldn't really hear what he was saying to me. I'd have to ponder it when I felt better.

The fragrance of the pines is so fresh and strong it calls me to the door. The yard is Van Gogh lit with stars. The pale brown oak trees are shiny their green leaves virescent.

"I'm BI, and TRI," he calls back." Love threesomes," but I don't let it interfere with selling clients. First comes the magic, then comes the money." *It's amazing how you can know people and not.*

A few shots of light brand the dark earth as he departs. I go inside the dreaded studio. My neck feels stiff. I swallow a painful lump in my throat. My oncologist said I should call if it doesn't go away after 5 days. I cough, blot my mouth, noting a drop of blood. Oh I feel so hot. The doctor said if I had a fever higher than 102 degrees, I should phone. But I'm too tired to go inside to take pain medication to decrease the sore throat and achiness.

Johannes Brahms Symphony # 2 in D fills my head with sound, no place left to put blood thoughts. Brahms who was rejected as a conductor in 1862, Brahms who permanently moved to Vienna in 1868, Brahms who took more than 10 years to complete and present his first symphony. Brahms who remained a bachelor, though he was in love with Robert Schumann's wife.

I grab a painting stool, sit, my back to a blank easel. I imagine Christine on the makeshift cot-bed there. What a frail, easily hurt, rather pathetic thing her body seems now in my memory, naked; somehow half-complete! After the baby, she lost too much weight.

I study the canvas, Christine's failed reflection in the middle, her too flat hair, the too pale sky, too muddied water. I hear Christine's voice as if calling from the painting itself. *"Be vigilant. You're never allowed not to be vigilant."* I again pick up the brush, squint at the canvas trying to see the big shapes and movement in the image.

I try to tone the rain falling about Christine in the painting, working past discomfort in my upper body. Using a big brush, I paint in burnt sienna. But Christine is too bright in the foreground. I lean into my canvas, sweaty and shaky and pick up a brush. My eyes are moving from place to place, unable to decide what the focus of the piece is. I use a tiny bit of dioxin purple to darken sienna for dark darks of the rain, and roughly paint them in. I check a photo of Christine to try to see the image already there. Weather has changed. The sky is a tumult of giant rain waves. It's too dark so I open the blinds. The oak tree appears an angry burnished black. One of its limbs has been split off.

CHAPTER 9

The next morning, I'm tense. I see what I don't like in my painting, the highlights in the eyes are too big. I scrape off paint, bleed more purple on the canvas. Monica's back and has been watching me. She doesn't bring up the episode at the museum. Thank God. I put down my brush.

"Don't watch," I say. "You agreed. I'll take my meds then you must leave."

She walks over, moves back a disarray of items on my worktable, watercolors, a sketchbook, a can of rubber cement, unpacks some medical supplies.

"What was she like? That woman in the painting?" Monica says, taking my pulse.

"Christine?" I struggle for a summary word, every fiber in me recoiling. "Loquacious, I say finally."

I hurry through my temperature taking and pills and retreat to the canvas. Unnerved, I'm hoping for an almost sinister privacy, but Monica follows me, points to a tiny swaddled thing in the painting.

"What's that?" she asks.

Tightness in my stomach. "Nothing," I say. Look I need to get back to work."

She leans into the painting. "It looks like a baby," she says. "Yours?"

I don't answer. I stare at the painting dazed, unable to talk further. Monica looks around in a perplexed manner and leaves.

I stand frozen, dazed remembering, the word "baby" exploding inside me. "In 2012, we finally did have a son." I sit on the wobbly stool. Wind howls around the studio. Christine wouldn't let me name him. I could pick the middle names. I suppose it was because it was something that could last forever. Afterwards, the baby slept between us."

There's a stunned silence in my heart. I'm so shocked by the reconnection with that pain, I'm unable to think clearly. I rest for a moment on the cot, scrolling through my cell for diversion. Once again cold sweats take hold, stinging in my thumbs and toes. I feel faint, slump back on the cot with my eyes shut, listening to the rain, whipping debris about the studio. I plan on napping until I can bear to open my eyes again and look at that image of my son, shrinking inside that canvas, turning inside out. I just want to hide in silence, stare out the windows, where the rain's already dripping through the oak trees.

* * *

But Ma bursts through the studio's timber door with a shawl bound tightly about her head, her face stark, white, and tight, microstructures of rain all over her Chanel suit.

Servants coming across courtyard entering studio delivering a coffin follow her. Imagine my horrified expression as it unfolds.

"It's awful," she says, "your gallery director at the CAC sent back all your—" Her voice cracks. "Paintings in—."

I place my feet on the floor and slowly uncurl my head.

She strains for words, "A casket."

Suddenly, my head is spinning. I hope I don't pass out.

"I want to kill that CAC director," Ma says. "Write a seething letter to *The Advocate/Picayune*." Ma's eyes jump toward the sound of approaching footsteps. "The servants are bringing the COFFIN out here. I couldn't keep it . . . inside."

Two yardmen drop a coffin onto my sun-speckled floor.

"Apparently, they are discounts for mailing coffins—" Ma says, retreating to the swan chair.

I manage to lean over and unlatch the lid of a casket of reinforced 3/8" plywood. Watercolors languish on the cotton muslin interior, barely separated by tissue. Paintings I've given half my life to create. Gotten up in the lonely dawn hours, before light lit the sky, or traffic hit the streets, or sun baked the houses to make. Should I white knuckle it and retrieve each work in tissue paper? Or bury them all in one go? Telling myself not to hear those drawings, pastels, oils politely crying.

I collapse on a bench, hunching over. "Please don't talk about my . . .my past," I say. "I'm trying to think future and keep what little identity I have."

"And what is that?"

"I don't know."

"What do you want to be?"

"Something bigger.

"I'm sorry, son," Ma says, backing away, darting off under a flapping black umbrella to the big house.

I stand in the doorway feeling the rain's sharp scent, everything spinning around me. I tell myself not to feel, to think, about the relics of my art. I steady myself, pivot toward the Christine painting but there she is laughing and holding up the baby. Just as quickly the mirage vanishes inside the canvas.

I go outside. Although it's 55 degrees and too cold to paint, I like it when I'm freezing. When I can't think of anything but getting warm. I sit on a bench and the dampness pushes my pants against my thighs. I look up at the frosty blue sky. The Van Gogh blue raging sky. I relax into the wet bench back, close my eyes. Oh to be one with nature and not think. The moist air wraps me in chill. There's no consciousness... the trees are all sleeping. The birds shivering silently inside the leaves.

Some time later, I slide inside the cot's clammy sheets, turn on Rachmaninov's *Piano Concerto no. 2 in C minor*, and look up Yeats, The Second Coming. Yeats the last poet who made a real living at it.

> Turning and turning in the widening gyre/
> The falcon cannot hear the falconer;
> Things fall apart; the centre cannot hold;/
> Mere anarchy is loosed upon the world,
> The blood-dimmed tide is loosed, and everywhere/
> The ceremony of innocence is drowned;
> The best lack all conviction, while the worst/
> Are full of passionate intensity....

Institutions have been destroying artists for centuries. Not consciously but by making them invisible. How many museums would we need to sustain all our great painters? To hang art. Upkeep it, even store it in the basement. The majority of works in most museums is not contemporary.

Tomorrow, I'll get an enormous amount of work done. Tomorrow, I'll get myself up at 5 a.m. I'll finish that last painting.

But Monica arrives, rain and a gust rushing in after her and insists I go inside. She pales, horrified as she spots the coffin box.

I explain.

"Dreadful," she says, scrunching down, lifting the ebony lid, the color of her scrubs squeezing out paintings, unrolling them in the light.

"The wrong people had these," Monica says. Quickly, she calls friends for help. Shortly afterwards they come, unpack my paintings, and take the coffin away.

I swallow unnecessarily, holding my breath, regard the returned paintings. It took me ten years to make those paintings, now strewn discretely about my studio, like ghosts, thin, moaning, embarrassed trying to slip inside the walls.

"I'm still in shock. That that director could do that," she says.

"It's called retaliation," I manage.

"He's hard-hearted. Demonic lets say what it is. I hope this will drive you to paint more now than ever. We have to fight evil with action."

I reach for the cane. But it's no good; I'm dizzy, and I sit back down. I'm not abnormal in terms of a lot of artists. Usually it takes a blow to wake us up.

"I just need to sit alone somewhere for a few years and think," I say.

"It's pretty fabulous that your work was under review any way. Don't you think?"

"No."

"Be strong. Be courageous," she whispers and leaves, not understanding I fear my painting is me, it's all the identity I've ever really had.

I want to call her back, but instead I clutch my cane barely making it outside.

CHAPTER 10

Back in the day room, I find myself walking slower than normal—avoiding the bump in the Oriental rug, our dog, Boon, stretched out, the unpaired dove moaning in her cage. By virtue of their melancholy call, mourning doves have been fittingly named. My body caves into the aqua armchair, Christine's armchair. She would sink into it, fall asleep bent down, or lie back her jaw swung open. Sometimes a tear would dry on her cheek. Other times she'd call on me to play something on the spinet piano long gone from this room. *The Moonlight Sonata* was her favorite.

I stare at a mockingbird on the rug. My wife would come in here, I think, loosen her hair, eat pecans, and drink wine. I press back into my chair. The velvet sooths my aching spine.

Monica comes in, runs the vitals machine. "I like that chair," she says.

"So did my wife. She sat right here, in this chair. Nights she came in here and drank."

"She was an alcoholic?" Monica asks.

I hesitate. "I think so. Yes." And she had a cat called, Christmas."

"Really."

"It was a feral cat. Its ears had been burnt in a fire.

"My."

"Every night that cat waited for her outside the studio. And she'd carry it under her umbrella to this room. When my wife left, Christmas got in here and tore the room apart. Wadded the drapes. Knocked everything on the floor. Howled. Tonight, I feel like Christmas."

Monica takes my pulse. Her shirts sleeves expose her thin firm arms.

I imagine her, naked white with sunburned face . . .

"I'm in mourning for my paintings," I say, suddenly overwhelmed by grief. How do you accept loss?" I say.

She clears her throat, pushes her hand down in her pocket, and pulls out a flimsy Kleenex. "I don't. I'm still mad about things. The last year with my husband was a battle I lost every day and started the next." She looks away. "My husband wanted to die. He couldn't stand getting weak. He was strong before. Raced motorcycles for the thrill. He didn't want anyone to see that he couldn't walk, so I'd help him down to his motorcycle, and he'd drive it to the mailbox. The bike roaring beneath his thin legs. He'd come back to the stairs, exhausted and sit. And when no one was looking, he'd ease himself up one step at a time. I smiled from the window—so attentive to what he was doing, merged with his courage. But finally the world of matter faded away, and he gave up, and I gave up."

She folds back my bed sheets; her hands are narrow and slim. "I have faced sadness, too."

"Oh, yes . . .how did you cope?"

"I was a network of nerves. Every night there I was on the internet looking up cures for his cancer. But it wasn't hard till the end, cause I didn't accept it at first." She unravels her Kleenex and blows her nose. "Speed was too thin; I see it now . . . "

"How did you deal with his death?" She's resistant but then, when she comes in to take my pulse, she blurts. "My husband knew he was dying, but he hid it from me."

"What did you feel when you found out?"

"Betrayed . . . The first day he died, the lights in my room would flicker when I walked by our wedding photo with Speed lifting my veil. Monica looks at me with troubled eyes. "Then came the visits. Speed scattered through my dreams that first night after his death–coming in and out. I would feel his strong long arms above me, reach down for my head but when I went to grasp them, they faded into the air." She turns her blue eyes away from me. "The second night, at six pm in the evening he came back, wouldn't say anything, but left."

"Did you see him?" I sit on my bed and hand her a fresh Kleenex.

She takes it, moves away, a little stiff. "No but I know my husband."

"What did he want?"

She looks at me sharply. "Permission to leave." She spreads wide the Kleenex, blows her nose.

"What did you tell him?"

"I said, 'No.' He came back the next evening, the third night after his death, at 6 pm. He asked the same question."

I lean forward on the bed. "What did you say?"

She turns away from my face. "I told him, 'Not yet.'" I couldn't let him go even as a vanishing spirit. When I met him I knew I was for. That's the sense I felt, sensed, smelled, touched, lived for. The thought of him kept me safe." Her voice breaks. She goes to the doorway, leaves quickly into the bright light.

"Not yet," the words spin inside me.

She kneels down and pets under Boon's raised head. "Try to keep working. Don't think. Just create. We can help each other. One term, we nurses use is called a mutual hold. Hopefully," she says, pulling the vitals machine back. "I hold you and you hold me . . . and together something good comes out of that for both of us."

"I can do that."

CHAPTER 11

Strangely delighted by Monica's sharing, I make it to my studio. The yard embraces me with its delicate scents: lavender, honeysuckle, the ground's fastly drying in a sparkle. The sky is pinkish, tinted red and blue at the edges. When I look up through the web of tree branches, the leaves stencil themselves against the sky. I merge with everything. And yet, I see sharper. The sun, the rain, I smell the grass in the garden. I can almost taste the resurrection ferns, the green leafy plant on tree branches.

Inside, I turn up the sound system. Music lifts through, "Because of you, there is a song in my heart ....because of you my life had it start."

While I'm humming along, Skye calls telling me he'll be in town next week and wants to see the Christine painting. I begin to work on it, can't stop, get angry with myself for not being able to capture what I need. I noodle, pausing, setting the brush down and backing up, repeating strokes on the same spot with no thought, praying the painting will narcotize me like the great outdoors. I soothe myself, trusting the need to cling to Christine will lift. I paint in one place so long that I wear a hole completely through the canvas, swear uncontrollably, toss the painting aside.

I adjust the easel, decide on a tiny brush with hog bristles and perch on my stool. Christine scowls at me, from inside the painting her feet slammed into the dirt. I watch the painting, and I'm inside the rain, with earth and wind drifting here and there, cool moss and water punching through. Sensations pass directly into the mind. I look how Christine shields her face from the curious, won't admit me into her emotions, but still she does. I feel her reaching out, as if she is holding on to some unseen huge winged creature that keeps her suspended. . .

"Why not give in," she whispers. "Be sad. Sob. Paint what you feel, see . . .."

"Our … son?" I say. I like to hold on to his expressions.

"Draw him," Christine says from inside the work. She lifts her slender white hand, and cradles his head. "He's alive in your mind. If you don't draw his face, it's like he is forgotten."

I paint without stopping, forcing myself to keep the thread. I recall that tiny boy, his little image inches from my face, his big blue intelligent eyes, saucer-like taking in the world, his full lower lip, and dimpled chin. And then the canvas paints me.

I tell myself to face what I don't want to see. Blind my mind. Try to get drunk in her spirit. Then suddenly there's Christine in our world in Rhinebeck.

2012 baby joy, Rhinebeck

Christine is at the workbench, an early century Oak Farmhouse made with thick planks, that's been with us since Yale. But our drawings are pushed aside for a bassinet and Christine is juggling our baby. Blood vessels tighten, causing a "head rush." Ah yes, we're at that table but in Rhinebeck.

"I just realized for the past three months, I've been happy," she says. The baby cries and she shifts it from one shoulder to the next. "I'm grateful now for the time to think about all this," she says. "We've been so over planned."

I blink. See black spots. I've been checking my coat pockets, looking for my commuter train ticket. Oh goodness. How could I have clung to that commute?

"Busyness," she says, "Allowed us to overlook important things. Manhattan was a total time waste. Having had the baby, I want to rest and enjoy him. Later on we can go to Paris or Rome or Chicago. Later on you can do more shows in New York."

She puts the baby in the carrier, grabs her keys, and trudges to the door. "All I need is the three of us in Rhinebeck. Maybe a picnic on the Hudson or a hike down Poet Walk."

* * *

Back in the present, I try to keep painting, blues, violets, purples. I didn't recognize how self centered my work made me. How many times have I refused to trust women in situations that were rough?

I sink myself in the blackest rain colors… stroke on cleverly devised patterns of nagging little images.

I thought it would be a short trip to fame but it was a long trip to nowhere. An obsession to work can be repented of, but it can't be forgiven of. I glance at my unringing phone. Don't grieve the world of Christine I tell myself.

CHAPTER 12

Finally I fall asleep. But Christine rises in my dream her hair wild, her face wrought. She's knocking on a window in an all glass room.

The wound I experience is called a transverbaration--the piercing of the heart. Sometimes love, like an arrow, is thrust into the deepest part of the heart and the soul doesn't know what has happened or what it wants. The pain remains unabated for hours, but even after that I continue to feel the torment of an open wound that reaches to my soul.

I soothe myself with the lush orchestration of *Madame Butterfly* blasting through my stereo, feeling for Butterfly who loses her son to the new wife, mourning the doomed Puccini dying of throat cancer while writing the opera.

I awaken that night on the floor, a gash on the right side of my forehead. My face is swollen; circles line my eyes.

Inside, the studio, I listen to *Danse Profane* by Maurice Ravel to pump myself up and go back to the Christine painting. Ravel, for whom music was a kind of ritual, having its own laws, to be conducted behind high walls, sealed off from the outside world, and impenetrable to unauthorized intruders. So what if he never married and had few friends. At least he didn't die like Purcell at thirty-six having caught a chill after returning home late to find that his wife had locked him out...

I collapse in the swan chair. Nightmares take over. I'm pushed through a vast, dark, empty purple sea. I try to scream, but a coin rests in my mouth. I raise my freezing hand and note my fingernails are pulled out. Am I on the course, death? I force myself awake. A crochet blankets strangles my feet. I grab the sound monitor and Mozart's last symphony, *Jupiter No. 41* wails its strident finale.

I grip the armrest, stumble up. But I can't make it. Another pain hits. My eyes land on the crucifix on the wall, noting the bleeding of the head.

A little later, I wake up, headachy and gloomy on the cot. Monica is sitting across the studio, her hair rather mussed and damp and her face pale and worn. She clips the oxygen monitor on my finger announces I'm breathing at eighty-two not ninety-eight percent.

"Do you want a little oxygen?" Monica says.

"No."

Her face darkens all brightness and color melting away.

"Please," I say, "let me be treated by meds only and not in a hospital with more radiation. Or more chemo."

She touches my arm, "I'll phone the new doctor."

"That Swedish army Nazi--? No," I say, clenching my chest.

She sweeps a thermometer over my forehead. "I'm getting you admitted to Tulane," she says.

"If anything happens to me," I say, "will you promise you'll get my paintings in my studio and take care of them?"

"I thought you didn't care about paintings."

"I do… just don't tell people."

"Nothing is going to happen to you."

"If it does?" I say numbness spreading in my arm.

"Then don't worry. I'll protect them."

"Same as if they were yours?"

"Same as if they were mine."

"Don't call the doctor!" I say.

But she does.

The Triage doctor arrives, a fading red head says, "You're in accelerated gas distress. You've probably got a pre-existing condition of irritable bowel syndrome (how awful) that chemo has super aggravated." He gives me injections for increased white blood count.

"No hospital," I say as I fall asleep.

Suddenly, I'm with Monica but on a shut down of some sort. I'm dizzy, weak, my mouth won't cooperate. Words blur. Monica's face looks confused. I tell myself to talk or imagine something. But I can' find a way back into connection. This time, I fall into this paralyzed state where I can't tell anybody what is happening to me because I'm not able to speak or to move or do anything like that and yet it is exactly as if some fiend of a butcher has thrown me on a tombstone and taken a horrible meat cleaver and just slashed my entire body open

As the pain mounts, it is so shocking and horrifying I simply can't believe I can be completely conscious, gasping for air, but unable to express myself. The sound that's finally killing me is the pain that my body can't bear any longer, it turns into sound. I turn into this North African Swift bird, which mates and sleeps on the wing. "Be not afraid." It says, "At every key moment, God says, 'Be not afraid.'" I sleep soundlessly endlessly. Am I dead?

The next forty-eight hours are a blur for me. They keep me in bed. My energy gives out.

CHAPTER 13

Then I open my eyes in a hospital and I know I'm back in this rotten body.

Monica wipes her hands on brown towel, sweeps past a wheelchair and walker in my hospital room, surveys me with tight lips.

Knifing stomach pains! I can't talk to her. Oh lord, I want nothing to do with her.

"They gave you a transfusion. Two transfusions," she says, distressed. She puts a Rosary in my tube-studded hand." It drops on the sheets. She bends over my bed, makes a sign of the cross on my forehead and says. "We're so much greater . . .than who we are . . "Stay connected to God."

Oxygen in my nose makes speaking difficult.

She puts a statue of the Blessed Virgin on my hospital tray. "Pray."

But the hospital nurse--a black girl with an Egyptian wig-- shoves the tray aside checking my vitals. She feeds some medicine into an intravenous bag, checks the reading of my oxygen tubes.

"You're breathing at 65," the Nurse says. "We need to fix a second oxygen mask on you."

Monica touches my hand. "Should I call a priest?"

"No, YOU pray for me."

My blood feels cold, my hospital room claustrophobic; the wall picture of a sunset isn't calming.

The Egyptian nurse breezes over with a fresh gown. I'm covered in angry red hives. She checks all my tubes: oxygen, water, morphine and leaves.

Monica puts a crucifix in my hand,

I put the cross down.

"You have a soul, and your soul is thirsty," Monica says.

I stare at the raised Venetian blinds. Clouds loom dark and heady

"You need to get well and do more art." She closes the blinds. "I brought your supplies." She gestures to the pale green chest of drawers before me, topped with an enamel crucifix, pencils, paper, sketch pad. Drawing is your oldest friend."

I commit to completing a new painting. One specialist gives hope, suggesting complications from surgery a month started a simple bacterial infection.

But that night I'm violently feverish. Does it matter how we exit the world? Some are melancholic, some angry. My uncle curled up in a little ball and refused to talk to anyone.

My friend Skye arrives, in town for an opening at the Ogden museum. He sneaks in with some Godiva chocolates, tells me he has landed the post as dean and then as quickly zips out. What I recall is being stunned at his offering me a tenured teaching position in studio art. Two courses. Two days a week.

I'm pondering the offer, when Ma enters, red-faced. She stands by my breakfast tray, picks at a boiled egg in a cup, (afternoons she may down one or two to keep her appetite low.)

"Ok," she says, eyes small, mouth wide." I just passed that Skye character lurking in the elevator. I made sure he knows you can't accept any painting work at this time."

"What?" My heart rages. "On whose authority?"

"He must have learned about the CAC fiasco," she says, tears welling up "I brought you some reading." She removes magazines on selling art from her unzipped Gucci purse, then dives for a Kleenex to blow her nose. The purse falls onto the floor, taking down a small carton of milk. "Oh I'm an hysterical mess," she says.

"You don't need to work," Ma says, pushing back in her green pleather chair, clearing her throat, her grey eyes red blotched from crying. "Soon, the family trust will resolve, and you'll inherit all your father's money. Alternatively I could die. I've already had two heart attacks."

I blink, turn away, look through the venetian blinds at a blank sky.

She sits back with a weighty movement, "I simply won't allow you to go." She blots her skirt. "I've no influence."

I bypass the ache in my stomach go inside my sheets. I ask her to leave. She ignores me, closing her eyes, stretching out.

"Ma, this opportunity could be my last chance!"

Ma is still pouting, strutting about in Gucci black (short fitted coat, polished double-G belt, and enameled tiger-head buttons) shaking the coffee cup absconded from my tray. "My priest--who probably wants my money--told me to create a little box in my heart nobody could get to, including you." She stares at me through cloudy eyes. "I'm on anti-depressants, five heart pills, and you won't listen to me. You don't have any compassion at all."

"Look, Ma, I'm not going to end my life as if nothing matters."

She raises her cup in the air. "I know. I know. You've been given this gift that you need to do something with." Water rushes to her eyes. Even at her age, she can't understand sacrifice. Art cannot be understood without sacrifice.

* * *

I wake up the next morning sweaty but cool when the loud speaker says: "Mass in Room eight in five minutes. I manage to bribe an attendant to unhook me briefly and take me to Mass. But it's a painful ride, slippery and cold in the hallway.

In the chapel, I sit in a rear pew. I look at a creamy white statue of the Virgin Mary, her robed arms spread wide and think, God's the whole truth about everything. ...Then it hits me that I'm in hell, physically, mentally, spiritually, psychologically. Every possible way you can be in hell.

The priest sermonizes: "Do you know what hell is? It's the utter absence of Hope, which is God. No Hope. On earth, there's Satan's presence but there's tremendous presence of God, so we get God and Satan all mixed up, and we can choose God here as much as we want. Ask Archangel Raphael, the angel of healing for help. Grab onto every godlike thing that enters your day. Try to make a little heaven on earth for yourself where all you see is God."

A few days later I'm sent home from the hospital, only to find that Monica no longer lives in our guest quarters. *Surprise. Shock.* I knew she was relocating from Ma's, but I didn't know it'd be so soon. Ma says Monica's on vacation for two weeks. I'm uneasy she didn't explain, but tell myself she'll call in the next few days.

I try to say the Serenity Prayer, on a prayer card Monica has snuck in my pocket. "Lord make me an instrument of thy peace..."

Back in my bedroom, I find myself walking slower than normal— avoiding the bump in the Oriental rug, our dog, Boon, stretched out, the unpaired dove moaning in her cage. By virtue of their melancholy call, mourning doves have been fittingly named.

I retreat to my studio to make sense of what has happened. Black clouds sprawl over dreary oaks, their branches swaying in the strengthening gusts, dropping their leaves without a fight.

The soil that was fried so hard last summer is mushy with rainwater. Outside the grass looks normal but one step forward would tells an angry story. After the rains any pressure will bring up the water, soaking the foot. For a second I imagine Christine walking across it with her suitcase, every step causing a temporary puddle.

When Monica doesn't answer my calls, I call upon Brahms, turning on his *German Requiem*; Brahms, who played for income at bars; Brahms who was jilted by his only love Clara Schumann and died of cancer shortly after her death, Brahms who damned what was found on earth and embraced death as a relief from the material world's excesses and pain.

I look around my studio, this nowhere space where I dream. I study the painting of Christine that never got finished. Inside it, the sky is low and gray, spilling wide rain over Christine and a baby you can barely see. Indecision is visible on the canvas although it tries to pass for subtlety. I realize I'm a half artist, giving myself to almost painting him, and waiting for something to embolden me. Never going deep inside the pain, breaking off when walls start closing in, living with unclear questions rather than see hurtful answers. Like a falcon only resting on the owner's glove long enough to feed. My adult life spent mid-air. Paris, New York, Boston, Rhinebeck, Philadelphia, Berlin, Princeton, Pennsylvania, New Haven, New Orleans. Even when I lived in one place, I was always commuting to another.

I put on *Un Sospiro* (a sigh) by Franz Liszt, a beautiful concert study, trying to soothe myself. Liszt who wrote over a thousand pieces some of such exceptional high quality, the astounding acrobatic handwork that only a handful of players in the entire world were good enough to perform them.

I move my hand across the sketchbook. I'm remembering the Virgin Mary statue I saw in the Chapel hospital and testing a new take for the Christine painting, asking god to hold me up. I capture the fold in the gown, the hands. But the pencil slips through my fingers and I've no energy to hold it.

A hard wind sends a fierce cold through me. Bitter rain batters the studio.

I turn on Brahms, filling my head with *Symphony Number 2 in D*, no place left to put blood thoughts. Johannes Brahms who was rejected as a conductor in 1862, Brahms who permanently moved to Vienna in 1868, Brahms who took more than ten years to complete and present his first symphony, Brahms who remained a bachelor, though he was in love with Robert Schumann's wife.

I return to my painting stool staring at the wind through the trees, the high branches drooping through teary skies. At the window, a bird is splashing, jumping, drinking below a blackened tree. The oak trees brood in the wetness. Everything changes in the shadows. . . . Colors change and certain leaves are lit up, darkness growing into light. The purity at dawn, the stark reality at noon, and the romantic red of sunset, the final burst of color before blackness. Then twilight--the hour of gentleness-so mysterious, so sad. I don't know what color it is.

The next day, I perfect a small part of the painting: Christine's right hand. I rearrange a basket with pencils, send Monica another futile email, trying to sound hopeful. I look at my unfinished rain painting propped on the back of it by the wall. Christine standing in the dampness, clutching our son. I erase the baby in the painting and try replacing it with a toy of his—a stuffed bear with the a stitched mouth.

Dr. Miles comes out to the studio and I quickly hide the project, having been warned not to resume painting, and knowing his collusion with Ma. Still my devotion to Monica demands a confrontation even if only a slip of information can be gathered.

Rain rattles all around, steaming through the windows. I bang about, picking up different colored pencils and checking them against the weary light.

"Thanks for coming," I say. Miles can be two-faced, I know but still has the remnants of compassion.

"How are you?" he says. He takes in my red puffy eyes and pallid complexion.

I pause by the worktable. "Not well. Since Monica left. I've no idea what's going on. Ma is completely evasive."

"I know." He clears his throat, his eyes shifting behind thick glasses. "Try to bat out bad thoughts because they'll make you feel ill. Some things heal themselves and some through time evaporate."

"What are you talking about? She's completely left. I don't know if she's working any more at all. I'm like stunned although you had warned me."

"I did. When?" Dr. Miles says, scratching a cheek, watching me from a corner chair in my studio.

I sit, make firm, precise movements in a sketchbook, determined to control my temper. "Tell me what happened?" I insist. "Do you know?"

He shrugs.

"I saw her 3 days ago," I say. "What can I do?"

Miles tilts back. "Your Mom said she needed time for personal reasons. That's all I can tell you."

I shake my head, break out in a sweat. I stand up. "Traitor."

Miles' face turns sallow. He seems troubled. "Look," he says, "Monica's life is taking a new phase. Say to yourself, 'Something perfect is waiting.'" Peering over his glasses, he says, "Set the scene. Just like you do when you're painting."

I recoil.

Miles smirks. "Periods with people end. You can't hold on to a life, a house, a pattern."

Indigestion takes hold. I want to scream. "Tell me one thing. Should I confront Ma or would that worsen things?"

"I advise patience." He stretches back, mopping his glasses. "Monica may return. You want to keep your mother-son relationship neutral, like Switzerland."

"How do I reach Monica? Her cell phone doesn't answer. She left no note."

"With Monica," he says, with a measured expression. "You'll need compassion. I'm sure she'll contact you in time."

My pulse speeds up, veins, capillaries, arteries, all racing. I restrain further attack.

He puts his glasses back on. "With Monica, you want a smooth, nice and easy business relationship like you had in the beginning." He slithers on a raincoat and slips out inside a blackening sky.

CHAPTER 15

Two hours later, I clomp to the dining room. I breathe deep. Beethoven's *Moonlight Sonata* plays, Beethoven, who at eight, allowed his father, a court musician, to mold him into a second Mozart.

The help bring Ma a silver tumbler of Bloody Mary: ice cubes, tomato juice, okra, beans, caper berries, and three jiggers of vodka into my room and for me a Bloody Virgin.

Her hair is mussed. Her riding boots scuffed. She shoves her new caramel shiatsu off her lap. He chirps. The rescue place she got him from cut his vocal cords. Her Chanel suit is tinged with funereal tobacco. When Ma is really low she smokes little black cigars, which she does now. "The doctors told me . . . They need to monitor your walk, your blood count. But you missed your appointment. How could you do that?"

She drifts to her shelf with Hummels on alcohol-numbed legs. Ma loves the porcelain child statues a nun created in World War II to pay for the orphans she housed. "I read about an artist, who exhibits Hummel heads," Ma says, lifting a cherubic boy with a flute. "This man buys them in fifty head lots. He also exhibits baby doll limbs. Even Hummel parts attract buyers." Her grey eyes go moist as she studies a figurine of a boy and girl under an umbrella. "Hitler hated Hummels. . .Couldn't take their innocence." Her eyes fill with tears." All this business about . . .needing to paint . . . isn't . . . the real problem. . .Your sickness . . is getting worse." She breathes deep, flattening a hand to her chest to hold in a sob.

I order a Perrier with lime, hoping I won't have to resort to a real drink.

Her lip curls. "Your body's . . . breaking down." She wipes a smudge under her eye. "You haven't got long. And now that you've started missing your transfusions, it'll get worse. You're not thinking clearly. You're worn out." She sniffs, blows her nose. "You've already had one setback."

I focus on the dog crawling under the table.

"A RELAPSE!" she says with a strained voice. "It can happen again . . soon, any time."

"There're worse things than . . ."

"I want you to stay ... inside . . . Near me." Her face constricts.

"That's what I can't take. I need to be outside."

"Lets go for a ride," she smiles, a darkness in her eyes. "I pay the chauffeur whether we go or not. . .And the new pup should have an outing."

* * *

I tell myself to be strong and courageous as Clarence backs down the drive. We bump down cavernous Prytania Street. My eyes salute a pigeon with crust in it mouth, students, biking around potholes. Ma's Shiatsu squawks, and she knocks it on the floor. "I want to compliment you on that woman. Mo-ni-ca. She could con the whole family under the table sequentially."

Oh no it's going to be an attack ride. Sitting tight, arms at my sides, I'm captive in the Cadillac. But haven't I always been captive to someone or something? A treacherous diagnosis. A gallery closing. A fickle patron?

I slap the armrest. "Don't berate Monica."

Ma chugs her tumbler. "No. Who's this nurse? I'm not convinced she's ... What has she taught you? You run off to your studio. . . acting rash," Ma's hand twitches as she grasps a letter from her Chanel bag and sticks it at me. We bump down the oak-shadowed street. With a sinking feeling, I squint at the letter, with bright blue cursive script.

Dear Mrs. Dubonnet,

It is with regret that I must resign from your employ as of today, March 15, 2019. Please don't try to contact me. My old phone is changed. My mail will be forwarded. Give my best to Rooster.

Sincerely, Monica Falcon

"What in God's name is this!" I say.

"You've got to accept these temporary alliances. Medical people don't stay. Soon as the money's threatened, they go." Retrieving the letter, Ma tucks it in her purse. Ma removes her gold Chanel compact, purses her full lips, replenished with Botox, examines her high-filled cheeks.

I try to think of some crisis I handled successfully. Outside, the blood brown skies are infinitely heavier than before. Tchaikovsky's *Death Symphony No 6*, "*The Pathetique*" wails from the car. I grab my cell phone, start to dial.

"She changed her number," Ma says, tucking her compact into her Channel bag.

I try to breathe. I listen to the rings.

"Have you phoned her today . . ." Ma scoops the shiatsu onto her lap, grits her re-veneered teeth. "How long was Monica at it, before she knew you were under her sway . . . Using this hocus-pocus spirituality?"

"Don't speak about her," I say. "Accuse her."

"She's an impostor."

"I don't want you saying her name."

Ma sticks her red nails into the dog's fur. "Don't tell me she didn't try to seduce you."

I bite my lips.

"It feels like everything is 'available' every time I look at her." Ma diverts the chauffeur and the car cuts left, taking Riverbend to the Fly, the last strip of green by the Mississippi River.

I look outside at a boarded-up house. Nothing I say (I've been coached by the best) will make any difference when she is in this emotional pitch. She's out for blood. Before, I threw phrases at her using intellect to calm her, but it was like throwing raw meat at a starved tiger. "Where is Monica now?" I ask through clenched teeth.

"She doesn't want to be REACHED!"

I'm sweating, hands hot with anger. "You're behind this resignation aren't you?"

I seize the armrest. "You concocted this. . .scheme to rid yourself of . ..her...!"

"She's blinded you. I told Doc Heymann, your fly-by-night nurse was NUTS... Pushing you to stay up all night, paint till you collapsed. Then swearing to me you were improving when I see you stretched out across that cot. . . .Monica won't be the first girl thrown from nursing for hysterical excess."

"Did you fire her?"

"I told her to leave quietly when you came home from the hospital."

I cough down water from my bottle, wipe my mouth.

"Or," Ma says, "I'd report her to the American Medical Association."

"For god's sake. She could lose her license. You know--"

"I do know. And she should."

I grab Clarence's shoulder. The car swerves. "Stop. I'm getting out," I say.

"Drive on, Clarence," Ma says through slit teeth.

I lean against my door. "PULL OVER."

The car halts. I grip the door handle, swing myself out. I move over the soggy grass, driving my cane into the field over the levee and down towards the river.

Ma chases me, gold braceleted hands flying, screaming, and frightening off a boy firing a Frisbee. The leashed shiatsu pants behind her.

A boat of fatted tourists are unloading along the dock. Skinny, tall, young and old are crossing a gangplank onshore. A couple pushes a pram–across the shaky gangplank. I wobble after them onto the boat. Ma reaches the dock just at the gangplank goes up.

I collapse onto a bench, drink in the fetid air of this crowded mercy ship of strangers. I grab the side rail, getting in a good position for rough water.

Ma stands waving, lost in her hatred, black and forbidding like some medieval falcon.

I stare through strong head winds at choppy water. We pass a rotting possum. Fur and bones stuck to a log. And sooner than expected unload in the French Quarter.

CHAPTER 16

Jackson Square is burgeoning with Tarot readers, leaning back in their folding chairs, stooped over arrangements of cards. Black clouds lurk. Soon the rain will weep on these muddy stones. At an umbrella-table, an old gypsy in a bright green turban waves, her robes swirling with a gust of wind. "Still grieving over a lost friend?" she cries.

My feet give way at her truth and I reground my cane. "No," I say.

"But you are," she says. "You want to talk about it."

I walk over.

Sitting, she yanks off her black fingerless gloves, flips a card and says, "July. You should be careful then."

The first drops fall.

"About what?" I say, ducking under the umbrella.

"Come see." Her smile reveals a diamond studded gold tooth.

I rub sweat from my neck. "I don't want a reading." Or to learn about my bad health, and worse future.

"No reading then. Just a strategy session." She aligns a black velvet cloth between us. "Do you want to get your friend back? The first five minutes are free."

I sit on a folding chair, in the blackening square. My legs ache. Monica liked Tarot cards, believed in them. The gypsy opens the tarot box.

"Did this fr-ie-nd," she says, playfully, stretching out the words, "have a long-time lover?"

"A husband. I think so. He died."

The gypsy tightens her shawl around her. "Don't under any circumstances go into this relationship until she's free emotionally." The gypsy lays three cards face down and nods for me to pick one. I do.

"Nine of wands," she says. Nine of Wands shows a beleaguered man in a red tunic holding on to a wand. Eight other wands stand behind him on a blue horizon. "You've been hurt," she says, "but it's important to stand your ground. You're stronger than your foes."

Ridiculous, I think.

The gypsy flips a card of a golden queen on a throne looking off in the distance, her silver sword contrasting with the bright blue sky.

"Who's that?" I ask.

"Queen of Pentacles means relocation.. . .houses, property."

"Impossible. . . ."

"Everything is possible. Your five minutes are up." She taps the deck of cards in finality.

I give her $30.

She shuffles, cuts, and restacks them, frowning at a blue card with stars. "The Star Tarot card," she says, "This girl's on a different trajectory. Draw a line with her. The gypsy fans out seven more cards, flipping one with a skeleton in black armor, riding a white horse.

"The death car ?" I say shrinking back.

"The skeleton survives long after life has left the body."

"Am I going to die soon?"

Her throat catches. "The armor could mean strength. You can fight death. You ride a white horse you can live long. Death isn't necessarily physical death. Radical transformation or change is also possible."

I draw my chair closer.

"See," she says, "the rising sun and child in the back of the card. They promise a new tomorrow if you end some things. Rebirth, happiness can also occur."

"Like what?"

"That depends . . .

"Cancer has my body. The only thing I have left is my thoughts."

"Go home," the gypsy says, "and let no one in until you figure out what to do." The wind picks up. "Everyone has a white horse." She points to the animal on the card.

After leaving the gypsy...I sit on a bench in Jackson Square. "Palm trees sway overhead. I've never seen so many birds: seagulls soaring, sparrows swooping. The birds seem to be talking to each other, their lightweight skeletons with hollow bones lifting at will.

Some time later, I go back over cobblestones bulging and damp. It's late, and the gypsies are flattening their umbrellas, folding their tables, leashing up their supplies. A breezy darkness spreads over Jackson Square. My gypsy is just blowing out her candle.

"You're back," she says.

I sit on her sweaty stool.

She rolls her small black eyes, relights the candle. "The nurse?" she asks.

"Yes."

She fans out a spread on her musty velvet square and points to an image of two waving figures before a castle. "This card means journey," she says. She nods at another card of a cloaked figure leaving golden cups for a barren land. "Eight of Cups," she says. "You must find the courage to strike out in a different direction. A new house. It may not be a new address but leaving something behind," she says, biting her lip. "Walking away in love." She points to a Six of Swords where a woman and a child are being rowed in a boat. "See how their backs are to us. I get the feeling that there's a big loss. . . An awful loss." The gypsy peers through slit eyes. "Maybe something from the past?"

I wince, think of my painting of Christine and my son, so incomplete.

"Where are they headed?" I ask pointing to the figures in the boat.

The gypsy pauses. "Where do you want to go? Think about getting a place for yourself. . . ." The gypsy lays down another set. "You have gloom to deal with."

"What?"

"That's you--mourning for what has been lost." She turns more cards. "There's the Nine of Swords: a person sitting up in bed, head in hands, losing sleep. And the Five of Swords – with three figures, one with all the swords. Who does this make you think of? Yes, your grieving is from the past. It's not over. Something . . . "

"You're not hearing me," I break in. "I want to talk about the present, the future. The nurse, who's left."

"Pick a last card," she says.

She turns a picture of a corpse face down swords in his back. "Ten of swords," the gypsy says scooping up her cards. "She's in a graveyard. Periods with people end. You can't hold on to a life, a house, a pattern." She stacks the cards, puts them into a box, blows out the candle.

"What am I supposed to do with that?" I ask.

"Work on yourself. What's dead can't be brought back. Move forward."

CHAPTER 17

Cabbing home, exhausted, I want to go to my bedroom but the help insist Ma is still waiting at the table. I inch into the dining room with its impervious Oriental of vast gray, its bleached walls darkening inside the wail of Bach, *Concerto for 2 Violins in D minor* moaning through the speakers, its chrysanthemum, lily, and sweet olive centerpiece, ripening on the table. Ma in her Gucci leopard robe draws up her green leather armchair.

I sit, to her left, lifting my eyes to a lesser supposed painting of Cezanne. A cloaked skeletal figure nears a bridge riding a white horse. The image reminds me of the gypsy's card. The skeleton must cross the bridge to life on the other side.

Ma unrings her monogrammed napkin, rushing through Catholic grace. I tell myself, "Don't cave in, her behavior towards Monica is unforgiveable." Fried oysters with crumbled blue cheese arrive. I unfold my napkin trusting Ma will be nice at first. But she spears a crusty oyster and jabs, "I was so happy for you, son that you had an amiable nurse."

I grab a piece of buttery garlic bread. "Don't start."

Ma tests her blue cheese. "But you have to face the fact that Monica was proposing a whole different living arrangement than what I'm used to."

"What are you insinuating?"

She pauses twisting a diamond earring, as Cook serves us both asparagus salad and seafood etouffee smothered in a thick sauce and ladled over rice. Once cook leaves, Ma says, "The problem is you ... you're weak, son ... weak and fragile and..."

I seize my fork, slicing my asparagus, staring into my arugula lettuce. "One afternoon I'm going to breathe a moment and go away. I don't want Monica not to be there--"

"Stop!" Ma say. Tears drip down her face.

I swallow a hunk of crawfish, choke, tap my chest. "To be here alone," I say. "And. . . and to be so mad . . . I find myself reeling."

Mascara leaks down Ma's cheek.

"I'm not going to die like this." I dip into my rice. "I want you to call Monica, grovel if you have to, and get her to come back."

"Calm down," Ma says.

The skeleton card and white horse march through my brain. "That's what I can't take. Staying locked up here . . . Till I become helpless."

Ma puts a finger to her lips as crème brulot is served. "You haven't got long and I want it to end sweetly." She pierces the hardened caramelized sugar dessert crust. "I don't want this woman, this sometime hysteric . . . Nurse imposter . . .riling you up." Ma thrusts her spoon into the rich custard. "

The maid, Margaret trudges in with two demitasse coffee cups, pre Civil War. Tiny white cups with a gold and blue trim. Cook follows with sugar lumps and cream.

"You know Ma I'm feeling rotten loving someone who says these sadistic things... You're jealous. And I don't know if you can stop."

Maid, Margaret and Cook flee to the kitchen.

"Don't let the help see you . . .you bully me," Ma says. "Apologize."

"I can't." I pour water from the silver pitcher. "You nursed me through the cancer," I say, "and that was far worse than the cancer. It was like peeling back a scab. And now you're doing all you can to stop me from growing...from having a relationship. And do what brings me joy."

"How can you say that!"

"You never cared for me. My painting was a way for you to stay young and beautiful with a close bond to art."

"Not true. I gave most of my life --"

"To . . .volunteer Boards at Tulane, the New Orleans Museum--Bla Bla--"

The door flickers open and Margaret serves crème de menthe. Ma idles with her liqueur glass. She glares at me. "If you're going ahead with this painting . . .I'll monitor everything." Her chest heaves.

I gulp water, choking, "I don't want you to! How can I work with a tyrant who abuses my friends . . ."Married to Dad." Yes, I say his name with contempt. "A serial. . . A serial cheat. You were fascinated with his money, wanted to display it like diamond earrings. And Dad looked perfect, like Adonis and gave you everything. Long as you kept his secret. Promiscuity."

"How dare you! It's this woman who has--"

"You're jealous. And I can't stop it. You have no friends. Only a voiceless dog and paid servants. Wanting to keep me to yourself, like royalty. Making me abandon the work that brings me delight. . . .Cut off from friends."

"You're selfish, an overgrown child."

"Keeping . . .Keeping ready at all times for another doctor's visit, MRI, transfusion. The only way I can bear it is to grit my teeth and over medicate!"

Margaret enters quietly with a tray and Ma screams, " I didn't call for you to clear." Margaret quickly evacuates and I rise strongly sans cane, and shoot my napkin back in its ring. "I'm moving out, going back to a little apartment and my imagination. I'm going to keep painting for a profession that is out to demean me every step of the way. And when the end comes, I'm going to try to face it with dignity and in high spirits."

CHAPTER 18

Alone in my studio, minutes later, I smash on classical music by Satie, Satie whose one relationship was with a trapeze artist. I want the icy loneliness of his sounds to empty me. Its single bass phrase to focus me.

Twisted paint tubes flank half finished canvases.

I liked having an intimate like Monica who believed in me because I wasn't sure I did. But I didn't see her slowly weakening heart. Slow transitions, I didn't see them. I was so arrogant. I didn't want to change for women. They were supporting characters. I knew relationships were treacherous. 80% of my class at Yale left the art world in NYC in the first 3 years due to "family obligations."

When your first instinct says, "Don't couple up," then you can't do a relationship. Your gut is telling you, "Stay out." You don't talk yourself into it, try to finagle or maneuver it. Eventually, the woman isn't going to respond the way she did when first infatuated. Tenderness, intimacy was chucked in favor of the dramatic. I was looking to these women to be a muse, to fuel my art and not vice versa.

By zealously guarding my time, I could make all these canvases on rain. I learned to do without. The partner, the child. I steeled myself to feelings, to touch, to softness. My skin hardened like leather. Creeping along the ground like an alligator, resting in place with eyes rolling on the top of my head, waiting to slide along quickly at the smell of meat.

Creative time is alone time. You can't paint when people are yapping at you over your shoulder. I felt I was big enough. Strong enough. Deep enough to feel everything I could. I lifted a brush, and depth would fall out on canvas.

My stiff neck begs me to go back to bed. I concentrate on the nightview out the window. Outside, it's damp, damp. Bone wet treetops tilt this way and that, resisting the moist breeze. Birds scruff inside branches looking for a dry perch. Then a shadow, a sunken body shape, of someone tiptoeing toward the studio. *Oh no it's Monica.*

She slips in, sliding back her grey rain hood.

I freeze, breathing in a faint smell of musk, rain, and sadness. Who could have predicted it? I'm completely taken aback.

Her eyes moisten. "I don't know . . . how to . . .what to say." Her voice starts and stops. "How is your painting?"

I should tell her my concentration is poor. I'm indecisive. Exhausted. Only have a good four hours a day. "Great," I say.

"I'm sorry for . . . what I'm putting you through." She hides her face with her hands. "You see, I didn't know before. But I do now . . . for sure and . . . there is no question." She pulls up tall. "I can't be near you now." She blots her forehead. "I'm not finished mourning for Speed."

I step back off balance. A muscle in my leg starts to tremble. "How long has this bothered you?" I ask.

"A while." Her face changes, frowning eyebrows. "Speed and I were married for nine years. But we were childless. So he was everything." She dips her hand in her pocket for the Kleenex. "Speed knows ... about my affection for you... Even though he's dead."

"How can you say that?"

Her voice falls. "He knows." She's quiet for a second. "Speed and I used to walk through this cemetery near where we lived on Camp Street. . .We got used to going there as if visiting a park. It's is full of beautiful carvings on the family tombs, old trees and the pleasant singing birds. There was so much to learn about New Orleans of the past.

The families, where people came from, the times when disease took many...." she says, massaging the back of neck. "Huge headstones and crypts. Speed's buried there."

"Why are you telling me this?" I ground my feet in the floorboards.

"After his funeral," she says. "I continued to walk there. I couldn't sleep, eat, cry, but the sunlight on his warm tomb and the leaves falling soothed me. . .made me feel whole. . . You see Speed left me so . . . quickly. He breathed a little moment and went away. It was just a breath, it was very calm."

I look down at splotches of dried paint by my feet. I (just) can't get over what she is saying.

Her eyes grasp mine. "But the last time I visited there," the sky went dark, the ground turning to shadows." She paces then stands in a permanent position. "I felt Speed's presence," she says. "in the cemetery. I'm sure he was there . . ."

"You were praying for him?" I ask, tensing forward." And you imagined him there."

"No." Her voice rises. "More than that. She bites down on her words, chewing the inside of her cheek. "I have never experienced him to that extent before." A cloaked look comes to her eyes. "I know Speed came back," she says, her face stiff and immobile. "I clearly saw shadows in the aisle by the tomb and something called my name. I didn't see him. But . . .But I sensed him. . ."

"What did he want?" My heart goes faint.

There is a deathlike pallor on her face. Her breathing is labored; "Permission to go."

I clutch my fist. "What did you tell him?"

Her eyelids raise, tense. "I told him, 'Not yet.'" She pauses, scratches a cheek, blinks. Her look is overly intense." I went through a period of disbelief," Monica says. "How can you tell anyone that you heard this dead man, solid as ever, talk to you?"

Her nostrils dilate. Her face is masklike "Then Speed came back again. I was asleep around 2 a.m.," she says, "when I snapped awake. He was standing over me. He smiled and said, 'Everything will be fine.' Then he said, 'I'm going now.' He looked concerned his eyes fixed upward yearning. So I greed, 'OK,' I said."

Monica's voice is strained and blocked. "It's not your mother's fault I left. I need to be alone to think. To suffer through certain things. To pray." She turns, pulls a hood over her head and leaves. Some cloistered life is stealing her away from me.

She leaves swiftly like a grey bird flying low opting to skim the earth when a storm approaches. My brain sobs for what she feels.

I drag out the Christine rain painting. Turn on *Pavarotti* singing "Forever," on the sound system. At some point you have to order yourself into a canvas. I look away, out the soggy window. But rain can't soothe my heart in all its abundant weeping.

I put the canvas back.

I take it out again.

I open a file drawer and remove the death photo, kept next to Benno's bear. I nuzzle its fur, the red stitched mouth, say my son's name. Memories loom like uninvited ghosts: the baby's bedroom, soft blue like fresh air, his toy truck in a corner nook.

I pick up a paintbrush, rearrange my paint tubes, dip paint on my brush again.

Little Benno waits in the photo.

I don't go out.

I don't drink.

I'm determined to finish the baby's face. I stab the tip of my brush into practically undiluted paint, and jab it onto the face to clarify it, squash out some with the brush -- but it's no use. A sorrowful grey claws through the face. I have to scrape all the paint off and cover my work up.

Oct 31, 2013 The day my son died.

I was at the New York City gallery hanging my show. Christine phoned me from Rhinebeck. It was a mournful sound. The phone is never good news to me. The wind was whistling round the gallery. The glass on the windows slapped back and forth.

"I'm at the train station," she gasped into the phone.

"You're where?" I heard her retching. Oh God, Oh God. "What's wrong?"

She caught her breath and wailed "I- I -I had to run to the train station. Bring him."

"Bring who?" I said.

"The BABY!" she screamed. "When I found him, my hands were shaking so much," she shrieked.

"Back up, Christine. Talk clearly."

"The baby. Our baby. They took him," she cried hysterically.

"Who took him?"

"I ran to the train station with him," she repeated, "because my hands were shaking . . .so much . . .I couldn't dial the phone. . . ."

"What happened?"

"They got me an ambulance," she blurted into the phone. "He's . . .dead! I'm sorry. Your son is dead!"

"What? What? WHA-A-A AT!"

That day, the Rhinebeck hospital seemed so large, white, muscular. But the doctor was tall, bald, curt. He stepped forward a warning glint to his eye, then he extended his hand tentatively. His soft fingers wrapped around mine. "We did all we could," he said through thin lips. "We lost him. I'm sorry."

We both sat, silenced by the event. My eyes spun over the walls of the doctor's private office. Not seeing color, just beige. Searching, seeking, desperate for something to look at, something to numb the ache seizing my chest.

"How did it happen?" the doctor said, taking a skinny pad and pencil from his desk.

"I wasn't home," I replied. My voice had suddenly caved in.

He posed his pencil over the paper. "What did your wife say?"

"Nothing. My God, are you taking notes? What is this?"

He bristled, eyes tight. "It happened . . .accidentally, I suspect," he said. "90% of infant mortality syndrome has to do with that. A blanket. A bumper. A toy placed too close to the face. Ten seconds after the heart stops beating the brain goes dead." Cautiously, he opened a bag on his desk, removed an eight-inch fuzzy brown bear with button eyes and a red stitched mouth. "My guess is this smothered your son. The emergency squad found it in the crib."

I gasped recognizing my son's favorite toy, long straggly legs, striped scarf. I imagined the baby's head pushed up against the bear.

"My wife never left the baby alone."

The emergency room physician in charge of resuscitation frowned. "It only takes a few minutes," he said, "for a baby to suffocate on his stomach. "Do you want to see a grief therapist?"

"No. Why would I keep regurgitating the story?" I want to forget it. Bury it with the body.

"I'll dispose of the toy," the doctor said.

Where? In a dumpster? A garbage can? Goodwill? "No, let me have it." I said, clutching the brown bear then stuffing him in my backpack.

"Time will bring comfort," the doctor said. "Your wife said she didn't want a cuddle cot."

"Ah .. .what?"

He looked helplessly into my face. "You have the right to take the body home."

"Why would we...?"

"Some parents tell us that spending time with their babies at home before the funeral helps them with the grieving process."

"I don't know." I completely broke down.

After I saw the doctor, it was hardly necessary for me to speak long to Christine, paralyzed as she was in agony and disbelief, horrified at the idea of taking home the body.

Christine's brother came and took her out to eat.

I stayed behind with the excuse I had to speak with the hospital billing department. I waited in a windowless room in the hospital basement, and they brought the baby to me, wrapped in a thin blue blanket. Dead child slung like a sack in my arms, blue eyes sealed shut, brown hair pressed flat to the head, skin palest white. His toes were cold, and I twisted a sheet round his feet.

I told myself if only I had been home I might have seen something . . .done something . . .averted something...

I took his picture. I didn't want to, but I had to preserve the memory: the wide forehead, full lower lip, dimpled chin. The photo would keep my child whole. It was something I wanted to have for later. It's the one I would paint from.

I came home, numb. The daisies were still blooming on my desk. Christine's red puffy eyes tormented me. She'd awaken nights sobbing for Benno. Once I found her on the floor. She'd tripped on one of his toys. That night, I walked with painful steps, following her around the house as we put them all away.

The thrift shop wouldn't take his stuffed animals, so Christine stored them in a plastic container on the top shelf of our bedroom closet along with his favorite clothes.

"For the next baby," she said.

In the days following the loss of a loved one, they say your chance of death goes up twenty-one times.

* * *

His ashes arrived in an initialed urn and the words *Baby Boy*. We put them on the mantle and argued about where we would empty them. She said the Hudson River. I said, Poets' Walk in Rhinecliff. And so, they stayed on the mantle. A constant reminder.

A memorial service was held on November 1. I froze inside this bomb of terror, moving like a ghost through the house. The day my son died, I had been in New York City. After, I kept going there off and on . . .mindlessly for three weeks. I was walking the pain out. His death was like a closing of the chest.

After his death, everything became very, very small. People passed me down the street in Rhinebeck and left me alone. Every time I entered the grocery, the café, someone left.

In the month after, I found myself fleeing into the wild grass and stonewalls of Poets' Walk. There I could allow myself to cry on one shaded, streamside path, buffered by almost eight hundred acres of land and the notion that Rip Van Winkle had fallen asleep there. If only, like him, I could collapse and not wake up for one hundred years. I'd never really felt like a dad. Even when we had the baby and I had all the stuff there for Benno, he was more hers than mine. I didn't spend enough time holding and caring for him, cuddling him, taking him to the park, walking him in a pram, or pushing him on a swing. I was pushing my art, thinking I'd have time later, when the kid was older.

I pounded the fields, painting until I was out of breath, mostly birds of prey flying above waiting for something to drop dead. My paintings didn't resemble my others. They screamed with black, green crusty textures and dollops of red everywhere. Moments of fury squelched into paint.

Meanwhile Christine turned inward, closing windows, blinds, doors, sketching our caged doves. Even when it got really warm, she would sit under a hot light, using a magnifier and stenciling tiny black birds.

"Are you going to Poet's Walk again?" she said, hunched over her wirery obsessive sketches. "I've been thinking that maybe our teachers didn't have it all wrong. First you run to the gallery, then you're off to the country. Maybe you do suffer from a lack of focus."

Christine and I still sat there on the couch but more and more we retreated to our cushions on either end, me in a book and she in her computer. Something in us didn't allow us to make contact. We used to watch TV and lay Benno between us, and we'd both rub his back and he'd fall asleep and our fingers would touch.

I tried to be affectionate, reaching for her hand, putting an arm about her waist, keeping my lips on hers a little longer for a good night kiss. Christine stopped making love to me in the house on Rhinecliff Rd.

"I'm sorry it has come to this," she said.

Why couldn't she allow herself sex? I never knew. Was there some deep anger controlling her on and off switch? "Be patient," she'd say, her eyes flashing red. "Or give me time." Or, "I just don't feel anything yet."

Frigid fall evenings she wouldn't come to bed, sleeping in the rocker in Benno's room, a blanket up to her chin. Eventually I quit trying to lure her beside me.

In December, my mother flew up to take Christine shopping at Saks, lunch at Tavern on the Green, and to see *Mary Poppins* on Broadway. Ma's efforts worried me at first. She hated all death related things. Never went to funerals. Avoided hospitals. Shunned anyone in the mortuary business. But this time, Ma's presence was a relief. In fourteen days, Ma and Christine dined at all twenty-eight restaurants in Rhinebeck. She followed the scene in New York.

"There are so many wonderful plays," Ma said, reading the *New York Times*, and circling them with her pen.

Christine smiled, halfheartedly, sipping the chicory coffee Ma had brought from New Orleans. Beads of snow were already sailing outside in late November.

Ma would check on the weather each morning to make sure Christine and I were warmly dressed, the driveway clear of all debris, leaves, sleaze. When she had "done" Rhinebeck, she said, "Let's have a cab drive us to Hudson to a few restaurants and art galleries. Or Woodstock?"

At the window, Christine shook her head seeing the gloomy clouds of snow like thin, white sheets covering the whole sky. Her mother had been dead a long time, and her estranged father lived with his new wife in Australia. Occasionally Christine dipped into a vacant need for distance.

Ma went and put a hand on her shoulder. "It's dreadful that you have to worry about the weather. The New Orleans house is big enough for all of us. You shouldn't have to face the brutal winter alone." Christine sat by Ma on the couch and Ma held her and she cried for three hours until she fell into a sleep that lasted a night and a day. Christine's fierceness subsided and, although I was opposed, fearing Ma would suck us into her web of control, I noted a glint of joy lit Christine's eyes when Ma talked about the tropical birds in Audubon Park. "Because of you, there is a song in my heart" came through the sound system. Tony Bennett, wailing, "because of you my life had it start."

Christine accepted Ma's proposal for us to live for a year in the art studio at her house. I agreed to go because I felt we had to leave the memory burdened Rhinebeck house. Christine said she couldn't stay there and I felt guilty.

2014 Restlessness in New Orleans

In New Orleans Christine and I shared a double bed, touched feets, hips, even spooned once.

Christine was happy if superficial. One day she came through the door, taking off her rain hood, and shaking her blonde hair. We'd been in New Orleans nine months and restlessness was taking hold.

I looked up from the sofa where I'd been sketching. "What this time?" I said.

"Your mother's trapped me into another debutante tea." Christine flopped by me, slipped off her high heels, threw her leg over mine.

"You don't have to go," I said.

"I know I also accepted a makeover at Saks and a mud bath at the Ritz. I gave in to your mother. All these 'flimsies' gobble up creative time."

"Ma admires you."

"That makes it worse!" Christine sat up tall, ghastly and blank like a person losing her mind. She shoved on rubber boots. "You can't be an artist here. There's no time for depth!" She made her way direct and sullen outside, releasing her mourning doves whose wings made their usual whistling sound upon take-off.

"We're going to make it," I said, raking a hand through my hair. "We just need time."

She sat opposite me at the table, which no longer enshrined our son's photo.

"Where's the photo," she asked.

"I don't know. Maybe it dropped on the floor."

She scrambled about, searching. "You moved it. Didn't you!"

"Okay. I put it away. I'll give it to you in three years when…"

"I hurt less."

"It will never hurt less. I want it back tonight you hear," she screamed.

"Calm down."

"You think I killed him."

"I told you. The doctor said it was an accident. Come. We can pray without a photo, just you and me!"

That night she slept apart from me.

I didn't blame Christine for Benno's death even though I knew Infant Death Syndrome was largely the cause of unattended babies, babies who couldn't move and smothered from a blanket, a toy, a bumper pad. Then too my commuting to NYC had left her to care for the baby alone.

At Mother's I hid the photo in my chest of drawers. I wanted to keep looking at it till I wore myself out from it. But one day,

Christine discovered it. She froze there, her face ashen, then went into the bathroom. I found her, bent over the sink. I wondered if she would hit me. Instead she whispered. "How could you hide this? She leaned further over the bowl, coughing up phlegm. "I … can't …. believe … it's not real." She got in the shower. Turned it on high and sunk straight down to the floor where she stayed till I hauled her out. She clawed me as I dressed her, then gasped, "Why did you do that? Are you sick?" she said. "SICK."

After that things only got worse. She retreated more and more into birds, became obsessed with drawing them, from the pigeons in the French Quarter with the iridescent neck feathers, to the occasional happy bright red cardinal in Audubon Park. She started applying for residencies at the American Academy in Rome, Bellagio Center on Lake Como, the DAAD in Berlin. I was aghast.

"Shouldn't we discuss this?" I asked, unnerved.

One day, Christine checked a mail slot on the side fence, and returned waving a letter. Your work just didn't do it for the Stern gallery," she said. "I told you, you weren't ready. There's some lie people sense. If you can't go deep, you need to go commercial, design wall paper, towels, pots." That wasn't meant as an injunction. She actually thought wallpaper and noncommercial art had equal value.

Again her career began to soar. I didn't think she'd get a big award so quickly. But a month later she was opening a large envelope with light-filled her eyes. Even though she'd been relatively in hiding for months she'd landed a six-week award.

"I got it!" she rejoiced. "A residency at the Irish Cultural Center . . .in Paris."

"No kidding?" I said, a fist to my mouth, imagining her triumph in Paris, fearing I would lose her.

But when I took the letter and scanned it, my heart lifted. On rereading it several times, I realized there was something actually nice about the residency—a chance to work with other artists who knew nothing of Benno's death. Most wouldn't even know she'd been a mother. Hadn't heard her crying in the night. I sniffed back a sudden congestion. Blew my nose. The trip would be a buffer from the day-to-day darkness of our place.

She was both worried and cheerful saying, "Do you think I'll need my little umbrella?" or "I'm rewarding you with a hot stone massage my departure day."

I wanted to see her happy. I told myself, my problem would go away, when she came back healed.

She wanted to take Benno's ashes. I begged her not to.

She clasped her hands together and looked up, her throat choking. "I'm sure in Paris I can find the courage to scatter him, as surrounded as I'll be by creatives I love."

"You can't take an urn on a plane."

"I'll send it through wrapped carefully in my suitcase. . . .I won't do anything without telling you. . . . I can't bear for you to keep looking at me that way." She grimaced, leaned back on the sofa, and drew her chin into her neck, totally anguished. "Oh let me. It'd be such a comfort to scatter his ashes in a place I love."

I agreed. Perhaps Paris would help Christine find joy, peace, and heal. I wanted to help grow the tiny part in her that loved me. Just having her a little in my life was better than not at all. I knew the drawbacks of her leaving; I didn't know I'd get cancer. Not all storms are in the forecast.

I remember the day she left, the hallow sound in my heart as I made myself watch her getting into a taxi with two unmatched suitcases, pink and black. I saw her go down the drive, with hesitant step. No sound. No flutter of birds. No dog barking. The lawn mower screaming next door. I closed my eyes, pulled up tall, forced a final hand wave. She smiled as the cab backed out the drive. I eased inside the screen door, my sockless feet, rapping over the cold studio floor.

Christine got everything when we divorced, I think. At the end, the only thing I had left was my feet. The world of art joined us, fed us, and in the end took all.

* * *

Back in the studio, in the present, I wrap up the canvas, slide the photo in its envelope and put them both in a large suitcase.

I watch the sunset fling shadows on the walls. There's a special light that comes from a different state of being. It's almost blue-white. Colors I've seen in Florence and Rome around the cathedrals at night. I get a bottle of *Cotes du Rhone*, Camembert cheese, fresh ham and salami slices and *fromage blanc*, let the rich food bloat me.

Later that night, I go out in the back yard in the rain. Let it pour over me as I sweat and dig, dig and sweat. I'm determined to bury the suitcase, despite the sweat pouring under my armpits and rain screaming down my back. I jab at the earth and thrust more and more dirt on top. Soon instead of the suitcase, there is only blackness and me sitting gasping for breath on the hard sealed off earth.

CHAPTER 19

Ten nights later, I'm living in the Vieux Carre in my own apartment. 760 square feet of my own space, my bed in one corner, my art supplies in another.

Outside the window, palm trees and magnolias sway in a night breeze with a pale silver sky. I hunger for rain, real rain, thick and slick with a texture like cream. A bell gongs from St Louis Cathedral, sparrows rustle behind clumps of leaves.

Inside my eyes spin over the bedroom furnishing. I took some from Ma's but had to get a new bed. That was Christine and my "skeletal" bed. Was purchased on whimsy. It didn't bear fruit. I wanted to take it. If you always do what you want to do you will end up where you don't want to be. Lurking in the shadows of that bed is someone I no longer valued.

I recall the gypsy, now only blocks from me. A graveyard, she said was where Monica was. I had taken that metaphorically. I was so distracted then by protecting myself. Perhaps what I really want lurks in a realm I rarely explore.

Particular cranky and jaded images of cemeteries begin to compel me.

Metairie Cemetery with its Elk-topped mound and house tombs soars in memory, followed by Lafayette Cemetery tucked beneath the storied oak trees of the Garden District, a place where Monica said she liked to pray.

The next morning, I forge through the gates of Lafayette Cemetery, past a dead tree, rows of wall vaults, roses and gladioli ripening in marble vases. I plod under some magnolia trees, catch my breath in the shade of their large showy flowers. I breathe deep the smells of soil, moss, old flowers. I turn down a dusty alley, move past a slab covering an entire family that died of yellow fever.

Overhead the sky presages early rain. Thunder rumbles. It's just noon and a storm is coming. Birds land on grave houses. For a second, I imagine Christine feeding a sparrow. I shake her off.

I plow past a row of wall vaults, not identifying their residents, nor considering that before they retired into the night, they might have shared a meal, held someone close, or tried to paint a masterpiece.

Someone hunches before a tomb praying the Rosary. Monica. I tiptoe to her, putting my weight on the cane, trying to silence the crackle of a leaf. I wipe my nose, rush a hand through my hair, blink. She's still there. What a mistake to desperately need her. I won't tell her, my blood count is bad. Mornings I awake with evening pain. I wait till she puts the rosary in her pocket, then inch closer.

The raised "house tomb" before her reads, "SPEED FALCON, LOVING HUSBAND, 1984-2019."

She wipes her eyes hurriedly. If only Christine cried for me that way. I breathe in a damp smell, tombs drying in the sun. I'm a man. You know how much we can ache for tenderness and then you don't ask the question and the woman is gone.

She turns, eyes and mouth opened, eyebrows raised.

"How are you doing?" I ask.

I can feel her nervous breathing. "Fine," she says.

I hold back a rush of nerves. "Please …forgive ….me," I say. "For …all I did…" My throat catches." To make… it difficult for you." I sit. Nearby a magnolia tree, is holding on; its fallen white flowers with strappy petals still trying to breathe. I hand her a wide faced spongy flower.

I don't tell her I have spinal issues I neglected, discs are degenerating, my back pain worsening, transfusions increasing. I use a cane in places where I walked freely before.

I sit on a bench beside her, discretely catch my breath. "Where are you staying?" I manage.

Perspiration beads her lip. Her eyes flit to a puddle before us already stagnating. The smell of exhaust from a passing car lingers. "I'm taking care of an elderly lady," she says.

"Please work for me again. . . .I'm on my own now."

"I can't. My relationship . . .with you . . .has disconnected him."

"Maybe he's comforted. . .Let me care for you."

"Speed never got 'back to himself.'" Monica says, ". . .I couldn't save him. How can you expect me to stay with you?" Her body goes rigid beside me.

I tense, breathing in a faint smell of ashes and stone.

Monica goes to the tomb; around it, the grass isn't growing. The breeze brings a hint of recently turned mud.

I stab a dead blossom. "I've moved to a new apartment: my own studio on St Philip in the Quarter."

"I fear it would be too much…too soon."

"At least come see it. Ten minutes? Saturday."

"Maybe," she says. "I have to go now. Her small feet crunch some dead leaves as she departs, passing a blighted tree, rounding a bend, of tall cement tombs and sky.

I pass mounds of raw earth waiting to cover sealed bodies, large house tombs temporarily opened for beings unable to crawl out. How do I find someone to lead me toward the world of the dead?

I bumble past an angel monument with one wing ripped off. Ahead, the statue of Weeping Woman groans for me to stop by her barefoot hunched self. To touch the statue's snooded head, feel the clutched urn, in her chiseled hand. I never had time for reflection, meditation. I regret that. I told myself I could tolerate a walled marriage, an estranged child, a rebuffed friend. There'd be time to fix it later.

Suddenly thinness in the air signals a downpour. I flee the cemetery for Commanders Palace Restaurant, its teal blue and white canopy galvanized against the downpour. I hail a cab. Inside, I move past a broken umbrella, a coke can littering the floor, cigarette stench. The *Carmina Burana* aria wails from the speakers, reminding me I'm not the first tormented human. Humans have been destroying each other for centuries.

Outside the blurred glass, rain falls like pellets, water dripping off edges of scaly houses and umbrella-bearing pedestrians.

Back home on the patio, I drag out a stool easel, and blank canvas from under the circular stair leading to the second and third floor units, hobbling on my stool. I turn up the Vivaldi. Vivaldi, who squandered his wealth and was buried in a pauper's grave, balance myself on uncertain legs and do a simple wash of green.

Tchaikovsky's *Death Symphony No. 6 Pathetique* rages on the sound system. I clench my brush, flinching at a shoulder pain, leaning back and judging the greenish-black. The painting doesn't work back! Why can't I redirect myself? Plot out a worthy piece till I die, floating to the ceiling to review the canvas.

CHAPTER 20

A little later, my gypsy, now calling herself Madame Tissot, shuffles cards with an insatiable fire.

"Still some grieving over that lost love," she says, one eye closing in rebellion. "You want to be cherished," she says, hands hanging limply on the soft felt tabletop. "Ah ha. . .You're opening secret . . .feelings. And so the person you'll attract is a person who loves that secretness in you." Her eyes zoom from card to card. A candle flutters on the table. "A prone stabbed figure is not good," she says. She points to rain and a heart on the card. "You also got the Three of Swords."

The chair knifes my back.

The gypsy studies me, sweeps up her cards and growls, "You don't need the cards."

My mind spirals out of control. "But you're a tarot card reader."

A single groan passes her lips. Her top row of teeth gleam. "Nothing in them cards is going to fix you. You're doing something wrong--.not allowing yourself to see something. . . ."

"See what?"

"Here, take your money back," she says emptying her wallet. "Something's got to give." She fingers a card, pulls it to her heavy slothful eyes.

"Show me," I say, half in anticipation half in dread.

She holds up that card with a woman and child fleeing in a boat. "The Six of Swords," she cries. "More and more swords cards. Let go or be dragged down."

CHAPTER 21

Late that afternoon, a polite knock at the door drifts over the wind. My buddy Skye jangles the steel gate. He's in town for like a minute, and finds me to have a celebratory drink. I wander down the central patio tunnel, designed by some Frenchman to forestall rain. How do I get Skye to leave?

Before my condo on St. Philip St. a Voodoo tour guide caws out to tourists. Why don't I like Skye now? He's my friend, my advocate but I want to get away from art today. A hint of cologne drifts in with Skye, dressed preppy stylish, khakis, t-shirt, blue blazer for the *Jammin on Julia* arts event.

He funnels in politely behind me, mumbling, "I don't know how you could leave the Garden District. It gave you such prestige."

I wince. "How did you find me?"

"Your mother, naturally."

Down the blue tunnel, into an empty palm court and swimming pool we go.

"Nice," he concedes, a spark in his gait. Rambling slave quarters now condos horseshoe a huge pool. "Where are the other residents?"

"Houston, Washington, Shreveport.

"None of them live here for real," Skye smiles.

At my patio, I flick on the wall fan behind us and turn my easel sideways.

His piercing green eyes study me, as if he knows something is up, his lids flickering every so slightly. "What were you working on for me," he says.

I ease out a crick in my neck.

Tossing his straw hat on a table, he sidles over to my easel, lifting his Ray Bans on top his head. "Can I peek?"

My skin burns. "Soon," I say, twisting against a sudden cramp. "When it's finished."

"I've got some interest in your paintings now. There's a Southern series at Yale."

"Southern?" I say.

"New England has plenty of New York painters. Louisiana is still exotic, you know."

My heart soars.

"Those slides of your work, really turned colleagues on. Especially this couple visiting from New Haven. "If you let me do an exhibit at my gallery, I'm sure I could sell something."

"Take one or two of my paintings with you. But about a show, I don't know."

"Next year when I team up with the university as dean, there will be even more possibilities." He runs a hand over his blond hair, stretching tall. "Again he squeezes my shoulder. "You need to be back east. You're doing everything on your own here, that's why you're a target for rejection. You forgot the power you have."

I bask in the compliment.

He takes out a Perrier and sips. "Imagine living in Connecticut. Amazing art galleries, museums, theatres. Farms, waterfronts. Something perfect is waiting for you …Near Stanford," he adds.

"Nothing perfect waits near Stanford," I say.

We laugh.

He borrows trunks and strolls to the pool. His arms are strong, his shoulders broad, legs well shaped. I remove my loafers, dip a toe in the warm water, jealous of his body that functions effortlessly. After a few laps, he lifts his lanky body poolside. I pass him a towel. "A couple of classes and full time pay, he says with a twinkle. He shows me pictures of a sweet farm town, a studio, the university. "We got really smart eager students."

I break out in a sweat, move under an umbrella, out the glare.

Skye frowns, "You can't stay in a place, that decays your talent. Let's face it, this city is a swamp. You'll sink here. Why are you stalling."

A second line band bursts from the street. Several yells from drunken tourists.

"Well, there is a woman," I say. "I'm stunned although you predicted it." I update him on Monica and that she is already employed elsewhere.

Shaking his head, he says, "I don't think a nurse in New Orleans is prepared for all the issues in any artist's life." The outside air oozes about us tense and thick. "No," he says, "you two would be arguing, --."He grabs his cell phone and says, "I think the best example you can give her is of a man who takes care of himself."

The Saint Louis Cathedral angelus clangs, 6 pm. I blot my eyes and clawing skin. The humidity is vicious despite the breeze from the Mississippi River.

Skye goes inside and changes his clothes, then comes out. He smiles curling a lip mischievously. "Think future. A year down the line, you'll probably be moving. Not true for locals, very rooted here," he says, grabbing his hat and perching it on his head. "We were raised by people who didn't change so we don't expect to. Don't become one of them."

He slips out his keys, slides on Ray Ban sunglasses. I note his Peter Pan blonde cut has a sliver of silver, which looks good on him. He is aging gracefully.

My heart beats light and timid at the thought of Connecticut, students watching me through skittish wide eyes as I walk in the studio. "I got to think about it." I say, tensing my jaw.

Moments later, I wave goodbye to Skye inside his red convertible, financed by the university bolting over drizzly pot holed streets.

CHAPTER 22

The next morning, I'm barely able to get up. I'm uneasy. Discomfort is back. Indigestion and bloating make walking difficult. I sit with a cup on the living room sofa. The plastic ghost chairs shine at me, ghost chairs for friends, artists, strangers still to come. This portrait of my mother at thirty-five, way younger than me at thirty-nine greets me as does my baby self. Me at three, so cherubic clutching a popsicle (not painted in) to keep me still. I push my feet into the red oriental rug wondering how many times my feet rested here.

I grasp coffee from the Keurig, walk toward the French doors, look out at the blue pool, the palm trees jittery with sunlight, the crows flapping atop a tree, the Saints football floater collapsed on one lawn chair. The sky is a jumble of grays. A canvas waits untouched, hoping. First and foremost I must paint. I can't, won't do that to myself again. Bury another painting.

I step outside onto the empty patio, remembering my son's cheek, how pale and cold it had been. How to paint him? Was my son dreaming of seahorses and sailboats?

Perhaps if I hadn't gone to NYC that day.

I turn on Schubert's *Fantasy in F Minor,* created during his dying year, Schubert who worked as a schoolteacher by day and composed music by night, Shubert one of fourteen children of whom only five survived, Shubert who died of syphilis and had no offspring.

I take a few steps onto the patio, into the still-moist air, squint at the sunshine streaming in. I glance under the stairs. I retreat to the window ledge, removing paint from a brush by whisking it along an old rag.

I continue to the staircase, pause before the rough canvas where I've outlined a new painting.

A sparrow swoops by, flushing over dust.

The painting in place, I reach for my brush, feeling more determined and I'm able to paint intensely for a time. Pink salmon colors and abalone colors, thick paint, shell shapes, strawberry shells, white cup shells, pink rose cups. And large conch shells of mother of pearl.

* * *

I'm having lunch, fueling myself to return to the easel when I'm distracted by the beep of the intercom, 11am. I buzz the door open and Monica trods in, her pinafore dress array, her hair scattered about her face. I step back, breath accelerating.

Her face is sad and beautiful with weary things in it, weary eyes and a weary sensual mouth. Her bulgy umbrella droops with moisture. She holds it out. I take it, making sure not to touch her hand.

"I had breakfast at Croissant d'Or round the corner," she says. The muscles in her chin tremble. "I thought I'd say hello." Another surprise visit. I step back delighted.

I accept a wet Cici's coffee from her, my palms sweaty. "Thanks," I manage, noting the intelligent eyes, the high forehead, the sincere smile.

"Lovely house," she says. Her voice is wooden. She glances around, not focusing on anything

I turn on the lights, exposing the wow fourteen-foot ceilings, built-in bookcases, scarlet Orientals. Old world beauty to distract her from my crippled body.

She inhales the breathtaking sparkle of the huge crystal chandeliers, antique Swedish piano, French doors streaked with rain, paintings and mirrors crusted in gold.

I look toward the French doors, top bare and open, bottom shuttered from St Philip Street as if rain-splattered light could soothe me. "I can't stay." Her voice fades off.

God, don't let me beg. "Sit," I say, "while I drink the coffee."

Her face is a dull shade of white. I expect her to flee, but she doesn't.

"I liked working for you," she says. She clenches her jaw, averting eye contact.

"Come back."

Her eyes are red. She looks past me toward the sofa. "I'm not pleased about quitting. But I had to."

I watch her through glassy eyes, grasping for words. "Why did you come?"

She licks her lips, gives an uncertain smile. "To see your work as you requested." There's an awkward silence.

The dull chandelier spreads slimy light. I sit, urging her to join me, lean back into the grey sofa between two musty matching lamps from Rhinebeck, New York. For a moment I see Christine breastfeeding our son there.

But Monica goes to the bathroom. When she comes out her eyes are bloodshot, her eyelids puffy. She isolates herself on the end of the sofa. A gold-leaf mirror full of contrasting colors faces us. We sip our coffee allowing the heaviness in the airtime to clear.

She blows her nose. "I want you to know I hurt too. I feel terrible saying goodbye." A tear spills down her face.

"It's like a death," I mumble, retreating inside my coffee, the container crunching inside my fist.

"Yes," she says in a suffocated whisper.

She glances around, not focusing on anything, eyes wandering aimlessly, as if lost. "But where are your paintings?"

I dig my nails into my palms. I don't want to show her anything so I say, "I'm not painting much now."

"Oh," she says. Her lips grow thin and firm. "Where do you work?

I rise slowly, with the coffee cup, slouch to the patio on my 4-prong cane. I sit on a stool, gravity-drawn, shoulders spent. The area comes alive with her presence and the upside-down reflections after the rain: the soft illumination of the palm trees, the dark ground around the glistening pool. The earthy smells.

"Is that yours?" she says pointing to that dark preliminary painting by a succulent plant.

Sweat trickles from my forehead and armpits as she lifts the painting off the easel, holds it to the light. I get a cleaned paintbrush, and rinse it under a water spigot by the patio, reshaping my brush bristles. I store my brush to let it dry. I walk rapidly with head down to the window, remove any remaining solvent on the brush on an old rag.

"My. This is good," she says.

Is she lying? I look down at a spider on the windowsill, down some coffee.

Her eyes take on a hunted look burgeoning with tears as she looks at the canvas, and says, "It's raw but wonderful." The scene is of a small rowboat on the sand, abandoned to rot in the abrasive and damp air of the beachfront. I wipe my brow, rise with difficulty, yank on the overhead fan.

She finds the initial sketch stuck way under the stair well. She studies it, her eyebrows lowered. Every aspect of the drawing focuses on a little boy who stands between two grown-ups. My son, if he were alive.

Raindrops strike the already steamy patio, pitting the surface. Wind picks up, howling. The first crack of lightening rents the air and she returns the sketch to its safe keeping place under the stairs and within seconds she's inside. I'm burning up, palms oily as I grab my claw-footed cane and follow her through the French doors, past the bedroom, down the hallway with built in bookshelves of hard covered art books.

Into the bathroom she goes, then comes out, eyes redder than before asking for water, and sitting on the sofa. She closes her eyes, downs the water. "I've got to go," she says, her voice edged with tension. "I hope you understand. I can't bear to see you like this. . . I can't go through another. . She gulps, hiding any sound from her mouth. ."And I can't allow myself to overdo things. "

"I'd like to be with you," I manage. "As long as I can."

"No, no." Her body grows tense and her breath goes thin. She pulls herself up tall, striking her knees with a determined pat. She adjusts her purse and gives me a half-smile.

I grin back, from beside her on the sofa.

"I want to remember this place as it is now. . ." she said.

"For when?"

"For when you ... for later."

I try to speak. To form my lips correctly to talk to her. Appropriately a soprano sang, "Un bel di vedremo" from *Madame*

Butterfly and I think, Should I drown myself like Butterfly did or blow my head off like Treplev in *The Seagull*?

I stand, but my leg is asleep. I trip. She catches me, and we make it back to the couch and sit, me hunching over embarrassed, then crossing my arms as if to say, "This is not happening."

I say, "I dreamed I cut a hole in the floor above me, and you could reach your hand down from the bed upstairs, and I reached up and we held hands."

Monica scratches her neck, her oval eyes locking on me. "What will you do," she says.

"I don't know," I scrunch down so she can't see me. "Life's a peculiar blend of starting over and using the scraps."

"You feel sad, don't you?"

"Sure." I say, close-lipped.

"That's not what I mean. You feel sad in here." Monica places her hand on her chest. Tenderness! Followed by an ache. Before, Monica would come running to me if she saw me suffering. Now, my sadness is met as an observation. What went wrong?

"I'm going to look good," I say, shrugging off, "When I leave here. But I won't be."

She tilts her head back, lips parted slightly, looking down through long lashes.

"Skye visited," I say, voice tight. Anything to keep her there. "My friend from the Connecticut gallery. He offered me a job. He's just landed a deanship at a university." I clear my throat, swirl the last coffee in my cup. "All these people on the periphery ascending." I shift uneasily. "On the other side of art, the purveyors, the critics. He wants me to teach. Actually, to be in residence there."

A flush of color warms her cheeks, she returns to the sofa, sits. "Do you feel up to a residency? What did you tell Skye?"

"He says there's physical access and facilities on campus for the dis-abl-ed." I stumble on the word, fingers poking the sofa armrest. "They have to do that you know, to get funding from the Feds. I suppose I could teach if I went with a companion."

She fidgets in the seat. "Well that's a good thing. . . . What does your physician think?"

"Which one?"

"I think you should go."

"Accept . . .Skye's . . . offer?" I stammer. "Why?"

"Chance to grow. Change of scene. Possibility."

I stall. "I don't want to go on a w-w-w-walker," I stutter. "I don't know how long I can stand on a cane?"

She looks down, looks up. Her eyes are cast softly upon my hand resting on the claw-footed cane.

"They make larger four pronged canes—," she says.

"I know. Then you walk with two canes. Do I want to do that with students?"

"Live day by day and give them the best of what you have," she says with a soft, close-lipped smile. "You know so much. "You don't even know how much you know."

"But to go alone in this condition?" I say.

"You could get a companion." She rises goes for the door.

My stomach recoils and I follow her with hesitant step. Paderewski's *Minuet Célèbre in G* plays on the sound system. Paderewski, whose beloved wife died in childbirth one year after they were married. I know what Monica's suggesting. Someone else. "You mean a nurse, an attendant?" I say.

"Yes. Plenty of nurses and aids would love to travel with you." She hides her face in her hand, as if looking into my eyes is difficult.

I blow out a heavy breath. "I leave May 10th . . . in two weeks. Come with me."

"I can't," she says, looking about for her umbrella.

"I'll get tickets and text you the flights. You could meet me at the airport."

"I'll think about it."

She fiddles with the umbrella, making a strangled noise with her throat but saying nothing, smiling goodbye.

I release the button on the gate. She clanks it open, glides out. A soft ache hits my chest. I step forward to watch her. Her auburn hair sways over her shoulder as she dips under the umbrella, then vanishes into a crowd of tourists. I wonder if it's the last time I'll ever see her.

CHAPTER 23

An hour later, the doorbell buzzes. I release the gate with a pizzazz, and Dr. Miles bolts in, blue morning light following. He is spruced up in khaki, Bermudas, shorts jacket, crinkled shirt with a thin but daring striped scarf. When people visit the Quarter, they like to "do it up a little," get sassy with beignets or tea, look a little spry. He hangs his raincoat and hat on a rack by the door, sits on the sofa, face tight, glasses fogged.

"Did you forget our therapy appointment," Dr. Miles says, crossing a leg and motioning to me.

"Sorry," I say, setting my jaw with determination. "I did . . .yes. So much has been happening. Mostly for the good."

He takes a pen from his pocket.

"I'm thinking of moving," I say.

"Again?" He scratches his nose, perturbed. "You just got here."

"Moving away to Connecticut?" I say.

"Connecticut." He releases a crick in his neck. I tell him about Skye's offer. He pushes his sweaty glasses up his nose. I'm regretting his visit and seeing I don't need him.

"Are you prepared for all the medical issues should you relocate?" he hammers.

"I can handle it." I place the lid back on the empty cup, sit.

"I don't think Connecticut is a good idea. Down the line, you'll be . . .be more compromised."

"We don't know for sure." If only he would leave.

"Yes, we do." He coughs. "I've been your friend."

"A paid friend." I rest a moment on the sofa, quelling the heat in my voice, back pressed into the cushion, defying the shock in his face. "If I'm in a happy place with people who admire me, I may live better, longer."

"Or it may cut your time short." He sticks his pencil behind his ear.

My head burns. "I won't be seen everywhere as Mr. Cancer." I claw at my neck.

"Your disease will follow. You can't escape it or leave it behind like a suitcase."

"I just want to do my work, smell paint, dab oil on canvas, talk 'art' and not worry about what comes next."

"But do you know for sure this is true inside." He tightens the scarf at his neck. "You . . .you have serious   . . . limitations."

"OH BE QUIET. I don't need the incessant reminders . . .the doctors visits. . .the precautionary responses." I stand, legs wobbly, but jaw fierce. " I want to walk into a room of shining students that admire me. Look at a painting and feel it. Just do the work. Move forward fearlessly."

Dr. Miles rises, eyes soft behind his glasses. "Well, it seems you've made up your mind."

"Yes."

He marches to the hat stand, squashes his hat on his head, "You'll have to tell your mother," he sighs.

"You do it!" I snap. "Reporting is what you are best at."

He leaves with a glum smile.

Tchaikovsky's *Valse Melancolique* wails from the sound system. Tchaikovsky who was passionate for Mozart and suffered numerous emotional breakdowns, Tchaikowsky who based one opera on a poem by Pushkin, Pushkin who died of cholera after drinking a glass of unfiltered water.

I roam through my cell to see if Monica has called. No texts, no calls, no voice mails, nothing. I phone her in hopes that she'll answer. She doesn't. Who knows may be she will show up at the airport? I go back to the easel and then I call Skye and accept.

Ma calls the next morning at breakfast. I answer knowing if I don't she'll keep ringing.

"When can you come to dinner?" she says. "Or at least cocktails?"

I sit on the bed, brain hot.

"I've fresh crabs?"

I tell myself the brave thing is to face her. Eventually I'll feel guilty if I don't give her this one last goodbye. "Tonight," I say.

I get there early, but Ma's walking in the park. The azaleas, camellias, bananas trees still thrive on her lawn, and one random pink hibiscus. The magnolias full branched sway slightly, their brown bellied leaves cringing from the sun. I sink inside the porch swing. Once it cradled me from the huge fern baskets that hung like monsters' heads from the overhead gallery and from the distant bamboo, which I imagined were beanstalks that Jack climbed to the sky. I'm back in the Garden District. . . . It hurts that I love it so much.

I savor the thick smells, the heat, the weight of "home." Even so, I don't want to die in New Orleans. If I stay here, I'll die sooner.

Footsteps approach. Margaret comes out with ice tea and a wide-eyed smile. She catches her breath, as she savors me, pulling a Kleenex from her pocket, wiping her eyes. "How you feeling, Mr. Roo?"

I nestle a moment in her calm arms, smelling of rose water and mild perspiration.

More footsteps. I break into a sweat.

Ma swanks in, swathed in Gucci: jeans, shades, and baseball cap. She gives directions for drinks and crackers, hands Margaret her voiceless toy poodle who peeps wildly as they leave the porch.

Ma hooks her cap on the doorknob, swings her pageboy hair do (Sassoon in NYC), cranes her neck for a kiss. I haven't seen her since I agreed to a birthday lunch at Commander's.

"You're early," she says as she removes her sunglasses. Her skin shines pink, weekly facials and a mini lift having over-sensitized it. She burrows inside her Gucci tote, for a cigarette. Her new haircut makes her look even younger, but ashamedly she's resumed smoking, perching the cigarette on a shell ashtray and only raising it to inhale. "Don't say anything, I know I shouldn't smoke," she says, sitting before a window on a green wicker chair. "Your leaving completely unhinged me. I'm glad you've decided to come to your senses and move home." She blows out a smoke ring. "If you'd warned us, Margaret could have cooked your favorite meal tonight."

I sit back on the swing, rocking firmly. Out of the blue, the skies open. Rain gushes, and batters the lawn, oak trees cringing, banana trees shriveling, camellias bursting open and falling.

Ma inhales deep all the way through her fingers to her toes. She cranes forward smarting, tapping the big shell ashtray, assessing me. "You look awful," she says in her deep throaty voice.

I crack my knuckles glancing toward an oak tree. "You over-anxietize. "

"Over-anxietize?" She shakes her head and inhales.

I breathe deep. "Dr Miles says—"

"Oh no. Are you talking to him again?" she chuckles. "You missed your last appointment. "

"How do you know?"

She squeezes her cigarette pack. "I called him. What am I supposed to do? Guess what's going on with you? Talk to your voice mail?"

"I can't believe you called him. Doesn't that violate . . . some . . . some confidentiality," I blurt.

She cocks her head. "Aw come on. I'm a mother."

I'm boiling inside.

She smiles. "Miles told me about the job offer. The sup-po-sed (she 'syllabulates' gleefully) residency in Connecticut."

I stretch back, pushing off the swing, my brain sizzling. I focus on a thousand-leg spider circling a column.

"It's interesting," Ma says, "that you've done . . . the same things in the past . . . when your art failed."

"What are you talking about?"

"Rooster! There's some point where you have to decide if these relocations will suffice? When you're living with so little energy you can barely walk?"

Margaret rounds the door with Bloody Marys in iridescent glasses with raised Venetian clowns and Beluga caviar. I pass.

Ma lines up the two drinks on her end table. She leans sideways, aggressively flicking her cigarette, hair curtaining her profile, blowing out the side of her mouth as Margaret leaves.

I sit forward, feet muscled to the planks. "Skye came by to see me."

Ma bites her cigarette, baring her teeth. "Skye? Ha. Is he still hawking art?"

"He's a good soul," I say.

"Maybe Skye *was* a good man. But whom does he demonstrate that to? He's always sniffing around at fundraisers. I know you need friends. But Skye? Think again." Ma twists a Tiffany neck chain of gold crusted rubies. "He's an opportunist."

"He wants to help."

"Pshaw," Ma says. "Artists don't want to feel people are egregious, so they make up a story and deny their real response."

"Not true!"

"Well ... you and Skye can drive to the Country Club, dine on me, and talk art. But don't let him get too close. The key is to let ME help you with your own autonomy."

I grin, shake my head. "Do you even realize the absurdity of that statement?"

She lights a cigarette from the first. "Poor choice."

"That was offensive."

"You're overly-sensitive," she says

I move to lift myself off the swing.

"I know I shouldn't have said that," she says. "I don't want to talk about Skye."

I look at the overhang, painted blue to keep bugs and birds from nesting. I've been fooling myself that I could get closure. "I'm moving to Connecticut."

She lets loose a smoker's laugh. "You can't be serious." She shoves her lighter in her purse, raises a brow. "Connecticut. What is it really? A postage stamp by New York. Cold winters, high taxes, no amenities."

"Skye's going to be dean. Of a thriving arts school. . . .And he wants to hire me. Teaching there will be easy for me."

Her face blanches, white, stark. "What are you talking about?"

I tense forward. "I've accepted this job."

"Preposterous. You can't teach. You're delusional. You can barely walk." She reaches for her drink. "You've got to figure out what's easy for you, son."

"I'd like to postpone dying as long as possible."

"Don't use the d word." Ma's grabs a cigarette, pinches it in her teeth.

"If I can make it to Connecticut. I'll teach students to paint their best work."

"Oh Rooster, you know that position's a bribe. That university just wants a bequest."

I push a foot into the plank porch board. "Why are you so . . .so narrow?" I say.

Ma's lip quivers. "I thought you were moving back home. You can't teach college students, son even if it was a valid offer. They're utterly exhausting." Ma shows her teeth. "You must rest. Give up the glory for now. You've had your . . .your time in the sun."

I rise, sweating, the swing slapping my leg. I came to see you because I thought I owed you this last thing. "

"Skye is only doing this for you . . . out of some . . . some calculation. You must realize that? What people see in you is MONEY. Your clothes, your vocabulary, your arrogance. Friends can impersonate goodness. They say they really care about you, and at the same time they're stabbing you. Skye's looking for an endowment."

"You don't like Skye or anyone—"

"Taking you from your home, your medical protocols. "She drops back in her chair, blots perspiration off her lip. "Have you even talked to your doctor?"

"Last week. He says he'll connect me with a clinic up east. "I grab my watery Bloody Mary. "I'll see him again before I leave."

She blows smoke rings. "And when might that be?"

"Two weeks. . . Tuesday morning . . . nine am flight."

"Impossible."

The rain has ended. Light streams through the oak trees, snaking over the gallery. I try to slow my breaths. "I need to surround myself with other creatives."

"Don't emote. It's pretentious."

"I'm leaving Ma." With one swift movement, I push up. "I came here because I thought I could reinvision something." I grip my cane, plunking it down. The deck crackles as I walk.

"Oh I'm so sick of all this. Sit! For god's sake. You haven't . . . haven't . . . even found a replacement nurse."

"I'll get one if needed..."

"No you won't. You'll be too busy—" She squirms in the porch chair. "With this painting that you should NOT be doing."

"Please, Ma."

"You're disabled. You need rest, a servant. That's what I've been."

I know she's right, but no one should endure her abuse.

"Well," Ma says, "I won't have to serve you any longer."

I turn away, downing two dry aspirins, outrage searing my face, warning myself not to explain.

"Look at me when I'm talking," she says. "Is that Monica lunatic involved in this? Answer me! Do you want to see the medical bills for her services?"

I stomp across the front gallery, sweat fueling me, brain fire taking hold.

Ma squishes the cigarette butt in the shell. "I'm sorry I don't like Skye, but he's such a fop. Encouraging your self-idolatry. Once you get to Con-nec-ti-cut," she elongates the syllables. "If you don't fawn over him, he'll find you useless! I've seen his type in my volunteer work." She stretches back, lynching me with her eyes. "God, I hate being your mother." She curls up in a ball on the chair.

I bolt across the gallery, stomach cramping, brain screaming, diving inside the big house. I find Margaret in the kitchen preparing gumbo. I won't let the smells of okra, shrimp, crab whirl me back to childhood. She puts down her big stirring spoon.

"I'm leaving for good, Margaret. Moving east. Needed to tell you goodbye."

She wipes her hands on her apron, squares me with her eyes. "That's good," she says. "Make us proud."

"I can't understand how you have put up with Ma for so long."

"You go and get well again. Don't worry. I'll take care of her."

Margaret inhales deep, gives me a hug. "Don't come back here."

My heart pounds fast. I can't think. Or swallow as I return to the gallery.

On the porch, Ma ruffles her hair, peeping out through puffy eyes, face drained, burdened, sore. She rips cellophane from her new pack of Kents, cursing herself for wanting to smoke, ignoring the Garden District tour group huddling before the house observing her every mutter.

"You're consumed with yourself," Ma says.

I grit my teeth, uttering to myself the word, "Calm," my cheeks lifting to force a smile. "Goodbye, Ma."

Ma starts to sob, throat catching, thrusting her hand to her face. "Oh you're so mean to me. Putting me in this impossible situation. I'll have to worry night and day, travel when you get worse. And for what? For you to pursue some talent you think, but never had."

The dinner bell rings. Ma grabs her cigarettes, downs her Bloody Mary, shoulders rigid. "Now you're a good teacher. Talking about art. You're really good at that. But the art itself? I stand before it, and stare. . . . It doesn't satisfy. It never has. Christine took you as long as she could but you were too selfish for her too."

Tourists stare.

Ma rises bent on the dining room, her face strong and wild. "Never answering phone calls. Isolating yourself with your sketchbook. Not noticing when Christine had pneumonia."

"That's a lie."

"The baby had high fever, or even if I had a stroke."

"Psycho babble!" I grab the porch railing needing to feel the familiar strength of the moist wood. I'm not caring about the crowd creeping closer or Ma's sneering face. I shout. "You… you… you, neurotic, paranoid narcissistic, borderline, post-human sociopath. You hate me because I keep growing."

She glares at me. "Meanwhile you're just sitting here every night, pickling yourself on Bloody Marys."

"Get out," Ma screams. She grabs the ashtray and hurls it across the porch.

I fling open an umbrella. "I'm not going to give up like you did. I'm raising the bar. Leaving." I forge down the slippery stairs, chin to chest, the metal cane thwacking each step. The tour group parts as I burrow toward my car, turning up the stereo, Benedictine monks mercifully chanting *The Liturgy of the Hours*. I hit the gas, thinking of Margaret's words, "Don't Come Back."

CHAPTER 25

That night in my apartment, I pour myself into packing, Schubert's *Ave Maria* on the radio, swinging clothes into a suitcase, opening the doors to the rear patio, letting the clawing humidity and a breeze from the Mississippi River embolden me. I buy and send Monica a plane ticket.

My phone rings. Skye's name appears on the screen. "I got your classroom set up. And a great cottage nearby. You have six students enrolled," he says.

I exhale, collapse by my suitcase on the bed.

"It's a hand picked master class," he says. "Two graduate assistants will assist you daily to see what you need. I'll meet you at the airport."

"I'm doing the right thing, aren't I?"

"Absolutely," Skye says.

I make a packing list. My eyes blur with the weight of looking. The portrait of my mother holding me, the red Oriental rug, the ghost chairs, cobalt blue lamp from Christine. Do I want these "loaded" objects to surround me?

I sit on the sofa between antique funnel lamps. Should I sell them or donate all to Good Will. These lamps that lit Christine's face, my son's feet, Monica's hands. These lamps still standing on their gold twisted poles with bulbs promising ten years of light.

I text Monica. No response.

* * *

The next morning, it's hot, hot. No rainbows. Steam rises from the wet pavement. Despite my swollen eyes and stiff back, I'm up. Outside, the sun's already peeking through the trees. Swallows scruff inside branches. Treetops tilt in the warm breeze. I text Monica. Again.

By eleven am, I'm packed. I swoop up my silent cell phone to see if it's on. Beethoven's *Moonlight Sonata* plays. Beethoven whose *String Quartet No. 14 in C-sharp minor, Op. 131* was what Schubert asked to be played while he lay on his deathbed.

I walk out the gate onto St. Philip Street one last time. The French Quarter has been a place of dreams for me, since I was 19. I carry it in my heart, my blood.

I tell myself I don't need the cobblestone streets, the tightly sealed dormer cottages trying to claim authority with their crumbling blue, yellow, pink, purple walls, the creeking gates, the lizards slinking around fountains and pools.

I skirt the old and the homeless skulking along the sidewalk. I step inside St Louis Cathedral, appreciate its vaulted cream ceilings with frescos, step out to Jackson Square with its slate tiles, bulging vegetation, statue of Andrew Jackson on rearing horse. I tip my cap to the defiant gypsy guarding her cards before the bloody brick Baroness Pontalba apartments.

I don't tell the gypsy I'm leaving, but her pointed stare as I approach her tells me she knows. "Will I come back here?" I ask.

"Ever?" the gypsy says. "This isn't the time to think about that."

My eyes tear up as I stand before the grey shuttered French windows of 524 St Philip. I tell myself, "The reward for leaving. . . is time. To do something, even small with the gift of it, I have left."

The handicap spot before 524 St Philip, usually clogged with a junk car, is surprisingly empty. Two speckled terriers on a balcony and the long haired blond, who descends at noon to walk them and insists she makes her living as an "organizer," stare at me. Her blank cold look so differs from Monica's encouraging smile.

Ma's chauffeur pulls in front, hands me a fat envelope, which feels fat with bills. I open it to find money, my grandmother's ring, and a note that says, "Just because . . .Ma." I pocket the ring, give the chauffeur the money, decline the ride. I'll live off my salary in Connecticut and get well.

Moments later, I toss my backpack, cane and suitcase in an Uber. I've arranged for all my stuff to be donated to Habitat for Humanity and dropped the key in the mail earlier that day. We bolt over drizzly streets, reaching forty mph in seconds. Tchaikovsky's death *Symphony No. 6 Pathetique* rages through the vehicle, the driver bragging about using *Classical 104. 9 Radio.*

Light streams in through the concave glass window, as we pass cafes, bars, stores, the curiosities of New Orleans. My body relaxes. If only Monica will show up at the airport. I pause, lean my head back to let thoughts of her in. Stretch my shoulders wide.

At the airport, I try breathing slow. Inhale, exhale one, two, three, four, five. . . I close my eyes and breathe in—progressively. Exhale six, seven, eight, nine—If only my brain would cool. I ask myself. "WILL SHE BE THERE?" Exhale ten, eleven, twelve. My wonderful and beautiful Monica.

But as I stand to get out the car, my heart seems to pound even harder.

Inside the airport, Delta attendants thrust me a wheelchair. I decline though the terminal seems excessively large, bright, loud. Polished floors. Gigantic chambers. No sign of Monica.

I get my ticket and check my bag. I'm curious if the routine flight to Atlanta (impossible to fly direct) is different from the one I had before when I came home and they found the lump. I present my boarding pass. I tell myself it's good I've found the power to come here alone despite my queasy stomach.

I go to security and take off my shoes and socks, put my carry-on bag in a grey bin, and take out my laptop and my cell phone. I hand over the bottle of water I've mistakenly brought with me. Again no sight of Monica.

I take off my watch, my Jesuit school ring, my Celtic cross, my belt, and put my change in a dish before going through the metal detector. My possessions survive the x-ray machine. I put my shoes back on, get my belongings. I veer around, scrutinizing the pathways.

"She won't be here," a voice in my head says. "This is what death feels like."

I shake off the thought, go to gate C6, grateful I've only five gates to walk my cane pass.

Down the hallway is a little nook with coffee and tea. But I can't spare the energy to stop. I make it to a waiting area with wretched overhead TVs, gray chairs, gray rug. II get some water, collapse in a chair.

Moments later, I get up and steady myself, look about for Monica. Half hour to boarding.

Bluesy New Orleans music plays, sounds meant to ease anxious people waiting to board a metal tunnel in the sky. A pretty black girl with perfect Egyptian hair comes in with haunted eyes and very long lashes. I wonder if she is going to New York. I retreat to a spot overlooking the runway. I see a man with a streak of grey hair in the reflection of the glass. How could I look so old at thirty-nine?

Outside the glass wall, a blood brown sky sinks over low planes, crouching like prehistoric creatures, grown lazy in the dark light. Soon I'll be leaving the blustery semi-tropics. No more ninety-five degree days and rain attacks.

I check my cell phone to see if Monica's called. No texts, no emails, no voice messages, nothing. I know I said I wouldn't hope, but I do. I wait, watching shafts of light shadow the rug. I pop a mint to cool my throat.

I check out three more people waiting nearby: one with a magazine, one with legs crossed thinking, one with flip-flops kicked astray scrutinizing her ipad.

A crack of thunder. Awool. The rain is having rain. I don't want to look out and feel death in the clouds. I grab my sketchbook. Pushing the pencil point into the paper, I keep my hand moving across the page. Drawing, my old friend.

Every few moments, l check my cell phone, palms sweaty. For 30 seconds my eyes crawl from the floor to the seats and the aisles.

My flight is called. I stand in line, face steamy, armpits moist. I wait for nine minutes straight, looking about hoping, light draining right out of me. The attendant scans my ticket and I board the plane.

Outside the small oval windows, the rain floods, but, undaunted, a valiant seagull sails by. We need to say goodbye to so many things in life in order to grow. At some point, we say goodbye to life itself. I smell lavender perfume.

"Is this seat taken?" a sweet voice says.

I open one eye. See a woman's hand, a green dress, long neck, auburn hair, turquoise eyes. I reach out to make sure she's real.

She holds the boarding pass to her slightly opened mouth. "I'm sorry. I'm late," she says. "Please forgive me."

Monica looks at her watch and says, "We've ten minutes before the plane leaves."

I say, "Yes."

"The next one's mine."

I smile, "All of it?"

"Every minute."

We are playing word games again and I like that.

She places her purse under the seat and says, "I plotted out our relationship, and I feared it was going to be real sexy."

"So?" I smile.

"Every time I came near, I felt embarrassed, had to move quickly off to the side, keep you exercising and moving. Eventually it was too much and I left."

"Why didn't you say something?" I ask.

She blushes. "I didn't want to ruin anything between us." I felt ashamed because I'd wake up in these hot sweats and I needed to act like a nun." She flushes stretches her neck back. "I'd such sexy ideas in such an utterly nonsexy place."

"Did you—well."

She attaches her the seat belt. "You knew it. Huh? Every morning when I saw myself in your eyes, it reminded me I wasn't buried with my husband."

"You never told me?"

Rain blisters the windowpane. She looks out. "It's started to rain again. Your deciding to go to Connecticut told me how strong you are. Your determination bothered me, kept me up at night. I knew I had to go with you." A tear drips from her eye.

I turn her to me. "Are you . . .?"

"I'm crying because I love you so."

"Marry me," I say.

A stewardess closes the luggage racks overhead.

Monica looks away, "You'll soon be working nonstop, free of the concerns that worried you."

She leans over and I kiss her. "You like rings?" I take my grandmother's ring from my pocket.

"What are you doing?" she says.

"I'm putting one on your finger."

The air conditioner speeds up. The plane doors shut. The engine rolls. The rain begins to pour again.

We are inside the rain and lifting off. The best rain can't be contained. It is lustful. The plane lifts into the joyful roars and frequencies of the wet diamond sky.

THE END

SWEET OPIUM

Soline McClain, actor, *Sweet Opium*
Photograph by Christian Raby

Photograph by Mary Anderson

Photograph by Rory O'Neill Schmitt

PROLOGUE

This is a story about a family in Pass Christian, Mississippi before it vanished and all that blue gray water before the house, the mansion with steel post construction and red brick from St. Louis that was flattened by Hurricane Katrina. The town that is no more. There is only rubble ten miles back from that blue gray warm water with sea gulls flying, crushed brick and one statue of Our Lady, arms wide standing by a church.

The mansion called Serenity was built to withstand 200-mile-an-hour winds. It had roof flaps that popped open so wind could ripple through. The former house leveled in Hurricane Camille had burst open like a Cracker Jack box.

They say trees stand in front of Serenity now branchless red-gold, ripped of their leaves and moss. They say snakes swim along the beach in that cool gray water now brown from the debris and dirt.

Who will take the miles of rubble away? Who will purify the water? Who will have the courage to rebuild again? The coastline has eroded and oil rigs have exploded into the Gulf. Who will clean it all? Who will stand under the stripped oaks, charred and smelling of soot and feces? Who will wear a mask and keep digging, holding their breath and knocking with chain saws to bring the green earth and the fresh salty air back?

CHAPTER 1

July 3, 2005
Fifty-seven days before Katrina

All Sissy could think about was sex, moving to Grandma's just before Hurricane Katrina hit. On July 2, 2005 the family gathered in Pass Christian, Mississippi with its lush foliage and waves that made her feel ripe. Sissy Leger was seventeen, and her hormones were fiery and depleted like that coastline. The villa, which her grandmother had named Serenity, loomed over the Gulf of Mexico like a mausoleum, defying August hurricanes that threatened to suck beach mansions into the waves like surreal icebergs. Other manors had succumbed in 1927, `47, `69. But the twenty-year span that birthed the big hurricanes had passed, and people felt safe.

Sissy was from New Orleans, ninety minutes away, and New Orleaneans in the ancestral tradition had expanded family compounds for recreation. Most were within two hours of New Orleans on the Gulf of Mexico in Mississippi. Serenity was the biggest and most impressive on the most exclusive strip, Pass Christian. Built of steel post construction and St. Louis brick, the house rivaled the *Titanic* in construction.

That day, the chauffeur, Clifford, walked Sissy over sun-parched grass, his navy uniform crisp over brown skin. It was already a hundred degrees. They passed police dogs lounging on the gallery. One snarled at Clifford and showed its yellow teeth. A black yardman had thrown stones at the dog and made it hate Afro-Americans. Clifford marched on.

Rockers rattled in the breeze, and windows reflected uneasy trees. Sissy's mother had waved good-bye on this gallery before running off with her lover over the timeless gray sea. She had brushed back her daughter's hair, soft fingers soothing her temples, and promised they would be together soon, if only Sissy would visit her in Paris.

Clifford heaved back the steel door, spilling out cold air, and smiled. Had he learned of Sissy's expulsion from school? He was kind enough to avoid hurtful subjects. He led her to the chilled morning room, with its swags of dreary olive fabric and silk cord. The expensive furnishings were upstairs on the second floor, higher than the surges of Hurricane Camille in '64. Serenity, built farther back than the old mansion, was twice as big, with twelve-inch walls of old-plantation brick.

A portrait of Sissy's twenty-eight-year-old uncle startled her. Today, in the silence, he seemed so close, almost breathing. His soft doe eyes looked down as if to say hello, boyhood lending sweetness to a brooding smile. It carried an edge, which defied his hair, loose and tumbling against his brow, and huge hands, defiantly useless, resting on china-white slacks. Sissy wrote in her diary: *Uncle took twenty years to rip off that suit and run off to the French Quarter. How long will it take me?*

From upstairs, Sissy's grandmother Irene Dubonnet screamed a greeting. She was a petite woman with red hair who, even in stifling Mississippi, dressed as if going to high tea: designer suits, pencil-heeled pumps, hair swept in a tight French twist. A widow, she wore the style appropriate to her husband's career.

Sissy met her grandma on the balcony. Her fierce gray eyes took the girl in with a dismissive stare that told Sissy she was deeply hurt.

Sissy pecked Grandma's forehead, which reeked of Chanel perfume. To others, she appeared unemotional because she used calm, as a shield during a crisis. They sat on the coffin-gray chairs, the girl slouching, the matriarch shielding a newspaper before her face, her skin sensitized by weekly peelings and facials.

Below, Sissy's white German shepherd, Greta, lunged at Clifford, who leashed her and took her whimpering away behind the house.

Nature seemed uneasy, the sun speckled and hot, the Gulf too quiet, the moss thinning in the oak trees. Drilling offshore had eroded the marshlands that surrounded the villa and dirtied the water out front.

The family didn't talk about global warming in New Orleans or Mississippi unless it was to raise the A/C when it was getting hotter or to negotiate a better contract from the oil companies drilling in the Gulf out front. The family owned the water rights in front of Serenity and leased them to companies that paid a good price and drilled discretely beyond sight.

Grandma appeared calculating behind intense eyes. Had she received Sissy's report card? "Beastly weather! Boils the flesh!" Grandma said. "Your Uncle Blaise doesn't seem to mind. He likes it."

Sissy's pulse quickened at her uncle's name. She fantasized a sexual explosion between them kissing underwater, then a rendezvous at midnight in the guest bedroom. Though no one knew of her desire for him, it didn't squelch the guilt. If she didn't meet some young men soon, Sissy feared she'd lie down naked before the first gardener she could find. Put down that spade. Spade me, spade me.

Sissy looked out. The grim gallery of oaks screening the house forbade approach. Behind them, a shiny highway coiled before the sallow private beaches of the Gulf of Mexico. Few boys would have the nerve to visit here.

Grandma loved to spend time socializing. "I'll line up some sailing lessons for you." she smiled, lips tight over pearly teeth, and handed Sissy the yacht club schedule. "Your uncle will take you the first time."

Sissy's heart skipped. Blaise preferred regattas and champagne to jeans and Pepsi. He'd studied at the Philadelphia School of Art and shocked the family by painting nudes in the New Orleans French Quarter. How was she deal with this man whose brushstrokes captured breasts and thighs, who sculpted women in oils so he could touch every curve in their bodies?

Grandma nodded down at Clifford, who washed the Cadillac daily, the dripping hose loose and familiar. Oh how Sissy wished she could talk to him and not Grandma. With her, Sissy always felt isolated. Perhaps the sternness in Grandma's voice came from the heat and not that rotten report card.

"Cadillacs suit any occasion, Sissy. Weddings, funerals, divorce. What was that thing your uncle drove?"

"A yellow sports van."

"A banana truck. Far be it for me to judge your uncle. The older he gets, the less he resembles me." Grandma poked at the brace that squeezed her torso. Her car had slammed into a pothole, racing to report Blaise missing to the Coast Guard when he took the sunfish out during a squall. "Blaise is totally unreliable."

"Unreliable?"

"Defends your mother's running off to Paris. We won't discuss this thing. Your mother's affair thing."

"Yes, Grandma."

"I don't like that word. It's 'Irene.'"

"Irene." First-naming someone so old felt disrespectful, like a funeral director nicknaming a corpse.

"I don't like 'Sissy' either. Why not call yourself Edna, after my mother?"

Sissy's real name was Edna Irene Leger. Theodore Roosevelt had called his grandchildren Sissy and Buzzy, and Mama had hoped to honor him. "Popular girls have nicknames," Mama had said. "I'm Kitten, you're Sissy, then there's Aunt Bitsy, Cousin Peaches, Tootie, Pudding, Muffin."

"You're Edna to me, and I'm Irene. Besides, your mother is pubescent. Leads a self-centered lifestyle. I hope you pray for her, because I can't." Grandma straightened the pearls between her breasts.

Outdoors wind picked through Sissy's hair from the choppy waves a thousand feet away. For a moment, she was thirteen, squishing wet sand into a castle while her mother sunbathed and read *The House of Mirth*. "You need to build up your soul with books. You're going to love Edith Wharton," Mama had said, her voice resonating to the red splashes of sunset:

Her heart was beating all over her body—in her throat, her limbs, her helpless, useless hands. Her eyes traveled despairingly about the room; they lit on the bell, and she remembered that help was on call. Yes, but scandal with it—a hideous mustering of tongues.

Was Sissy's mother lonely then? Had she already given up on Dad?

Sissy's father had strolled over, hadn't touched them just walked down the beach. Mama had raked her hair back in a slow sweeping motion. Sissy supposed she could go the rest of her life without talking to her father. Millions did. Still, sometimes she missed the pale blue eyes that shone through you. His touch rattled her heart. But she could do without it if she had her mother.

Grandma handed Sissy a card from her mama in Paris heralding the Luxembourg Gardens: luscious roses and Greek fountains. Mama lived in her body and not her head. If Sissy got lost when they visited Paris, Mama had promised to meet her there. On the card was the giant fountain where nude powerful Cupid reached for his beloved Psyche. Water streamed down their moss-encrusted faces, chests, and thighs. Did Mama read Ronsard to her lover there? Did he appreciate the poet of chivalry who eulogized the child named Rose? *"Rose elle a vécu comme les roses. L'espace d'un matin."* (Rose who lived like roses. The spare of one morning.)

Sissy's mother loved American beauties. When she'd get a bouquet from Sissy's dad after some transgression, she'd pick the sweetest one and perch it delicately on her dresser. *Rose elle a vécu comme les roses . . .* Sissy kissed the card.

Grandma winced as if she too missed Mama. "For each action there is a natural reaction," Grandma said. "Mine is different from yours because you've your mother's sentimentality. If I'd known the pain that woman would cause, I'd have aborted her. Goes to the best schools, makes her debut, then runs off to some foreign country and sends a monthly card."

"Don't talk about Mom."

"She called from the French Riviera," Grandma said vaguely, her blue-veined fingers threading her pearls.

"Did she leave a number?"

"No, she and that man are off . . . to London. To visit the birthplaces of the Romantic poets."

The Romantic triumvirate. Byron, Shelley, Keats. Better than Ronsard. Lighting bonfires in Italy—like that counted, like it counted that her mother went back to college, that she rose at four a.m. to read philosophers with weird names like Teilhard de Chardin, except on Saturdays, when her parents' locked bedroom resonated her mother's "Come back later." The realm of pure form had evolved into simple sweat and rut.

What had her Dad done to her brilliant mother behind Saturday morning doors? Had he found her secret self-wanting, or used that knowledge to procure wilder pleasures with ladies at the Broadwater Hotel in Biloxi, down the road? Paint that, Uncle Blaise.

Clouds clumped over the Gulf. "Remember when Mama recited poetry?" Sissy said. "She'd end with Richard Cory. The man glittered with charm but he put a bullet through his head. Mama was depressed then."

Grandma held her head high. She felt responsible for her daughter's failures. "Exhausted. Blaise thought she'd improve if we left her alone."

"Does anything improve if left alone? Animals die. Flowers wilt."

"I offered to pay for that Mississippi sanitarium. My mother-in-law and mother went there. Fragile women need to replenish themselves. They are always in danger." Grandma sat up tall.

Sissy smoked. She'd started at eleven, wearing pink lipstick and echoing old Bette Davis movies (her mother said red lipstick was for whores). Once Mama had answered the door nude, when Sissy came home unexpectedly. The confrontation had called for red lipstick.

Grandma changed the subject to beauty so she could use her expertise. Sissy felt sure report card had come.

"Girls look smart with tobacco in their hands, if dressed correctly," Grandma said. "But change those shredded jeans. You look like the yard boy. I remember when girls suffered to look pretty, squeezing into waist cinchers, girdles, and strapless bras for boys in navy blazers and striped silk ties, whose privates hung behind expensive tweed. Aren't you going to dress for dinner? You must present yourself correctly to attract the right caliber of people."

"Who's coming?" Sissy said.

"One never knows. I've put the word out with all my friends. Plenty of wealthy girls vacation on the coast. Attorneys' and surgeons' daughters. Rich girls have rich brothers. Your uncle proves that. You must be cutthroat in choosing friends. You're looking for a mate."

"No I'm not!" Sissy feared losing her deviant love for her uncle Blaise. The chaotic unpredictability of his presence excited her.

At one p.m., Sissy and her grandma dined, 'Irene's' ivory-handled fork rasping across the salad dish. She liked to plan meals down to the smallest luxury, almonds in silver shells, individual crystal salt and pepper dishes. A deep longing for love and connection filled each choice. Eating became the spiritual Communion, so when fewer and fewer relatives called on her in the country it was hard on her.

That day, Irene cut her steak in cubes, inspecting them for fat. Her daughter's elaborate napkin ring idled by Sissy's plate. Irene kept the table set for four, with Blaise's place by hers.

Sissy petted the heavy initials on her mother's wide-looped napkin ring. Clifford said her mother left quietly in a limousine. She looked peaceful, as if the idea of quick travel had come suddenly. She left Sissy a note with a white azalea tied in blue: *I need time with my sweetheart. Hope you understand* it read. Funny how Sissy wanted to get to know her mama, when most girls hated theirs. Perhaps it was her outlook on life— taking the days in huge bites-- or simply her beauty. Her mother was mysterious. Men noticed she was different from any other woman. And wanted her alone.

Grandma gulped her water. Mama was a seductive muse and Grandma an iron butterfly.

"Your mother is ungrateful," Grandma said, reading the girl's thoughts. "You'd do best to forget about her as she has about you."

Sissy scraped Béarnaise sauce from her filet mignon, dumped some steak into her napkin to feed to the hungry swamp ducks.

How could Grandma say such awful things?

Grandma stabbed holders into her corncob. "We won't discuss your refusal to live with your mother. I don't care for her new companion myself. And your father. I was amazed he kept you till the house sold. Now he has vanished, leaving me to face the report card. I hid it in my file drawer of volunteer activities under 'F."

Sissy's ears went silent. All this time Grandma knew. The brilliant sunlit shapes of table dishes burned at Sissy's eyes. The food in her plate looked like weeds.

Thousands had been spent to get Sissy into the school from which Irene had graduated valedictorian. Dark lines like barbed wire crossed her brow " 'F'" she said, "in every subject but comportment, in which you got a 'C.' I'm so humiliated. All those counselors, something's very wrong with you. I should never have gotten you that television. Are you watching too much TV?"

"I need late shows to put me to sleep."

"Fade out to the toe-tapping of Ginger Rogers? Is that what you do?"

"In class, I keep dozing. I and this other girl whose mother died and whose dad ran off, sit along the wall. We don't bother anyone."

Emotions surged behind Irene's stoic face. "You're floundering, because you want to. My mother, grandmother, and great-grandmother were Ursuline valedictorians. I got you in as a legacy," She said. "Do you know the sacrifice involved for those women's grades? No recreation. No missed homework. Even when I had the mumps and a hundred and four degrees of fever, Mama smothered my face with powder and sent me to school."

"She could have killed you."

"I've enrolled you in Saint Joseph's Academy here on the coast. At least no one but the teachers will know of your disgrace." I've disconnected your cell phone for a month. Time for you to reflect on the consequences of your choices."

Sissy checked the dead phone in her pocket. "You didn't cut off my cell phone?"

Grandma looked at her watch with an apologetic expression. As of ten minutes ago … I tried to give you the least punishment I could because I want you to like it here with me."

Walls closed in on Sissy. She'd been at Ursuline for four years and she had a few friends there. Now she might lose touch with them all. She found solace at the convent in the creak of the shiny wood floors, the dimly lit halls, portraits of Our Lady lining bluish white walls. The Ursuline nuns had opened the first Catholic school for girls in New Orleans. Once ten thousand French nuns taught there. Now only five remained, childlike crones who understood Sissy's need to rest in the infirmary or help out by cleaning the vigil lights. She'd sneak off to the pantry to dust the midnight blue glass, smelling of wax and incense, then duck outside to a rampart and watch the boys in Mustang convertibles or Impala coupes lining up to meet their girlfriends.

Sissy's eyes roved to a wall, dressed with diplomas from Harvard, University of Pennsylvania and Tulane, and a shadow box of gold medals. Her throat burned. She wanted to be contained like her grandmother, speak only when controlled in a nonreactive way, but Grandma's words hit her like a balloon, the hold broke free and she went flying in the wind, charging from the table, screaming, "You lousy witch."

Sissy grabbed the elevator that the heart specialist had made Grandma install and rode all the way downstairs to Blaise's room. Just the smell of him might give her power.

The room had an early-evening dark, but even that couldn't hide Blaise's warm, cloying scent. It was like a spoor Sissy could track, a mixture of Givenchy Gentleman, a woodsy smell, and leather. A dull glow lit the room. Sissy could barely see the raw silk bedspread, the colognes and tanning oils on the dresser. Grandpa's chesterfield sofa, ponderous drapes, and bearskin rug were stuffed into the room. Blaise's huge closet was empty, his fishing caps were gone.

"You didn't throw out his clothes! Why?"

"I had to put Grandpa's stuff somewhere," Grandma said entering the room. "We closed the New Orleans office after the funeral. Besides, Blaise has his own little house."

"A garconniere, he never uses that," Sissy said.

"Punishing me because I wouldn't let his friends drive up and down the grounds after midnight. You want me to encourage his deviant side?"

Grandma aligned herself only with powerful men, and when Blaise got caught living for the moment and not planning for the future, he got reprimanded.

Sissy half-closed her eyes till she saw nothing but a faint blur and the lightest and darkest shapes.

"Don't look away when I'm talking," Grandma said.

Blaise had told Sissy, "When you feel yourself breaking, leave, inhale the sky, taste the air."

Sissy bolted outside. Fantail pigeons scattered, sending up dust. A palm tree wafted its ragged edges in the bleached sky. She wanted to scrape herself against the tree's brown-gray bark. If Grandma was being mean to Blaise he might stay away forever. A single peacock cried, clawed at the dry earth, its brown tail quivering in the July heat.

A dozen peacocks and twenty flamingos once pranced over the lawn with soft delighted cries. Starving possums and vultures from the poisoned swamp had killed them. Peacocks, nuns, mothers, and uncles were all disappearing.

Sissy hurried under the oak tree where every family valedictorian had stood, decorated in gold medals, tasseled cap shining.

Clifford, who also had a gardening business, stopped clipping a hedge and came over. She fended him off. She had to leave to stand up for herself.

Branches snatched at her as she passed the moss-crusted statue of Venus in the reflecting pool where she'd once spotted Blaise naked. If only she could draw that firm body over her and stroke that back Enjoy the fiery sensation down her legs. Nights, her sheets were sweet with the shadow of him, his imagined body more real than the darkness that came over her, which made her fingers run wild in forbidden places and brought wetness between her thighs. God, Blaise was eleven years older than she.

She broke through elephant ears, and confused azaleas exposing their purple blossoms to the July sun. The path drooped with oleanders, their soft skins slipping to the ground.

To the right, rose blistering swamps. Sissy could lose herself in the squealing of those wild ducks, swishing cattails, musty marsh, in some secret connection between her and the remnants of the Gulf. She threw hungry geese the steak bits fetched from her pocket, and they nipped at her fingers, attacked her ankles, bit her heels. She waved off Clifford, who yelled for her to come back. How could he understand her strange nature?

Memories of Uncle Blaise kept chasing her like a breeze. He was part of her earliest touch of the place, of the heron, the seagulls, and the swamp. Sometimes she felt he lived inside the wind and she'd never shake him from consciousness. She crept over paths made slippery by moss and ducked under waxy magnolias, their leaves shining like patent leather umbrellas.

Sissy slung back the fan gate of the family pier, the wood weathered salty black. Gulls lining the railings screeched and fluttered off into the bleary air. Maybe they were the souls of weary ancestors. Or of those bitch valedictorians, condemned to fly.

Blaise said the loud waves talked to him while he painted. At night they said, "Don't forget how cool I feel when you close your eyes."

Sissy remembered when Uncle Blaise took her swimming off the pier. She'd jump into his cool slick arms, relishing the touch of skin, the surge of water, thick with salt. He'd dive through those cracking waves as if he could subdue the turbulence.

Once, Sissy found Blaise's T-shirt on the pier and she was so happy to sleep in it, but not before she had smelled it, explored it, checking the seams, the armpits, the neck, pulling it on.

Sissy stepped onto the hundred-foot walkway. The salty air stung her nostrils. She heard a shout. Was Clifford shouting again? His shrewdness was so annoying. She checked her dead cell phone again and threw it in the Gulf.

She imagined Mama on her sunfish, sailing alone on the spongy, greenish brown water. Wind splayed through her hair. Once, Mama had told her the moon, a symbol of Diana, the Huntress, had a menstrual cycle. She rolled around every twenty-eight days. All the unborn were stars, blood drops of the moon.

The constantly shifting waves made it difficult to capture her fragmentary memories. Sissy was afraid to become her mother and afraid not to. When Mama had read to her, had she thought of Sissy's future or hers? A random sentence from *The House of Mirth* haunted Sissy:

As she moved beside him, with her long, light step, Selden was conscious of taking a luxurious pleasure in her nearness: in the modeling of her little ear, the crisp upward wave of her hair—

Was her mother hinting that she was the strong and fine one and Sissy was dull and ugly and needed to be sacrificed?

Waves pounded the pilings, churning up images of Mama. She was deep in the sea like an angel floating down, down, and Sissy couldn't see far enough. She leaned over a railing. The water sucked and slapped foam all around. Sissy heard nothing, not the pier rattling or the gulls shrieking. Waves below swept around the barnacled pier posts, swirling gray, black, spitting up foam at the brown murky water, ripping it open, layer on layer. She held out her arms to dive into the shallow water. Moments later, Clifford was at her side, in his old shirt. He yanked her with a thud onto the pier. Sissy tried to break free but he held her firm. Cliff was shy and somewhat restrained, but that day he really looked at her. "What you want to lean out like that for?" he said, his hand strong on her shoulder. "Few months and your mom be back."

"Course she will," Sissy said. "She could come back tomorrow if she wanted to."

"Your grandma expect a lot." Then he gave her such a sorrowful smile; she saw he knew she'd flunked. "You the only grandchild."

"Less Ma and her lover have a boy."

Clifford handed Sissy a Camel. She looked up, thankful for his understanding that had buoyed her through many a lonely summer. Clifford sang, his rough voice blending with the salty sea breeze, 'And he will raise you up on angels' wings'. . . Your grandma take care of all of us," he said. "She paying for my daughter's veterinary college in Starkville." He pulled out a frayed book. "Then she's sending me to ministry school. I'm learning a page each week in this here dictionary."

"You're not leaving!"

"Not till Clotilde graduates."

Sissy's throat tightened. "When's that?"

"Not for a while."

They sat on a bench turning pages, pronouncing words. Serenity dissolved into a stretch of oaks, pines, and an oyster sky.

Sissy lifted her face against the damp air. "Perhaps Blaise could help me bring Mama back."

"Leave him be."

"Why?"

"Your uncle not doing good. Suppose you know about his leg."

Oh no, what was being hidden by her relatives now? Had her gorgeous uncle had a physical setback? So sensitive was Blaise as an artist, the least turmoil attacked his body.

CHAPTER 2

July 4, 2005
Fifty-six days before Katrina

The next day, a yellow Mercedes towed a shiny yacht through the gates. Most wonderful! Her daddy, Quint Leger, was there. Sissy hopped onto a three-wheeler h had bought in good times, and raced the police dogs toward the gate.

She passed the beautiful marshes with their golden cattails and long-necked blue heron; vines crawling over red-brown soil, through crushed roses, magnolias, and strange blossoming violets flung down by a Gulf storm; simmering honeysuckle; limp, overripe pear trees; deep thick grass.

Dad flung a Brooks Brothers jacket over his shoulder as he got out the Mercedes. A crisp shirt offset his blond hair. He had a strong will to get things done and wanted to unhook the trailer while maintaining a sleek appearance. He waved off the dogs that snarled at his pants. "Tie up the dogs, why don't y'all? Good-for-nothing guard dogs won't let you in your own yard. I love Mississippi. If I had fifty dollars, I'd buy it."

Sissy peeked into the glistening car, which smelled of cowhide and lemon while Dad detached the trailer. He felt every rejection intensely and compensated with extravagant purchases.

"Most cars, you look out, you see the road," he said. "This car, you look out, you see the hood."

"A rental?" she said, getting in.

"They repossessed the Jag." The sound of crushed gravel drew Sissy's gaze to the black Cadillac approaching.

"Your grandma drives the largest town car," he said, "so she can hog the road. She never haggles. Doesn't know the word 'sale.'

A bigger car simply replaces the old one like a changing of the guard. How do you talk to someone that spoiled?"

Grandma hollered over the window, "We'll eat when I get back from Mass. Take your daughter to church."

Guilt overcame Sissy as she jumped in her dad's car. She imagined Blaise's naked body sleek against her sheets. She couldn't go to Communion when she lived for her impure thoughts.

Snapping on the ignition, Dad swerved out the eagle-crested gates. If only Blaise was there.

"Let's get your uncle," Dad said, almost telepathically, and the engine rushed in applause. At forty miles per hour, they passed a "20 mph" sign and skirted a raccoon mashed on asphalt. Sissy grabbed her seatbelt; she found some woman's gaudy earring and slipped open the glove compartment to put it up.

A dark shadow edged Dad's mouth, and he grabbed a listing agreement that slipped out. It was for a huge tract of swamp to the right and rear of Serenity, land that had been in Sissy's family for generations.

"Your grandpa promised the swamps to me," Dad said.

"You can't sell them," Sissy said.

"Look. All I've made money in is shopping centers, tract houses, and re-tilled cemeteries. This swamp deal is complicated. These government guys can limit drilling. Stop the oil seepage killing fowl and polluting everything. Your Grandpa wanted this sale despite your mother's lies."

"You promised not to talk bad about Mama."

"She has blackballed me in the family, but fine. I made your grandpa a dying promise to turn the swamps into a wildlife preserve. The Gulf is dysfunctional. I don't want to argue with you. It's hard enough coming here. Thank God, Blaise doesn't hold a grudge."

Sissy's heart jumped at hearing her uncle's name. His artist's body was firm, his arms long and sinewy. How many nights had she slept imagining them around her? Blaise had said the primary sense for a painter was touch. Did he have to touch things to paint them? If only his paintbrush would shape her legs or her breasts.

"But Blaise won't do much good today," Dad said. "Poor fellow's in Hancock Hospital."

Sunlight prickled Sissy's scalp. A deep longing for connection with him filled her heart. A truck clanked past in a rush of rubber, metal and dust. She grabbed a cigarette. "What's he got?" she said, lighting up.

"Smoking! You're sixteen."

"Seventeen."

"Smoke. Kill yourself," he said. "Hell, I'll join you."

They braked at a convenience store, a glassed-in 1950 s service station. Clifford drove past them, probably with a bottle of Blue Nun to sedate the adults at dinner.

A glass case of boiled crawfish, burnt claws and tails shuddering, greeted them. Behind it, a print of the Sacred Heart of Jesus peered through stacks of Bull Durham tobacco. Dad ordered vodka, raw ribs, aspirin, Camel filters, and a receipt.

The clerk, with flat blue eyes and a pencil mustache, wiped his hands on his stained apron, then handed dad NSF, non sufficient funds, checks. "Miss Irene won't cover them like before."

Dad smiled through steel teeth and wrote a $320 check, near a tattered sign that read, "Positively No Checks Accepted." He put a $20 bill in the tip jar and said, "An icy soda for my daughter. "

Coke slivers soothed her throat when, minutes later they eased up to Hancock Hospital, a one-story cement building. Outside, her uncle limped back and forth through broad, sharply defined sunlit areas. He wore a rumpled white linen suit and held a book, probably of his favorite poet, Wordsworth (the Romantic poet who lived longest). Charming and easygoing, even when out of sorts, Blaise smiled at Sissy over steaming air. Her heart beat in quick uneven strokes.

Tall, muscular, he looked slighter, thinner. The sun shone on his wavy brown hair, and sweat glistened on his angular cheek. She had last seen him in April standing by Grandpa's casket. Blaise's dark eyes had held that strange tension of a son who both loved and hated his father.

Blaise loped to the car with the smooth, graceful movement and regal bearing of a cat.

Sissy managed to cover her shock when he opened the door, his complexion whitish and his breath deep. He called out to her father "Do you mind playing chauffeur? I want to catch up with your daughter."

"Fine," Dad shouted back. "Just close the door. You're letting in hot air."

They sat in the rear. Blaise's eyes walked down her body and she was floating on the sea without a rudder. She felt the shame of her randy thoughts because although Sissy often felt like she was an orphan, the two of them were blood relatives. Her breathing picked up and she crossed her arms to hide her breasts, which one maid had referred to as grapefruits.

Blaise eased over; his fine linen jacket hugged his wide shoulders. Oh, to be cloth against that skin. Would Sissy were silk, undulating to muscle contour, cascading down, He stretched back on the seat and pointed out a red stain on his pant leg. "In Mississippi," he said, "people don't notice you're drinking unless you do something tacky like spill red wine on a white suit or trip over a body."

He handed her a gold pelican pendant, its strong beak perfectly shaped. "Your Fourth of July gift," he said. He tousled her hair, her scalp simmering at the trace of his fingers.

Sissy had read somewhere in *True Confessions* (passed on by the all-too-believing upstairs maid) that if a man is in love with you, he will give you jewelry, not a practical gift. If you don't get this or something romantic--flowers, weekends in the country-- you might as well call it quits. Sissy checked the card. Yes, he had signed "Love" instead of "Yours."

Blaise stretched his leg over the seat, exposing a heavy bandage under his cuff.

"What's that?" Sissy asked.

"Spider bite," he said, suddenly moody and morose.

Dad glanced in the rearview mirror. "That's not the cancer?"

Sissy said, "No one tells me anything."

"A little basal cell," Blaise said. "On the side of my nose. And on my neck. Starts like a patch of rough skin. Here on my hand. Sun worshipers have to expect these little carcinomas."

She told herself Blaise wasn't really ill. He was just being his artistic, overly dramatic self. And God knows, in the country someone had to be eccentric. They needed entertainment. Still she knew something trivial to her could actually be earth-shattering to him.

A bit later, Sissy slid out the car at Serenity. The sky was a glaring bluish white. Warm lights bounced off every surface. Wind sprayed a hot stickiness over her cheeks. Dad got out and checked his Rolex even though the empty driveway signaled Grandma was at church. A Texan, he was always trying to approach her in the best way, but he never knew what that was. He sniffed his cuff. "Something smells like dog. Sissy, get me a new shirt. Don't just stand there."

Inside, Dad changed into a madras shirt and sipped a Bloody Mary in the giant foyer. "I know about your grades," he said.

Sissy looked up at his reddened cheeks. Had confrontation done Mom any good?

"Answer me," he said. "How did you flunk high school?"

"Whatever you do, Daddy will resent you for it," Mama had warned "Don't say too much. The person who talks the most has the most to lose."

Dad darted to the paneled window framing the entryway, his face pale. He flailed his hand toward the marshes. "Blaise's only home for an hour," he said, "and we have to catch him. God, he's off for the swamp."

Sissy dashed outside, stomach queasy.

"Come back," Dad yelled. "Once you get your uncle, come back. I'm not finished with you."

Outside, Sissy passed the slimy fountain, where lizards squeezed in cracks like little vampires, living on borrowed time in the splintering sunlight. She looked for meaning in the seemingly trivial to keep herself focused.

Sissy's earliest memories were of Blaise fixating on some wild creature, finding a crow with a broken wing and feeding it drops of milk, throwing stale bread to the hungry ducks, or befriending a wounded possum. She wanted to save the swamps, champion Blaise as if he were a hurt animal. Like her mother, who hung in her study the sign, *"Possible d'avancer,"* Sissy believed all was possible.

She pursued Blaise to the grotto framing a six-foot statue of Our Lady of Guadeloupe. Her dark skin was flaked, her gray veil caked with mildew, her hands melded together by rain and heat.

Blaise stopped suddenly, as if sick to the stomach. Sissy touched his back. It felt hot under her palm. Where was the sweet shadow lover of her reverie, more real than the bedroom darkness around her?

"Why do you walk back here?" she said "Didn't you say you had cancer?"

"I'm a hedonist living in a state of disadvantage. Polyester dust. I'm allergic to practically everything," Blaise said.

"Remember when I took you to Pere LeChaise Cemetery in Paris?" he said. "That graveyard felt timeless. As does this grotto. That's why I come here."

He swatted a wood fly, grabbed her hand, and steered her through the woods toward a mud pile, like a huge sponge, coated in marsh. Imbedded in it were liver-shaped mushrooms, water lilies, and moss-bearded wood. The sight of the grotesque mound smacked her squarely in the face.

Blaise pointed beyond the heap to an abandoned open-air structure. The construction created a frame for the distant woods. His face fell and, like his skin, his white suit seemed a jaundiced yellow.

"Ma's stopped building the wildlife refuge. Seems your dad misused funds. She's ignoring Grandpa's promises," said Blaise. "Someone needs to tell your dad."

"Not me!"

Blaise turned, his broad shoulders burrowing under a branch. At first, Sissy thought he was playing a practical joke, his movements were so spontaneous. She hated to see the heron swooping from tree to tree seeking shelter, the rabbits, legs sticky with oil, scooting across the swamps. If something wasn't done to stop the dredging, God knows what creatures would die and what natural barriers would be destroyed.

Blaise and Sissy crept by pine trees and walked close, weighed by the warmth of being together even if they confronted odious things. She felt moody and morose despite her deep-down sense of her uncle's love for her and the land.

A pinecone bumped across the grass as they neared Quint baiting traps beside the boathouse. He was deliberately always by his boats or on the water. The weathered cypress building on stilts was perched above the marsh like a sacrificial offering to the next great storm.

Blaise touched her shoulder. I can handle your dad, his gesture said.

Before Blaise could speak, Quint shoved binoculars at him.

An outdoorsman, like Blaise, Quint paid a lot of attention to animals because they couldn't help themselves. "Look," Quint said. "Birds everywhere are searching for marshes. Their habitat's vanishing. They'll be moving into the house like parakeets."

Blaise peered through the binoculars, wiping them off, looking again. He sent Quint a smile and said, "You upset about something? You're the closest thing to a brother I've got."

"Brother-in-law," Quint snapped.

Blaise said, "What's the difference?"

"Rules are different for in-laws than family." Quint scooped up some rope, slinging dirt, and huffed to a bench. "The old man's estate is screwed up. When he was alive I had input, but now I'm the pariah."

Morning sunlight reddened his cheek. "Now Blaise's here, I've another job. I can't just come for dinner, to see my daughter. Fine." He scooped up a tackle box. "Irene wants to talk about Blaise's future. God knows, she doesn't give a damn about mine, but since I'm a broker, she figures she'll use me." He walked toward some crab traps, which smelled of shrimp. "What are you planning to do exactly?" he said, eyes sharpened on Blaise.

"Paint."

"To make a living," Quint said.

Blaise grasped the rope of a hammock and swung it. "I thought maybe I'd . . . I'd . . . I'd go back to school and study criminal law."

"Do you want to wash your hands after shaking your clients' hands?" Quint secured hemp to a trap.

"I'm twenty-eight," Blaise said, "and I've never had a job that could support me. I open my fridge and I see my reflection in the rear wall. Maybe I should get a master's degree in social work."

Quint snipped string for bait.

Blaise breathed in deep and sat in a lawn chair. He clutched the metal armrest. "I'll tell you something, if it wasn't for my analyst, I would have killed myself. What is your advice?"

"I don't give out hot tips because someone looks friendly," said Quint.

"I thought maybe I'd travel. Start my own gallery."

Quint unwrapped the soggy bait.

"Sissy could come too," Blaise said.

"Terrific," Sissy shouted.

Blaise smiled in her direction and her head throbbed. *If this is a dream, oh God, don't wake me up,* Sissy thought.

"Y'all are not doing anything this summer," Blaise said.

"Sissy's not traveling with a sick man. And I can't leave." Quint diced the bloody bait.

It was suddenly very hot. Blaise's chair sliced the parched grass. "My paintings would sell in Puerto Vallarta."

"Listen, Dad, just this once."

"We could live there cheap," Blaise said.

"Aw. If your work won't sell here, why would it do better in a Third World country with no plumbing and a worthless currency?"

"We'll have specialty items," Blaise said.

Sissy lifted off the ground. A cardinal flew into the pine tree. How wonderful to go to exotic places with her uncle. She imagined herself wearing a winged cap that flashed her over the beach to

Mexico's El Presidente Hotel. Ice-blue swimming pools, thatched huts, sparkling restaurants, coconut drinks and late-night swims. Sissy fingered the gold pelican on her neck. She would buy a gold loop big as a silver dollar and wear all her charms from Blaise.

"I'll start an arts festival and hold weekend exhibitions," Blaise said, with a mysterious half-concealed grin.

"You should have gone off with your sister," replied Quint.

"Don't mock Mama," Sissy said.

Quint walked to a wall of fishing supplies and scrutinized them. "What about the cancer?" he said.

Blaise slid back in the chair. "Everybody has some run-in with the Big C," he said. "I've become flexible, now I've hit twenty-eight and had a nervous breakdown. I need money but I don't know how to approach Ma."

"Take the nipple out of your mouth," Quint said, "and ask."

"You're so negative, Dad."

"That's right, blame me. There's nothing attractive about cowardice, Sissy."

Blaise's face wasn't dead white but a collection of pale values. She felt his pain as her dad stacked the traps.

Moments later, she looked over, but Blaise was gone. His shape vanished behind yellow fountain grass that stood like great swords along the marsh.

The wind had picked up, gnawing through the pine trees. Sunlight greased her dad's forehead. Despite his rudeness, he roared strength and the family leaned on him. "I don't want to hurt your uncle's feelings," he said, "but I can't say okay to some hare-brained scheme."

Sissy gathered up a wire box three feet long. "I'll lay the traps," she said.

"Irene is right," her dad said. "She claims her children are narcissists."

"Dad, you promised--"

"Fanatically neat, chronically inattentive."

"Don't start --"

"You make nice and they hire a therapist to downgrade you." He secured the traps on a three-wheeler. Sissy mounted it. Wind gnawed her ears as she charged off, skirting the grassy textures of a plateau where flowers were growing, blanking her dad from consciousness. "I didn't say you could go!" he called out.

She floored the pedal, hot air knifing her hair and called Blaise's name over the breeze. Her body was on fire. She had no skin. The gray sky glistened with brightness. *Oh, when could they again be irresponsible, fun-loving, naïve.*

Freeing her dog, Greta, Sissy whizzed past a green snake sunning itself and a squirrel scrambling over an oak tree root. She ducked under moss-draped oaks, rode out through golden pampas stalks, to the peat-dark bayou where baby alligators floated like logs. A great egret lunged for a minnow.

In her mind, Sissy was elegant, Blaise was healthy, and they had six sons. They made love every night, exploring each other's bodies like uncharted territory. No need for red lights or scented candles. They fell asleep holding hands in sheets limp with love. The moon hurried to peek through the window. Thirty seconds without touch seemed too long.

The three-wheeler jolted by a Spanish dagger plant and Sissy bounced back inside her body and haltered the vehicle. Grandma had planted the sharp barbed plants below Serenity to stop beach trash from parking there. Transients from behind the railroad tracks were taking over the beach, leaving their trucks with Styrofoam chests of chicken and beer everywhere.

Greta bounded over the slick highway, across two hundred feet of sizzling sunlit sand. Sissy hoisted heavy crab traps around women sunbathing, their buttocks spilling from string bikinis.

Even so, her eyes skipped over thighs and heads searching for her uncle. The question of who she was and why she had this attraction rang endlessly in her ears. She pounded over squishy sand bars to lay the heavy crab traps. She looked for him, past slapping waves, past glittering catfish thrown back by fishermen, past seagulls screeching for fish. She hurled a trap into thick knee-high water, watched the falling and lifting operation as waves devoured it. Greta paddled about. Sissy needed to decide for herself what she wanted with her uncle, as opposed to what other people wanted her to do.

There was a mystery about his childhood her mother had never finished explaining.

CHAPTER 4

Minutes later Quint stormed out to the beach, waving a court summons. He would bother everyone till he got to the bottom of things. He steered Sissy inside the blue and white family tent, its sagging canvas straining to sustain another Fourth of July. Clumps of gray-white sand singed by salt air created a feeling of drabness. He took a Heineken from the cooler.

"So early?" Sissy said.

"Bracing myself for the lawyers. I've been vaporized. Corporate slang for terminated. Dead."

"Does Grandma know?"

Again, he flailed the summons. "She's the one who alerted my creditors. This is the real fear in life, being framed by your family, persons of supposed integrity with your interests at heart, not losers."

"Didn't you and Grandma patch things up?"

"We're in Mississippi. More people are killing relatives here than rats." He downed the beer.

"What are you going to do?"

"Hide in the country. Freeze in place. Search for a weak link in the chain of relatives."

He torpedoed the can out the tent, barely missing Blaise, who limped inside. A flash of wind and sun followed him.

"God, watch it!" Blaise stammered.

Sissy jumped up, hugging Blaise's broad damp chest. "We couldn't find you," she said.

He patted her head with rough regular strokes. A warm darkness came over her.

"Down," Quint said, motioning for her to back off Blaise.

The tent buffeted in the breeze. Blaise hiked up his squelchy trousers and drenched cuffs and sat.

Quint frowned. "You go in the water?"

Blaise changed the subject. "What's in that envelope?"

"When someone gets screwed in this family," Quint said, "it comes on legal letterhead. There's a world of private decisions being made around the swamps." He gestured to the house "Your grandma is inside her cathedral, and we're out here at the bar." He popped another beer, his lips drawn tight like barbwire, and said, "Your mother's hired a man to frame me. Guy Levert. He's caught me before, and he's going to get me big now. He'll shut my firm down and send me to jail."

"What'd you do?" Blaise said.

"I took out a note against the family insurance policy. I'm vice president."

"You stole money?" Blaise said. "That was for Sissy's education."

A bolt of anger gouged her stomach. *Oh God, the man had gone and spent her college money. He was a bastard with a body that was all.*

"How could you, Dad? I don't believe it."

"It was a paper deal," he said, his eyes misting with uncertainty. "The account was flush. Look, this family's been cheating Uncle Sam for years; now the estate's being scrutinized, the attorneys need a scapegoat. . . . I'm telling y'all my neck's on the chopping block, and you're sharpening the blade."

"Be patient. You'll outlast Ma," said Blaise.

Quint plopped in his chair, laughing. "You're living off her and advising detachment? That's good. Fine. You're sucking tit and I'm supposed to get lost."

"Look, I'm an artist," Blaise said. "You're the businessman."

"You're not going to weaken your position to help me. You're an artist. Because you can't think, you can't play politics, you can't zip your pants."

Blaise rocked back. It was family life as usual, and he was emotionally heading under. "I don't know how to say this, but I agree with the attorneys," he said. Sissy saw that his eyes were dark, like before his nervous breakdown. He blinked and wiped his brow, jittery, staring at the ground. "I recommended they cancel your inheritance and slip you money on the sly."

Sissy's heart knocked about.

"We're saving the land for Sissy," Blaise said. "Those papers are a formality. We are trying not to put you under pressure, just to let you know how we feel. "

"You're a loiterer, a pest, someone feeding by." Quint seized a bamboo pole, releasing the smell of fish and waved it in Blaise's face. He screamed, "Levert's set up an irreversible trust to lock me out."

"Ma will give everything back," Blaise said, heated redness in his eyes,

"Uncle Blaise shouldn't talk," Sissy said. "He's sick."

"Not too sick to think of his own interests," Quint said. "Your grandpa and I were partners, but that was never enough, because your grandma couldn't control me." He imitated her high, thin voice and said, "'Don't worry, I'll help you if you get desperate. You can live in the servants' quarters and repair the villa.'"

"Stop it, Dad!" Sissy jumped up.

"It's my fault. I trusted this family," Quint said. "A warning light should flash on whenever y'all approach." He released a mean swing; he was purple faced, with inflamed eyes. The blow whizzed above Blaise, blurring Sissy's vision.

Blaise hollered, "Watch out."

Sissy struggled for the slippery pole. Quint yanked it away, whipping it with mounting frenzy. She spun off balance into Blaise's leg. He let out a violent groan, grabbing his ankle. She cried, fell to her knees.

Blaise dove out the tent and walked knee-high into the water, waves surging over his slacks. She scrambled after him, past sunbathers and some guys launching a sailboat. The sky sizzled and men cawed.

Quint charged up to Blaise and sliced the pole above his head. Blaise stood defiant, hollering, a fine slender vein pulsing on his brow, "I'm on your side: Honest!"

"Titty-sucking mama's boy!"

Oh God, was Dad going to kill him!

Adrenaline ran through Sissy's body. She seized the pole, swung it upright, and whacked Quint on the forearm.

Oh God! She had hit him!

He reeled back, shock restoring his rage, and then he pummeled Blaise.

Her uncle doubled over and crawled ashore, gagging while men clustered around him.

"You struck your own father! You no-good kid," her dad screamed. *If only she could lift overhead, ascend out of the situation.*

Quint stumbled inside the tent, where he grabbed his Gucci loafers and the papers. He looked like he was going to tip the tent over with his stomping, and then he walked off.

Blaise dragged himself up and sat crumpled over by a sandcastle some dreamer had left. Overhead gulls cried, their soft bellies and stiff wings sailing through the damaged sky.

He let Sissy help him up, put a hand on her shoulder, his fingers hard and yearning. They walked together, his damp chest pressed tightly against hers—as if they were one seagull, belly and wing on cloud and sky.

He stared at the big house. "So much has changed since I was a boy. Maybe I've changed."

They walked under the high clouds. To Sissy it seemed as if the beach expanded, to keep them back. In the glare, he and she traveled to some faraway land, emerging like Icarus, with huge wings, soaring toward the light.

An hour later, Blaise changed into linen slacks and sat beside Dad in the dining room. Now Grandma's face was silent, her mouth still, the gleam once anchored in her eyes gone. She had gotten up at six a.m. to arrange the meal and smiled with a tired mouth. She said nothing about her complicated procedures because no doubt the men wouldn't have been interested. The oak table was done up in Irish lace, George Jensen silver, and Lenox china. She tapped her knife against a crystal glass to signal quiet.

Dad, his arm in an exaggerated sling, winced as he drew up a chair. He stared at the foliage of a large tree, which cast a shadow over the table. Sissy had barely finished saying grace when his phone went off. With a panicked look, he left for the veranda.

Grandma lined up her butter knife on the bread plate. She could have forgiven Sissy's Dad if he'd let her overhear the conversation. "Why go to the trouble to serve a good meal?" she said.

"For me, Grandma."

"Your father is a promoter hawking his wares. My grandfather was a surgeon in the Civil War."

The slow way Blaise swished his gumbo around made Sissy nervous. Lord, she hoped he wouldn't have to go back to the hospital.

Grandma broke a biscuit on spindly fingers. "No wonder your mother became scattered: philosophy classes, Jungian therapy sessions."

Sissy fingered a snag on the tablecloth, where the white face of a fragile flower was exposed. She took out her gold-leaf travel journal and leaned against the table. Every interaction must be carefully recorded and her mother's innocence preserved.

"What are you doing?" Grandma said.

Sissy concentrated on the subtly textured marks on the shaded paper. "I'm writing things people remember about Mama, her shoulder-length hair, chestnut blond, and her Opium perfume. Mama said opium is a narcotic made from poppies."

"I wear Chanel," Grandma said.

Sissy kept writing. She would remind others that her mom had tried to be a good wife and mother. Sissy didn't mind her ma leaving if it meant her soul could be revived and the sweetness at her core wouldn't die. How could Sissy resent her having the warm tender touch that she so craved? Still, when Mama defined herself, the family made her feel guilty.

"It's impolite to write at table," Grandma said.

"When did Dad first meet Mom?"

Grandma let out a hopeless laugh. "Your dad was smitten when your mama was sixteen. He loved her painfully through two years of high school."

"Was he drawn in by Mama's melancholy or her detachment?"

"Both," Blaise said. "She could sense your feelings before you told her."

Where Grandma had been hesitant, she was now eager to talk. "Before her trip, Kitten said, 'I can live with my husband only if I need nothing . . . If I think he's an invalid.' "Grandma cleared her throat and said, "I suppose I'm jealous. I feel guilty because I spoiled your mama so much."

As her Grandma talked about her mom, it seemed pieces from Sissy's liver, heart, and lungs were being cut out and laid on the floor to die. She locked down her tears, but "Crying is a sign of weakness," Grandma told her.

"It's nice she misses her mother," Blaise said, "so do I." Seizing the heavy gumbo tureen, he limped into the kitchen.

"We should have sent Sissy to that military school in Alabama," Grandma called out. "Where the colonel comes to your house to get you." She prided herself on her voice, which at full blast could reach any part of the mansion.

Grandma went on, "Sissy was voted the girl most likely to die a violent death. She was the ideal child till she turned fifteen, but St. Joseph's Academy on the Gulf Coast said nothing in her application sparked their interest. Course the school sparked a-plenty when I made a donation."

Blaise returned with a platter of peppery steak. Smoothly dodging the subject of grades, he clustered each dish around Grandma. He leaned into Sissy's hair. She feared a blush had seized her cheek.

Sissy started to eat when Grandma raised a hand: "It's impolite to start the main course till all guests are present."

"I'm just serving Sissy," Blaise said.

"What am I paying the help for?" Grandma said with a voice that could confront anything.

"What help?" Sissy said. She headed into the kitchen, scooped up collard greens, and then set them on the table. "They've all left for church!"

Grandma shook her head. Dad kept pacing, peering in occasionally from the veranda.

Since no one was eating, Blaise got a pad from under his chair (he carried a notebook everywhere) and sketched grabbing another pencil after he'd dulled the first. His eyes were fixed on Sissy.

He kept sneaking looks at her, this god-man, with wondrous eyes and facile hands and mouth. *But how long would her craving last and would it satiate itself if they touched deeply and their souls entwined? Wouldn't guilt strangle desire?*

He sipped his water slowly, gazing at her, transforming his goblet from a glass to a transparent love object with his reflection.

Oh it was all too repulsive. She couldn't validate her feelings without being condemned to hell.

Blaise passed Sissy his sketch, his eyes lingering on hers. His version of her was of a girl with full lips, thick hair, piercing eyes so big they made you cry. *Was that what he saw? Did his soul sob for her as hers did for him?* Nights her heart cried for him to purge her fantasies with the stroke of his real hands.

Dad's voice jolted her back to the dining room. "I'm not King Midas. That's why I understand money is key to everything else in America." Putting up his phone, he popped in suddenly.

Grandma put down her weighted water glass, ice chips shriveling inside. "For God's sake, come eat," she said. She needed to have some progress toward her dinner goal and not have it once again postponed.

Dad walked over, his dynamic gait complementing the angular static shape of those at table. The phone call had given him a plan, a vision, a possibility of something that might go. "The feds are taking their checkbooks out," he said, sitting. "Looks like they want to spend billions to put nutrients back in the marshes." A pile of peas curved inside the weight of his eager spoon.

Outside gravel crackled on the drive. "Who is that?" Grandma said, looking toward the French windows with annoyance.

CHAPTER 6

A bronzed redhead got out a cheap taxi and strutted by the azalea bushes, shoulder-length hair speckled with gold. Her features were flawless: full lips that beckoned, ice blue eyes, and a chiseled nose. "Aunt Jasmine." Sissy hadn't seen Mom's foster sister since Jasmine visited with her Hollywood entourage months ago and was refused entry. She was an actress on a time machine. Still, she was living her dream. Her persona had not been denied. And it was flattering people said Sissy resembled her, though there were no blood ties.

Dad and Sissy went down and found her sitting on red luggage under the portico, quiet as a bird. She knew everything about Grandpa's death but couldn't talk about it. She stared at the burglar bars: "This house is a fortress: all that metal work. Looks like a fat lady who's been to the orthodontist."

"We're broke," Dad removed the sling. "But safe."

Aunt still looked exquisite, like an Arabian doll, almond-shaped eyes, high cheekbones, wild mane of hair. Still, who was Jasmine really? The line between fiction and nonfiction blurred with non family members who acted like blood. Aunt Jasmine had quit high school, and snorted cocaine while Mom had become valedictorian, a debutante, and an equestrian.

But Grandpa never refused Jasmine, so she grew up thinking all was possible and wasn't influenced by her stepsister's helpful opinions. Jasmine was like a flower once cultivated now growing wild near porches of abandoned movie studios. She clung to weathered men.

"Kiss, kiss," Aunt Jasmine said, pursing her lips and sending Opium perfume about. "I flew home via New York," she said. "Elizabeth Arden. They sent me through the revolving door, and voilà."

"*Voilà*," Dad said, as if waiting for something.

"I believe one should always dress as rich as possible. I want my clothes to make a statement, and these clothes definitely talk."

"Arf! Arf!" Dad said.

Jasmine tightened her turquoise jumpsuit. "It's from a shoot in Australia," she drawled. "I don't like to encourage foreigners, but I do like variety in my clothes. I like dressing up and dressing down, I don't like dressing in the middle. I've joined Debtors Anonymous, a group for recovering shopping addicts. But I can't stop myself. I was born to shop. It's better than sex and more reliable . . . It's so nice seeing you again, Quint."

"It's not nice. It's necessary," Dad said.

Deep dark shadows appeared under Jasmine's eyes. She would have to move carefully and quickly before seeing Grandma. Jasmine's face flooded with color. "Look, I've run up an incredible bill on Pete's company Visa."

"Pete?" Dad said.

"Daddy Dubonnet," Aunt Jasmine stammered, referring to Grandpa.

"You said 'Pete'?" Dad stared at her, finding meaning in the off hand remark.

"I'm such a wreck. I depended on the old man. Look, I need massive plastic surgery, liposuction, and a million dollars."

"Is that it?" Dad said.

"Gosh no. Let's not forget I'm financing my sister in that damn sanitarium upstate. They're scavengers – they'll put her things on the street. I have no life. No plan. I don't want to sell all my stuff, but I'll have to."

"I don't get it," Sissy said.

"Papa Dubonnet paid all my sister's expenses. Now the bastards are talking me out of all my money. I'm supporting this institution, swear to God. I can't get my work done, but I can't leave her."

"I forget," Sissy said, "about your sister."

"I come from a line of perverts. When we were little, our father used to come into our room . . . I bought a bat and nearly knocked him out. One night we fought by the Mississippi River. Muffy and I fell in. Muffy was in a coma for a week, then left to rot in a state institution. Daddy Dubonnet was put on our case. I was eleven. Don't you know this? I wore maternity dresses 'cause I ballooned up from all that water. Mama Dubonnet read horrible things into the situation 'cause from then on Daddy Dubonnet never wore his wedding ring. When Pete adopted me--"

"Pete?" Sissy said.

"I meant Papa Dubonnet. My . . . oh, I've lost my contact," Jasmine cried. She dropped down, looking about, her perfect rear inviting touch. Baby doll helplessness invaded her gestures, and she purred; it was a contrived way to make men feel powerful and it worked, disgustingly well.

Dad got down on his hands and knees, found the lens. Familiarity passed between them as he put it in her palm.

Her eyes fluttered about. "I want a ride in your big, bad Jaguar."

"Gone," he said.

"I can't think of you without a Jaguar," Jasmine said. "It's part of who you are."

"I should have sold my interests in the family company. Then I could drive my own car, instead of a leased vehicle."

Their chuckles, warm and low, echoed other times, as did their dark casual glances.

Sissy recalled when Aunt Jasmine and her dad got caught in a storm and the yacht rescue squad called her his girlfriend. Sissy had hoped something would come out of all that confusion.

A two o'clock sun simmered overhead. Sissy walked away. She felt lost, angry. Jasmine had no boundaries with men, and for so many years Mama couldn't do things spontaneously. She had a little girl to take care of. Somehow, no matter how it hurt, Sissy would bear witness.

In the rear hallway, Sissy cringed, looking up at the portrait of Grandpa's mother with a parrot on her shoulder. (After his death Grandma had dethroned the dark-haired peasant woman from her altar like place in the front hall.) Angular features, high forehead, brown eyes too large like Blaise's. Mama was eleven when Great Grandma died. A year later, in ironic celebration, Grandma gave birth to her only son, Blaise. There was something abnormal about his birth, but still no one would discuss the details. As for her own birth, Sissy had been born in Paris, her mother so drugged she couldn't recall the time of day.

Great-grandma's eyes bored through Sissy. Some of her face was lost in shadow. Now she was pure spirit, she could lead Sissy through her confusion.

"What should I do . . . about Blaise?" Sissy asked.

Admire your mother, the portrait said. Sissy stared at the lime green parrot nestled near the woman's throat.

Moments later, Dad and Jasmine drove toward the rear service door, rarely used since the servants insisted on entering by the front. He was protective about walking Jasmine to the house, making sure her high heels didn't sink in the mud. He unpacked the car, placing baggage on fragments of sunlit grass before bringing it inside.

Inside the murky hallway, Sissy moved carefully around the old forgotten furniture. She nudged Jasmine toward the painting and took out her journal.

"What do you know about the parrot lady?" Sissy said. "Grandma won't say a thing."

"Your grandma believes birds are the sign of death, while your great-grandma had two parrots and huge doll-like cages built for them in the backyard. One of the birds was named Friday after Robinson Crusoe, and the other was called Dixie because she had taught it to sing 'Dixie'."

"Perhaps if Mama had a parrot to play with, she'd still be here."

"Don't blame your grandma for hating the parrot lady. She sent your grandma to fertility specialists, to get her to conceive a son. There's a lot of heartache around it all-- no one knows what really happened. But the parrot lady willed her heirlooms to your mother, skipping a generation, and died. That, after your grandma took her in for twelve years, and sat silenced at table. Grandpa always sided with his mother."

Sissy looked down at the gold and peach love seat embossed with fairy tale scenes, rosy cloudlike shapes, and large masses of flowers. She noticed how a few bluish weeds curved around a weighty castle. Soft stains on the fabric slid under her finger. "Do you remember where this love seat came from?" she asked.

"Your mom's sixteenth birthday at the New Orleans Country Club. Your mama believed in fairy tales. She said when she was born fairies gathered around and called out 'Kitten' because she was delicate and shy. And I came out to a passion flower, Jasmine, because I have a warm soul." Aunt Jasmine blinked back a tear. She pressed a ring into Sissy's palm; its stone was full of light and dark pinks. Sissy touched it with a gentle, rhythmic stroke.

"A gift," Jasmine said. "You admired it once."

"Not your opal ring? This ring's famous. Grandpa bought it in that estate sale! You wore it on <u>General Hospital</u> and <u>One Life to Live</u>."

The ring still smelled of Opium perfume, like Jasmine's hand, for she imitated all she could about Kitten.

"These hands are worth two million," Aunt Jasmine said. "If you're a hand model, your fingers are your greatest asset. Mine are insured against chapping. But the ring is too tight. Hands are the first thing to go. God, you can't have a hand lift."

Dad interrupted their conversation by coming over and clanging them into the casket like elevator with its faux mahogany walls. The cranking and lifting operation matched the annoyance on his face. Grandma never paid for anything she could get family to do, and when Dad carried luggage upstairs he felt like her slave. The elevator creaked up, stopped, and they walked out. Sissy hoped Jasmine's arrival might add variety to dinner. But an empty dining room greeted them. Edginess filled the air. The help had arrived unexpectedly and were clearing the table, a few dark forms surrounded by whiteness – tablecloth, draperies, and white linen-covered chairs.

"What's wrong?" Sissy said.

The grumpy seventy-year-old cook, Andrew, looked at her through murky eyes, one brown and one gray. "Your grandma been lonely, mean," he said. "She mad at your grandpa for dying, your mama for leaving, your dad for losing his money."

CHAPTER 7

Sometime later, Sissy met Aunt Jasmine in the tearoom, where long Bloody Marys, caviar, and crab dip were set before wicker furniture. Aunt Jasmine sat on a fanback sofa that loomed like a stork.

A basket chandelier of Venetian glass bathed her with pink light. She fumbled with a compact, her face dark and exotic-looking when women wanted blond hair and an ivory complexion. Her eyes varied in intensity from a pale gray green to cold blue black. Melancholy slipped through her glance.

"Sorry I missed your grandpa's funeral," she said. "We were taping. No one would accept my calls. Did Irene like the red blanket I sent for the casket?"

"She said you charged it to her," said Sissy.

"I'm paying her back."

The air conditioner buzzed, quivering a rose in a thick-rimmed Steuben dish. Sissy sank inside that sleek glass, floating with the soft petals, remembering Mama. Sometimes she would appear in a shadow, then vanish. Mom's shadow would reappear in strange disguises: the lapping of waves, a rush of sunset, and the softness of silk.

Aunt Jasmine shaped on coral lipstick. "Did Mama Dubonnet miss me?"

"Grandma just talks property all the time."

The door swung open. Dad frowned in the doorway. "Relatives are not like property. Property is valued in this family." He had changed to crisp tan slacks and a soft blue polo shirt that emphasized his blue eyes. Sunlight further defined his strong stance.

Sissy flipped up her parents' wedding photo. When people made Grandma mad, she turned their photos facedown. Still, the darkened front of the picture brought coldness to Sissy's fingers.

Dad picked up a frosty glass that shone by a silver ice bucket. To Grandma, food presentation was the essence of culture.

"Have a Bloody Mary," Dad said to Jasmine.

"No thanks. I react violently to liquor."

He lifted a silver pitcher of tomato juice. Late afternoon sun filtered over his face. "How about a Bloody Shame?"

"Just ice."

Aunt Jasmine unsnapped a box shaking at her feet. A mouse like dog popped out and sniffed at her ankles. "My Pomeranian," Jasmine said. "Cornelia Brontë Shambles. She's the smallest dog alive."

"Not another pet," Dad said.

"I need to be touching something," Aunt Jasmine said. Cornelia jumped under the sofa and peed. "She just lifts her skirts and goes anywhere," Jasmine said.

"We'll have Pomeranian for supper if Irene smells that," Dad said. He eased by Aunt Jasmine, sitting and wrapping his arm over the sofa.

"Sissy," Jasmine said. "Go put the dog in my drawer. She won't wet there. My underwear is more sacred to her than all your grandma's Orientals."

"No, take it outside," Dad said.

The hot little dog went limp in Sissy's fingers, its skin tight under pads of hair. Ducking through French doors onto the screened porch, Sissy threw it into its box. She rocked on the glider, brushing her feet against the tile floor. The glider swing hummed, reviving the memory of Grandpa eight years ago. *Oh Lord, why did she have to think about that now? She wouldn't go back to that smelly memory, too thick and greasy and white-red, blinding her eyes, like wind rushing over waves.*

Aunt Jasmine had returned with clips from her film when Sissy had spotted her and Grandpa on the glider. Sissy couldn't make out what she was seeing in the shadows on the sagging couch. Her aunt's skin had shimmered in the breeze, and Grandpa had kissed her, coiling around her and unzipping his fly. All Sissy could remember was Grandpa's bright red jacket and the disturbing intimacy of their figures.

Sissy had found Grandma at her desk, by a lamplighted window, her face gray, shallow tears filming her eyes. "Do you know where Grandpa is?" Sissy had said.

Grandma stiffened. Her stone cold shoulders wouldn't let in the thought of Grandpa's betrayal. She ordered Sissy to leave her alone.

Sex was something Grandma never discussed. "Your grandpa has a high libido" is all she would say.

How could such a long-ago memory still haunt Sissy now? Her eyes leaked, lips hot, images forcing through, impossible to dissolve.

Sissy kicked the rough green glider back and forth, releasing smells of dust and sweat.

CHAPTER 8

Through the door panes, Sissy watched Grandma march into the tearoom in a self-contained rage. She walked by Dad, who was already deep into his Bloody Mary on the sofa, and Jasmine, who was nibbling a cheese puff.

"Don't wait for me," Grandma said. "Serve yourselves."

Jasmine put a hand to her breast to deflect the insult. She was there for money, because otherwise she would have said the "F" word.

Grandma tried to be tactful at first. She let her Bloody Mary ooze down her throat, and contemplated Jasmine. "I have the latest edition of Emily Post in case anyone is interested."

Dad leaned forward to change *Sports Illustrated* for *Yachting*. Jasmine licked a crumb from her finger and waited for Grandma to continue. She had learned not to talk back; that much was good.

Jasmine dunked a large cracker in crab dip.

"Didn't anyone teach you to take a bite-sized piece?" Grandma said.

"I'm not going to eat it," Jasmine said. "I just lick the sauce, Mama Dubonnet." Grandma had capitulated to letting Jasmine call her Mama Dubonnet, refusing to be called plain Mama, which implied kinship, or Irene, which signaled equality.

Grandma tried not to be reactive as Jasmine munched a cheese straw, wrapped it in a napkin, spattering crumbs on the floor. Everyone knew as Jasmine's career had petered out her eating disorders petered in. She shredded a Kleenex, not noticing bits falling on the pale straw matting.

Grandma started to ring for the maid, Ruthy Mae, reaching for her silver angel bell, which awaited her in each room.

"You're on a diet?" Grandma said.

"It's not a diet; it's a way of life. I can eat as many nuts and fruits as I want." Jasmine slipped out a banana, passing it to Dad to peel.

Sissy hurried over, seating Grandma in her one-armed wicker chair. Sissy drew up a stool, trying to protect the others by focusing on Grandma.

"You look beautifully middle-aged," Sissy said. "That was a compliment."

"It's a Dior . . ." Grandma said, tightening her svelte rose jacket. "I bought it for the Young Men's Fashion Luncheon. Still, it doesn't make me feel any younger. At twenty, beauty was easy; at forty it was an effort; at sixty; it's a commitment." Grandma was seventy-one but she had removed a decade from her age since she turned fifty.

She watched Jasmine, whose allure was very Hollywood: backless silver sandals encrusted with glass beads, and turquoise knit pants with Blackberry at the belt.

"What's that outfit?" Grandma said.

"A jumpsuit—it's the look," Jasmine said. "What would you call it?"

"Grotesque."

Jasmine turned off her Blackberry, which beeped. Grandma hated the Blackberry more than her cell phone because when people weren't talking on it they were playing on the internet.

"We don't allow gadgets in polite society," Grandma said.

"I'm not talking. I'm checking."

"Well, put it away." While Grandma had no aversion to cigarettes because she thought they made your hands look attractive, she was hurt actually when family members made electronic gadgets more important than her. Grandma's face looked flustered. She hated not accommodating everyone and was irritated she couldn't solve the problem.

"I don't know where we're going to put you," Grandma said, "now the help use your room. They need someplace to change uniforms and occasionally sleep."

"Actually I'd like to stay in the nursery," Jasmine said. "If that's okay?"

"Don't be ridiculous." Grandma said. She had kept the white lace nursery by her bedroom sacrosanct with its rocking cradle and canopied baby bed. She always missed what she left behind when she was a young mother. Sissy had slept in the baby bed till she was twelve and her feet stuck out.

"I'm saving the nursery for Blaise's children," Grandma said. "Quint has commandeered the tomato cottage to the left. Blaise has his garconniere full of paintings, though he sleeps all over the house. The downstairs bedroom is full of his Audubon books, which we can't move. Sissy has her mother's old girlhood room. I would put you in the servants' house at the rear but Clifford and the visiting help from New Orleans have taken over that. Cousin Ralph has locked up his house and spends his vacation in Florida."

"Jasmine can stay at my cottage," Dad said. He buried himself in a *Sports Illustrated* with deep-sea fishermen on the cover. *People* magazine was harder to hide behind.

"Or share the room with me," Sissy said.

"Arrivals should be better planned. Jasmine, you still live in the same postage stamp?" Grandma said. "You've got to drive thirty-five miles into the brush, Quint, to get to her house."

"Why do you care where I live, Mama Dubonnet?"

"Because I've an investment in you. I'm the one who raised you, who financed that two-bit beauty school on Canal Street."

"I don't have to take this shit!" Jasmine said. "I don't want my throat sliced out like your—"

"Careful," Grandma said. "I could cut y'all from Pete's will." The word "will" flew like a dagger across the room. Grandpa had died in April, Mama had left in May, and Daddy had sold their home in June. Long as Grandma was executor of the will, and her cousin the attorney, they held the family hostage. "I know I'm worth millions, but that's not why y'all like me, is it? I don't want ya'll contesting the will."

Sissy drew her fingers to her mouth, and then stopped herself from biting the cuticles. Dad uncrossed his legs, put down his magazine.

"Y'all know I moved to Mississippi because I don't have to treat anyone equally," Grandma said.

Dad added vodka to his Bloody Mary. Jasmine choked on a cracker.

"Louisiana is guided by the French Napoleonic code," Grandma said. "Didn't they teach you anything in school? You have to leave all your children the same amount, unless you can prove they've done something awful like a murder. But in Mississippi you can will any child, adopted or natural, whatever you want and cut anyone out."

Blaise burst in, his hair matted against his forehead, his eyes intense, as if he had discovered a secret from God.

He pulled Sissy to the porch, where bluish light reflected off the ceiling, walls, and tile floor, and directed her toward the mud-gray Gulf. Sissy never realized how dark and light-fired his eyes were. "What started as a walk, ended as an adventure," he said. He pointed to white dots out on the lawn. "See those specks. A gaggle of geese is headed in the wrong direction looking for fresh water. They have to cross the highway and ride salty three-foot waves without drowning. Storm tides and wetland loss have screwed the geese up. Four geese are already battling the waves. You can barely see their skinny necks above the crests. They're going to drown! What's worse, Ma has totally canceled the Reserve project your father wants. She says your father counts on our family too much. Each year he needs more."

Was this a practical joke? Some days Grandma changed her mind just to keep table conversation lively.

"My goal is to develop kindness," Blaise said quickly. "Who can do that here?"

"I don't understand," Sissy said.

"They are cutting your dad off. Ma is trying to slip out gracefully, saying your dad should contact new donors. It may be hard to save the swamps. The next step depends on how badly we feel for the swamp creatures and for this Reserve ourselves."

The dinner bell rang and they all went to the dining room.

Emotions affected Blaise's immune system and he was already too worked up. He moved to the white grand piano, where he slammed out a Chopin Polonaise.

Grandma swanned in. "For God's sake, Blaise, don't bang!" She pushed a button, and a cathedral window rose on a gush of warm air. Grandma generally came around to fairness. It just took her longer. The overhead sun cast high contrasts of light and shade. Perhaps Sissy needed to learn about finances. Still, money conversations were tinged with woe.

Stepping onto a balcony, Grandma shielded her forehead as she showed Jasmine land given other relatives. Grandma looked tense as if embarrassed she had already succumbed to family parasites. Afternoon heat weighed the tree limbs and stiffened the grass. Houses of various relatives checkered the estate but each faced Serenity, a reminder of who stood boss. Grandma expected relatives to dine at the main house, to pay evening calls, to keep her from being bored.

This vista of homes, made the family compound timeless. There was Cousin Ralph's house, built on stilts, where his father (killed in WWII) once played. Blaise's garconniere, refurbished so he could have parties and Grandpa wouldn't be disturbed. While other families jumped into vans with TVs and headed for the wild beaches, nightlife, and loud music of Florida, their clan still had Serenity.

In the hottest part the day, Dad, Sissy and Aunt Jasmine stood anxiously beside Grandma as she talked.

An old mallard flew out from the parched cattails and grasslands on the right, skimming the balcony. Dad turned back his cuff to check his Rolex, finagled from the insurance company to replace a cheaper match lost skiing. Jasmine blotted her forehead. No one wanted to talk about the property given to others and Grandma's possessions.

"Jasmine! Look at my favorite oak tree. It's so fat its arms drag the ground. "That tree's so old we've named it John Darling after my great-uncle, the Confederate general. It's nice to have *important* ancestors, Jasmine, to have your trees registered in the National Oak Society—"

It seemed like Grandma was being mean, but actually her ancestors were the only identity she could count on. "John Darling, my great-uncle," Grandma said. "That was his name. I never knew him but my grandma referred to him as John Darling. For years I thought 'darling' was a term of affection, but it was his last name. John's mother thought nobody was good enough for him, and every Sunday she would entertain his potential brides. Well, that's what men love, Sissy. Pleasures."

Grandma moved her hand freely, reciting from memory. "One Sunday, as the story goes, the balding John Darling brought a spinster schoolteacher to the table. The schoolmarm minced her carrots and peas, while John went on about the wife he wanted: 'My wife 'will have to be beautiful, intelligent, well-traveled. She must be stylish and passionate, thrifty, well-read. I need a cultured woman, a good cook, a fine mother.' When he finished ranting, the old maid put down her fork, blotted her mouth, and said, 'And when you find her, John Darling, she'll never want you.'"

Aunt Jasmine and Dad laughed, the story of John Darling making them feel included. They were trying to relate to Grandma, to get the inheritance due them.

CHAPTER 9

Moments later, a flushed Blaise joined them on the balcony. Sweat skimmed his face. "Andrew has left for church," he said. "I told him I'd serve." The cook, Andrew, was a preacher in the First Congregational Church of Christ on Highway 90 and could not be bribed into missing a service.

Blaise took Sissy inside the glassy air-chilled kitchen, where sparkling cabinets and tall windows overlooked oak limbs. Alone with him she felt she was swimming in sunlight, her heart casting complicated shadows. It was a relatively small kitchen. Grandma never cooked, but it was wall-to-wall luxury: trash compactors, commercial refrigerators, and dishwashers for heavy entertaining. All items were provided, to stop the help from taking the elevators downstairs to the second bigger kitchen and forgetting to work.

Sissy tried to concentrate on the shape of dishes and not on Blaise standing beside her. Pots brimmed with butter cream potatoes, and mustard greens, tangy and salty-smelling, enough to feed twelve. Oh God, Sissy hoped the parish priest wouldn't pop in sermonizing over dinner. But fewer people dropped by now because Grandpa had been the kindly, generous one.

Sunlight streamed through the window and silver platters magnified the sheen. Although she lived to inhale his joy, her thoughts tortured her. The sauce suddenly looked like blood, like a map of vessels ripping through flesh.

Sensing her anxiety, Blaise did a little jig and swept her around the room. "I went to this wedding," he said. "Down the road on the beach. At sunset, Can't you see that red glow on the beach and the girl's gown?"

"I don't know . . . didn't people get hungry by six o'clock?"

"They set up tents on the beach, case of rain. Hired a jazz band."

Sunlight got hotter, even in that cold kitchen. Sweat dripped down her sides, between her breasts. Was she allergic to heat, to her uncle, to thinking? Her skull burned as Grandma jangled the dinner bell.

Sissy went for a tray of spicy redfish courtboullon but it slipped and sloshed boiling thick tomato sauce on her foot. She felt nothing, her pulse raced so badly. She was always doing that, when he came near, bumping into something, tripping, she went so dizzy with the smell of him.

"Here, I'll get it," Blaise said, wiping her foot with a linen napkin. She could sense him kneeling beside her; his man hand on her ankle.

I'd like to touch you, his hand seemed to say. *I know your life isn't settled. At least you know I'd like to touch you."*

Her brain made her steady the tray of red fish and hot pepper, okra, and tomatoes, and get to the dining room. All this time, she could feel Blaise behind her, with his big shoulders, huge hands, and strong eyes. Bridling from the warm china, Sissy centered the dish on the table. She kept her eyes averted lest her cheeks redden like the fish.

Grays and yellows shadowed the professionally starched tablecloth. Grandma had the fine lace sent out, the help refusing to iron it. Blaise moved the two-foot centerpiece Andrew had designed from garden flowers. Grandma had paid for him to take a course on TV (Andrew couldn't read) rather than finance the florist, who kept putting her on hold and asking her to check his Web site.

"I've always thought of gladiolus as a funeral flower," Blaise said, "and when I sit, I can't see Sissy's face."

Fragrant smells of Creole cooking-- okra, greens, buttered biscuits, and blackened redfish-- buoyed up the thick air. "This is the first time we've been together since Grandpa's funeral," she said. "Blaise, take your father's place."

A shot of panic crossed Blaise's face as he walked to the head of the table. The seat with imprints of so many family patriarchs wobbled as he sat.

Dad winced at Blaise. He figured since he was married to Mom and the eldest male, there was a certain entitlement.

Jasmine mumbled a mantra, removing herself from the situation.

"Where do you want Jasmine and me?" Dad said.

"Down there's fine," Grandma said, pointing to the far end.

Sissy felt a little bullet fire from Grandma's mouth, through Dad's skull. For so long, Grandma had felt herself lucky to have Mama close by. She didn't know it but she missed the sparkle of her daughter.

Dad retreated quietly to the foot of the table. He was on several bank boards and had learned patience when millions were at stake.

Her dad awakened that Richard Cory poem Mama liked in Sissy's head.

Whenever Richard Cory came to town,
we people on the pavement smiled at him,
He was always dressed from head to crown,
clean-shaven and imperially slim.
And he was always quietly arrayed.
And he was always humble when he talked.
But still he fluttered pulses when he said,
'Good morning,' and he glittered when he walked.
So on we slaved and tolled, and went without the meat and
cursed the bread.
And Richard Cory one calm summer night went home
and put a bullet through his head.

It was a tradition to have the youngest at table say grace, to make sure they knew the rudiments of Christianity and wouldn't become pagans. Grandma was a member of the church altar society (never went to meetings but bought monthly roses) and treasurer of the St. Vincent de Paul society. Clifford counted the collections and reported that income to the parish council.

Sissy raced through a Catholic blessing, the others mumbling along with Victorian piety.

"I doubt any of you go to church," Grandma said, as she put her napkin on her lap. "I don't blame Jasmine. She is already in Hollywood, one bastion of male power, why would she kowtow to another. But Quint! It seems like you might like the Jesuits. They have a villa up the road and are always talking expansion and acquisition. Lord, the Catholic Church owns half the property in New Orleans."

Dad gulped water, his foot tapping the floor as if anxious to leave.

Sissy buried potatoes under crests of gravy, dark forms flooding the white.

Blaise looked at her with a goofy smile, prepared to perform if joking was required to avoid a family member being sacrificed at dinner. But Dad had passed Grandma a matchbook. "I wrote my business calls charged to you inside the cover," he said. "Tell me when they show up on your bill. I'll pay them."

"How?" Grandma chewed fish in uneven bites.

Dad shoveled down greens. "I won't respond to that."

Mama would have lightened the mood, talking about lilacs, or quoting Edith Wharton, her chosen mentor, who'd had the strength to leave her rich husband after he went insane. Sissy had hunted for passages from *House of Mirth* that exposed the conflict between what we wish to be and what society insists we become.

The telephone rang. Jasmine checked her Blackberry, while Dad almost tripped getting the landline across the room.

"It's for me," he said, his brow prickled with sweat. He snapped into the phone, "Levert wants a what? Dun and Bradstreet?" He went out.

"It's rude to leave the table," Grandma called out. "The help tell us when they'll work and in-laws lack manners. I suppose we'll just have to wait." She molded her glass to her coaster.

Blaise hummed Chopin's Prelude in E-flat minor, and took a pad from under his chair. He sketched, lips dry, eyes drained of fire. Sissy wondered if he was drawing a mass of lilies. A light wash of yellow from the window overlooking the marshes brushed his shoulder. Sissy imagined blank sheets erupting into ragged palmetto leaves, mirror like reflections of sun on water.

Sissy's heart shook, stricken by the intensity of his concentration. Watching his hand, she felt a mad throb of intoxicating liberation. He was so lost, yet found in the world of creation.

Sissy took out her journal, scribbled a phrase she recalled hearing Ma say, *We are only here for a short while. There should be more time . . . for silence.*

Moments later, Grandma showed Sissy her edition of Emily Post, flipped to a marked passage, and read: "It's rude to leave the table without being excused and to pursue another activity during the meal. It's all so rudimentary."

Blaise kept drawing, seductively, a warm darkness to his cheek.

Dad returned. He adjusted his chair, diced a ham hock, and apologized. He felt it didn't lessen his power if he showed empathy. His best tactic was to repeat what he wanted. Grandma would close her eyes as if she was too sleepy, too near death to respond.

"It's hard," Dad said. "But we must discuss Pete's estate. I know the will is still in probate," he said.

The will would freeze in probate as long as Grandma could keep it there. Her uncle's will had stayed in probate for twenty years so Grandpa could extract commissions as attorney and executor.

"You said Sissy should have the land, and I'm her guardian," Dad said. "I would never have left her mother. No matter what she did."

"The person who kicks the dog never leaves. It's the dog that runs off," Grandma said, dabbing her mouth. "Besides I'm making Blaise primary heir," she added.

Jasmine downed a fistful of vitamins. Dad dropped his fork and pushed back from the table. "My God! Blaise can't pay for his own apartment. He's never driven a lawnmower. Balanced a checkbook. God, if the yard man doesn't turn on the sprinklers the entire grounds will dry up."

Grandma's eyes roved over the silver serving platters. "The garlic bread's getting cold," she said. "I told Ruthy Mae I wanted baby croissants, but she does what she wants. She's been well schooled."

The breadbasket stopped before Blaise. Grandma pushed a bone to the gold rim of her plate, where it joined a fatty morsel. She waited for Blaise to enter the cockfight, but he just cracked a joke: "What's the difference between illegal and unlawful: Ill eagle is a sick bird."

"Perhaps Quint is right," Grandma said, pressing her spine into the chair. "Blaise comes to the table like a clown, hair askew, his gut sticking out."

"Don't start picking on Uncle Blaise," Sissy said.

Blaise scrunched over and stabbed some fish. "I've plenty of ice in my fridge," he said, "but no booze."

"You eat with your fingers--" Grandma said.

"My cheap fridge won't hold two bottles of wine."

"Talk with food in your mouth--"

"Whenever I rent a DVD at the appliance store they say, 'You're late on your payments for the fridge. Shall we bill your ma?' " Blaise slugged wine.

"Don't drink like a pig," Grandma said.

"It's Gran Sangre de Toro"-- he waved the bottle-- "great blood of the bull. I fill up here so I can starve on my own money."

"There's a code of behavior," Grandma said. "In acceptable society. But you . . . think backwards."

"Stop, Grandma."

"She doesn't care how she offends you, kid," Blaise said. "I need booze to sit at this table. They're blowfish all over the beach. Being polluted to death. They swell up because they're terrified, expand until they pop. But it's not worth it for one lousy dinner. For one lousy meal, it's not." Blaise flipped his plate, letting turnip greens slide onto the table.

Dad jumped back from the table and Jasmine ran for a rag. Blaise limped down the stairs and out the door.

"Uncle Blaise. Oh! No! Grandma, see how you pushed him!" Sissy cried.

Grandma looked up surprised. "This is between me and Blaise. Quint, if your daughter gets any ruder, it'll have to be boarding school."

Ice picks jabbed Sissy's skull. They weakened her soul and broke her resolve.

Grandma leaned back, blotting her mouth. "It's Pete's fault, always spoiling your uncle. Clean up, Sissy."

Sissy stared at the grimy greens and gravy leaking onto lace. "You do it," she said. "Our meals are getting more and more toxic. I can't sit by and let you go at him like a bird of prey."

"Cut the drama," Grandma said. "The older I get, and I don't say that word often, the more I realize we must challenge rudeness. The fact Blaise is angry is a good sign. It means my boundaries are working.

"Quint and Jasmine can look for Blaise," she added. "You've nothing better to do." Dad cringed.

Jasmine and Dad exchanged knowing looks as they left the house. Blaise was someone who had to be watched. His problems were not in the "Oh my God" category. Still he acted from a strange place. Sissy asked God if Blaise had a problem to make it the least of anything wrong.

Sissy's hands picked up plates while Grandma talked. "I'm the easiest person in the world to get along with. Ask my dead husband!"

"Why can't you just keep quiet?" Sissy said.

Grandma said: "I can't allow Blaise to act like a moron." Suddenly she grasped both armrests, her eyes bleary.

Was she feigning an attack? Oh my lord, was she having a real stroke? Sissy leaned close to her waxy face. "You need your heart pills?" Sissy said. "Should I call the doctor?"

"No."

"Ruthy Mae? Clifford?"

"God, no."

"Can I get you something? Walk you to bed?"

Sissy stood there stunned, her stomach tight. It was like five years ago, when they rushed Grandma to Touro Infirmary in New Orleans.

"You and Blaise have killed me. You didn't mean to, but you killed me," Grandma said. A shallow tear dripped down her cheek.

Grandma rose on unsteady feet. She stood up skeletal yet strong, and careened out the room like a ship ready to capsize.

Oh Grandma, don't lay that guilt trip on me. What was Sissy doing, hating the only person always there for her? She needed to talk to someone, anyone from Ursuline. Without the Internet and cell phone, which Grandma despised, Sissy was barely alive.

Sissy retreated to the baby grand piano, which glowed grayish pink in the dusky light. Sinking onto the purple velvet seat, she retraced the keys Blaise had touched, feeling his wide hands atop hers, sensing the warm sun on their skin, a good sweat on the fingers, the pearl keys caving in ecstatic release.

"Everything's a question of power," Blaise had said. "Southern mothers have had it for centuries and they won't give it up easily. When adult children start loving themselves, some moms don't take it well."

Possibly literature had revived Sissy's mama. A reader for Tulane's literary magazine, she chose thirty of the nine thousand poems that came in.

"What do you look for?" Blaise would say.

"Passion, authenticity, and brevity," Mama would reply. Sissy'd find her mother emerging late from her room, strolling barefoot down the beach. In a real way, Mama had felt God in the thrill of letters on the page.

Sunlight tinged Sissy's hands on the purpling keys, vaguely shadowing each finger. Mama had got them to play games like Scrabble, Trivia, croquet. She had kept conversations light.

"Remember," Mom would say, with an uneasy glance, "you do not walk alone. I'm as close as thought."

There was a good chance Mom would come back because it was the motherly thing to do. Sissy had taken Mama's red leather jewelry box to her room so she could touch the tan suede interior and remember her scent. Sissy supposed there were girls all over who never saw their mothers, and were fine with that. Still, at night, they say, the cavemen went home, and if the mother wasn't there, they couldn't feel safe.

"Sometimes you have to let people go," Blaise had said. Sissy pressed the keys so hard her fingertips burned, unlocking softness in her heart. Afternoons, Sissy needed to see Blaise, be with him, and talk about things that were important. Nights, she'd lie back, imagining his bare chest on hers and her legs spreading out.

She heard a knocking on the piano top and looked up, expecting to see him, but no one was there.

She left the piano, sunlight turning it the same burnt red as Mama's gold-rimmed jewelry box, and headed for the veranda.

CHAPTER 10

The sun strained from behind a cloud while Sissy sipped espresso on the veranda. She watched a sugar lump fall apart, like a blowfish, like Blaise and her.

"I'm putting it in your hands," she told God. "I'm clay. Mold me."

The sky was salmon and white: a tangle of trees cast intricate shadows on the lawn. The distant water lay gray and flat. Uncle Blaise was nowhere in sight.

Oak trees stood quiet but vigorous, determined to face turbulence or the violence of Blaise's brush. He would paint for hours a mangled branch or the eroding coast line. Long before dawn or after dusk she'd hear him on the stairs.

When she thought of Blaise she didn't choke up the way she did when she thought of Mama. Sissy imagined his tall strong shoulders, his muscular hands, his voice saying "I want you for my love." *First cousins could marry with a dispensation from the archbishop. What about a niece and her uncle? God no, that was disgusting.*

At five thirty it was a hundred degrees. Hotness seeped through Sissy's skin and into her bones. She wished to God she could catch heat stroke. Her T-shirt stuck to her sweaty neck. She thought she saw Blaise. She blinked and he transformed into a pear tree in the yellow green yard.

A match flickered under Sissy's palm. She hid in a cigarette; others didn't understand the weight she carried trying to figure things out.

Aunt Jasmine disturbed Sissy's thoughts, plunking down a coffee service.

The familiar garden table looked gruesome as Jasmine perched on it. "Quint's still looking for Blaise," she said. "Being around this family in the country, it's the saturation that gets to you. Your grandma blames me for her chest pains. Says *adopted* children don't know when to shut up. Meanness keeps her alive. It creates a primal energy."

"Can I look at your Blackberry?" Sissy said, shifting the subject.

"God no. That thing is my life." Jasmine dialed a number with a spoon and said, "Is this the Hilton? The Hilton that has the rain forest?" She shifted, shielding her eyes from the sun and snapping into the phone, "Don't put me on hold. Shit. Get me Chuck Feingold, Big Star Productions. No, I won't wait. This is long distance."

She strangled the sweaty receiver. "The receptionist from hell! Chuckie, you've got me climbing the Valium tree. . . . Donate my salary? What am I, the Red Cross? Okay, sweetie. I'll have your baby."

Jasmine had already had so many abortions: thirteen some said. She would sob when passing a toy shop. Rumor had it she'd actually had a child in Europe, but it had died in the hospital.

"Chuckie's an agent," Jasmine explained. "You've got to flatter these people." She rattled into the phone, "But I have no meeting with my stepfather. Any meeting would have to be in the cemetery. I told you, he's dead." Jasmine hung up. She could kill or make something beautiful in a flash.

"Unless I bring something to the table with this film," she said. "I'm tomorrow's nobody. A depression is going on in L.A. Phones fading in and out the Hollywood hills. Now five hundred producers want to cast the same ten bony adolescents."

Sissy passed her a cigarette, damp with heat.

"You shouldn't smoke," Jasmine said, taking it and dragging, her skin caramel-colored and shiny. Sissy's lips were full like her aunt's, but Jasmine barely moved her mouth when she spoke because she'd read Marilyn Monroe did that. "I'm not supposed to pucker my lips. Or squint. At the Actors Studio, my teacher says confidence is key. 'Course, he hasn't had a lead role in years. This cigarette is toxic. I should have gotten my G.E.D. How long can a good figure, face, teeth support you?"

"Dad says, 'After forty, y'all have to hang up your spurs.' "

"I've peaked. My hands are old. I'm two years older than God. Nature discriminates. Men discriminate!" Jasmine worked heavy cream into her palms. "Anti-aging cream by Estée Lauder. 'Le Couvert des Minons.' France. A steal at ninety bucks an ounce. My agent says beware of age spots. I say, beware of agents . . I'm fat. To get back into a size four, I'll have to jump on the trampoline ninety minutes a day, run six miles on the track, and do an hour of weights. Is it worth it? I can die thin and firm or live fat and ecstatic with night creams of lavender and acacia."

Below, a peacock with worn blue and yellow feathers scooted by. A dazed squirrel ran through a bramble patch. Jasmine grasped a demitasse cup and took a sip. "I need money for a movie," she said.

"How did you pay for the others?"

"Daddy Dubonnet advanced it from my inheritance. A thousand dollars to him was like a tip." She opened up a pouch, smearing Nivea on her face and hands, unfolding a broad-brimmed hat. Her face was lost in shadow.

"I'm in big trouble," Jasmine said. Your grandma moved her permanent residence here to disinherit me."

Of course Sissy recalled the dinners where Grandma plotted disinheritance. Sissy didn't want Jasmine to sink into her quagmire of cocaine. "Get a lawyer," Sissy said.

"It has cost me thousands in therapy. I'm in such denial. On a one-to-ten stress scale, I'm at eleven. Daddy Dubonnet promised to finance *Midnight Lady*."

"Sounds too—" Sissy tossed her cigarette off the railing in an arc of sparks.

"—dirty. After I do each script, I throw it in the fire to purify myself. I sell my costumes and donate the money to the Vincent de Paul Society."

"Grandma says you shouldn't pose naked."

"I'm *partially* nude, but it's done very tastefully. They are real delicate about the situation. They just spread out some red velvet and have me lie down on it."

"How do you get to the velvet with your clothes on?"

A warm drizzle dampened Jasmine's hair as she put down her coffee cup. Dad walked under the veranda waving up, in khakis and blue jacket. With the festiveness of his best Victorian manners, he offered them mint juleps at his cottage.

Jasmine accepted his invitation.

Moments later, Sissy caught up with her aunt, struggling through sudden gusts, bending an umbrella over her petite body. Last July fourth, Sissy was with Jasmine and Mom on the beach with her artist friends, gray sea all around and Ma so beautiful in her red bikini. Blaise had lit a Roman candle.

"What about you?" Jasmine now teased. "Any boyfriends?"

"No." *How can I date when I love Blaise?*

"If only you and Blaise were strangers," Jasmine said, with a twinkle. She considered herself better than "Dear Abby" in spotting romance. She encouraged any affair, seemingly unperturbed by Sissy's kinship to Blaise. Nothing about love was ever sordid to her. "You need someone like Blaise. You're mature, and an older boy would appreciate you."

"You think so?"

"Oh, sugar," Jasmine said. "You are walking in this new world of light and sex on baby limbs."

"You're embarrassing me!" Sissy looked at the marsh swans and thought about chasing them. Running off was what she wanted to do when the whole issue of boys and sex came up. God, I couldn't speak to Jasmine about Blaise. It was too disgusting.

"Romance will come in time, honey," Jasmine said. "Be patient."

Wind rattled the way it had the night before Mama's trip as if the sky knew and was trying to stop her. Mama had left Sissy a lace bookmark with a quote: *We stand on either side of the sea, stretch hands, blow kisses, laugh and lean. I toward you, you toward me, Mama.*

She and Sissy had climbed atop her organdy and red-roped bedspread. Mom had said love kept her from stepping off the precipice. Before that, she said, she was saved by travel, new places, and friends, like the poets at the Theatre de La Huchette in Paris. "Come with us," her mother had said. "You adore Paris. Remember those banana splits at the Café de la Paix."

Sissy and Jasmine neared the tomato-colored stucco cottage. The grounds were flat, patches of shrubbery providing shelter for wildlife and barriers from the winds which otherwise would have made a clear sweep across the yard. Grandma had given Mom the bungalow as a consolation prize. "The main property worth eight million shouldn't be divided," she said. "It should pass through the male line."

An electric connection passed between Jasmine and Sissy as if her aunt sensed Sissy's pain and they were both orphans. The rain slowed, spider like splotches hitting the umbrella.

Before the cottage stood a headless cherub. A plaque read, "The original family lived here – then as assets grew, built the main house." *God, Sissy couldn't go inside. All the little Sissies drifting about, from summers there!*

"Who uses this place?" Jasmine asked.

"Nobody." Sissy's friends vacationed in Florida, where their moms rented time-shares with maids by the week. "Blaise says only stubborn people from New Orleans have summer homes in Pass Christian. They keep them 'cause they want to be thought of as old money."

"Your mom always kept the cottage so nice. I should have my own house and not be passed about," said Jasmine.

Sissy didn't want to explain why Mama left. Through the screened porch, she could see tiny fragments of her family landscape, with a different image for each screen.

Lightning split the sky, casting a blazing line, from a sudden July storm. A broken branch flew by and slashed Sissy's face. She rubbed her raw skin. "Was that Indian Joe?" she said, hoping for distraction.

"Who?"

"The last Cherokee of Pass Christian," Sissy said. "Don't you know Serenity was built on this Indian burial ground? Rain causes the spirits of lost souls to wander around. Sometimes they get confused and think they are alive. But that's okay. Blaise says the truth is utterly necessary and any route souls take toward it is a sacred one."

CHAPTER 11

Sissy and her aunt entered the wrap around screened porch. Strange how they looked alike, with thick hair they both clipped back, and blue eyes. But Jasmine's values were so different Sissy couldn't share deeply with her. Sissy told herself she had to get well for the world, to develop the strength to make it through life. In the living room, antique wicker grayed with dust sapped her energy as if her mother's lover had walked in.

Sissy closed a window with yellowing lace curtains. She counted the raindrops stuck to the glass like blisters and the rivulets moving down the pane. If only she could fly out and alight in the branches, clinging to the softness of wood and leaves, subdued by the dripping rain.

Her eyes avoided pictures, which lit up like lanterns. Sissy, with a sports cap at two, on a pony at five; with her dad on his yacht. But the pictures dwindled as Sissy grew. A picture of Mom showed her, blond and nineteen, with vibrant blue eyes. An empire wedding dress with lace sleeves disguised her belly, where a baby waited. If Mama hadn't gotten pregnant in that convertible maybe she would have seen Dad differently. Beware of parrots, convertibles, and yachts.

Oh, there was a photo of Uncle Blaise, seated with Sissy on a bluish purple carpet and handing her a rose. Blaise said flowers, like children, if nurtured would bloom. Sometimes he'd lose himself in the rapturous violet of a morning glory or the startling yellow of honeysuckle, and recite, "It was many and many a year ago / In a kingdom by the sea / That a maiden there lived whom you may know / By the name of Annabel Lee"

She would join Blaise quoting her favorite lines: "And neither the angels in heaven above / nor the demons down under the sea /

can ever dissever my soul / from the soul of the beautiful Annabel Lee."

Perhaps Blaise would walk in any moment and hug her, in a sweet pause. The right person needs to say so little. In a breathless second, she could smell his Givenchy Gentleman cologne, tang of mint, herbs, on male skin. She didn't want sex with him, just affection but would that lead to sex?

Jasmine wanted to see Sissy's room right away. Any place Grandma could enter unexpectedly was dangerous, and Jasmine had to take her joys where she could.

With Jasmine, Sissy could be forthright because Jasmine respected women who were assertive, but Sissy reverted to her baby self. She couldn't go there, see the toys dawdling on the bed: the Raggedy Ann with buttonless shoe; the rag doll with face chewed off by her dog, Greta; the vanity with marble knobs, used for Barbie dolls.

Instead, Sissy went to her folks' room. The white drapes, made by Mama's black seamstress, still smelled of her Kent cigarettes.

Rain streamed down the windows, a rough mourning rain breaking up shapes outside. Sissy thought she saw Mama in the blue-tinted glass. Her eyes shone, and she was in the cashmere robe she always wore at night. Sissy wanted to untie it, to peel it off and keep it with her so she could smell it, touch it, and have it always.

Rough sounds invaded her thoughts. Dad stomped in the next room and shook water from his umbrella. A scent of wet leaves and honeysuckle wafted in with him as Sissy hurried over.

"The weatherman said little rain," Dad said. "I'm out there and it looks like biblical proportions, then it dries up."

"Did you find Blaise?" Sissy said.

"I'm not Houdini! If he doesn't show up in five hours I'll call the Coast Guard."

Dad got a beer from the fridge. "What makes your family think inconveniencing in-laws will make things better?"

"You're too responsible," Jasmine said.

"Experienced. Predators are everywhere." He sat by Jasmine on the sofa, stretched back, lifting his foot on a stool. "Before you see Irene, phone an attorney."

"It's the Fourth of July, Dad."

"I need a lawyer, too," he said. "I'll have to find someone to work on retainer. I can't trust anybody."

"Where's Kitten?" Jasmine said.

"Her mother left me. Sailed to France with her new independence. Maybe lover number two will thaw her out. He can borrow my blowtorch. . . . Once Kitten went back to college, she never came to bed."

"Don't talk bad about Mama."

"That woman went nuts over poetry. Studied transgressions; even put up signs around the house. 'Be cheerful, strong, quiet.' Counselors blamed her for Sissy's bad grades."

"That is not true," Sissy said. "Sometimes she'd fuss at me for watching TV or talking on the phone."

Dad slurped his beer. "The woman fell asleep reading Longfellow to Sissy, some sad tale like Evangeline searching for her lover throughout Louisiana. 'This is the forest primeval. The murmuring pines and the hemlocks . . .' How many times did I have to hear that!"

"I'm not going to agree all the way," Sissy said. "Really, I want to scream."

"I should have left my wife, but Sissy fell ill. Wasted away to a pile of bones on a chair. She faked a backache at ten and wouldn't walk. Did you know that? Her mom hovered by with a thermometer, which we later learned Sissy pressed to a lightbulb so it read 104 degrees. We had to coax Sissy out the bathroom and take the thermometer from her hand. After Sissy stopped eating, I got her Barbie dolls, blue jean purses, rhinestone jewelry. I visited soon as I got home from work."

Lord, Dad was twisted inside but he cared. Maybe Sissy should act sick again.

CHAPTER 12

Later, in the bathroom, Sissy studied Ma's sleeping pills, cupping the blue dots. When did Mama take them? How much drugs had she used?

Jasmine knocked on the door and came in for a towel.

She always showed up when Sissy felt low, as if she were her fairy godmother. She had changed into Mom's white swimsuit and actually looked better than Mom in it. "I'm a real redhead," Jasmine said. "Red hair. Tan skin. I swim at night. I can't even *think* sun."

Boy, her size D cups were amazing.

"I don't want to get caught in Mississippi," Jasmine said, "checking the weather reports, fixing my face for another trip to the grocery. How can hand commercials support me?" Jasmine looped herself with a red towel.

Suddenly there was a lot of screaming from the yard and a voice growled. Jasmine stopped talking, alarmed because her dad had set off the barking dog device her mom bought after banning weapons in the house.

Oh God, was another creditor chasing Dad?

CHAPTER 13

Ducking under her mama's Tulane cap, Sissy trailed her dad and her aunt out back. She couldn't see but she could feel the glimmer in their walk. Sissy dodged tissue-soft camellias and scarlet wisteria. It was so hot that summer that rain dried out after it landed.

Sissy feared she'd be trapped into defending Dad and borrowing money from Grandma to smooth things over. She and Mama had done so since she was five. She crossed a cement seawall crusted with mud and hurried over reddening sand that caved like powder beneath her.

A hag with a bull terrier panted up, waved a mutilated envelope and yelled. "You, Quint Leger's kid? Ten-dollar check he wrote for bait done bounced. He don't pay, he's going to jail."

It was too humiliating! So much upset for small transgressions. Sissy hated how his little checks tortured little shopkeepers. Blaise always knew how to handle his income, no matter how spare, sometimes living off apples and peanut butter for weeks.

Sissy darted down the beach, skirting a gaggle of boys screaming "Happy Fourth!" and sending chaser fireworks and bottle rockets. One boy cackled and fired a cherry bomb that exploded two inches away. She peered through the haze, watching him weasel away. Another declared himself at her disposal to teach her to ski. *Oh, where was Blaise?* Somewhere inside her, a voice called, "I was a child and she was a child / in this kingdom by the sea / but we loved with a love that was higher than love, / I and my Annabel Lee."

Hungry seagulls soared and keened in the reddening sky. They dove at sandbars unaware that oil spills had killed off the minnows.

Sunset was sliding into the gulf. Sissy felt herself slipping into its darkening maroon. When she closed her eyes, she could feel Blaise leaning over her. She imagined the toughness of his rib cage. Was she fabricating illusions to stave off loneliness?

She looked for Blaise at a pier whose lights had popped on, like a string of bulbs. Few piers had been rebuilt after Hurricane Camille, when pier costs soared. She sniffed the air like an alien; smelling the pollution, longing to commune with her uncle, be with him in a happy stupor, lose her equilibrium so she and Blaise could stagger away, hands connected to color and sound.

"Sissy," a voice shouted. In the distance a shape materialized. The loping walk made her think it was Blaise. Had he been drinking, then?

CHAPTER 14

But it was Cliff waving his chauffeur's cap. A pinkish tint shined off his face. With fewer servants, her grandma overworked him. Grandma lived in terror her children would drown, when she was little, her best friend's brother had dived into shallow water and broken his neck.

"Your uncle still ain't home. Go with me to find him?" Cliff said.

This would not be the first time they hunted for Blaise. A manservant could get more help when he searched with his mistress's granddaughter. He was dressed impeccably in his navy chauffeur's uniform, which he always wore unless he was working in the yard, and Sissy wondered what had happened to him at a young age to create the fear of being in ordinary clothes.

Cliff shook his head as they walked past rusted cars and discolored trucks, back toward Serenity. Few bordering plants could survive the boiling sun, shifting sands, and salt-laden winds. Cliff took pride in the place, and he would have to describe the increasing destruction to Sissy's Grandma.

Sissy sat in the front seat of the Cadillac, although Grandma had forbidden it. They drove by oaks with flaky limbs, lawns 300 feet deep with sprinklers hissing full tilt, pavilions guarded by Roman statues, their marble countenances bleeding, yellow-rayed weeds with dark disks. Sissy couldn't recall such a hot summer. Rock shapes rimmed secluded areas, yards drying in the sun, and "stilt" houses like Cousin Ralph's raised for protection against storm-generated high tides. But was safety before such a mass of water truly possible?

At Pass Christian Harbor, the Gulf swelled under distant thunderclouds. Sissy tripped over an orange folding chair and a couple necking. Blaise had taught her to ski in that water, how to straighten skis that shot up at impossible angles. Love and belonging were all around her then.

Back at Serenity, she and Clifford searched some more, driving down the gravel road framed with ankle-deep grass. Sissy asked Cliff why people give up. He said some people are just too sad to draw another breath. *Was Blaise going mad on his way to being a better artist?*

Cliff's gray eyes were coated with fear. "The young pear trees have done badly," he said, changing the subject. "We're getting more and more wind and heat. Lightning struck the new fig tree."

"I can't talk about these things."

"Come with me and talk to your grandma. She be praying the rosary all night."

Sissy defied Cliff and went off alone on her motorbike. She skirted the hundred-acre lawn, marshes, and eighteenth-century gardens. As a child, she had joined Blaise watching wildlife in the wetlands, from Mississippi to the Atchafalaya. So many of the fish and wildlife were now disappearing.

Circling the house, with its barred windows and too bright lights, she floored the bike, howling Blaise's name. She supposed her attraction to him had begun because of his looks. Always taller, more stylish, more clever than other men, Blaise lit up a room. Grandma used to call him her matinee idol.

Sissy skirted the snake pond, tore through papyrus, past the potting shed to the brackish grotto where stones loomed around a statue of Our Lady with the eyes shot out.

A banana limb whipped Sissy's face, hitting her hard with a burning sensation that grabbed her groin. She'd gotten her period that morning.

If only Mom were home or one silly friend Sissy could talk to. Ma'd slipped Kotex in Sissy's drawer when she was nine, knowing some of her friends were developed at ten. Ma blamed the growth hormones, on frozen meat.

Sissy used to unwrap Mama's Kotex. The caked blood repelled her at first. Then she relaxed with it and the sick smell of womanhood. She couldn't ask her grandma's advice about something so valuable; Grandma might send her to a course at the convent or break out in a rash trying to explain something never talked about. Grandma had advised her when her "visitor" came to eat well and sleep as long as she could. Mama left condoms and an IUD in Sissy's drawer. Lord, was Sissy supposed to use all that!

Blaise said women are homicidal because of confusion of the times and a "failure to thrive."

Sometime later, Sissy clambered to the roof of the big house and mounted the widow's walk. Fog hovered over the parapet.

Oh my God, that can't be Blaise—painting near an oil lamp, and some Jack Daniel's. The intensity of his posture recalled his breakdown six years earlier, at DePaul Sanitarium.   Blaise wrapped himself in Baudelaire's souls rhythms. Baudelaire, who searched for God in Poe, who translated him and died lost and alone.   Baudelaire, this God soul voice of France, who stopped speaking the last year of his life.

What emotions was he feeling to do this?

A great dead heron, cold scaly legs curled, its beak bent open, was strewn on newspaper by Blaise's feet. Nearby a sketchbook showed all shapes of deranged wildlife.

He pushed paper under the bird and said, "I'm making this dirty heron something bigger, finer, and bolder than it was. In large birds focus on the beak, the leg, never the whole." With a flat knife he slapped gold onto the canvas, shaping the beak here and there, the ripped feathers, the outthrust neck, bent wings, and pasty orange feet. He streaked the painting with rust and quoted Yeats: "There's no man may look upon her, no man." _He looked with yearning at Sissy.

She couldn't respond. It felt so good to find him. Her heart buzzed. Her legs went limp.

"I always gain something when I see you. Perspective, delight. I can be me," he said.

"You're a good person, Uncle Blaise."

"I shouldn't have flown off the handle. I'm a mean little wizard."

"You're talented, smart, but you have no power. There's no way you're going to control Dad or Grandma."

Fireworks shimmered in the distance, leaving pocked dust and singed tubes and the reminder that they should be happy because it was the Fourth of July.

Gold, silver, and pink fireworks streaked the sky, bursting into an umbrella, a crescent, and a star before shredding into nothingness. Sissy imagined herself floating, an angel with silvery wings drifting into the pale light. She wondered which fireworks ended with a tiny parachute, a teeny tissue toy slipping across the sea and sinking to the bottom.

CHAPTER 15

Grandma must have heard a noise, for she stalked onto the moonlight-whitened rooftop, walked right by Sissy at the parapet railing, and screamed, "Blaise." The only way she could get his attention was to repeat his name. "Blaise." She wasn't going to apologize.

"Is this the nine o'clock cry?" Blaise said. "Every twenty-four hours, Ma screams from the heart."

Grandma stood, crane like, fixing Blaise with a level stare. What would Sissy have to do to shut the woman up -- sprawl out on the floor anesthetized with alcohol? True, he said words that knifed out the color in her cheeks. She had been perceptive about making sure every part of the meal was something he enjoyed. Their relationship more than any other was always undergoing change as she tried to turn him into Grandpa, a man she never liked but married for money. "It's just as easy to fall in love with a rich man as a poor man," she would say. "Your grandpa owned forty pieces of real estate when he married me. Grandpa bought me jewelry religiously, diamond bracelets, Majorca pearls."

The parapet took on a haunted look with the amber from the lamp and shadows streaming over cement. Through the glare of the lamp, Grandma studied Blaise, who painted.

"Help me find my pearls, son! I've lost my pearls," she said.

"He heard you," Sissy said.

"Don't let the normality of my life interrupt his creativity," Grandma said.

The moon paled and the sky grew ashen. Now and then a dog bayed, its howl edged with tension. Grandma wrung her hands as if annoyed that Blaise continued to paint. "You're at it again," she said.

"This isn't me," Blaise said. "I'm standing in for a friend. Do you know who I am? Well, neither do I."

"I've had lots of experience with weepy, eccentric people," Grandma said, "spoilt, we used to call them."

Sometimes Grandma doted; sometimes she shot an arrow to the heart.

Sissy sent Blaise a withering smile. "It's going to be a starry night," she said. "There is a blue moon. The second full moon in a month. They said forty percent chance of rain, and it is beautiful. Remember that game we played on the pier? 'Light my Candle.' One person runs from corner to corner saying, 'Light my candle,' and everybody switches seats behind him screaming, 'Next-door neighbor. 'Y'all want to play that?"

"Quiet, Sissy. It's easy to start these projects, son. But when do you stop? The wee hours?"

"It's better to paint with steam coming out your ears."

"I read about a commercial artist who makes three million a video," Grandma said, squeezing her French twist. "He's outlined five steps to success. Be brief, be winning—"

"If there are only five steps, Ma, why isn't everyone successful?"

The hairs on Sissy's neck stiffened. Why did Grandma have to beat him up?

"Some artists are happier," Blaise said, "if they don't see their paintings hung."

"It's time to switch from painting when you start losing your hair. I'll give you a scalp massage tomorrow, son. My beautician uses this soap and a little brush."

"Leave him alone!" Sissy cried. Couldn't she see Blaise's muscles twitch? His face was turning chalky.

Her grandma didn't know the children she'd given birth to. She thought Blaise should be a lawyer, doctor, or if worse came to worse, a priest, if she pushed enough. Couldn't he create on the side? She had taken drawing in Newcomb College's art school. She had blushed gold leaf on pottery. It didn't take that much time.

Blaise rested on a hip, guzzled liquor from a flask.

"Did you call Ricardo about a haircut? Did you?" Grandma said.

Blaise looked up in disbelief. He was constantly seeking to understand her. "When did this shrinkage of your mind occur, Ma?" he said. "You started out smart. Valedictorian. But you've been thinking the same thoughts for thirty years. I've no more status here than a parlor entertainer."

"I hoped you had enough distractions with that grade school textbook," Grandma said.

"Drawing fish skeletons?" he said. "I'm not completely healed from . . . my nervous breakdown."

"Ssh. Depression," Grandma said.

"I need a few days off to recover each week," he said.

Mosquitoes came out with that eerie blue moon to eat flesh. Blaise let them hook onto his skin, so focused was he on the canvas.

"Let's go inside," Sissy said. Blaise shoved red paint onto the bird's eye.

CHAPTER 16

It was dark now, except for the oily yellow lamplight coming from Blaise's lantern, one side squashed from when he went floundering one night. This summer before Katrina was so, so hot. Her grandma pulled up tall, impatience in her overheated posture. She wanted to understand his need for self-actualization, but it was so far from what she had planned for him. She had long ago given up her personal dreams and didn't know what her own passions were. She scrutinized Blaise's canvas, wrapped up in herself and at the same time overly sensitive to his volatility.

Fireworks blasted the sky. One spray swelled and pulsed excessively. Sissy's stomach contracted as she heard Blaise clasp and unclasp his brush.

"You've got to face reality," Grandma said.

"What reality?" Sissy broke in.

Blaise retorted, "You think people flew the Atlantic, Ma, or landed on the moon by facing reality? I'm like Cassandra. I've the gift of prophecy and the curse of madness. Despite blistering heat and hurricane winds, I'm drawing every species of wildlife. I've penetrated the thickets on my knees and even lain in lagoons to sketch right."

"Pipe dreams," Grandma said. "Who's bought one drawing but me?"

"You've a bad mouth," Sissy said. "You say cruel things to people—"

"Truthful," Grandma said. "Blaise's got to paint in a style closer to the center where the majority is. The curator of the museum said his style has no appeal."

"Blaise always knows what to paint," Sissy said.

"That director promised to hang one piece," Blaise said. Beads of perspiration shone on his forehead.

"If I give him two hundred thousand dollars," Grandma replied. "It's my connections he's after."

"Can't we talk about something else?" Sissy said. Of course Grandma was right. The famous painters were dead, and most had been so poor they painted the food they ate. But Grandma was starting to have one of her dour fits. They began when she was tired and excited and fears for Blaise's well-being overwhelmed her.

Blaise moved the lantern closer so orange glare spilled on the canvas. He painted in wide strokes, streaking violet here, maroon there. He whipped up a coppery color and squashed the brush in, adding more oil till the canvas bulged contorted and grotesque, the heron shape growing scarlet and swollen.

Sissy's toes curled in her shoes. She was sure family relationships could improve if they were more intentional in how they talked.

But if there was any chance of being heard, Grandma would fight for it. "You said teaching interests you, son," Grandma said.

"I don't want to associate with those people!"

Grandma walked around the canvas, craving reassurance. "Well, you could work at your dad's agency."

"With those sharks?"

"There is a need for testimony," Sissy said. "Painting helps you become a more aware human being, which the world needs." She twined her fingers through her hair. "Uncle Blaise's so talented," she said.

"Talent's something the world decides about us, when we die," Grandma said.

"Shakespeare, Moliere, and Michelangelo were successful when alive."

"They weren't from the South," Grandma said. "We celebrate our dead heroes."

"What about Faulkner, Mark Twain, and Grandma Moses?" Sissy asked.

"I practice over and over to get it right," Blaise said. "Surviving as an artist. That isn't easy because the laws of the sea don't apply. Out there, the predators have names: the electric eel, the swordfish, and the hammerhead shark. But humans are perverse. They poison the artist through emotional blackmail. You've got loved ones like red-bellied piranhas hungering to extract your talent, going into a frenzy for a drop of genius. A piranha's teeth snap like a steel jaw. You don't stop one by patting its head. I survive by keeping a low profile, pressed to the sea floor. I was born normal, but my eyes have rolled to the top of my head from crawling along the bottom."

"Quiet, " Grandma said. "Have you seen my pearls, son?"

"These?" Blaise said, pulling pearls as large as mothballs from a newspaper. Disturbance claimed his eyes.

"You're drunk."

"I'm drunk. And you're a bitch. But I'll be sober in the morning."

Blaise hammered his supplies in his painter's box. Darkness pressed down, with its slow sounds of crickets, and seabirds settling for the night.

Grandma watched him, and her hands fidgeted. She hooked on her pearls, stiffening at the touch, as if disapproval from all her ancestors filtered through those gems. She tried to regain her compassion. But the rules of her parents were being violated, and there was no replacement son. Hadn't Cousin Malter left to be an actor in New York City and died in squalor in a sixth floor walk-up? Didn't the museum have an emergency health care fund for food for artists? Hadn't she paid the fuel bills for the sculptor who made that Virgin Mary statue for Star of the Sea Church?

Blaise left, his footsteps fading down the stairs. "I could always humor him, Sissy," Grandma said, once he'd gone." But to save his life is my job."

Grandma peered at Blaise's sketchbook red-eyed. "Violent drawings," she said, "necks twisted, wings crooked, legs shriveled in death, throats bleeding, eaten away. Look at this: popped eyeballs, and broken bones. A circle of buzzards like three-year-old children waiting for bodies to arrive."

"It's his anxiety, Grandma, like the life of these creatures is unstable."

"Watch your tone."

"When he pushes away, that's his soul, screaming, he can't respond."

"Painting takes him off the hook, but it comes with huge costs. He'll be broke all his life."

"Isn't he going to inherit anything?"

"I'm talking about now. Since Blaise was born, I've ceased to be Mrs. Dubonnet. I'm Blaise's mother. I live with an inner panic button stuck on 'Alert,' waiting for a car accident, a drowning, and a plane crash. I realize, white males are no longer considered useful in some parts of society, but this family needs one."

On the beach, bonfires shot up, tongues of fire. Bottle rockets buzzed, children shrieked, and hounds leaped and howled.

Dad burst in with finger sandwiches, and pink petit fours from Gambino's bakery. "It's a war zone out there," he said. "Smoke bombs and bottle rockets."

"Even this high you can smell the ashes and beer," Jasmine added, exuberant and expansive. She trailed him with champagne. When Jasmine and Dad were together their lively bodies enjoyed newness.

Grandma needed a time of withdrawal, pulling in, shutting down, and saying the rosary over a glass of wine. "I can't take one more forced celebration," she said, checking that the mayonnaise was spread evenly on a sandwich, the turkey had no gristle, and Jasmine and Dad weren't touching. Seconds later, she left, turning the sharp corner of the stairs with uneasy preparation and heading toward the bonfires.

CHAPTER 17

Fifty five days before Katrina

The next morning, Sissy walked outside into air so hot you had to pause before moving. Walking on the morning beach increased her tension. She searched the darker ridges and planes for sketches Blaise thought he had lost there. The wet sand glistened with shadow reflections of starving sandpipers and debris. Uninhibited, she tried to capture one, but feared her rough touch might kill it.

"Long before the white man set foot here," Blaise once said, "Indians did. There are stories of arrowheads buried on the coast, and pirate gold buried on Cat Island."

Her skin shrank from the white heat. Last August, Blaise had left for the Naropa Institute in Colorado to study Buddhism. He said he felt like he was committing spiritual adultery, betraying his strong Catholic roots. He pursued inner questions, waking up to the world behind his eye instead of just before it. That's what Sissy yearned to do.

Later, in the library, she searched the bookcases and dug in the rose print chairs for the sketchbook. Her emotions turned inward and she worried what to say to him.

Blaise labored in with Greta, her white hulk sideswiping the furniture. His face looked shriveled, his eyes small from sleeplessness, his smile too wide. He faltered by the breakfast service on the coffee table. Sissy was uneasy but she knew she could get further with him by pretending she wasn't.

"A three-doughnut day," he said. "Got to jump-start the body." He sucked at a doughnut, spilling jelly on his loosely tied purple silk robe, and on his chest hair. His gruff exterior covered a gentleness best seen in his eyes.

A tingling sensation claimed her legs. At weird moments she would start thinking about sex and look at Blaise's crotch. *God, she had to stop doing that before she got found out.* She hunched on the pink toile sofa by a scene of a gallant and a lady with a falcon. Nearby hydrangea plants trembled their bluish cotton-soft blossoms in sympathy.

Dad came in, skirting Greta and a cachepot of salmon geraniums. Dad's greatest value was he was assertive and could put any situation in perspective by emphasizing the horror of another. He dumped some brochures at Sissy. Preppy kids in sweaters, books in hand, strolling over blanket lawns. The boarding schools were up north, even though she hated cold weather.

"Back up schools, case you don't make it here," Dad said. "You know I wish you could live with me."

"You're barely in my life and you want to boss me."

"I'm trying to help." Dad opened his arms. He always liked an excuse to be cuddled. Sissy ignored him. He plopped in a black lacquer club chair with arms like snakes, and scooped up a *Sun Herald*. "Another drowning. Kid jumps off a ferry on a dare. That's what happens if you've no plan for your future."

"But I do have a plan. I'm leaving here soon as I can. Perhaps, I can stay with Mama."

"After she left us."

"Left you."

"For us to relate we need some semblance of respect. What is important to you, sugar? I don't even know."

Was Dad bluffing or was bankruptcy making him compassionate.

Blaise lifted his ankle onto a stool exposing yellow skin oozing with stale-smelling pus. Sissy wanted to punish him for hurting his body. Dad's sarcasm increased. "When did you change that bandage last?" he said. "The doctor says you could need a transfusion."

Blaise shoved off the sofa, the bandage unraveling like a kite tail. "I've got to reconstruct my life over the past twenty-four hours," he said.

"Why do you rush around?" Dad said. "You've got a lump like an orange on your ankle."

"I lost my sketchbook," Blaise went on. "I need it to see where I left off with my life. It's got all my memories, like the images of leaves when the sky turns white at noon, or the wind turns yellow."

"Sketch them again," Dad said, scanning Mississippi Wildlife magazine.

"You think my memory can sustain these details? My sketchbook's not a fucking calendar! "See the dentist, repair the car, have lunch with Ma."

Blaise was too sensitive and critical of others. Everything with him was an extreme experience -- eating, swimming, and finding sketchbooks. Sissy stood up to help him. They turned the room upside down, running into Jasmine, who came in sporting binoculars and a khaki bird-watching outfit: English riding pants, long jacket. A bitch, with a body. It wasn't normal.

Her high boots were designed like Marilyn Monroe's, one heel taller than the other so her hips naturally swayed when she walked. She had had beads sewed inside her bra like Monroe to make her breasts look erect.

Jasmine waved binoculars. "Quint," she screamed. "Your new dog, Gunner, has another bird in his mouth. Why can't you get a nice dog or keep yours in the pen?"

"He's a killer dog," Dad said, "raised by the New Orleans police."

"Come outside and feed the terns," Jasmine said. "Let's watch the sandpipers, lesser and least, going extinct, mating on the shore."

Dad seized the binoculars and looked out, "Oh, no. A helicopter. It's circling the grounds, checking us out. Damn. Someone's on my tail." Before Dad could give Blaise and Sissy orders, they were out the door.

CHAPTER 18

Sissy and Blaise stomped through the high grass with Greta, as the helicopter zoomed away. Sissy loved strolling beside Blaise, the top of her head barely reaching his shoulder. He was kidding around, bumping into her and knocking about. When she was with him, the world became a bigger place.

The hounds stared up glassy-eyed as Blaise unlatched the dog pen, its paint chipped from the rugged sea environment. He put up Greta, pausing for a second to watch the dogs cavorting as if he had an increased understanding of being caged. Then he peered at Sissy, so her heart throbbed in her chest like a tightly wound clock.

She longed to press his body to hers. In her mind he was on top, making love to her, slipping off her shorts, hand between her legs, and she fell into him, into the darkness of his life, into her fear for him, fear of losing Serenity, fear of all these squalls.

While the dogs thrashed, as if sibling rivalry with humans had taken hold. Blaise's black shepherd, Boone, lurched out. Blaise was off after him, seizing Sissy's hand as he headed for Scenic Drive.

There he was pulling her and his weight felt like lightness and she couldn't stop giggling through the breeze, the soaring birds, and the twigs skimming the yard. She wanted to make that moment last forever as wind fanned the bushes and trees, and grass crackled under her shoes. In time he would prove himself valiant and true, if Sissy would forget their blood tie and give herself over to him.

Blaise probed around live oaks, magnolias, pines, pecan, dogwood, and cypress. He pulled back underbrush with tangled limbs, trunks, and roots with his big man hands.

Sissy felt as if her skin was off and afire. Boone sensed their connection and circled Blaise protectively, a wolf like gleam in his eye.

Passing vehicles whizzed along the bare ocher beach. Beige sun accentuated the sauna like heat over palm trees and sea oats. A rust-eaten truck, a weathered convertible, and an SUV sped down the highway, accelerating where just last week a nine-year-old had been run over.

"Think I might take a trip to Club Med," Blaise said, waiting for cars to pass. "I went to one outside Paris . . . It's this singles spa."

"Why go to such a god awful place?"

"People pay thousands for their fountains, steam baths."

"Old guys go there to pick up stray cats."

"You think I'm old?"

She pulled away. It was fine for him to go there. Men could get away with what they wanted. But women were branded with shame and embarrassment. What about Hester Prynne, who had to wear that scarlet letter?

Sissy's cheek burned with heat, which was everywhere. She was bored with walking under oak trees, chasing down stuff for Blaise, yellowing grass dead around her. They were about to cross the highway when a Cadillac drove up.

Oh, no, Grandma was already back from daily Mass.

Light ravaged Irene's ivory complexion, but she wouldn't ride in a car with dark windows lest someone think she was with the Mafia, those crooks whose beachfront casinos chased off the shrimp and oyster people. In ten years, they had turned Mississippi into the third largest gambling state in the country and knocked out the fishing industry.

Grandma screamed, "Get in!"

Blaise darted with away with Boon, across the road and into the sunlight. Sissy grabbed the hot metal door handle.

"Hurry," Grandma said. "Selfish. Selfish. Blaise doesn't care. I've outdone myself to fix a lovely meal. He runs off. I don't understand the boy." Mealtimes were high points of her day. She got up at six a.m. to plan them and by noon was starving and irritable.

Sissy crawled in behind her grandma, swathed in black; a six-foot scarf circled her neck. She had always liked dark colors but since her widowhood wore them with authority. Her car inched through the gates.

Grandma's tension could be felt in the way she muttered through her teeth. "I wish I'd time to loaf like a heathen. I prayed at Church we'd find Blaise's sketches. And could have a decent meal. Father Fannen talked about starvation. Families living in cardboard boxes. Blaise's losing his sketches is not the end of the world."

"It's not the end of the world," Sissy said, "but he can see it from here."

Grandma flipped open an Estée Lauder compact, raised one finely arched brow, and checked her marble-size stone necklace.

"Fake beads?" Sissy said.

"No, real onyx. They're so big they look fake."

The Cadillac stopped in front of the mansion. When she was little, Sissy had called it a hotel.

Grandma marched through the bright hazy light, hat in hand like a shield, her vertical reflection dulling the salty gravel. The help were sure to be annoyed because of dinner's delay.

Inside, she lowered the air conditioning from the ninety-degree setting used when she was out and checked her diamond-faced watch. "Ten past one. The help will charge overtime."

Upstairs, the noon meal was underway, with Andrew directing one white and three black servers. Equal opportunity had come to the kitchen. Grandma had hired one middle-aged tobacco-smelling white woman along with Andrew's sturdy mulatto wife, Ruthy Mae, and her black daughters. The fifteen-year-old with the drinking problem flicked the TV off and filled water goblets. The fourteen-year-old, eight months pregnant, hid behind a door.

In the kitchen, Clifford sat down to a plate of roast beef and gravy, a custom Grandma promoted to eliminate leftovers, insisting nothing ever be reserved or reheated.

Sunlight shone on his sagging face.

"We might as well go get Blaise now," she said. "No one can enjoy dinner. When the boy's upset, he punishes everybody."

"I'll go," Sissy said.

"I don't need you when I pay a chauffeur."

The kitchen staff looked at Grandma with bleak eyes. Pots brimmed with potatoes, beef, pepper, garlic, and mushrooms. Ruthy Mae dragged a spoon through some gravy. Andrew, already irritated by his high white starched jacket, threw a fork into the sink. His daughters leered at each other, hoping to slip back and watch the big TV.

Grandma and Sissy took the elevator downstairs. Inside the car, Grandma gave Sissy her black straw hat to hold and pressed the *Times-Picayune* newspaper against the window. Grandma said, "Blaise is oversensitive. The last meal ended in his being a jackass. Why can't he get over it, accept his own failures, and join the group. No one prefers aloneness to being with family. But tell Blaise to eat and you are interfering."

Shadows crept over the cropped lawn as Clifford drove out Serenity. The sun vanished behind a bruised cloud. Everything -- water, posts, piers -- quavered under the foreboding rust-spotted sky. *Where was Blaise? Taking a long swim, flirting with white trash on the beach?*

Sometimes storms were bad; sometimes not. During hurricane season, from June through October, the family stayed prepared to evacuate if a big one came.

Sissy hoped a bad squall wasn't coming. Not with Blaise out there scavenging the beach. He was addicted to work, it was true, but could anyone become a great artist otherwise? He needed to know and understand the depths of what he painted. Once he had survived a small hurricane by tying himself inside an overturned canoe on Ship Island. Of course Blaise was aggressive, silly, evasive, a show off, but his works were magical.

She wondered why there couldn't be more pleasure, more enjoyment in their lives. Serial crises seemed to be hitting Blaise, exciting his perfectionism.

That day, the beaches were curiously empty of wave runners, sailboats, wind surfers, catamarans. They combed the twenty-six-mile area called the Southern Riviera, searching for Blaise. Sissy scanned the heaving water, trying to forget it takes three minutes to drown, filled with the realistic worry of an accident in waters where many had drowned.

The car passed brightly painted beach cans in Ocean Springs, Biloxi, Gulfport, Long Beach, Pass Christian, and Bay St. Louis, made by artists each year in a "Paint the Can" contest, Mississippi's great artists celebration.

Nearing Waveland, Sissy saw Blaise way out, battling waves. Boone paddled around him, surf burying them in folds. Sissy's mind raced, her hand fidgeting with the door handle.

The Cadillac jolted to a stop. Grandma yanked off her heels, tucked up her skirt, and grabbed an umbrella. Her hat flapped like a mammoth bat. Clifford ran in front though he couldn't swim and had a catlike terror of water.

"Are you a lunatic?" Grandma screamed as Sissy ran past and plunged into the Gulf. The current got faster and colder, tearing at her sides. A squall was moving in.

Competitive and stubborn, Sissy pursued Blaise and Boone up a barnacled pier ladder, slimy with seaweed. Boone panted once he got atop. Less resourceful than Grandma, Blaise couldn't manage his feelings well.

Blaise once said what saved him from a shriveled heart was watching the storms. He loved how thin sounds became high and wild, waves gouging the beach, water smashing objects into bits. "A squall lingers long after it's gone," he said. Water fontained through the pier slats in hard raw slaps.

Blaise bent down, letting his foot bandage skim the glassy water. A singular pelican from that near-extinct species paddled valiantly, her weight causing her to sink inside the man-eating waves.

The walkway quaked from the weight of Clifford, angling an umbrella over Grandma. She looked frightened and mute.

"Dinner's getting cold," Clifford said. "Ruthy Mae made a fine roast."

A wave rushed below, Grandma quivered, her face fixed downward. "I'd like to talk with you—son. Come inside. You and I were close before."

"Before, I did what you wanted me to do."

"You've drawn too long."

"People are things, Ma," Blaise said. He gestured toward a sunbather wearing the famous Bobbie's bikini, originating in Biloxi. "Artists. Ax murderers. There are bodies with paintings in them stretched across that beach. No one's told them they're artists, so they're drinking themselves to sleep."

Sissy was afraid Grandma was hiding his sketches. Once, Sissy discovered she had stolen a paintbox, brushes, and a book.

Suddenly less afraid, Blaise pointed to a roach with large, nervous wings. "Roaches survived the Ice Age. They're immune to poisons. That one is Japanese. German roaches have black faces."

"Why study foul things?" Grandma said.

"You're so discouraging," he said.

"And you're looking for an excuse to do nothing, son. I want to discuss certain concerns. But it's never the right time . . ."

"Did you find my sketches?" Blaise said.

Grandma attempted to replenish her meager smile. "Son, you're punishing yourself over something no one cares about. You artists have placed yourselves in an opposing camp. Like deranged soldiers, you're fighting your own kind, believing the worst about those who support you. You've got this narcissistic idea that you can do what you want when you want. All human beings, even artists, must face reality."

"Quiet! Bitch!" Sissy said.

That insult threw Grandma for a trip. She was so fixated on Blaise. Sometimes Sissy had to say some god awful thing to pry her loose.

CHAPTER 20

Moments later Blaise rose, tightened his robe, and hobbled toward the pier house, olive green in the storm light. The air looked bruised under threatening clouds and a prune sky. Waves struck the pier with haunted blows. He retrieved a pad from a trunk and stared out, sketching a tattered shrimp boat.

Sissy was sopping wet and cold from being in the water.

Oh why couldn't she take Blaise inside? Instead, Sissy and Clifford stood like viewers at his wake.

Grandma was pleased when she pleased others, but she was also unafraid to hurt them.

"Cliff, give me that bag from the trunk," she said.

Cliff pulled down his chauffeur's cap.

"What's with the hang dog face, Cliff?" Grandma said. "I found Blaise's sketches. I'd hoped to get them repaired . . ."

Cliff passed her the bag with a despairing look.

Blaise pulled out scraps crusted with sludge, an image, drenched in mud. "When did you find the sketches?" he said.

"Hours ago."

"And you waited to tell us? Oh my God," Sissy said.

"I never realized there was a time clock for artists," Blaise said. "I feel like I'm in this river of fire with millions of artists screaming, 'Help.'" He walked to the end of the pier where water ran fast and deep, stepped on a rail-less tract. "I need a new business. Caskets. No start-up costs. Millionaires drop dead every hour." Blaise flung down the sketches on a metal table used for gutting fish. Wind fought for the scraps.

Grandma pursued him and chattered a lot till she saw his face.

"You tore my sketches up, didn't you, Ma?" Blaise said. "What's yours is yours, and what's mine is yours. You were afraid my artwork might bring me glory. Independence."

"You're so narcissistic, son. You want to blame someone? Blame me. I can take it."

"Stop," Sissy shouted.

"You gonna make it worse, dern fool," Cliff said, pulling her back.

"Son, I'm trying to protect you. Do you want to go back to the hos-pi-tal?"

"Vulture!" he said. "You go through the motions of motherhood, the meals, the stories, the meetings. But beneath the fuss, you're a buzzard. You feed on the dead. I wish you'd never given me life." He struggled up on to the table, took out a flask, his face gleaming fiendish ocher. "If I thought my life was real, I'd blow my brains out."

Grandma took hold of Clifford's arm. Dull light furrowed her brow. "I'm too tired to recall what I've done wrong," she said. " I could always lie to Blaise and tell him he'd a future as an artist. But isn't telling the truth and saving lives a mother's function?"

Off she and Cliff marched. Serenity shone red in the distance, yellow windows in brick sockets. At least Sissy thought, Cliff wouldn't placate her the way Ruthy Mae did, saying all white children persecuted their mothers.

Blaise sprawled on the table, staring at the waxy sky.

"Don't let her get to you," Sissy said.

"Cruelty doesn't come with age," he said. "All old people don't act like that. They eat their young here." His eyes burned into hers in such a lost way that the heavens broke loose and poured.

When Blaise wouldn't budge, Sissy lay by him and imagined rain melting them into one. For a moment, she imagined he had been dead for a week. Blaise's lips looked almost brown. His roughly shaven cheek brushed against hers, feverish like the squall building overhead.

He wasn't sick. He was resting. He always bounced back. He would walk around a couple of weeks alone. Then one day he would take her for a drive and they would talk softly all the way to New Orleans.

When Sissy was older, she'd join the military. They'd fly her overhead, parachute her into crisis situations so she could resolve them. For now she'd try to live each day as if it were her last, with some integrity to her choices.

She wouldn't run away and let her face become an inevitable mask of guilt.

She wouldn't think about Blaise fading, wouldn't imagine it. Couldn't see him leave, them not together, not in the same room. No chance of warm touching, flesh soft and moist, no walks outside, the smell of spring, lilacs in the air, falling buds crushing under their feet. No sky, no trees, just absence, no touch no sweet smells.

One of her weird friends had told her when they embalm men they get a hard-on. Was that true? Another said your nails and hair kept growing, six inches or longer.

God, she must scare these notions away. She was too far in the future. She was young, Blaise was young. They had both survived cigarettes, drugs, and alcohol.

But his breathing was slow; it caught sometimes and she feared it would stop. And death did come sometimes the way the Bible said, like a thief in the night. Friends had freaked--boom, crash—in car accidents, on drugs, her cousin with a rifle at thirty-four.

God, she must stop worrying about so many things. Was she ill now—she herself.

She lifted her head, but the rest of her was lifeless. Nobody at seventeen ought to have to think of a loved one going nuts. The world should be a bigger place, and she should feel omnipotent.

Here she had these thoughts of stripping Blaise, putting her hand in his pants, pouncing on his erect body, and she would be eighteen in a month, and he was almost dead, and she loved him. Maybe her passion had invaded him, killing his immune system like an infectious disease.

CHAPTER 21

Tuesday, July 12
Forty-eight days before Katrina

For nearly a week, Blaise ran a fever, and Grandma forbade visitors and isolated him in the tearoom. She had inherited a love for tearooms from her grandmother, who used them as a lady's full sitting room, Victorian gentlemen gathering separately. All sorts of parlor games were kept in the closet there: Monopoly, Scrabble, Clue, and stacks of cards.

When Blaise and Mom were little, Grandma would play with them for hours. Grandpa stayed in the city, working in the summer, while Grandma, her children, and as many friends as they wanted headed for the Gulf Coast. Nightly games of canasta were common, as were competitions of who could paint the best flower.

This tearoom climbed with sunlit greenery and faced some marvelous banana and crepe myrtles, but Sissy hated it, for it was also used as a sickroom, and the walls held that wrinkled darkness.

A week after their stormy confrontation on the porch, Irene sat at a wicker table clipping camellias their pale pink blossoms, tissue-soft and trembling. She pressed up tall in her "Davis chair," which had once belonged to the Confederate president, and stuck out her tepid cheek for Sissy to peck.

Shadows spun over the net canopy, that was drawn back on the 200-year-old sleigh bed while Blaise slept. Irene angled over her table and fluttered white and green specks over the Steuben ashtray. She refused to wear glasses. With one eye she could see long distance, and with the other she could read, but at dusk both eyes bothered her.

Her gaze roved over the summer matting, past a *New Orleans Bulletin* from 1860 that declared, "Unanimously at 1:15 o'clock an ordinance of secession was passed," and stopped at Sissy's outfit.

"Why the garish shirt?"

"I thought it would cheer Blaise. He's been asleep all afternoon. And why do you keep him here? Mom says tearooms are for celebratory occasions: afternoon scones, or mint juleps," Sissy said, pressing her feet into the buttercup-colored carpet.

"Tearooms are for what I say they are for," Grandma said. "Blaise's room is jammed with paintings and here there's sun and fresh air. Most patients improve at home. My great-great-grandfather was a surgeon in the Civil War and he knew that."

How could Grandma make wise cracks when Uncle Blaise looked awful? Had she downed toddies? She had high blood pressure and took pills on the sly to appear in perfect health. She was panicked by the onset of arthritis. Her hand movements had improved, but she had no fine finger dexterity.

"I've never liked motherhood," Grandma said, amputating a petal with difficulty. "Only thing I've successfully nursed is a bruised camellia." She gestured to leaves shriveled around a plant base.

Blaise's plants were showing their resentment for being moved by shedding leaves. Living from trauma to trauma.

Hearing Blaise's twisted breathing, Sissy crept over shadows to the bed.

Oh, God, no. Blaise's cheeks were flushed, his skin chalky and blotched. Wisps of hair matted his forehead. Sissy wanted to touch him, soothe his uneven breathing.

Now his eyes caved in to grainy circles. *Was Grandma so dumb she didn't see how bad Blaise looked?* The damaged ankle stuck out from the sheet. A purple lump swelled up from the bandages, reeking of pus. Sissy wanted to burst into tears. "Can I wake him?" she said. "If he sees me he'll get better. Maybe I could distract him . . . recite poetry or put on classical music, Mozart or Debussy?"

"The sick need quiet. That's why hospitals limit visitors. I'm a candy striper. I know."

How could Grandma know? She wore that pink designer uniform and asked to be assigned to the maternity ward.

"Sissy, get the cucumber sandwiches and chess pie. It's so light. You can eat it with your fingers and not get crumbs on your clothes. And bring the white tea, Fortnum and Mason, the Queen's blend."

"Why don't we take Uncle Blaise to the doctor in New Orleans?"

"Because he is not that ill. We can get all his medications here. And Blaise prefers it."

"But he looks --- rough."

Grandma decapitated a blossom, creating a trembling in the chandelier. Its hurricane glass was etched with Confederate insignia, not American eagles.

Sissy wanted to cry. She drew a long breath. Her head felt like lead. "I'm scared he's lost the will to live. Every time he 'veges' out, I'm afraid he'll never come back."

"When you feel bad go to a holy place," Grandma said. 'Philosophy stretches the mind but beauty stretches the soul. Let's pray. Lovely Lady, dressed in blue, teach me how to pray, God was once your little boy, tell me what to say. Did you lift him up sometimes, gently on your knee? Did you sing to him the way that mother sings to me?"

The sun had gone behind some clouds; amber light drifted on the camellias. Grandma pruned. Every few minutes Sissy checked to see Blaise was all right.

A train rumbled in the distance. Sissy imagined herself airborne, on its mournful whistle. She spun through a side window with Blaise, sun running over their bodies, holding his hand as they flew. Mist-like heat turned the sky gold. Oh, how she loved heat. Light washes of orange and white gave the world a celestial atmosphere. The shine embraced her, lifted her up, and slowed her heart.

They flew over a fountain that looked like Blaise as a little boy, a cherub with a crown of curls. It was yellow-gray green and drenched with blackish dew. Beyond it, the five hundred acres of lawn, gardens, marshes, and trails were clouded in steam.

Suddenly the sky spun heavy and leaden, metal hot, the oak trees calcified like turrets. Outside, a nervous pheasant squawked, her feathers molting from the heat.

The tearoom faded into shadows, into that dim space between night and day, between life and death, between youth and age.

* * *

After a few days, Blaise's blood and urine test were normal and his fever went away. He refused to go to New Orleans, so Grandma, who believed in humoring the patient, hired a chauffer to drive a specialist from Biloxi biweekly to her house. She had her plastic surgeon, who vacationed on the coast, over regularly to dinner and to take a peek at Blaise.

Every day, Blaise's ankle held more angry swelling, redness up the calf and down the foot. Sissy would change the pus-stained gauze and say, "Tomorrow, you will work."

"Good," he'd say, quoting Degas' tombstone, which read, "He loved to paint."

Blaise's adoring stares became weaker; his hopeful requests to paint were denied. *How could he work when he couldn't stand long? What was she supposed to do, tie a brush to his wrist and lay canvas over the sheets?* The specialist read the thermometer, his hand trembling. "Blaise's temperature's down." What did that mean? Doctors had no guilt about confusing family members.

Queasiness overcame Sissy whenever she changed those seeping bandages, noting the size of the lump, the color of the purplish skin, the swelling of the leg. Perhaps her instincts were wrong and he was getting better. Some days he would walk with vitality, and other days he was drained of energy, complaining of a dry mouth.

Sun blasted the coast. No one went outside or even to the window between ten and four. People waited to no avail for rain. Glare clambered up the vines, over the cheesecloth, crabbing through shadows. Even with the air conditioner on super cool, they needed extra fans.

Sissy blotted perspiration from Blaise's forehead, cooling his clammy palms. She told Grandma to call Mama.

"I'm not going to alarm Blaise by phoning her. Nothing bad is going to happen. We're an hour and a half from New Orleans." Grandma's voice was hard, but her puffy eyes, soft. Deep down a sweetness resonated between Blaise and her. Illness infantilized him, and, though once a man, he was twice her child.

CHAPTER 22

Wednesday, July 20
Forty days before Katrina

A week later on a steamy afternoon, Grandma laid a run of spades on the table. Amber light from the chandelier lit her cards. Daily Solitaire was her way of contributing consistency to the family.

Sissy plopped down pie and tea. Her eyes flashed at Blaise's cheesecloth-tented bed. *What if he died?*

Grandma sliced one card behind another. "You should learn to like cards and amuse your grandmother. I come from a line of women who perfected Solitaire. God keep me from retirees talking about illness or death. Solitaire's a game for one person. Thank God, since that seems to be the direction the world is headed. Solitaire's the American name; the English term is 'Patience.' You play one card at a time into this tableau. Her, I'll show you," Grandma said, jangling her bell.

Sissy twitched. "Ruthy Mae's left for choir practice," she said.

"I've no use for Ruthy Mae. Her nursing degree's a waste. She just sings spirituals and wears a bandanna. . I have to keep three maids, case one doesn't show and one needs to be fired. Still I'm continually compromised."

Blaise turned on his side with a painful moan.

"What are you giving him, Grandma?"

"Tylenol. He doesn't hurt much when he sleeps, and he sleeps most times." Grandma placed another card. "The Queen of Hearts, the red suit looks good."

"Let me speak to the doctor."

"You're a child. I can't confide in you because you might share the information."

Sissy braced pillows under Blaise, her heart cold. Deep pools of yellow creased his face. She hated the change in him and the way Grandma acted all-powerful. "Uncle Blaise looks worse."

"Don't remind me of his frailties. Leave."

"Uncle gets sick because when he's well, you won't let up on him."

"Grandpa warned me about letting you get too bossy. But I felt sorry for you because of your vile mother not realizing how alike you were."

"Don't insult Mama."

"The doctors are taking Blaise to Oschner Clinic tomorrow for tests."

"What -- That clinic killed Grandpa! Needles and tubes everywhere. The smell alone . . . You remember? What did you sign Blaise up for--"?

"I'm ringing for Clifford!" Grandma clutched her angel bell, its one wing busted from an angry gesture.

"Call him. I won't let you send Uncle Blaise to Oschner. You sign the papers, he's mincemeat."

"All that matters now is for you to be obedient."

"So it's final then. What the hell— you're going to let those specialists work on him? I hope you remember what they did to Grandpa. You hear that?" Sissy said, calling at Blaise. "She's sending you to the clinic. Blaise hates hospitals."

"Not true!"

"Not when you're there, of course. You nudge the buzzer and the nurses fly in like hawks. It's your money they're after."

"I'm not worth that much."

"You want to torture Blaise? I won't let them use him like a test case."

Clifford responded to the appeal for Ruthy Mae and brought a steaming kettle of beef bouillon made from the blood of baby calves.

Blaise scrunched up in his bed, for he could still feed, wash, and dress himself.

Cliff let out a tired breath, and then hummed some silly gospel song.

"Clifford shouldn't be working late," Sissy said.

"Real women don't complain," Grandma said. "I'll feed Blaise."

"Let me," Clifford said. He propped Blaise on pillows, laid a napkin on his chest, and measured soup into a spoon.

Grandma took a step closer, tightening her blue suit. She was capable of sympathy and had gotten up at four a.m. to prepare the perfect bouillon. She was always ready to distract the sick with stories of her European adventures or recent movies seen.

Sissy took the spoon, sipping the greasy liquid. "Remember when I was a baby, you used to pretend each spoon was a landing plane. Now, it's your turn to eat." She dove her hand like a plane and said, "Whoosh! Spssh! Zzzz. The airplane is flying around—ready to land—one for Clifford, two for Sissy, three for Jasmine."

Sissy shoveled bouillon in Blaise's mouth, but he coughed. *Oh, God. He couldn't swallow.* He fell back, choking uncontrollably, sticky liquid dripping on the pillow.

Did he want to die? Or was he trying to get away with mischief? Sissy felt unreal. Was she floating above herself or was that Blaise's body lying like a cadaver? Blaise, the man who'd taught her to walk and encouraged her independence.

CHAPTER 23

Thirty-two days before Katrina

July 27, Thursday morning, the alarm went out, "Mr. Quint's here." Dad drove through the double sword-crossed gates, punctual and cheery, in his two-thousand-dollar suit, determined to incarcerate Blaise in Oschner Clinic in New Orleans.

Sissy thought, you had to admire Dad's leap from the bottom of the ladder to the top. A great strategist, he could offer the vulnerable what they wanted so they crossed to his side. Mama was the only one who could force him into things, often because she could make home life a living hell. His pride was devastated when she left, beauty intact, with a younger man, imitating a pattern he had begun . . . after their wedding.

At Serenity, Dad took over the care of Blaise, and the help and Grandma went out of their way to abide by his instructions. He ran the house like a general and treated Sissy like a slave.

"Don't take him. Don't," Sissy said, as Dad oversaw the packing of Blaise's bag. That moment was so powerful in her life that everything after it was a great shift. Her brain scattered about her head as she said, "What are you doing with him?"

Dad controlled Sissy with a hug, ushering her to the window to watch for the ambulance. Sun streamed through the glass. She wanted to turn into a coward, run away like Mama.

Mama had left her husband after eighteen years. Packed a suitcase and gone down the back stairs. Left her grandmother's green Victorian house on Saint Charles Avenue in New Orleans, which she had inherited and he had taken over, and her seventeen year-old daughter in her pink bedroom, which she had designed. Left with one suitcase, and did it for all the forty-year-old women who couldn't leave their trapped situations, who couldn't demand respect, kindness, and consideration from their mate. She gave away most of her clothes: all the furs, the ball dresses, and the Carnival costumes stored in the attic. All her jewelry: divided it among friends, daughter, and cousins. All the history books, her library books donated to Tulane University, her collection of Tennessee Williams's tapes to its English department. Gave all her photos and papers on her marriage to Blaise; left all the antiques, the paintings, the piano, and the china in a 6,000-square-foot house that had been in her family for centuries. Took her real jewelry, her laptop, and her soul.

Golden Ambulance sleeked over from New Orleans. Dad felt if you had to ride an emergency vehicle it might as well be deluxe. He too looked sad. But only for a moment. He tightened his jacket, finding strength from some Texas hardnosed gene extending back to God knows where.

Sissy said Mama's favorite prayer. "Oh my Jesus, forgive us our sins, save us from the fires of hell, lead all souls to heaven, especially those who most need your mercy."

Mama would go through her daily life as fresh and new as she could, till Dad came home and she stepped into the role of accepting wife. At least Mama hadn't committed suicide like Tolstoy's Anna Karenina, who threw herself under a train.

Eight attendants dressed in green crawled out a vehicle with flashing red lights. They looked like clowns, except Sissy's life wasn't a comedy. They strapped Blaise onto a plank, pressed on an oxygen mask. On this pallet, Blaise was carried across the yard, struggling to break free. Sissy ran up to him. "I'm with you. I'll be with you forever," she said. He couldn't defend himself now. Vitality had been his biggest gift. *Lord, let the enchanted world of their joined pasts return.*

Dad exchanged a worried look with Grandma, her left hand trembling, as the men lifted Blaise into the ambulance. Sissy tried to jump in, but Dad forced her back.

Oh don't let Blaise travel alone.

Sissy had lived naively, trusting her family could protect Blaise. She had the view that other artists would get hurt, attacked, or passed over but not him. Nothing terminal could ever happen to him. Life was fair and he would be rewarded for his efforts.

A rock, Dad needed his own vehicle to rule over and followed the ambulance in his newly refinanced Mercedes.

Clifford trailed him, and Sissy flattened her face against the car window so Grandma, Jasmine, and Ruthy Mae (who was tending to Grandma) could not hear her sobbing. The heat of the sun barely warmed her.

Mama said dying was like opening your wings and lifting off with the seagulls. *We dissolve into this ecstatic emptiness, this loving web between all living beings, which is our heart.* But who knew if she was right?

Outside, the pale sun peeked through grayish-pink clouds and a faint steam hazed the air, drifting through the mauve oak trees. Sissy visualized Blaise well, his arms swinging around her neck, a blue-white sky making her feel feather-light.

She tried to remain calm, let her body go numb, pinkness giving way to grayness as New Orleans approached.

What had happened to that man who got behind a creative project and worked for hours without losing energy?

At the admissions desk, Grandma tended to hospital business. She wanted to do things correctly to show her love for Blaise, but a room with half shower was the only private one left. She refused to let any relative share a room lest a stranger overhear her business. Grandma had a deep capacity to listen to the doctors because she knew how important it was for Blaise they not start out antagonistic.

That afternoon Sissy ran up to Blaise's room, telling herself that she would rather have a dull, long life than a short, more genuine one. She tried not to touch the urine bag or saline drip as she pressed by the bed.

Oh God, what was wrong with him.

A black nurse with high cheekbones and a thoughtful expression reviewed Blaise's chart and said they suspected he hadn't eaten. Wouldn't eat. Sissy tried to evaluate and hold on to this shocking new perspective.

"How long can a person go without food?" Sissy said.

"About three weeks --if they get fluid," the nurse said. She had a "nothing will work" attitude and wouldn't answer more questions. Maybe she had been disappointed or sued too many times.

After a few days in the hospital, Blaise's white blood cells went down, and his temperature spiked. Blood and urine cultures failed to reveal the source of the infection. Still, Dad remained exuberant, expansive, and highly positive probably to comfort Grandma.

They gave Blaise two transfusions, the strongest antibiotic, and heparin shots in his stomach to avoid blood clots. Then Blaise's kidneys gave out. Dad brokered Blaise's condition with ruthless persistence. Grandma was relieved. No one wanted to choose treatments that might lead to Blaise's death.

Sissy tried to evaluate and hold on to a positive perspective, but the only way she could keep from losing her mind was to think of Blaise nude under the sheets.

Late Monday afternoon, a Pakistani specialist, a short man with a blank expression, was called in, to give more tests. *How did he ever get to Louisiana*? Dad explained the smartest doctors there were Arabs or Indians. Most weren't Southerners with alcohol addictions. This doctor basked in the attention of the nurses, and thought he was helping by repeating, "I'm sorry. Ooh that hurts," as he drew blood from different locations for yet more cultures.

What had happened to the man who loved to play in nature and tell time by the sun?

One goofy nurse got Blaise to loosen up but drove everyone else crazy with her religious rituals, flapping her arms like wings over the bed and cooing some healing chant.

Then Blaise's lungs got congested and he couldn't breathe. When Sissy woke him, he was angry, but when she didn't, he said she was uncaring. Blaise seemed to be picking fights.

Once Sissy read poetry to him, Milton's sonnet on his blindness, and Blaise screamed out: "When I consider how my light is spent . . . They also serve who only stand and wait."

Friday a bald doctor arrived, cheery as if nothing was wrong. He read a report that indicated Blaise had cancer of the lymph glands, with a ten percent survival rate.

Grandma couldn't regain her poise. She sat in the chair clutching her armrests. Awkwardly upbeat, Dad insisted this was just one doctor's opinion.

Lymph glands. God, what were they? Did you need them to live, like the liver, the heart? Sissy looked up the evil words.

"Lymph— a nearly colorless coagulable fluid contained in the lymph vessels." "Cancer—a malignant growth of tissue ulcerating, tending to spread. "So lymphatic cancer was a malignant growth of colorless corpuscles.

Sissy steeled herself, submitting to Blaise's requests that she read to him from her summer required books to enter St. Joseph's Academy in the fall. Her deepening emotions created a lack of self-confidence. How could she get into *Red Badge of Courage* and *Pride and Prejudice*, struck as she was by her fear for Blaise? Hadn't Christ worn a crown of thorns? Hadn't Mary stood under the cross? Sissy had been initially attracted to Blaise for his intensity. Now that Blaise was weak, she still wanted to touch him, caress him, and love him. *God wasn't that disgusting*.

An insecure female oncologist, Dr. Boudreau, came on board on Wednesday, August 3rd. She had to know every detail before making a diagnosis, because most procedures for lymph cancer didn't work.

But a second opinion from the Sloan-Kettering Hospital in New York challenged the first and stated, "No carcinoma growth detected." Dad arrived with chocolates and roses, charged to Grandma, who enjoyed his humor and laughed out loud. Sissy was convinced Blaise's problems had been caused by his failure as an artist.

August 6th, Blaise and the family returned relieved to Pass Christian.

* * *

Sunday morning, August 7th, Sissy entered the brightly lit tearoom. Her emotions were extreme. She loved that Blaise was well and hated that they had all been put through so much torture. Her lively mind appreciated the newness and exaggerated grandeur of their home.

The half-raised floral blinds were a happy jumble of color, and the cheerfully naive country wicker furniture sparkled with light. Glare lit up the leaves of a palm; some looked lime yellow, while others farther from the light fell dark green. Sissy was like that plant, stretching for Blaise, needing his warmth. Illness had made their friendship stronger.

Blaise sat in the glare from a side window. *Oh, God, he looked wonderful.* The world around her swirled -- vines, wreaths, and books -- and a wastebasket of discarded envelopes turned into a speckled whiteness. His eyes sparkled with an unusual glow, as if he were seeking something different from their expressive bond before. She listened carefully, wanting to learn.

Sun streamed down his cheek. There was a sexual confidence in his bearing. His poise disturbed her, suggesting the sexual ambivalence and sacrifice of personal identity found in pictures of saints. Could illness have been an expression of his own particular martyrdom – his yearning for her? He toyed with the coverlet like a decorative plaything.

She could not see his legs, for they were under the comforter, but he was wearing a light fawn coat and blue silk pajamas. She drew into herself, excited by the closeness of him. Yellow and blue shadows dripped through the window. In her mind, she was in his arms like a nest, lying there like a limp baby and he the wet nurse feeding her. *God, this was sick.*

He took her hand, wrapping his shell-like hand around hers, making her feel like a little girl. A pot of azaleas trembled at her side as she crossed her arms over her sweaty chest. That's why girls gave in. It was the brutal softness of the whole thing. The air conditioner buzzed fitfully.

"I've been thinking about you, about the life we might have together," he said.

Was she hearing things? Her body was not under her control to do anything except go limp.

Blaise grabbed some pictures of Mexico, as a tension reliever. They were of the El Presidente Hotel, this beachfront hotel with three swimming pools, Latin bands, and couples drinking out of coconuts.

She could smell his Givenchy Gentleman cologne, a woodsy scent like pineapples and grass. He had taken her hand and kissed it. *Or was she imagining he had done that?*

He was excessively energetic, speaking at high speed. "I have wanted to be close to you," he said.

She attempted to back away, but he stopped her, sitting her by him on the bed. He put his arm around her so tight she couldn't budge, if he didn't want her to. That was when she realized he had been drinking.

His eyes went to her mouth. Guiltily she let them rest there, feeling the fullness of his stare.

"It's not illegal to marry your uncle," he said. "There is some precedent for it, actually."

She tried to move, but she was frozen with shame. She did not know if he was suffering from a physical euphoria, but her spirit to resist had left.

He leaned closer and she was lost in his slightly opened mouth.

Oh no, she was going to hell!

He touched her ear and the sensation burned. He was going over board, perhaps tempting her to squash him. But when he stroked her hair, the floor tilted beneath her.

She tolerated, no, she adored it. She fell against him, so glad for the closeness.

He smiled, as if wickedly enjoying her transformation and her giving in to his caress despite the distant way she had acted.

Was she really doing this? She thought their friendship was strong: how to repress the other thing? How could love and disgust be so intertwined?

The scent of alcohol drifted by. Perhaps it was his cologne.

Sensation was coming back to her limbs. *What had they done?* Her body was under his control. She was like a ball in his hands.

Was she really kissing him? Fear seized her, dark ghosts of her future.

His hard-knuckled hand was on her cheek. *God, she was going to hell, like all those fornicators in Dante's* Inferno. Humiliation howled through her ears. Sweat oozed down her thighs. He touched her breasts and she gave in to the woozy feeling of oneness despite the guilt clawing in her belly, the tension in her chest, the gnawing to leave the room.

How long had he been caressing her? She didn't know. Her thoughts dried up suddenly at the sound of footsteps down the hall.

Sissy breathed deeply jolted into the room by more footsteps and the reality of Serenity. The light about Blaise took on the dimness of a French church. His loosely belted coat gave the impression of an invitation.

Dad barged in. Sissy yanked away, her fingers barely under her control to pull down her shirt.

"Want to go for a walk?" Dad said. He was always pushing Blaise to over exercise as a cure all.

An unsettling look stilled Dad's eyes. "Leave us, Sissy," he said, fixing sapphire cufflinks in his pinstriped shirt.

Why didn't Blaise throw him out?

Dad brought Blaise real estate listings, encouraging him to invest, Grandpa having make his money leapfrogging. Dad brought pictures of galleries in Taos and Santa Fe, art shows on yachts that combed the world. He knew Blaise wanted to be treated as an equal to smart men in finance.

"When I came up the drive," Dad said, in his dramatic but normal way, "I thought, what lucky man could live in this house? And then I recalled that man is you."

Dad sat in a happy stupor, congratulating Blaise about his medical report, pouring him champagne in a Baccarat goblet.

Sissy took the drink Dad offered her and dumped it on the azalea plant.

"Why in hell did you do that?" Dad said.

* * *

That afternoon Sissy searched for Clifford and his sage advice, though he liked having her figure things out for herself. She found him in the stifling back hall, sweating while cleaning the sealed-off washers and dryers.

"What are you doing?" Sissy said, flicking on the air conditioner. "It's the weekend."

"Weekend don't mean nothing to your grandma. She need the most for her money." When there were no errands to run, Grandma had Cliff clean the house. He sprayed Lysol on the elevator door and rubbed off fingerprints.

"She's paying you, isn't she?"

Clifford hesitated. "She paid that tuition."

"So you can work overtime for nothing."

"I don't mind."

"You can't say no."

He took out a handkerchief and blotted sweat from his lip. "I feel fine," Clifford said.

"No you don't. Why don't you visit your daughter?"

"In Starkville?"

"I can't believe you're working weekends for nothing."

"Cleaning keeps me strong. Lease wise I'd get fat with gumbo, corn bread, and homemade ice cream." Clifford washed down the entryway, huffing now and then in the ammonia-filled air.

"Do you have to clean while I'm talking?"

Clifford rested the mop in the bucket. "Don't punish old Clifford. I ain't changed."

"Soon as you finish here, Grandma'll find something else."

Clifford laughed through sad eyes. "What's eating you?"

"I can't get along with men."

"You do fine with me."

"You're different."

"Don't your uncle listen? " Clifford dunked his mop in thick suds, which gave off a soapy alcohol smell.

"Why are Dad and Blaise so close?"

"Got to be something about money."

"Blaise doesn't care about that."

"His art shows cost a plenty."

"What can I do?"

"Wait," Clifford said.

"For what?"

"Blaise and your dad won't stay tight. They ain't kin, and they ain't alike. Now you and Blaise, you apples from the same tree." Cliff slapped down white suds in broad strokes. "Go on."

"How can I when everyone ignores me?" She started to stomp on the wet floor, then turned and ducked out.

Shortly after Sissy left, the air conditioning groaned off.

CHAPTER 24

Twenty-one days before Katrina

Monday, August 8, crepe myrtles withered under the hundred-degree sky. The dry, windy night had spattered acorn husks over the ground. August, the hottest month, was also hurricane weather. And Star of the Sea, Our Lady of the Gulf, and all the churches had begun praying to Our Lady of Perpetual Help for protection.

Sissy was talking to Clifford while he washed the car in the front drive. He liked humor and enjoyed being asked: "Is the car ebony or black?" His vocabulary had increased through reading a dictionary page a day. The noon sun on the transparent car surface cast shadows over the gravel.

Clifford stretched across the hood; his face gleamed and sweat poured from his brow. A string of ibises with molted necks outstretched flopped by. Suddenly his hand went limp, and he staggered and fell. His head was thrust back, one eye barely open; his face was waxy.

Sissy screamed.

Ruthy Mae hurried out, wiping her hands. She pumped Clifford's chest, blew in his mouth.

Andrew and Dad managed to lift Clifford, but Grandma blocked the entrance. "I called an ambulance," she said. "If he passes, it won't be inside. I can't live where someone's died."

It was hard to understand Grandma's fear of the grave. Maybe it was because her mother died when Grandma was eighteen and she had to watch her father die of throat cancer shortly thereafter. Sometimes, Grandma insisted, when she visited houses she saw the dead. At night, she triple-locked her bedroom door and hung a crucifix on the knob. The discussion of death was forbidden, because of her fear that mentioning the word could call forth its presence.

Dad tried to overrule Grandma, but Cliff dropped to the ground, stiffening into a crouched position, crossing his arms, and refusing to have his needs outrank Grandma's.

Ruthy Mae insisted they get to the hospital and "not wait for no ambulance."

The small bright emergency room smelled of disinfectant and dirt. The light was so strong, all the machinery and walls were tinged orange. One girl on a stretcher had a mask over her mouth and was completely ignored. *Was she dead?* Sissy wondered how they snuck corpses from there. Attendants in faded green hovered above Clifford. A long-legged nurse with a reddish face hooked Clifford up to fluids. Another extracted blood from his veins. Sissy knew she'd have to stay near him in this small-town Mississippi hospital. Just decades ago he would have been refused admission. Blacks got better attention when a white friend watched. The hospital was steaming.

The infirmary was curtained into cubicles. The man in the left one kept screaming for morphine and flailing, so the divider by Cliff shook. A listless Spanish woman on the right was wheeled off for an appendectomy, after giving Sissy her extra bottles of water.

Dad, Andrew, and Ruthy Mae left.

Blaise, who was not allowed heavily peopled areas, much less hospitals, phoned Sissy. "Do what you need to do to feel safe. I'll be over," he said.

Sissy had a terrible anxiety about being separated from Blaise, especially now. Still she said, "No! Don't come. Don't dare!"

Sissy moved Clifford to a private room, charged around-the-clock nurses to Grandma's Visa (a number she had already stolen), and prepaid for his daughter Clotilde's suite at the Holiday Inn.

Some time later, Ruthy Mae delivered sliced beef from Serenity, for when Clifford started to eat. She slipped Sissy a cell phone and Visa from Blaise, said Grandma had taken to her bed, and told Sissy to phone Andrew when she wanted a ride home.

After she went, a nasty glare seeped into the room. The dying sun lit a horizontal beam on the dusty curtain. Sissy opened it and looked at the Gulf with its raging waves of browns, mauves, and grays. The white male respiratory attendant put a pillow under Clifford to open his lungs and said that he had the breathing of people before they died.

Oh God no!

Sissy refused to go home, despite calls and notes from Grandma that Sissy needed to talk to her and "calm down." Sissy believed if she stayed good would happen and if she left, bad would take hold.

Early Tuesday morning Clotilde arrived, and she and Sissy began their practical relationship of tending to Clifford. Clotilde cared what people thought and always kept Cliff's sheets tidy, and the plastic gloves the attendants tossed at the trash pail picked up. Sissy became Clotilde's mouthpiece. "No, you can't feed him through the stomach," Sissy said.

When Clotilde took a break, Sissy phoned Blaise.

"They have put tubes up Cliff's nose," she said, "under his oxygen mask, and the light on the electronic box that indicates oxygen being used, blinks ninety-eight percent. Cliff is almost at maximum dosage --what if he needs more? Are these the best doctors here, or the ones given to colored people?"

"I'm coming down," Blaise said. "I know hospital procedures and—"

"No. If Cliff sees you, he'll get worse."

"Because I don't care what Ma or Quint say. You need me, I'm there."

"I can't have you die too."

"Okay," His voice got warmer. "Talk to me. Tell me what's going on."

"Clifford's heart is weak. One lung gave out. He can't keep ice shavings down. Clotilde tries to get him to eat. He asked for chocolate pudding, but gagged. Nurses keep changing, so I don't know who is in charge." Sissy lurched about the room, almost tripping over a light cord and bringing down the food tray.

"Get the doctor," Blaise said. "No, stay put, I'll get him."

Tuesday afternoon, a maverick doctor in cowboy boots and a red shirt turned up the bed light. He studied the nurse's notes and asked Clotilde if she knew a minister.

Clifford was going to die. Sissy had been thinking about his death, imagining if she could accept it, trying to see how she felt before emotions got the better of her.

At dusk, Grandma arrived, dressed in designer pink. In bad times, she felt it important to dress as cheery as possible. She was concerned about Cliff but scared that death was contagious. So she did exotic activities that other people couldn't allow themselves.

She filled the hallway with roses, so many they had to set up more tables in Cliff's room and give them to other patients. She checked to see if the twenty-pound box of Godiva chocolates she'd ordered for the medical staff had been delivered, then stood majestically in the doorway, light creating a nervous space behind her.

Suddenly the room buzzed with doctors, nurses, and attendants. Drips were hooked up, machines rolled in, lights punched on then off. Clotilde invited Grandma to sit in the one big chair. Grandma declined. She didn't believe in doctors or hospitals, perhaps because she came from a line of physicians. Her young mother had died despite her doctor husband's perfect care. Grandma said she knew her mom would die when she dropped the mirror by her bed and it shattered. Grandma lied and told her mom that it hadn't.

Like Jasmine, Grandma rarely went to funerals, finding some excuse -- the death of her dog, a migraine. Unlike Jasmine, she was lavish in her farewells, baskets replete with Royal Riviere pears, chocolate truffles, and mint chocolates, French champagne and American beauty roses.

Sissy hoped Grandma wouldn't be mean to Clotilde (as she was to most coloreds she didn't know). Grandma was more compassionate than Sissy gave her credit for.

Grandma surveyed everything, her misty eyes escaping to the patterns on the walls. She interrogated Clotilde about her family, prying into her grades and her plans for Cliff and herself in the future. Clotilde answered fitfully. Aware of her shattered appearance, she flattened down her hair.

But Grandma got tired of Clotilde's return questions about the how, what, where, when of Cliff's fall. She looked frightened and mute and fell into what Blaise called the sulks, reminding everyone she had financed Clifford's private room.

Clotilde nodded. "Sissy, go home with Miss Irene."

"The main thing now is supper and bed," Grandma said, her eyes dulling with anxiety about being alone in the mansion at night. She couldn't count on Blaise staying there from hour to hour.

Sissy pushed against the wall, while her heart screamed she didn't want to be with that bitch. *How could she sleep and wake up at Serenity with Cliff gone.*

Grandma gave Clotilde five hundred dollars from her gold money clip, told her to eat well, and left.

Sissy phoned Blaise. "Thanks for your cell phone."

"What you doing?" he said.

"Waiting for the sweepers, assistants, pill givers. They're coming as soon as Clifford is asleep. I bet Grandma tipped each one two hundred dollars like she did for Grandpa."

"You want me to come over?"

"Of course not. You're never supposed to go someplace festering with germs. Someone's here. Got to go." Sissy hung up.

Wednesday morning at seven a.m., the breathing specialist, a gay white man, told Sissy to hide her cell phone, as it wasn't allowed and would be taken away. He tried to help but his pumping machine backed up in Clifford's lungs. Sissy was not adept with managing conflict and even less resourceful in dealing well with those who tried to help.

She fled to the bathroom, frightened about Cliff's health but unable to make the smallest decision to improve it. Her eyes burned under the fluorescent light. She couldn't breathe in the coffin-sized room, with its paper towels, urine hat collector, and full garbage pails.

At ten am, Blaise phoned and they spoke till her cell ran out. His deep voice, like a midwestern newsman's, calmed her. Sissy couldn't recall what he said, but being connected to him made her feel better.

Clotilde relieved tension by talking nonstop with emphasis on "It's so awful" and reading the proverbs. Sissy suggested Psalm 100. (The happy one, Mama said.) "Make a joyful noise all ye lands, serve the Lord with gladness, come before his courts with singing . . ."

Most of Wednesday, Sissy stood by the bed waiting, staring at Clifford.

She rubbed cream on his dry hands and arms. The numbers on the oxygen monitor went down, indicating Clifford needed less oxygen: eighty-seven percent rather than ninety-eight as before. Oh, the power of touch! When Clifford breathed better, the numbers went down.

But that was only sometimes while Clotilde and Sissy tended to him.

At noon, a new respiratory nurse came in, an obnoxious witch who wanted to explore a new approach. She ripped off the face mask and made Clifford do blowing procedures to see if his lungs could hold air. Sissy escorted her out. *What was the point of torturing him!*

More and more Sissy checked the machines—making sure the line on the heart monitor ran in rhythmical blips, and the percents on the oxygen monitor stayed steady. Semi darkness took hold.

Around four o'clock, the cowboy doctor strutted in, face in a chart. He hung around for a while, looking away when Sissy confronted him with her questions.

"There's already damage to his brain and kidneys," he said. "One of the kidneys has stopped—" The doctor watched the heart machine. "He hasn't much time," he said, his boots clicking on the hard linoleum as he hurried off.

At six p.m., a young nurse crept in and took Clifford's temperature and blood pressure nevertheless.

Around seven, Clotilde took Sissy to a smoke-filled waiting room, furnished in fake green leather. When Sissy complained about the hospital, Clotilde broke in. "We got to prepare ourselves. I'm having a Marlboro. You?" She handed Sissy a Marlboro.

A crone trudged in on her walker, wreaking havoc everywhere. An old man scraped his wheelchair about.

Back in Cliff's room, an amber light reflected off the collapsed fluid bags, and the wheezing oxygen machine, now at 88, 90, 93, 97, and then 99 percent. . Sissy went into the hallway to get help, walked by five closed doors, ran back to Clifford's room.

"Don't give up," Sissy told Cliff. *Not before Mama comes home.*

Night made him worse. Oxygen was at 100 percent. Sissy realized she must journey with Clifford as far as she could. She stayed overnight at the hospital, conscious of the rules that weren't working and her rage at Cliff's body being so punished. Every attendant who came in seemed to steal vitality from Cliff and was unable to replenish his meager resources.

Clotilde ran back and forth to the smoking room, sedating herself with nicotine and scaring Sissy with her predictions (gleaned from veterinary school) that as the oxygen machine began to fail, Clifford would have more pain. Clotilde started calling family in New Orleans, Mississippi, and North Louisiana.

At dawn, Thursday, Blaise showed up. Thank God he did, because Sissy wasn't prepared for the flood of Cliff's friends who also arrived.

She leaned against Blaise's sweaty shoulder and let his low, peaceful voice soothe her. He said maybe Clifford knew he was leaving, and that's why he overworked himself. Death was his Paris. Cliff had come when Blaise was two and stayed as long as he could.

Sometimes Sissy didn't care what Blaise said so long as he kept talking. In Clifford's final moments, she felt she could do nothing by herself.

Blaise spoke on: "Clifford used to say, 'We've eternity to enjoy the rewards, a few sunsets to get the work done.' We are never ready for death, but I think Clifford is okay with it. It'd have been terrible if he had wrecked the Cadillac and been paralyzed. Only the rich who can hide humiliation should die a lingering death."

Teens, old people, adults trudged in casting shadows over the yellowing floor.

At 9 a.m., A Baptist preacher arrived, flailing a cross like a scepter. He needed privacy so the door was closed and locked. Particular about his grooming, he straightened his white collar before he began. Emotions ran high. Anger and tears took over the room. He talked about seeing a person's divine nature and healing the soul. He said Clifford may have been reluctant to be a manservant at first, but soon as he claimed that yoke, he stood up, and changed lives.

Bible in hand, the minister gathered loved ones about the bed, their shadows dulling the sheets. The preacher led them in the Twenty third Psalm: "The Lord is my shepherd, I shall not want. He maketh me to lie down in green pastures. He leadeth me beside the still waters."

The minister directed Clotilde and Sissy to take Clifford's hands. Light broke through the window, giving harshness to the room but luminosity to Clifford's face.

From the heavens, God swung down, caught his spirit, and lifted it away.

CHAPTER 25

August 13, 2005
Sixteen days before Katrina

Saturday morning, the day shone beautifully: a transparent blue sky, no shadows on the ground. A rainbow circled the sun. Hardly a day to dig deep and put Clifford under.

At one p.m., Grandma, Sissy, and Aunt Jasmine drove into Donaldsonville, Louisiana, where Clifford had been born and would be waked. The poor, largely black town two hours from New Orleans was once a place slaves congregated. The oaks and dark shabby houses looked familiar, but where Clifford had lived as a boy, no one knew.

Jasmine had insisted on bringing her Pomeranian, which was more like an extension of her belt, because the only thing Cornelia Brontë Shambles did now by herself was pee. Everywhere they went the dog required a pickup bag and a water dish. Jasmine covered her nervousness with dog potty jokes. Grandma said if the dog relieved itself once more, she'd throw it out the window.

Jasmine spun up the blazing cement drive of the United First Baptist Church of the Redeemer. Blades of high grass like old soldiers stiffened around the brightly lit parking lot. Men in black bordered the church door. *Oh, God, Clifford was really dead!*

Aunt Jasmine let the car idle while everyone collected themselves for the all-black service. Sissy phoned Blaise.

"What are you doing?" Grandma said. Midday light sharpened her face.

"Blaise said to call --"

"Hang up," Grandma said. "You're not supposed to use your cell phone."

"It's Uncle Blaise's."

"Hang up!"

Grandma's voice scared the dog. The flesh on its balding head quivered and Jasmine jumped out and let the dog pee in the parking lot.

Grandma was embarrassed by that, but even more humiliated by Jasmine's backless top.

"You're not going in church half-exposed," Grandma said as Jasmine got back in.

"I borrowed your Spanish mantilla."

"Thanks for asking, and what about that mutt?"

"I've trained her to be good," Jasmine said.

"You're not taking that dog in church!" Grandma said.

"She'll have heat stroke if I leave her in the car. It's 110 degrees."

"If the dog dies, it dies. You should have left it home. Well, for God's sake don't sit with me."

The dog snarled as Grandma got out, slammed the door, and marched toward the garage-like church. The best qualities in her had been brought out by Cliff: his love, care, and kindness. His death, with almost no forewarning made her colder than ever.

The morticians outside the door stood under umbrellas, their hawk like faces luminous, almost wet from the sun. Inside dirty, buzzing fans blew lilac perfume and incense about. The windows were bandaged with blue paper painted to look like stained glass.

Torch like blankets flanked a plain metal casket. Grandma had sent so many American beauties the altar seemed like a park. She seized Sissy and marched her down front. Jasmine followed – taking a seat behind them, bouncing the dog on her knee as if it were her child.

Clotilde sat before the casket, clutching her stomach and sobbing. Some fat woman in a white lace dress and hat threw herself on the casket. Nurses dragged her off. Grandma whispered to Sissy that part had been staged, blacks believing outbursts of grief reinforce the greatness of the deceased. *God, she was such a racist*.

The altar shook as eight women swayed behind the casket belting "Amazing Grace." Touches of crimson and yellow bounced off their shiny, too short purple robes.

Now, Grandma was tugging at Sissy's sleeve. She wanted to pray at the casket and leave. After the congregation had waited for them for an hour! She kept repeating, "I have to go." Grandma had run her father's house after her mom died, but never fully adjusted. Seems besides hospitals, Grandma also feared funeral parlors and churches. Who could she lean on, really? She never felt safe unless a man was in her line of vision.

The wretched dog barked and peed. People gasped. A man in a musty wool suit and a woman in rhinestone gloves left the pew.

Grandma rose. *God, she was using this as an exit.* Wrapped up in herself and very sensitive, she forced Sissy to follow her to the casket.

A lamp on a pole to the left streamed strong, steady light on Cliff's face. His smile was stone-like, fuller than life. His swollen and bruised hands were folded under an artfully placed cross and handkerchief. Still, Sissy knew how much his body had suffered and struggled to live.

"The spirit has been inside the body so long, it fights to stay there," Blaise once said.

Nearby were pinned school pictures of Clotilde and Sissy as little girls and Blaise as a boy. Tightness squeezed Sissy's chest. She turned away, uncertain of her own worth and strength, now Cliff had been kidnapped from her.

Then she saw Blaise walking up from in back the church. Her world expanded. He had come anyway, with armloads of American beauties. He did what was asked, staying home, then doubling the flowers Grandma had ordered and dropping them off.

Grandma hissed: "Don't come in here!"

Oh, God, it felt wonderful for him to make some important tribute. Blaise turned to the congregation, told them how much Clifford had meant to their family and how much they all loved him.

* * *

That Saturday night Sissy slept fitfully in her heavy oak bed. She had "going to sleep" problems, so excited yet overtired was she. She plunged into a nightmare where she was being chased down a dark alley. Suddenly Blaise was before her, drowning, swamp water oozing over his head. Maybe she wasn't taking his needs into account. She shouldn't have phoned him. What if he relapsed?

At eleven-thirty Sissy came to, sweating in her bed, weeping for Clifford and all the lost poets of the Gulf South. The room decorated in white for summer glowed in moonlight. She put her fists like hot compresses to her eyes, locked herself in her room. If only her mother was there to listen to her.

Wrinkled tissues and some wilted violets ringed the bedside lamp. She looked at the canopy over the bed, tufted with her mother's initials, KDL, and then she lit a blue votive candle that released a rain scent.

The lock turned. The faintest wash of blue framed Blaise's silhouette. *How had he gotten the key?* Sissy drew up the sheets, held her breath as he creaked over the straw matting. Sissy watched Blaise's sallow face. The shadows beneath his eyes seemed grayer. *Was he truly ill?*

He closed the light curtains of the once-airy room.

She felt him overhead, his shadow altering the sheen on the sheets. He regarded her through bright eyes. "Your mother would want you to have this," Blaise said, giving Sissy a rosary, once Mama's. The ice green beads shimmered as they had in her hands at Jesuit Cathedral.

Finally there were anchors in life.

"You think by locking yourself away," he said, "you can stop grief? You can't. The soul needs attachment."

Outside, a storm grew, disturbing the dark, night-flickering shadows in the room.

He sat on the bed, one foot on the brown footrest, and then turned back the patchwork quilt.

Oh no this was wrong.

She wanted to throw him out. He unbuttoned her nightie. She told herself she didn't like Blaise's rough hands, his firm grasp. *Oh, God, she didn't want him to touch her.*

He lay by her on the bed, the pillow faintly purple pink. His cheek invited touch. She was on the pill, and had been for a while. Mama had taken her to the gynecologist before she left.

She knew she'd be bad at sex. Blaise wouldn't like her naked, her boobs were too big. And then he did like them, and it frightened her. He unzipped his pants and he was already hard.

God, *had he been thinking about her before he came to bed? This was too perverted, too warped.*

"Is the door locked?" she said, frightened at the pace at which they were moving.

He got under the purple satin cover, wrapped himself around her. She felt his thing and they kept touching.

She'd read somewhere that some couples didn't fit physically together.

He caressed her breasts, kissing her nipples like he was paying homage.

But, oh, this was wrong and she was still a Catholic. Had she bathed and washed enough? The church Angelus chimed midnight as he parted her legs and reached down.

Time ran in and out of their rushing hands sometimes slow, sometimes hurricane-like, for she loved to turn away and be caught, and it ended like the dawn, full and pink.

They fell into a deep sleep, absorbing time.

She woke with a jolt to footsteps down the hallway. *Grandma? At five a.m.? What was she doing there?* Grandma had a great love of family and showed tenderness by checking on people.

Blaise fumbled out of bed, grabbing his clothes as he ducked into the bath. Grandma pounded at the heavy Victorian door. "Open up." Edginess fired her voice.

"I'm asleep, Grandma." Sissy had learned not to lie, because that always resulted in being found out.

The lock turned. God, she had a key! Harsh yellow streaked inside as Grandma came in. Sissy buried her face in her pillow.

Grandma walked suspiciously about, crossed to the bathroom as if aware of something secret now going on.

CHAPTER 26

August 15, 2005
Fourteen days before Katrina

Monday morning, Sissy found Grandma in the library. She stood by an original leather chair -- she claimed it was the sign of a wealthy merchant -- near high windows that faced the Gulf. Early morning light gave a purplish cast to her face. Outside, the earth was bitter dry. Trees had a whitish crust. Still, the abundance of red leather infused the room with a beautiful density. *Oh God, let Blaise come here! Especially now they had their hallowed secret. Intimacies with lovers were not shared with grandparents.*

Grandma took a book from an English desk, and angled herself against the bookcase, solid mahogany and airtight. It was hard to understand her taut expression, but Sissy told herself she'd try. She'd been watching her family for years and never noticed running off helped anybody.

Internally, Grandma seemed very busy even when her exterior was stagnant. "Blaise stayed up, working in here," she said. Tension was seen in her hands, for her nails were chipped and she needed a manicure. "He's drawing . . . and writing lies. You encourage this. Blaise's reading what you read, *The House of Mirth, The Awakening,* stories about sick women. You play on his delicate imagination like your mother did."

Sissy wanted to scream, have a tantrum, kick, bite, throw herself on the floor. Instead she drifted into fantasy. She imagined Blaise falling to his knees, sand on her dress as he burrowed his face into her stomach, his hands clutching her hips. God, he was pulling her down with the steeple of the Catholic Church shining white in the distance.

"Listen up," Grandma said, bringing Sissy back. *Oh where was Blaise?*

Grandma hadn't finished Sissy off yet, given her a good emotional wallop. She pushed the book at Sissy and read an inscription: "'As I breathe, beauty breathes by me, our lives should be one divine miracle after another.'"

"You shouldn't read Uncle Blaise's notes."

"Blaise has not fully recovered. Didn't you see that?" Grandma read more: "'If only we could go someplace where we're not known, or if I could meet a stranger like her. I'd rather die than touch her than have these feelings about her ever again.' Who is Blaise writing about?

"Vicious hypocrite," she said. "Duplicitous like your mother." Grandma stuck the book in a library case and left.

"What is that supposed to mean?" Sissy called after her. "Mama isn't vicious or whatever." The Towne grandfather clock struck the ninth hour.

Out in the front hall, inspectors were assessing the free-flying mahogany staircase, noting the full-length portrait of Irene and four generations of family on the buff-tone walls. Grandma updated appraisals to guarantee total replacement should a big storm occur. Interested in anyone who could improve her finances, Grandma offered them coffee and croissants.

Standing at the library case, Sissy dove into the book. Blaise had inscribed paragraphs. Words coming down the pages made them seem full and soft. Sissy slipped the book under an English bracket clock on a table inlaid with holly wood, for later inspection.

When Grandma returned, Sissy let her have it, for berating Mama unjustly, initiating preliminary steps in the adult world. Sissy kept moving, striking furniture in her path, tarnishing the lemon-waxed surfaces where her hand fell.

Grandma spied the errant book under the clock and returned it to the locked library case that protected books from the heat. Had Grandma figured out Sissy was in her first "serious" romance? Was she debating whether a safe sex talk would encourage her further?

"Don't emote," Grandma said. "We've serious matters to discuss. Your uncle's fever has shot up."

Sissy had to balance herself, command her legs to stand.

"Quint has driven him back to town to see the doctors. I think he needs something to live for. Grandma took an envelope from a Venetian marble-topped table. "I had my lawyers draw this up, to transfer all my Mississippi property to him. I don't want you contesting the donation or getting mad. The paper's been witnessed, notarized, and signed. Blaise's only obligation is to be candid with me about what he does and for whom."

Grandma unfolded the paper painfully. Giving money away was hard because without it, she feared she'd die a cold death.

"What would Blaise do with the land?"

"Call it a mother's sixth sense. But an artists' colony at Serenity might work for Blaise. There are none here like those he talks about up North. He can paint in the main house and build cabins for his friends. I've tried to like the country, but I can't. You can come with me back to New Orleans, visit here, and Blaise could will Serenity to you."

The room went quiet and warm. Sissy's head was spinning. She had merged her identity with Blaise, with her sexual choices, and now another loved one might be slaughtered. "How can you give Uncle land promised to Dad?"

Oh God, the properties that would stop Dad's bankruptcy had gone to Blaise.

"You're not giving Uncle the rear property?"

"I worry about your father. But I can't let him ruin the family."

"I'm calling Dad."

"That man doesn't care about you. You don't believe me, ask your mother. Traveling without him was her one right action." Grandma had always been more interested in money than family.

Grandma whipped another note from her English secretary bookcase, which displayed family treasures including a silk copy of the Act of Incorporation of the Confederacy and a first edition of <u>Evangeline</u>. Why couldn't Sissy live in quiet like Evangeline with those Acadian farmers? "A hundred hearths, the homes of peace and contentment."

Now that Grandma had terrified Sissy about Blaise's health and her father's solvency, she decided to give Sissy an important letter, apologizing for the fact it might cause her pain.

Sissy sank into a red Victorian tub chair to read the letter. *It was from her Mama! And she said to phone and left the number.*

"Did Ma call? Really?" Sissy didn't dare sound enthusiastic, or Grandma would be jealous.

"That's her phone at the Georges V in Paris. I know you think I'm hard, but the woman comes and goes like a butterfly. You can't count on her. Pretend she's lost."

"I'll never do that. I'll see you dead first!" Sissy retained an image of Mama in her absence and understood she would return, but Grandma didn't. Grandma was mad that Mama had left, but felt culpable because she wasn't sure she was free from some responsibility for it. To her, Mama's disappearance was random and terrifying, a reversal of wifely compliance, that linchpin of wealthy marriages.

Sissy searched about for Blaise, who had indeed left without a word to her. She wasn't sure if Grandma hadn't destroyed his correspondence.

Sissy found privacy in a small elaborate reception room off the main stair, with tiles around the fire depicting Shakespearian plays. Grandpa had liked holding court and reading excerpts from Shakespeare after dinner. The Wedgwood blue wallpaper caved in on her. *Oh if only she could reach her Mama.*

She picked up the receiver, put it down, and walked in and out of dappled sunlight. She was making the transition from child to adult. Her physical activity became smoother. This was a happy phone call. Light played on her arm as she settled in a chair. When she finally called, they said Ma'd just checked out. *"Rose elle a vecu comme les roses, l'espace d'un matin."* (Rose, she lived like a rose, the length of one morning.)

CHAPTER 27

August 16, 2005
Fourteen days before Katrina

The next morning Ruthy Mae pounded at Sissy's door. "Come on. Your grandma wants you," she said.

Sissy pulled the pillow over her head. While sleeping, she was developing some plan for herself, which she had just lost.

Ruthy Mae came in with a tray of grits, eggs, biscuits, bacon, and juice. "Your grandma say, 'Eat well. It just takes a little more energy and a little more money.'"

Minutes later Ruthy Mae put Sissy in the Cadillac, which was parked by a marble nymph in the garden. The car was stifling. You couldn't touch the sizzling steering wheel till the air ran for ten minutes. Inside, the sense of huge space and isolation defined the car.

Grandma got in, her face colorless from the short walk from the house. Aunt Jasmine jolted up the engine. She looked tired and lonely.

"I hate women drivers," Grandma said, "and Jasmine's the worst. But, you can't find a chauffeur in Mississippi unless you hire an immigrant, and they don't know where they're going."

"You're such a bigot," Jasmine said.

"You used to be so good-looking. Now, when I'm with you, there's just this scent."

"It's Opium!" Jasmine said.

Sissy stared at the sky, which darkened over the treetops. She hoped Grandma wasn't falling into that lying quarrelsome self-centered state she got into when she was frightened. Aunt Jasmine spun through the grounds, through dying summer grass. Global warming and rising labor costs made it hard to keep everything

watered.   The heat had hit the azaleas. Broken edges frayed the
bushes and blossoms collapsed in the wind.

"Slow down," Grandma said. "I want you to appreciate the
land I've given Blaise." *Lord, had Grandma handed Serenity over
to Uncle already?* "The cathedral-high pines and glamorous oaks.
That cypress and tupelo swamp."

Sissy shot the window up and down. "You talk like we don't
live here."

"What has gotten into you, child?" Grandma said. "If Jasmine
loves the land so much, she can go buy some. Plenty of mansions
are for sale."

Aunt Jasmine turned the car sharply, almost hitting the sea
wall. She zoomed ahead.

Grandma flicked on a raunchy tune. "That music's from
Jasmine's film *Ravaged at Sea*," Grandma said. "Your grandpa
saw it four times."

Oh, no, it was going to be a punishment ride! Sissy hoped they
didn't crash. Accidental deaths were higher when drivers were
fighting.

If only Sissy could fly out into the plantations and tall oaks
they passed, low horizons, a dominance of vertical lines. She was
sick of family issues: how could she find herself and claim an
identity with relatives always on the attack?

Oh, there was the Biloxi lighthouse! A white tower standing
180 feet above pearly sand. Its role, to warn ships, was most
needed in August. Everyone feared a big hurricane would wipe
them out, and a few families with century-old mansions would
brag about how their houses had survived the storms. For many the
lighthouse was a sign of invincibility.

The Cadillac headed for the Biloxi Yacht Club, with its blue
roof and crimson accents around porch railings. Every town had a
yacht club: Pass Christian, Long Beach, Bay St. Louis, Gulfport,
and Biloxi.   Southerners named yachts for parties (*Jubilee*),
weather (*Rainbow*) and lost pets (*Winston*) and mostly their
daughters: *Gladysanna, Eleanor-Ann, Florette, Oopy, Anaise, Jo
Pepper*.

At Grandpa's slip, Jasmine and Grandma got out. Aunt
Jasmine looked back, wide terrified eyes piercing her porcelain

face. She followed Grandma down the yacht's brass-trimmed stairwell.

Sissy had to face Grandpa's empty yacht, the *Night Hawk,* by herself. Purple and brown water gnawed at the hull. Docked nearby were a rowboat and Blaise's slender sailfish. Light bounced into the bottom of the sail and shone through the jib.

Nearby masks and booms counterbalanced wide boats, their images spinning on the hot water. A frail sun lent a disembodied glow to the frenzied seagulls, the lapping currents, billowing sails and yachts like large-breasted birds folding their wings for the night.

There were so many conversations she wanted to have with Blaise, but for some reason she had been cut off. Sissy dialed Blaise's number, but suddenly she was sick to the stomach and barely made it to the bathroom downstairs; 1920 s style with gold fleur-de-lis, the room still smelled like Grandpa's Armani cologne.

Her eyes looked dark and shadowed as she pressed water to her face, exploring for new imperfections, recalling her mother's flawless skin. How long does a scent linger, after a person leaves? Mama's smell turned up in strange places—a hat in a closet, a robe on a hook.

Hearing voices, Sissy cracked the stateroom door. Grandma moved under stuffed predators mounted on the wall with a random terrified expression on her face. They seemed to stir in apprehension as the boat swayed. The shark gnashed its teeth, the owl widened its glassy eyes, and the deer bowed its antlers crested with Mardi Gras beads.

Grandma scrutinized a photo, a beaten look on her face.

"Photos of you and my husband," Grandma said, "after your last birthday. The big forty."

"Who took those?" Jasmine said. "A detective?" Jasmine tripped, almost falling into the green bedspread. The overhead light made her look jaundiced. "Have you been spying on me?"

"It was more like fishing . . . about you and Pete."

"Our relationship was of no importance," Jasmine said.

"When was this nude shot taken?"

Heat lines broke out on Jasmine's face. "Where did you . . . get that? He was old."

"Not too old to humiliate me," Grandma said. She snapped a DVD into a TV console.

On the screen, Jasmine lifted up her pink sweater. An imaginary friend appeared who unzipped his pants and showed himself! He cupped Jasmine's breast, ran his wet lips all over her. *Had Grandpa paid for that film?*

"They say you're looking for nine hundred thousand dollars," Grandma said, tersely.

"I'm his daughter, legally."

"We're in redneck country. No judge will give you a dime."

"I'm not like your limp-wristed kids. I know where I'm going so you can't cut my hands off." Jasmine lit up a cigarette with a contemptuous laugh. She loved holding on to things -- men, cups of coffee, Perrier -- just so long as that right hand wasn't empty.

"My attorneys are concerned about how much you skimmed off my husband."

"Gifts. We had one interest you never shared." Jasmine blew out smoke. "Sex."

"You think your little arrangement shocks me? I was married to Pete for forty years, and him to me for seven, but not consecutively."

"Sometimes your husband would ask me to sit on his lap. We never did it."

"How much will it take, Jasmine, for me to never see you again?"

"Just the insurance money willed me." Jasmine drew out yellowing papers.

Grandma whipped through the policy, tension darkening her face.

"Nine hundred thousand. That's all you got? Well, you'll have to subtract that from the money you owe me." Grandma pulled checks from a safe. "DeBango's compiled a list of your loans and charges to my husband's Visa. Some two million. I'm deducting that amount with fifteen percent interest from any insurance money willed you."

"You mean I'll get nothing."

"No, you could owe me money. Or, we could call it quits. It's your choice."

Jasmine's hands began to fidget.

"Fine, you can't destroy the policy. I'll do it for you." Grandma put a match to the paper and it burst into flames. Overhead, the deer peered down; a permanently bloodied tooth seemed to grow.

"All these years," Jasmine said, "I thought of you as my mother."

"You should have put some savings aside."

"I hoped one day you would love me, too."

Grandma focused on her watch. "I've got to provide for my retirement."

"Like when you built me that dollhouse that some hurricane blew down. Everyone said it was a poor investment because I'd outgrow it. But it was there, a miniature of your house with columns, a gallery, and shutters. Inside I had your China dolls . . . Kitten didn't want them. But I loved their glassy eyes and cold faces. I'd rock them for hours, pretending I was you."

"I don't remember any dollhouse," Grandma said.

"It was there."

"Nonsense."

"You built me a little house like yours with blue rugs and pictures. You went inside."

"I don't remember."

Sissy clutched the door so roughly the knob almost popped. *Oh God, Jasmine was evil but she was lonely. She needed to be touched and loved in the wrong way. And so did Grandpa. So they took love from dirty hands. Sissy and Jasmine were orphan sisters.*

CHAPTER 28

August 17, 2005
Twelve days before Katrina

On Wednesday at, eleven a.m., the sweltering heat continued, and Blaise returned to Serenity.

It'd been four days, and she hadn't seen or talked to him. Had he gotten sicker? Did he still care? She had been neatly cut out of the clique. She didn't quite know what she did wrong. What was she supposed to think?

She was relieved to know he was in the house, even if Serenity was experienced as a place that was draining her. They had to steal an hour here, a half hour there. She wanted more than a brief visit every afternoon and phone calls. Sissy needed him close beside her without a phantom third party. She had fewer skills in making friends. She was aware of her body, of the perspiration between her breasts when he appeared.

He lounged under an olive comforter, inside the gracious greenery and warm light of the tearoom, reading Pascal's *Pensees*, a volume he once said he wanted to know before he died. He played with a pencil drawing and erased something in the margin, mumbling strained words of affection. This was unusual behavior for Blaise who had always drawn in quiet. Light filtered through the leaves and branches around him. Seeing Sissy he put down the book.

"Come here," he said.

She was sweating and smiling. Sissy planted herself in a wicker chair, discomforted by the drizzle outside that dried up fast as it fell. August weather usually brought more rain. Anxiety about their love blossoming approached like a ghost ready to incarnate.

Did Blaise still care?

She liked the way his gaze slid down her body. She felt ravaged by his piercing eyes that had examined so many torsos, and even more so now that they had made love. Guilt crawled over her when she looked at him, and she became very aware of her fast breathing. *Why had he left suddenly? What was he thinking?*

Sissy remembered the glow that suffused Blaise's cheeks when they'd finally had each other. She had to understand what was going on. She ripped open a carton of Femina mints, flipped a caramel over her tongue, sitting back. The mint soured in her mouth. *Why had she shared her body with Blaise, this man whose almond eyes wanted to control her weirdly!*

Dad walked in, disturbing their privacy. Smartly attired in tan Armani, he whisked champagne from a chilled cabinet. Light reflected off the crystal glasses he poured. Dad did a little spin, handed Sissy a half-glass and settled in an armchair.

Her eyes retreated to the bright yellow rug and shiny green plants. Sissy picked at the enamel finish on her chair. How could practical Dad delight Blaise, who believed "the road of excess led to the palace of wisdom"? Blaise was intellectually more curious.

Alert and imaginative, Dad sat up in the chair. "I've got a reward from Irene for $12,000," he said. "Can you believe it? She turned in some stock and is giving each child and me a distribution. You can gift anyone $10,000 a year tax-free. The IRS. It's a fabulous thing!"

The men exchanged knowing looks and downed their champagne. Sissy was jealous of their friendship, now Dad had such a smooth relationship with Blaise.

"Sissy . . . Did Grandma give you money?" Dad said. "This is serious. If you got some, we need to put it aside for your college."

"I'll pay for Sissy's college," Blaise said.

"I'm not going," Sissy said.

"Don't count on your uncle's money," Dad said. "He's been seducing—girls—up and down the Gulf Coast. Someone may hit him with a paternity suit."

Sunlight wove in and out, brandishing Blaise in light. It fired Sissy's hatred, reminding her of how morbid he was. Maybe if she could detach herself from him, she'd have fewer fears and nightmares.

"Cheer up, Sissy," Dad said. "I'm taking you and Blaise to dinner at the best restaurant. You pick."

"No need," Blaise said. " 'Cause grief's made Ma generous."

Grandma had given Blaise the land after all.

"I should get an Oscar," Blaise said.

"What are you saying?" Sissy asked, her head whirling.

"You know Blaise has always loved to act," Dad said.

"A dying invalid! That was my part!" Blaise said. " 'Course as I failed, the role became more taxing. It's hard to decline into a corpse."

Sissy glanced at Blaise's slimy satin comforter. "You faked being ill!" she said.

"I followed Quint's instructions," Blaise said. "I'm turning Serenity over to your dad to keep for you."

Blaise handed Dad pages, detailing, no doubt, dimensions of property lines and plots.

"I can't believe this." Dad said, with a discriminating smile. "You're giving me the entire estate?"

"Just a dot on the map of Mississippi," Blaise said. "I'm trying to be as un-extravagant with extravagances as possible."

Dad had to control his rapture. It was perhaps the first time any family member had done something totally generous for him.

Blaise inhaled a cigar, his gaze coasting past a spurt of smoke toward Sissy. How could she ever talk with him again about anything--sex, love, and friendship, the meaning of life? Outside, the drizzle had stopped and the sky was hot. Crusty tree limbs reached for moisture through the parched air.

"You see that oak," Blaise said, lighting a cigar and pointing outside. "It's been here since the American Revolution. And that pecan tree? Dad used to say, 'Winter's not over until the pecan trees start to bud.' I enjoyed being a boy here. Fishing at dawn, hiking with a stick, chasing geese. But some gifts have strings. If I don't detach myself, it'd be too easy to revert."

Blaise smiled sheepishly.

Sissy's insides churned like that thick black cigar burning into a carcass. She didn't want to think about how Blaise's actions related to her.

"Don't be mad," Blaise said. "I'm doing this for your future."

"I don't want a future," Sissy said, turning away.

"No need to explain," Dad said. "She's a minor."

Oh, God, this wasn't happening. Sissy, who dreamed nightly of pressing her cheek against Blaise, she too, like Lily Bart and Emma Pontelieux, had been betrayed.

"How could I tend to real estate?"

"Your namesake did."

"Wealth like that doesn't exist anymore." The compound's founder, Robert Blaise, his great-great grandpa, was a prominent portrait painter worth millions.

Money took on an importance in Sissy's mind, and plans to live apart. She had to free herself from Blaise and her family to find her own independence. If not, she might turn into a rebellious, ugly creature, gossiping and knifing relatives.

Now that Dad had Serenity, would he take a deduction, and donate all to the Saint Vincent de Paul Society? What would become of Blaise's portrait, Mama's piano, and the gold ormolu clock? These mementos deserved a respectful burial. If not, Sissy might as well rush to the water like Virginia Woolf, Kate Chopin, or Ophelia.

Sissy confronted her father. When Mama comes back, what will she think?"

Ignoring her, Dad dialed his phone. "Quint speaking," he said. "Roy Fatswell? The Lone Ranger? Roy, I got the papers. For Serenity. Bring Silver on over. Let's get hitched." Dad put his hand over the phone and whispered, "Roy's loaded, but he never says much. You never know if he's a genius or a complete idiot."

Sissy left the tearoom, their voices getting paler as they receded.

If only her uncle hadn't meant what he'd done. Blaise had once saved Sissy from drowning, diving through freezing currents unraveling her from the sail of Dad's flipped sunfish.

Grief rushed over her. *Try to stop a surge thirty-five feet high. That's a good one.* If only Blaise would have given Mama Serenity. Maybe she could have saved it.

The afternoon caved in to heat, the lush vegetation shriveling as sunlight expanded, Sissy wrote in her journal: *This is how cancer begins! Too much inner turmoil. I need courage! I don't want to join the line of girls screwed by male relatives.*

CHAPTER 29

August 20, 2005
Nine days before Katrina

Sissy knew why Blaise refused to talk about the transfer. All his ancestors in Metairie Cemetery would rise up. The aboveground tombs would crack open, toppling angels, Christs crucified, tearful Madonnas. Ancestors were important. Their concepts had shaped her adult viewpoint. Weren't they significant to the governing group now, or would a new order of values take over?

Blaise had failed her, fooled her with his soft smile. So much even now depended on men, because women wanted it that way. Blaise took advantage of her attraction as Selden had with Lily Bart in *The House of Mirth*.

"How pathetic," Mama had said. "Selden liked Lily less because she liked him." Sissy grabbed her forehead. She had no buddies to give her support. All friendship was tied up in him. Even when he was gone she talked to Blaise inside herself. She had tried drugs, cigarettes, and alcohol but nothing lifted her soul like him.

If only Aunt Jasmine was here. But she had fled with her dog, to a lawyer's in New Orleans, saying she felt better with strangers than here.

At five the next morning, Sissy awoke with restless legs. She checked herself in the mirror, horrified her breasts seemed bigger than the week before. She walked down the gravel drive to the beach, more to murder thought than to birth it. She needed a mutually shared good relationship with someone. Drizzle seemed to be returning, but all it was, was steam.

No, she wouldn't let herself cry, even though she knew she was becoming more and more egocentric. The refrain "I must go down to the sea again, to the lonely waves, and the tides . . ." came to mind.   Maybe poems were written about water out of some desperate yearning for understanding.   The tide was out. Mustard foam bubbled over the shore like a fungus prodding Sissy to criticize her uncle, father, and grandmother, even her mother. A ways down a heron picked at a rough tree root.

Sissy took off her shoes and let the crusty water lick her toes.

If only Blaise would walk out on the beach.

For a second, she imagined her idealized love a pop star. Sissy recalled learning that Greek boys stayed with the women till they were ten, then went to the men's quarters to toughen up.

At least Mama's lover supported her.   Still, he'd swept her into an enchanted world from which she might never return.

Sissy should have gone with them, even if it meant nights next to their locked lovers' bedroom. Sissy missed Paris like a child, the City of Lights, with its Place de la Concorde, Rue de Rivoli. Surely it was those lights that made buildings look like castles in a pink sky.

Even Sissy's memories of traveling now seemed someone else's. She understood why Mama quoted Dylan Thomas, "Time held me green and dying."

* * *

That night, Sissy trailed Grandma through a burnished corridor, with copper paper, gold sconces, and elaborate carved moldings. Her grandmother's cheeks were freshly powdered; her Chanel shoulder bag, containing a pear-handled pistol, swung by her hip. One out of three New Orleans women carried guns because of the high crime rate.

Amber light shone off the aluminum foil on a dinner plate Grandma carried: crab soufflé, butter-loaded mashed potatoes, and mustard greens. How she spoiled Blaise was sickening, especially when he rarely ate her deliveries, even when genuinely hungry. Blaise could barely tolerate the connectedness.

The guest bedroom, where Dad and Blaise conferred, was done up in waxed mahogany and thick scarlet Orientals. Blaise ambled about the high-ceilinged room, suitable to a hot climate, in khaki slacks and a raw cotton shirt. Sissy's eyes ran over his detestable profile, his full shoulders, and his long sinewy arms. The sentimental erotic strain she hated in her mother had taken hold of her.

Sissy experienced a pain in her groin. Thank God she was better prepared for the onset of menstruation. Starting her period at fourteen had made her feel one step behind, specifically when Grandma was always announcing, "Twelve was the average age of menstruation." Today, her period was a welcome visitor.

Grandma eased the dish onto the mantel, which was black African marble with the head of John the Baptist framed above it. She waited for Dad to rise and give her a hug. She too liked cuddling by family.

But Dad just nodded at her from his throne like maroon leather chair. Light from a standing lamp shone on his face, covering a softness sometimes seen with his dog.

He licked froth off his champagne.

"I was saving that for my birthday!" Grandma said.

"Some hurricane is brewing but it is headed for Florida," she added, attempting to change the subject.

Dad curled back his cuffs, friendly yet distant. "Doc Boudreaux says Blaise's been playing possum," he said. "He's got an ancient disease: gout. Hippocrates had it in 500 B.C. These crystals cause lumps, which go away when treated."

Blaise squirmed. His lips seemed slimmer, his muscles, taut. *Had Blaise been lying to Sissy all along? Was his conscience hurting him?*

"I'm calling Blaise's doctor," Grandma said, dialing a phone. "Oh God! The line's busy. I'm a hostage of Gulf Coast Bell. Being around y'all -- my heart gives out. Seizures of the main artery!"

Grandma redialed the phone. "I want Doctor Amelia Boudreaux. It's a crisis about my son, Blaise Dubonnet." She covered the receiver and said, "Women doctors are tougher than men, and she's the toughest woman doctor I know."

Grandma spoke into the phone. "No, the responsible party is not my son-in-law, Quint. Why are you laughing? Gout? That's what those lumps were?"

"The disease of kings," Dad said.

God, Blaise had that sickness people got from overeating. He was a liar, a hedonist. And Sissy had thought he'd a greater emotional life than her.

Sissy's eyes darted to the balcony where Dad had stationed himself with celebratory fireworks. He hurled a skyrocket at a 300-year-old oak tree. Blaise joined him, and the two set fire to paper reptiles that ate themselves up while chasing smoke.

"Sissy. Come out," Blaise called, from the balcony. The spontaneity in his voice aroused her sexuality, or was it the anger, horseplay, fear, all of which were puzzling to her.

Blaise lit sparklers that knifed the air with silver streaks, and Dad threw them at the bullfrogs, which thrashed as fire shocked their scabby flesh. Dad and Blaise let out hoots.

"Don't do that," Sissy called out, with an angry gesture. "Even frogs have souls!"

Greta bolted in. She spotted the plate on the mantel, leaped up, and toppled it, slobbering greens and buttered biscuit with gusto. Grandma shrieked. Greta skidded to Sissy, crabmeat thick on her teeth, her big flanks trembling as cherry bombs exploded on the balcony.

Evading Greta, Sissy found herself walking toward Blaise, so full was she of disgust and determination to set him straight.

CHAPTER 30

Blaise glared at Sissy through dark, alluring eyes as she walked out on the balcony. How could he look at her like that now? She knew his positive and negative traits, but suddenly she felt he had gained weight, and his sweat glands were pouring. Was he trying to seize power over her?

Did he even care for her? The great expanse of not speaking became their relationship.

Moonlight created shadows through the oaks. Nearby, lightning bugs sizzled into a yellow floodlight and were incinerated into specks. She looked down at the husks. She should invest more time in her own mind and less in his!

There was something so spoiled about Blaise, his Duck Head slacks, his Burberry shirts.

Better to abandon your lover and keep your sanity. That's what the hero in *The Age of Innocence* did. Even when his beloved awaited him, Newland Archer never went up. Sissy recalled the sad ending of Wharton's book. "He sat for a long time on the bench in the thickening dusk ... then got up slowly and walked back alone to his hotel."

"You're angry?" Blaise said, forcing her attention.

"I didn't say that."

"What is wrong?" He touched her arm.

"Everything. You, mostly."

"Sissy, my brandy," Grandma called.

Her orders always felt like interference. Still, it was an excuse to duck inside. Sissy had borrowed her mother's submissive behavior she once criticized. She fondled her crusted pelican charm, recalling how Mom had said, "It's okay to have an ending to something we thought would go on for a long time." But had she meant an ending to family, to Sissy's love for Blaise?

Outside, Dad and Blaise whipped sparklers in arcs, spurred on
by mild exercise. Dad spelled out D-E-A-T-H and Blaise spelled
out J-O-K-E. Supplies exhausted, the men came inside. Sissy had
hoped for an apology from Blaise but all he wanted to do was horse
around.

Dad headed for the bar, originally a French mahogany writing
table with Egyptian decoration dipped in gold. He poured a crème
de menthe, sucked the swizzle stick. For the first time he acted as
if his money would last and he wouldn't always be broke. His
humor was crisp.

"Sissy, how many times did you flunk out of school?" he said.

"Four, five, if you count kindergarten."

"This is losers' paradise," Dad said. "Jasmine's a 'hand
model.' Blaise's a hypochondriac. And I'm a hack. Last week, I
overdosed on Quaaludes."

"What?" Sissy said.

"But Blaise kept me going."

"How! God!" Sissy said.

"We boys concocted this plan."

Sissy's eyes raced about. Her brain went into physical and
emotional withdrawal.

"How badly hooked on drugs are you, Dad?"

"Remember Blaise used to be president of the thespian
society?" Dad said. "Well, we bleached his skin, shadowed his
eyes, and smeared ash on his cheeks."

*Oh God. Blaise had faked being sick! Wasn't anybody in the
family ethical, concerned with right and wrong?*

"Sissy, did you know this?" Grandma said, embarrassed. She
scrutinized Sissy's outer, then her inner self.

"Leave Sissy out," Blaise said. "It was done for her, but no
matter."

Dad pulled out stained sheets and bloody bandages from a
camphor-lined trunk. "It was a stellar performance," he said.
"Blaise practiced moaning and gasping. Antiseptic scents and
Preparation H made that pus smell."

Lamplight reflected an oily glow off Dad's face. "The
hospitals' diagnoses were sent to me," he said. "A cooperative
party—whom we shall call 'ghost doctor'--wrote the ones you got.

It's a technique, an over reaction. A doctor can make a patient's condition look a lot worse than it is, or a lot better. To have the right ammunition, they run a page of tests, use whatever results they want. Now when you ordered that second opinion from Sloan Kettering, that was tricky. We had to work quickly to find a 'ghost' who would write diagnostic reports that matched our profile. But there are so many cancer patients today."

"You will be sued," Grandma said.

"Aw," he said. "Even top-notch institutions are likely to slip, write inaccurate reports, and get confused."

"What about Dr. Boudreau?" Grandma said.

"She reads the reports. She doesn't know the names of patients. She doesn't know anybody. She spends her time before the computer and reading the doctors' diagnoses. She never answers the phone. Now if you had spoken to the nurses, you might have gotten somewhere, but then again I wagered you wouldn't deem them worthy of your time."

"This is preposterous," Grandma said.

"This is business," Dad replied. "All over the world, there are 'ghost doctors' who take bribes. A lot of mothers want to have their children ill so they can take care of them. No one got hurt. We had a happy ending. Yes. Our one-man show is concluding with rave notices."

Grandma sat rod like, her bones leathery tight. She fumbled with her diamond pin, bought last summer at Adler's half price sale in New Orleans. Her solution was to ignore them all, till she found some way to counterattack. When nervous, she was extremely sophisticated. "My father had his first stroke at forty-seven. So I don't approve of games by a sickbed."

"I did it for Sissy," Blaise mumbled, accepting blame.

What hog rot! How could Blaise's betrayal be for her? Sissy spiked her Coke. If only she could cool down, because, God, she wanted to kill somebody.

Enterprising, Blaise was figuring out a way to her. "Talk to me a minute," he said.   Sissy looked across the darkening room, deep purple creeping up the marble furnishings and fabrics, the Sheraton field bed, the eighteenth-century chest of drawers, the ormolu clock. *Oh, Lord. Don't let her be snapped up in his hypnotic excuses.*

The alcohol Sissy had drunk shot up to her head, spinning to a quick lightness. Did all girls-in-love feel stuck in dualisms between forward and reverse? Mom said the third thing was the most important. But what was that?

Blaise led her to the balcony, where locusts wailed. A barely perceptible foghorn echoed through the oaks, firing Dad with energy. Greta barked, and Dad whistled, "Off We Go into the Wild Blue Yonder," joining Sissy and Blaise.

"Can it be true?" Dad said. "After refinancing already refinanced loans, we're going to finally bail out?"

Across the distant water, Sissy glimpsed a phantom white hull. Moonlight dramatized the height of the ship. Dad seemed so comfortable looking at that boat. His boyhood dreams of ships, equipment, and periscopes that go up and down were finally coming true. Sissy wished she could have liked him. Until her parents' separation, she had joked with him sometimes.

The phone rang sharp and hard. Blaise left with a hangdog look, and Dad ordered Sissy to get the phone.

CHAPTER 31

Dad sat on a rare serpentine-back Windsor chair and sent Sissy a Chicklet smile. He had always dreamed of being a success at real estate and getting the attention he craved from Grandma. Grandma looked concerned. She cringed in the glow of a lion's head lamp with a red silk shade. Her butterball diamond flickered in the light.

"It's a Mr. Fatswell," Sissy said, passing the phone to Dad. "The one Grandma says sounds like a snake oil salesman."

"Yes, well. When you see a turtle on a post," Dad said, "you know some snake helped him get there." Dad took the receiver, unsnapped the white collar of his blue striped shirt, and looked about as if enjoying the room. "Hi-ho Silver. You want Serenity? Well, you've got plenty of money, Fatswell. You've just got to turn it loose ..."

Grandma toyed with a hand-carved statue of the Virgin from Paraguay, salvaged from the 1947 hurricane and placed nearby.

"No, my family is thrilled with the refinery idea," Dad said.

"Refinery?" Grandma said. All she could manage was a one-word comment.

"We'd need twenty-five. . .   Twenty-three mill. If you throw in your yacht."

"Why lead on these fool prospectors?" she said. Even when angry, Grandma would rather argue with Dad than sit alone. "These beach houses were designed for leisure, for people who like gardens and naps after dinner. You're drunk with debt."

"No, I'm drunk with life," Dad said. "I'm officially cutting the cord. Snip."

"The bank must have refinanced another loan. I don't have one note on any of my property. Don't come to me when you overextend yourself."

"The *grande famille* doesn't exist anymore," Dad said. "Soon these beach houses will be chopped up into one-room condos so somebody like you can get rich."

"Oh no," Sissy said. "You can't let that happen. I love this house and the grounds. You can't cut it all up."

"What about your daughter?" Grandma said. "She wants her children to live here."

"Sissy can go to an American school in Tijuana. I'll buy Blaise an art gallery there. He won't have to pawn his youth for a little 'blood money.' Even a mildly successful life in Mexico is better than the status quo here."

"I've already lived," Sissy said. "What else can I do, Dad?"

"Sunbathe on the Riviera. Cruise to Greece."

"Who's going to do business with a CPA who's one step ahead of the sheriff?" Grandma asked. Her pale worried eyes glazed over.

"You can't make a living in oil," Dad said, "but you can occasionally make a killing."

He went to the doorway, gesturing upstairs to where the finest furniture was placed to save it from hurricane flooding. "Imagine yourself," Dad said, "walking inside a painting, this house, that Gulf. Underneath is a money machine spewing oil."

"Preposterous," Grandma said. "Any oil would have gushed into our well."

"That's not what Roy thinks."

"Roy?"

"Roy, who wants to construct an oil complex, storage tanks for holding and housing for the workers. His rigs are way out there, in the Gulf. Now he wants to drill on shore. Who else has a tract this big in Pass Christian?"

"He's not going to ruin my land."

"Blaise's assigned Serenity over to me."

"He did what!" Grandma shoved back in her chair. Panic blurred her face; her hand clutching the statue trembled and went to her chest. Her solution was to punish them all, especially herself. Heart failure was an effective self-affliction.

Sissy's eyes watered. She couldn't breathe. "Yes, it's true. Serenity isn't yours, Grandma. But Dad wouldn't sell the house?"

Dad turned. "I'm holding everything in usufruct for Sissy," Dad said, picking up a paperweight and inspecting a hunting scene. He genuinely liked his daughter; it was just that money had his greater devotion.

Spurts of blood attacked Sissy's brain.

"You want to play hardball?" Grandma went on. "I'm on the board of every bank in Mississippi."

"Yes. But Blaise's given the rear land to me. And I've sold it to the snake oil salesman."

"Oil field trash," Grandma said.

"From Odessa, Texas," Dad said. "They put their pants on one leg at a time like we do."

Sissy guzzled some Coke down a parched throat. *Oh God, Dad, say something to make this pain go away.*

Sissy willed herself to change the rhythms in her head, open her eyes, glide over the hardwood floors to confront Dad, then Blaise. She thought she and her uncle had been so close.

Her dad seemed comfortable doing things totally hostile, even in a family group. Did he never think globally about world issues, like hunger, peace? Sissy figured her dad couldn't concentrate on anything but his own concerns. That analysis was true but not complete. He often prioritized the needs of his women.

A full moon brought out Dad's shape in vivid form. He had put on a khaki jacket. His eyes glinted under fierce brows. "I remember the parties we attended at Serenity," he said. "I actually liked the house boat week-ends more than your mother did . . . Don't be angry, Sissy."

"I'm not angry. I'm in a rage!" Sissy said. "Habitats are vanishing with all the offshore drilling. Lost heron swoop in the yard. Y'all must do something to save the land!"

"We'll hide construction behind palm trees, like in Beverly Hills," Dad said.

"Where will the heron go, Dad?" Sissy said.

"To Heron-ville." He chuckled. "I've developed a network of people to . . . uh . . . uh . . . act as our sounding boards, so . . . uh. No creature will be hurt. The oil company's donating millions to preserve sea life."

Grandma leaned back in her chair by a wicker pram, an heirloom from 1920. "Greed like yours is polluting the South," she said. "There is that preservation bill."

"Which will be reversed," Dad said.

"You can't . . . build more oil wells. It's illegal," Grandma said. "Immoral. You'll get nowhere. My family owns this town."

"Politics is a gangster's business, not a gentleman's profession. The South is run by bitty politicians with little bitty men's hang-ups. They will take my money."

He pointed across the moonlit lawn, past the oaks, pines, and laurels to a yacht, its slick hull glowing like a space ship. "Fatswell's taking the presidents of Hancock Bank in Gulfport and the Whitney in New Orleans to a very rich lunch. You get my picture. They'll be handing out a lot more than food." Dad waved an imaginary envelope of money. "I'm moving to Florida."

"Florida isn't the South!" Grandma said, rising. "It's lower Manhattan . . . Can't you wait?"

"Next week, we'll be on an international flight." Dad said. The overwhelming majority of his friends used drugs, alcohol, or cigarettes, so he felt his penchant for deluxe travel wasn't serious.

Dad walked over to the gracious French window as if trying to hold on to his perspective that he was doing the right thing. A strained relationship had developed, and while he still wanted to talk to everybody, it was easier to leave.

Sissy's eyes darted from him to Grandma, standing tall on her one-hundred-year- old Chinese rug before a watercolor by her great-great-grandfather, who originally purchased the land. She tried to speak, but the experience of being inadequate claimed her flesh.

"Get my heart pills," she said, her face ghostly, her eyes shriveled. "Downstairs. In my tan purse."

Scrambling to the day room, Sissy shoved back the Tulane rocker, tore apart the sofa, and retrieved the purse.

When she returned, Grandma was limp and barely breathed.

Oh God. The only solid person in Sissy's life was slipping away. And where was Blaise, wanting his freedom, eager to go?

Sissy pushed the nitroglycerine into Grandma's mouth. The pill fell. Sissy dropped to her knees, searching about.

Dear God, don't let Grandma die!

* * *

Doctors bedded Grandma, lowered the thermostat, and said it was heat stroke. That week a scorching sun baked the beach. The Coast Guard picked up bathers passed out from too much sun. Grandma wanted Sissy by her always, but when she was, Grandma demanded everything, appreciated little, and got insulted easily.

Sissy's nights were restless, full of nightmares of Blaise in which she was sexually active to varying degrees. She avoided him, though she had more desire to talk to him than ever before. She found sanity in foolish things such as phoning him and hanging up before he took the call. "I'd rather die than touch him ever again," she swore.

CHAPTER 32

Three days before Katrina

On Friday, two days before Sissy's birthday, the family ignored Hurricane Katrina warnings. Storm threats had multiplied each summer. Sissy walked to the cottage, appreciating its lush walls of West Indian coral and Spanish tile roof that had been that way for years. There, Mama's presence was the strongest.

Near the parched trees, locusts scraped their limbs, crickets squawked, a frog growled. Still, she thought in all that confusion, more things are alive than dead. The wrap around porch, shielded by pine trees, glowed under an orange moon.

Where was Mama? True, she hadn't left Sissy, she'd left Dad. But she wasn't here, was she?

An aroma of beeswax softened the waiting furniture, seashells, and patchwork cushions, and Sissy was stunned to see her aunt. Her polished flesh glistened in the moonlight, in clothes so tight fitting she appeared naked. Jasmine lit a vigil light, which stirred in the rough Gulf breeze. She acted as if Sissy had become very significant to her, and she looked for things to say to her.

Brahms's *Symphony No. 1* played on the stereo. "It's left over from your mama," Jasmine said. "Bit heavy. Still, it breaks the quiet. I live by candlelight," Jasmine said. "It's the only way to look good after forty. Don' tell anyone I'm older than thirty-five or I'll swear you lied. At thirty-six, Marilyn Monroe died, Marlene Dietrich retired. 'Course with plastic surgery, our generation doesn't have to grow old."

"I'm sorry. You didn't get your insurance pledge."

Jasmine waved toward the big house, its rust brick framed by trees. Her emotions were more brittle now she'd been lampooned. "Mama Dubonnet needs someone to hate," she said. "The day we met—she made me use the servant's entrance. The bitch. Anyway, I'm leaving tomorrow."

"Oh, Jasmine. Take me with you? I've three thousand dollars and Grandma's Visa. Everyone famous lives in Los Angeles."

Sissy silently begged to die every day if she stayed.

Rigid and confused, Jasmine changed the subject. "Look at that? My nails are breaking. When I'm bored, I pick them too much. Are you ready for this? That actor . . . I sublet to . . . set fire to the kitchen. So, I've no damn place to live. I may need to crawl to my agent's house and kiss up to the son of a bitch. Oh damn it, give me a cigarette." Lighting up from a candle, Jasmine dragged deep. "My agent is a jackass. He does absolutely nothing. Damn all agents."

"I could cheer you. You and I are alike."

"What do you mean?" Jasmine said, startled.

"We could form a shame group. You could shame me into studying, and I could shame you into getting good roles."

"My agent says I need a face-lift . . . And new photos. The man spews insults. I should tell him to take off his tight-fitting pants and go to the gym. My life is a catastrophe. My therapist says that's a sign the worst is over."

Sissy turned on a side light, powdered Jasmine's swollen face, and lined Jasmine's eyes with midnight blue.

"I hope you'll forgive me," Jasmine said. "I'm leaving before your birthday. This year it will be too hard. I know your mother has something special to send to you."

"Oh please."

"I guess I'm not breaking any rules by telling you she and I were pregnant at the same time. In Paris."

"My, I never knew."

"I don't like to talk about it. Makes me cry."

"Why in Paris?"

"My lover was an actor. Your dad was working at that French bank. Kitten and I were due at the same time. So we got adjacent rooms at the same hospital. Wasn't that something."

"Mama never told me about this."

"She promised not to because . . . I lost my baby. When I see you I think of the little girl I might have had. My girl only lived a short while. Something wrong with the spinal cord or the neck. I was going to give her up anyway but she left me first. I can't face your birthday this year."

"What does that mean?" Sissy said.

"I just can't do it, that's all. Be the person this family wants me to be."

Jasmine now joined Blaise as an object of criticism. Sissy's relatives simply couldn't prioritize her. Sissy was becoming more secure about freeing herself from all her past.

Outside, wind chimes flickered in the shadowy trees, a lost edge to their ring followed by a crackling sound.

It was Dad carrying a lantern. He howled when a hanging caterpillar bag hit him in the face. "Why can't they torch those damn bugs? Whenever there's a squall, fool bags fall everywhere." He stomped inside, brushing his shoulder.

Sissy turned, gazing outside through the brisk-smelling pines and the dewy roses struggling to breathe. Splotches of moonlight hit the lustrous parapet, poised on light-drenched brick.

Sissy needed to see the reason for her dad's changed rules. He loved glamour, and he had hoped one day their family would retire to Serenity. Now was he just going to strike it down?

Dad glared at Sissy and wiped his brow with his monogrammed handkerchief. His inadequacy was visible for all to see.

"You're dallying with danger," Sissy said.

"Just put on my tombstone 'He was fearless,' " he said. He headed for the master bedroom, with its furniture all hand-painted in a matching flower motif.

Sissy pursued him, smashing her heels on the floor.

"You're a traitor! I can't believe you've sold Serenity. I'm writing down everything before it goes."

Dad said. "This is the information age. Careers, not family, dictate where you live. This compound living in Serenity seems odd."

"Not so, Dad. It's unusual but . . . wonderful to settle down in the same place where you grew up."

"There's a closeness, a special connection to history and your people," Jasmine said.

"Don't start that holier-than-thou stuff with me. I can't save Serenity alone. The other relatives have left . . . there is no telling where your mother is. I've reserved use of the entire grounds twice a year for entertaining."

"Who wants to party around an oil rig?" Sissy said.

"Me!" Dad cried.

"You're callous," Sissy said.

"Repulsive," Jasmine added.

"Y'all don't have the guts to stand up to the old lady, so I do it for you. It's not yours, girls. No one gave Serenity to you. This place was meant for the family sons. I got it because the last son didn't care."

"If only I could never see you again," Sissy said.

"Y'all were raised to think you were owed land and service by birthright," Dad said, "this plantation mentality."

"You're so mean," Sissy said, plopping on her mom's white crocheted bedspread. Swirls of ivory fabric punctuated dark scrolls of cream.

Dad tossed shirts—cotton stripes, starched whites—and an alligator belt in a suitcase. He buttoned on a taupe linen blazer, and brushed a smile at the Victorian mirror. He looked at Sissy in a significant way as if searching for something to say.

Sitting by her, Aunt Jasmine stroked Mama's bedspread, imitating her mother's mannerisms.

Sissy looked at her hand, and saw Mama's. *Her dear sweet Mama, who had worked so hard to love Dad—never saying a word about her in-laws, or his indiscretions. She kept up her looks, her interests, and lowered her expectations. She spoke softly, and kept things the way he wanted them even when he never came home.*

Dad's cell phone rang. For a second, Sissy hoped he would change his mind, but most of his physical preparation had taken place. He hurried his suitcase to the porch, the candle almost gone out.

"Fatswell is docking at Pass Christian Harbor," Dad said.

"You just going to leave?" Sissy asked, her voice thick.

"Screwing your family has repercussions," Jasmine said.

Dad let out a slow breath. "The Gulf South is an oil-based, below-the-land economy. That's reality, girls. Once news of oil hits, these houses will be nothing but shells."

Sissy went from unself-conscious to brash. "We can't let that happen, Dad."

"Come with me, girls!"

Was he feigning love, knowing the best way to avoid it was to ask for it. Or maybe he was experimenting, asking them to go. Dad liked to get away with things, and he needed an audience.

Sissy stepped about the porch, hoping the mother smells and objects there would tell her what to do. She had always listened to her mother better than her father. Some said Sissy looked more like Jasmine than either parent.

Jasmine took Dad's arm with girlish tenderness. Suddenly she became very important to him, as if he was looking for something long-term. Dad identified with Jasmine, her boldness, facing Grandma's belittlements. "Marry me, Jazz," he said, with a wink.

Jasmine looked at Sissy tenderly, trying to evaluate what the girl would do. "You're not even divorced," Jasmine said.

Dad straightened his jacket. He was so particular about his clothes. "It's just a phone call away. I don't date the women I love. I marry them ... And there is such a thing as abandonment. Hell, if Sissy were younger I could probably get child support."

Some disturbance occurred in his face, and Sissy knew their father-daughter relationship would soon end.

"Buy me a big diamond, won't you?" Jasmine said. "What's the biggest they make? Thirty karats?"

"You'll soar past forty," he said, embracing her, "with more diamonds than Liz Taylor."

Sissy was no longer rebellious and critical as Jasmine fell into his arms.

"Sissy sandwich," Jasmine said, squashing the girl between her and Quint.

Sissy felt safe inside a couple hug. Even if one left, maybe the other would stay. But what if each became half a person?

"Won't you come with us?" Jasmine said. "You said you had to get out of here."

"We'll phone you," Quint said. He searched about awkwardly for something to do, finally giving Sissy a hundred dollars. Perplexed, the couple backed off, letting in the scent of honeysuckle as they shut the screen door.

Sissy's chest clamped down. She wiped her hand on her clothes, blindly discarding the sweet aroma. Dad and Aunt Jasmine were leaving Serenity. Like mourners at a grave site, they were running before the casket plunged. Sissy imagined Serenity gone: the grounds stripped, vultures the size of three-year-olds perching on metal rigs, swooping out to rip off a robin's wing, suck open a rabbit's throat.

Like Lily Bart in *The House of Mirth*, there was to be no comfort for Sissy.

Lily had no heart to lean on. Her relationship with her aunt was as superficial as that of chance lodgers who pass on the stairs. What Lily craved was the darkness made by enfolding arms, the silence which is not solitude but compassion holding its breath.

CHAPTER 33

The candles went out in the cottage and only moonlight streaked the porch. Sissy felt she was being smothered by the diffuse glow. Sissy had to learn to be more self-sufficient, now her loved ones were for the most part dead. She went for her diary. If she could keep pencil to paper, she could focus her thoughts. Outside it was mud black, the air so thick and sour, it silenced the katydids and terminated some part of her heart. Humidity singed her face, skin, eyelids, all bleeding for the past, for continuity, for the same faces. Despite her bravado, she was afraid of experimentation, of new limits.

Sissy wondered what treacherous activities Blaise was involved in, now that he had betrayed the land. Was he hanging out in troubled waters after curfew, or spray-painting strange herons on garbage cans? If only Sissy could seize her real identity and clear herself from Blaise. But only a small percentage of women in her family had ever made a self-driven detached choice.

Sissy heard footsteps through the grounds and the old weathered screen door swing open.

Oh God, not Blaise.

"I need to speak with you," he said, unzipping his jacket and sticking his hands into his slant pockets. He wore fitted jeans, which shaped and flattered his strong legs.

"If I talk, I'll curse," she said.

"That's not like you."

Her eyes took in his brown ones, the smooth tanned throat. Sissy's legs threatened to give way, her ears and her heart screamed. She wanted to forget every detail of his face and body. *Oh, let her hurt him.* Soon only the bleak moon would remain, taunting her to love him, no matter what his excuse. She could justify it, find a therapist who would applaud her daring.

If Mama were here she'd tell her to behave. It wasn't good to love anyone too much, for they'd certainly depart, either emotionally or physically. One crash, one fever, one divorce and your darling was gone. She read about a widow who loved a poet so much she exhumed his body to retrieve a poem from his pocket, a paper already thick with body fluids.

"You know you are my first serious romance," Blaise said. "I have not been experimenting with you. Everything I've done or felt has been true. But I need to become a more clearly defined person if I'm to mean anything to you. The conflict was separating from Ma and Serenity, never from you." He looked at her through sensuously soft eyes.

Sissy lit a candle of lavender oil. A mauve shadow glistened down her fingers. "I'm going with your father," Blaise said. *Down, her heart plunged.* "It's temporary but you must come too. There's a storm coming," Blaise said.

"Back up! You're doing what?"

"Painting the wildlife here is like killing someone. Creatures are all gummed up, molted. How can I have them remembered that way? When I draw them, I feel I'm failing an examination. One heron shriveled up by a pond where twenty used to play."

"Still," Sissy said, "I thought you wouldn't throw in our history."

Blaise tried to take her hand. "I feel awful about the sale," he said.

"You're only concerned about what you want for yourself."

"Sometimes your father seems like such a good person. Quint said he'd hold the land in trust for you."

"You believed that?" Sissy said.

"I was duped! Look: the tropical paradise we knew is gone. No one can find the money to fix it. Coastlands have eroded. Marshes are compromised. . . . I paint the remains and hope the universe will repay me for being a tireless recorder."

"So you can't create here?"

"Right. I could only stay here as an activist."

"So do that!"

"I'm an artist."

"You're selfish."

"No. Realistic. What little talent I have comes from work. If I don't paint mercilessly fifteen hours a day, I might as well quit."

"You exaggerate."

"Only the viewer enjoys art. I'm in a profession where he who suffers the most wins. John Sargent made some of his portrait clients sit eighty three times. The competition is fierce. Three thousand paintings rejected for every one hung. If you're not declared a genius, you die unknown."

"So you're leaving Serenity."

"Just for a while. I need to get a perspective on things. Travel will be a distraction. A pleasant narcotic—Mexicans worship artists. When you arrive, it's like Noah has landed his ark."

"So your career is your major concern."

"I must leave for another reason," Blaise said.

He looked at her and she felt like she was nude in public.

"I can't spend my life waiting for you."

"What are you talking about?" Sissy said. "Here's your cell phone. You never call."

"I can't. It's too painful."

"Blaise . . . I can't act . . . like you've done nothing wrong."

"I've been a jackass. In the hospital . . . I thought of you . . . and decided my confusion was a punishment."

"Don't say that."

Blaise touched Sissy's chin with an effortless stroke. The blue-toned ash light sculpted his cheek.

She turned away from the face she'd come to hate.

"I wanted to tell you everything," he said. "But I was afraid to – I yearned for you. But you didn't know. Why are you—?"

"Shivering . . ? I'm crying for Mama . . . who used to protect me . . . for Daddy and Jasmine, whom I don't trust, and Grandma, who acts so bad--"

"Is that all?"

"And . . . for all the things I want to tell you but can't."

She went for a walk, skirting patches of grass, where crawfish lay in wait under tall brown holes. Wind lapped impatiently through the grounds. A fierce moon glowed down on the John Darling oak. Could she die of love? "Men have died and worms have eaten them, but not for love," was Mama's favorite quote.

Hadn't Juliet killed herself for Romeo? "For never was there a story of greater woe, than the story of Juliet and her Romeo."

Blaise followed her, talked about being locked up when he didn't paint, his sense that his mission was to capture wildlife, but now he felt he was painting in a mortuary. Blaise said change makes individuals receptive to new people and ideas, and that's what he needed to heal and grow.

He had this instinct that, like Gauguin, he must go to a tropical place to heal, to experiment and claim a new life. To define himself as an artist, he had to move in the direction of a simpler lifestyle. Money would make Blaise more self-sufficient to do that.

Sissy had figured out some of it, but discussing the sale of Serenity wasn't information she could handle.

On leaving, Blaise wished her happy birthday two days early, said he would always be there for her, and added that some news she might hear from her mother would liberate her too. Sissy broke out in a sweat, wiping her lip nervously. *What was this birthday secret so guiltily alluded to?*

CHAPTER 34

Two days before Katrina

Saturday evening Sissy found Grandma on the balcony in sickroom attire of pink lace, a plunging neckline with sash-tie back. She wore the sheerest lingerie even outdoors. Flannel nightgowns were always a horror because she feared that in a hurricane the police wouldn't see her in her best. She toyed with his hair caught in a silk ribbon at her neck. She had learned not only was Quint sleeping with Jasmine but he was actually marrying her and reversing the hierarchy of Serenity.

Grandma made preliminary steps into a discussion of their departure by using the hurricane for an excuse. Old family traditions were vanishing, and she looked perplexed. "They say a storm's headed this way," she said. "Carrina or Katrina. Hope it turns for Florida." There was heaviness to her rich movements as she laid gold-rimmed cards for Solitaire. "Now I haven't a single trump card left except privilege."

Grandma glanced inside; noticing Jasmine had left a pair of jeweled high-heel slides with imported satin uppers, 3 ½-inch heels, and rhinestone medallions, probably worth a fortune. "Your dad and aunt are spoiled," she said, "so they'll be back." She stuffed a jack under a queen of hearts. "Once everyone wanted a home in Pass Christian," she said. "This was a place to be *from*."

An unexpected star bounced on the blue horizon. "Temporary stars destroy themselves in one explosion," Sissy said, changing the subject.

Grandma looked up, very concerned about her relationship with Sissy. "I belong to that rare breed of Southern women, going extinct," she said, "who dedicate their lives to finding rich husbands and having children. At seventeen, I attended noon Mass at the cathedral so wealthy bachelors would see me. Never wearing the same dress twice. At twenty, I married well, had two children, and decided I could either care for them, or I could cook and clean. And since I'd never cooked or cleaned, I devoted my life to them. Harmony, that's all I'm after. Peace in the family. Dissension jeopardizes the simplest things: a lovely dinner, an evening stroll. What is life but a chain of little pleasures? Breakfast in bed, fresh cut flowers, and fireworks on the Fourth of July?

"We've everything you'd want on the Gulf Coast," she continued. "Passion for us is having an affair with your eyes. Where else can you grow such glorious hydrangeas and hear a calliope from the church fair? I wouldn't live any place you couldn't hear the waves slapping the beach; see the shadows from the oak trees; where it is never too early or too late to have mint juleps on the veranda."

"The house feels empty," Sissy said.

Blaise appeared in a light jacket and tropical weight trousers. He plunked down his keys in an ashtray. Grandma adjusted the lingerie strap on her camisole.

His eyes, hard and pensive, reached for Sissy. The shimmer that originally caught her heart was no longer there. She dropped her eyes to his trousers just below the waist. She felt like the sweet lover of her dreams was dead.

He took out a cane with a pelican handle, and shuffled by her, his beautifully fitting long sleeves almost brushing her. She would remember the musk scent of his skin that she thought about at night when she dreamed herself to sleep.

He crossed one foot over the other, doing a soft-shoe and singing, "Give me the old soft-shoe and nothing else will do." He quoted Kierkegaard: "Don't finish with life until life is finished with you."

Sissy felt like her life was vanishing and there were no replacements for herself.

Everything was happening too fast. She was young. They hadn't really talked. The weather was getting wild. Wind warmed the air like some villain was approaching.

Then, Blaise brushed off his slim trousers that gave the appearance of legs that went on for miles. Certainly Blaise couldn't be leaving, because he was too ill.

"Blaise, you're such a ham," Grandma said. "You should join the St. Louis Cathedral Drama Society."

"I'd rather recuperate on that yacht." He studied Sissy for a second.

"Don't talk foolishness, son." Grandma loosened her three-quarter-length sleeves and flowing bodice. "My, it's humid and hot."

"Sissy should go with us to Mexico," Blaise said. "Travel is one way to learn."

"All animals can think," Grandma said. "What sets humans apart is our ability to deceive ourselves."

Blaise glanced down at some creamy blossoms in a pot on the balcony. "Water my plants, and feed the ducks."

A yellow SUV honked in the drive below, antique brass trim down its sleek sides. Moonlight gave it an illusionary quality. A touch of stretch made it seem oversized.

A hush punctuated Sissy's sobbing heart.

He gave a final lone wave, hesitating so strangely that even when he was gone, his distressed gaze lingered inside her. For a limited time only, Sissy might scream "Fire!" or call him back.

Sissy leaned over the balcony railing, its dark white paint sticking to her skin. She threw him his cell phone. She watched him stride over and get into the vehicle with some strange military-inspired walk. Her eyes drifted over the drive, bone dark and punctured with shells like her shattered heart. She tried to melt into the restless breeze that contained so much slate and purple. The van faded into dwindling orange taillights, heading toward the church steeple, copper, in the moonlight.

She wouldn't miss him, need to talk to him. God, her ears were burning. She felt like she'd been invited to a wake or a funeral but didn't know the person who had died.

Sissy remembered Blaise throwing his arms above her on the beach, the feel of his rough hands against her jacket, the double-breasted corporal coat he wore at Mardi Gras with its shoulder epaulets, button detail. There were so few things about him she could forget. The time he took her to her junior prom, when her date stood her up. Blaise wore a puff-sleeve tux shirt and told her, "You are an extraordinary woman, how do you expect an ordinary date?"

Grandma set up an elaborate game of Solitaire on a table on the balcony, predicting her future from what the cards implied. Her face looked as though she had been dead for a week.

Grandma would be with her, demanding care. But she wouldn't pry into Sissy's thoughts, crack her open like a clam and throw her out. Thank God the sensitive and stupid ones had left Serenity.

Sissy told herself it wouldn't be bad for long. She had survived her mother's leaving and Blaise's departure for the Philadelphia School of Art. Both had said they weren't coming back. They always returned, they just did. She sat by Grandma.

Wind slapped through trees, hurling twigs onto the gallery. Baby Katrina was growing.

CHAPTER 35

One and a half days before Katrina

Saturday night, Grandma led Sissy to the ballroom, where crystal chandeliers and gold sconces glowed brightly. But there was a lot of tension under the beauty, for the thick walls couldn't completely buffer the room from the storm building outside. Occasionally a light blinked and silver rattled on a tablecloth. Grandma had filled a handsome beverage bucket with ice and Sissy's favorite cold sodas. Peanut butter cookies were on the bottom tray.

Grandma lit a doberge cake, twelve chocolate crusty layers with a sugary inscription, "Happy Birthday, Sissy." Grandma always knew the cake, meal, drink, each relative preferred. How many centuries had women in her family been doing this?

Sissy remembered the great birthdays they used to have, replete with Shetland ponies, ballerinas, and fire-eating clowns. Blaise swinging her under the oak, lush grass blurring around her, and the day her mom left her dad's.

Mom would arrange to meet Sissy, having her to the bed and breakfast where she stayed and sneaking in to meet Sissy after school. Mama made several trips back home getting odds and ends, which she kept in a plastic bag in her car trunk. She moved from room to room in a bed and breakfast a friend owned and let her stay in cheap as long as she would take whatever quarters were unreserved. Now uncle, mother, father were all off traveling. Sissy blew out the eighteen candles.

Grandma grimly sliced cake, the chocolate shell cracking under her knife. She seemed too tired to notice wind shivering down the panes. Her face looked white, blue cold. She put the girl in a gold chair, handed her the cake, and drew a seat beside. She tried to listen and be patient, assuming a concerned facial expression, her spine lodged into the chair back.

Suddenly, Sissy missed Blaise, remembering how they used to swim in the gray brown water or play with an empty bucket with only a few catfish flopping. She was so bored and angry sitting with this cake, yellow candle stumps burned all around.

Her fork creaked, scratching the Lenox plate. "I can't eat," Sissy said.

"When home life is bad, people take it out on the person in charge."

"Remember when I went away to camp?" Sissy said. "You wrote me twice a day—"

"With a program for your career. You returned the letters—stamped 'addressee unknown.' The only way I knew you were alive was you kept cashing checks. It's not me you love, it's my function."

"That's not true," Sissy said. The hot salty air burned her cheek.

Grandma retrieved a packet of letters from her negligee pocket. They looked like they'd been opened many times, although she acted as if she'd just shoved them there. The parchment envelopes, embossed in blue were slit, head to tail.

Every day that went by, Grandma had thought of Mama as a corpse; that way her pain was less. Still, Sissy was shocked when Grandma said: "Letters from your mother." *Was it a total lie?* "And a birthday card, which I didn't open. She's pregnant."

Sissy could no longer speculate on reasons for her ma's behavior.

"Her prince errant has an heir," Grandma said.

"You read my mail," Sissy said.

"I'm trying to protect you."

"No you're not. You say awful things," Sissy said. "You make me feel terrible."

"I didn't leave."

Sissy opened her mother's card with difficulty. The back was taped and sealed shut with a note: "Private Material. Read and you will be sued." *Was this the secret Blaise had alluded to?*

Dearest Sis, I promised Jasmine on your eighteenth birthday to tell you—a secret only Blaise, she, and I know, bloodline being so important to Southerners. Jasmine and I both had babies the same day. I had been having trouble with my pregnancy. Her baby, you, was strong, mine died. So we switched babies. She buried my child and I raised hers. To me, you will always be mine. Destroy this letter as soon as you read it.

Love, Mama (Kitten)

PS Your father lost at sea was a sailor, Saul Reichlin.

Sissy stashed the letters in her backpack, fearing she would crack and fall on the ground. She grabbed the Derringer from Grandma's purse. She scratched the barrel, the size of a sparrow. Sissy pointed the gun at her temple, terror lifting her off the ground. "I'm living in some gray zone, Grandma. I have to hurt myself to get attention. Race a cycle down a silver cord. Flip from one trapeze to the next with a knife in my teeth. Here's to Dad, Mom . . . and Uncle Blaise."

"Don't shoot!"

"Our home life is hysterical. How long does it take for you to give me Mom's letters?"

"I didn't want to upset you . . . They're predicting a hurricane!"

"Don't you know I looked for those every day? Blaise leaves when I turn eighteen. And Dad . . . I've this pounding headache. I don't know where it's coming from." Sissy peered down the short barrel, hard-rock floor under her feet. Her lungs felt congested with mud and she wanted to vomit.

"Give me the gun," Grandma said.

"It's funny, but I can't recall Mom holding me as a child," Sissy said.

"I'm sure she did."

"Eighth grade graduation, everyone's parents took pictures and I was alone."

"Didn't Blaise fly home from art school?"

"My worst birthday was a third grade beach party."

"You got stung by a catfish."

"I cried all day 'cause I wanted Mom, but I blamed the catfish. I saw all these parents and mine were off."

"That's Southerners. We miss people we hate. This is your important day."

"At midnight, I'll be eighteen, but no one's here."

"We'll celebrate next week."

Sissy pushed back the safety catch. The gun creaked, clawing at her heart. With everyone gone she feared she would crack and topple to the ground, setting off the gun. She didn't want to go on alone, but she didn't want to bring her grandma down. "I feel like a jellyfish, flipping with no direction. Maybe I should move to Cozumel, work as a waiter, live at a hostel."

"You know nothing about hostels! You can't go out hawking yourself."

"I'll join the marines. I've got so much despair, it'll take boot camp to get it out. I want to go to dangerous places, where I have to defend things that feel right, even if I can't understand them. You'll never be far from me."

"I'm Old South. I'm seventy-one. We come on this earth for a short time, when you consider the centuries. We make a little tour and we're gone."

"I won't drop out of sight." Sissy put the gun to her nose, dust teasing her nostrils. Was this the only gun she would ever hold? Did she want to use this gun? It was this "I don't know, can't decide" path that made her lungs feel congested., made Sissy want to fall asleep and tumble off the chair of her long-gone ancestors. She yanked the pelican charm off her neck and threw it on the floor. Sissy didn't want to think about Blaise and Mama, that all along they knew she wasn't "blood."

"Stay till Katrina passes," Grandma said.

"There's this old anger I can't shake, because I trusted the wrong people. People who had power over me. Y'all told me things that aren't true. You made me feel nothing mattered except---."

"Put up the pistol! You expect too much. The only duty of a student is—"

"To learn well. I don't know how to gauge myself; I'm left with these false thoughts. . . I've too much of you inside and not enough of me. I'm not stable."

"I've been counting on you to lead this family," Grandma said. "You're our bright star."

Sissy hurried down the stair. Lush and full, its substantial railings once boasted garlands and flowers: poinsettias, magnolias, berries. Grandma followed, shoving Sissy an envelope. "Throw-away money. Talent doesn't pass from mother to daughter, but money does. The rewards here are fiduciary, not emotional."

Mother to daughter! Sissy couldn't even think about that.

"My favorite stimulus is panic," Sissy cried, tossing the bills. "Ta-DAH." She stood before the commode in the grand hall abundant with faux fruit and flowers in warm tones of bronze and burgundy. For a second she saw Mama in the Louis XVI mirror, and an ax struck her heart. Then Mama's face turned into Grandma's pale trembling one. Sissy whipped on her Tulane cap and locked eyes with all the tormented ancestors in the glass.

"I'd feel better if you'd leave the gun," Grandma said.

Sissy dropped the pistol into the Ming Dynasty bowl on the commode and looked up at the ornate gold leaf mirror that made such a grand statement, shining with light. She grabbed her backpack and denim jacket from the hall closet, and turned off the burglar alarm. Red dots like rat's eyes screamed the gates were unlocked.

With a full sweeping look, Grandma turned toward the day room. She scooped up a new box of magnolia-faced cards. Imperial as an iceberg, she slapped down a game of Solitaire, and smiled through pearly teeth. The cards were made of the finest quality non-color-fading paint, intricately detailed and constructed to shine year after year. Sissy yearned to run to Grandma, to hide in the predictable sameness of her ways.

"I'm not going . . . to stop . . . loving you, Grandma, because I'm away."

"Switch on all the lights and put the air conditioner on 'super cool.'"

Sissy hit the master switch and spun back the thermostat. "I thought you were saving money."

"For what?" Her expression fatigued, Grandma flawlessly coordinated the cards. "The queen of diamonds," she said. "Sometimes the queen must go into her tower and cry-- all great queens do. And sometimes she must say, 'Off with their heads!'"

Sissy heaved open the Palladian door and went out on the porch. Wind howled on all sides. She tripped on a tree in an urn flanking the doorway. The wind broke through other foliage before her. She trudged to the yard around grim pecans and angry bushes. Yard lights flashed on and off as she passed. Heat infested the mossy oaks.

At the dog pen, Sissy's steps activated the sensors, causing a change in ambient light. Her dog, Greta, reared up and turned her head, watching Sissy grooming her, petting her muzzle. "Bye," Sissy said, ruffling the dog's ears. Greta backed inside with a gentle gait, very obedient and serious as befitted a brave beast.

Sissy wandered by the mildewed fountain with its headless cherub, the result of a theft attempt. His opulent shape had been mounted on a pipe for durability. She hedged by the snake pit, crusted with marsh. Even in the heat of summer, a green, red, and gold botanical pattern brightened the black water. She breathed in the smell of wet leaves and earth.

At Scenic Drive, wind hit from all sides, no longer buffered by shrubbery and mossy trees. She paused at the sword gates originally made for a Louisiana Guard House. They had the rich look of the classics, yet were so easy to care for Ruthy Mae could wash them off. Sissy took out a sign with "Heading West."

"You can go down this highway to Hollywood," Jasmine once said.

Under the yellow lanterns pasty with moths Sissy checked her wallet, where $2,000 was lodged, airfare for a never-made trip to Paris.

Sissy crossed the highway, turned left, and blundered down the wet seawall. As she walked, moonlight became brighter and washed these beach-front palaces with a champagne-colored glow. Perhaps it was their windows that beckoned full and airy, their morning gardens and lattice vine gazebos. Maybe it was their pastel tones of sand and sky, the staircases that swooped to balconies, galleries shining like the decks of vintage yachts. She walked by a big house with green shutters and a wrap around porch. She'd buy this house, when she came back in a turquoise Porsche with white bucket seats.

Her thumb honed the air.

A van drove down the highway and stopped in a precise command. She couldn't see who was jutting out in the fog of the headlights A tall man motioned to her. Oh God, no! It was Blaise!

She ran across the road, slipped on sand, and steadied herself on the beach. Blaise caught up with her, his eyes shiny with intent. They passed a sand dune, its shrubbery rattling in the breeze.

Seagulls cawed, a tired truck raced by, a speedboat clanked behind a convertible skipping town.

Her sensors detected his every sound, movement, touch. She had been subdued asleep and now unexpectedly she was hungry for his voice, for his rugged, strained face.

Was she duplicitous or crazy? He swung her backpack over his shoulder, glanced at her doe-eyed. He pressed her against him, stirring her as suddenly as if he'd simply pulled open the box where her heart was in storage. For a second she remained standing, sand free, ready to do his bidding.

He was in full form. His dense hands easily lifted her face. "I couldn't leave," he said. "Your dad's closed up the deal with Serenity. I've got enough money . . . but I'm not going with him. I've shamed myself too much. I'm trying to find . . . some . . . some soft spot in you I can reach. I was cowardly."

"Evil."

"I apologize."

"Spare me!" Her mind wandered. She might give in to him after all, let her breasts stay stiff, not think about it, like the wind wrapping around her and slicing hair over her dampening face. She told him about the birthday card.

"You know," he said. "Finally. How do you feel?"

"Scared. Relieved." Why didn't you tell me? I could have kept the secret. I always felt strange here." She beat at his chest but he caught her fists.

"Your mother promised Jasmine. Your aunt didn't want you to be treated as a misfit like her. Adopted doesn't mean anything in this kin-driven South." He held Sissy quietly a moment. "We have to go away," he said, "get to know each other. I'm older, so I don't want to waste . . . a day."

"You're so screwed up," Sissy said.

"I'm not your uncle at least. Men are less evolved, but I want to grow."

"Liar."

"If Katrina comes, they'll shut the airports tomorrow."

"That's not what they're predicting, and what about Grandma?"

"She's got Ruthy Mae and Andrew on call. She'll be fine."

"First of all," Sissy said as she shortened the handles of her backpack, "I'm not a good girl, like you think. And secondly—I don't do well with liars and cheats."

"We've been living with nefarious relatives. True, I isolated myself too, sold my soul. Can't you forgive me? If we leave this hell, surround ourselves with giving people, perhaps there is hope. I love you," he said, scrutinizing her.

"Loving someone is not enough."

"I know. You must confront his complications. The whole business with Quint and me turned out to be a joke. But, I actually do need therapy."

"What! You're lying?"

"I want to undergo analysis in New York."

"Why go to New York?"

"It's where the best doctors are. The power. The glory. And the art. "

"You're not going to tell Grandma?"

"Let her think I'm a goof-off. If I'm with Mom, every conversation will create a ripple of anxiety . . . I did that whole ruse with Quint to change my life. Now I realize it can be more than I imagined it would be. The most important thing is we have each other."

"I can't deal with all these complexities. You're too old for me, too convoluted for me. I don't deal well with sickness."

"I can beat this thing, but I need to eliminate stress. I'll discuss everything with you later." He pulled her to him. "I've come to appreciate small pleasures that bring peace. Together we can rebuild our lives," he said. "After New York of course we would move to Texas or Mexico."

Sissy ignored his lips on her neck, his timid hand to her breast. They walked toward the waves, through the slapping debris. His big hand was under her shirt, unsnapping her bra, and then her shirt was off. Waves roared! Mama was gone but Blaise was there and though he had his limitations, he wasn't blood.

She felt her body go limp like the soft sand beneath her feet. Perhaps it was possible to rise above her circumstances and make positive changes in her life. She went deeper into the shallow water, letting it ooze over and under her shoes, sandal slippers that turned mud black and soggy. Knowing Blaise was penitent, she felt motivated and somewhat contrite.

Water crawled over their feet, and the wetness made her let him come at her, and forget the house lit up like a lantern one thousand feet behind them. They stood on the cold wet beach, his arms heavy around her neck. He owed her nothing. She owed him nothing. They owed themselves everything. In a day, Hurricane Katrina would hit. She didn't fear that then. A deep strength propelled her, so without making any promises, as an experiment in forgiveness and healing, she left with him for the airport.

Epilogue

One year later

Sissy and Blaise had much to be thankful for post-Katrina. Dad surprised Blaise with a big bonus check from the oil companies, a thank-you for the gift of Serenity.

What was difficult was many people just "disappeared." They scattered over the country, and Sissy and Blaise never had the chance to say good-bye.

Katrina was the first time Grandma ever evacuated. She did so because she didn't want to face New Orleans in August without electricity and air-conditioning. Her house on St. Charles Avenue in the prestigious Garden District was spared. Grandma lives, visits friends and family, and shops in this small, undamaged peninsula. Except for the majestic oak trees that were cut down, her world appears unchanged. To maintain sanity, she makes no trips to the devastated areas, which are basically eighty percent of the city.

Jasmine and Quint married bigamously in Las Vegas and, eager to capitalize on opportunity, opened a New Orleans restaurant and bar. TV coverage appeared on *Nightline*, including an up-close interview with Quint and Jasmine, eating roast beef po-boys.

Of the six hundred beautiful old wooden beachfront homes, only six remain in Pass Christian. On the ravaged Mississippi Gulf Coast, almost all houses, churches, and businesses from the beach to miles past the railroad tracks and highway were destroyed down to the slab. Serenity and her buildings were leveled.

Many of Sissy's relatives are buried in a beautiful 100-year-old Episcopal cemetery in Pass Christian, about one block from the beach. During her visits, Sissy and a friend who is a crane operator are trying to locate the granite headstones of family members so they can move them back near their graves.

Grandma is the only one in the family who plans to rebuild right on the water. She has purchased her land back from the oil companies at a greatly reduced price.

Blaise was successfully treated at NYU Medical Center. Analysis has helped him create effective boundaries.

Sissy and Blaise were engaged and married later in Mexico, in a ceremony that was announced in the New Orleans paper, next to robberies and arrests. They visited Texas looking for a place to relocate and decided upon San Antonio. The state of Texas found them a gallery and a house.

Sissy's surviving dream of Serenity is to have another wedding ceremony at the Shoefly, the large oak with wraparound porch that survived the hurricane. She would be the third to commit at the compound and the second to do so on that porch. Sissy has revealed the secret of her birth and the family has accepted both her and Jasmine. Since Katrina no one has the time to criticize, simply due to a lack of energy.

ACKNOWLEDGEMENTS

How do you ever thank all the people that kept you writing? These human links, to God, to hope, to promise, to peace. Angels who make you believe giving a huge chunk of your time to writing alone is worth it. Mostly I want to thank God who inspired people to help me and to believe in me.

Individuals who blessed me with their encouragement and praise include journalists Carole DiTosti and Meagan Meehan. Carole met me some decade ago in NYC at the National Arts Club and believed in me enough to cover all the dramatic readings I had in NYC. These one-night stands normally go unnoticed because once seen, they are gone.

Carole reviewed every reading and launched me from invisibility into the Internet galaxy. Following in Carole's mighty footsteps came Meagan Meehan who offered to write about any event I was doing, and true to her word, she did.

Readings in Rome, Paris, in Germany, all of which would have vanished after one sumptuous evening, are recorded. I say sumptuous because you have no idea how thrilling it is for us writers to hear our words read out loud, words we have mumbled alone in our rooms at night or at broad break of day in some coffee shop or private chamber.

Writers write after all to pass on something. For me it's the capturing of time and place. I write mostly about cities where I've densely lived like New Orleans and New York. I write about family and near death experiences. In NYC stricken with cancer I almost died. My writer's residency at the National Arts Club under

Aldon James secured me a great surgeon, Dr. Roses, and I survived to write these tales.

Along with the journalists who encouraged me I have to thank my family, observers who put up with my obsession to write, isolate, and record what is happening about me. My sister says she trembles at what I might say. I thank my relatives for letting me rift on them, though in this mad confusion of life, who knows what glimpses are true and which ones are fancy.

There is much of the Irish dreamer in us Southerners, us people of bayous, of rivers, and of enchantment, of the gothic houses, banana trees and silver rain.

I thank you readers for the time you spend with my stories. I hope they will help you live your dreams on this tightrope of breathing. Life is short and we are here for JOY.

A brief list of encouragers: Bob Harzinski, Anne Pincus, Rachelle O'Brien, Barret O'Brien, Dale O'Neill, Rory O'Neill, Jim Bosjolie, Bill Goodman, Mary Anderson, Steve and Pat Hartel, Jay and Sandra, Nix, Nora Wetzel, Rexanne Becnel, Allison Alsalp, CW Cannon, Tom Andes and the New Orleans Writers Workshop, Mary Ann McCray, Ann Jarrell, Jeanne Fayard, Irish Cultural Center, Paris, Tyrone Guthrie Center, Ireland, and the Amercan Academy in Rome, Actors Studio NYC, the Virginia Center for the Creative Arts. . . .

Rosary O'Neill
Sometime New Orleanian
and New Yorker
2021

About the Author

Rosary Hartel O'Neill, PhD, a sixth-generation Louisiana native, lives in New Orleans and New York City, where she writes screenplays, plays, and books. Her films include *Naked in New Orleans*; her *Vampire* screenplays, now in development at Herbert Berghof Studios, NYC; and *Edgar Degas: The Impressionable Years* (co-written with Rory Schmitt); for which she received seven Fulbrights. Her play *Degas in New Orleans* will be heralded in Paris in 2021. She is the author of twenty-five plays, most published by Samuel French, Inc., and seven published books.

Photo by DC LaRue

www.ingramcontent.com/pod-product-compliance
Lightning Source LLC
Chambersburg PA
CBHW031426240626
47154CB00001B/222